MW00577489

INTREPID FORCE: INVASION

Written by: Timothy D. Wise
Story and Characters by:
Timothy D. Wise and
Ivan S. Wilson

Published by:
Emporium Press
The Publishing Division of
Professor Theophilus' Emporium of Imagination
Magnolia, Arkansas

© 2005 by Professor Theophilus' Emporium of Imagination, Inc.

Printed in the United States of America

Published by:
EMPORIUM PRESS
The Publishing Division of
Professor Theophilus' Emporium of Imagination, Inc.
Magnolia, Arkansas

Library of Congress Control Number: 2005900769

First Edition
ISBN 0-9725549-1-2

DEDICATION:

I dedicate this second volume of the Intrepid Force saga to the fans who eagerly devoured the first book and irately demanded the second. For Austin, Paul, Cameron, Mike, Shellie, Girard, Felicia, Valerie, Dustin, Marguerite, and all of the rest of you-- here it is, folks. God bless you. I hope you enjoy it.

LITERARY REFERENCES:

The hymn "Amazing Grace" was written by John Newton, a former slave trader. The short story, "The Fall of the House of Usher" was written by Edgar Allan Poe. It is in the public domain. The song, "In the Air" was written by Phil Collins and Charles David and performed by Phil Collins. It is used with the permission of the Hal Leonard Music Company. The song "Ninety-Nine Red Balloons" is the English translation of "Ninety-Nine Luftballoons." The song was written by J.U. Fahrenkrog-Petersen and C. Karges and performed by Nena, a German rock band in 1983. It was translated into English by K. McAlea. It is used with the permission of the Hal Leonard Music Company. The poem "Ozymandias" was written by Percy Bysshe Shelley. It is in the public domain.

ACKNOWLEDGEMENTS:

The Intrepid Force owes its existence to a number of special friends. Ivan Wilson was there at the beginning when we began to dream up the characters. Dr. Kelly Farrar served as my faithful technical advisor in those days.

I was inspired by a number of writers. You may see traces of C.S. Lewis in the discussions between Sheppard and Gogue, some of Ray Bradbury in my use of metaphors, and elements of Frank Peretti, Dean Koontz, and Stephen King in the scary stuff. I continue to be grateful to the writers and artists at DC and Marvel comics for the Legion of Superheroes, the X-Men, and the Teen Titans. Their imprint is unmistakable. Star Trek and Star Wars had their influences as well. Thanks also to H.G. Wells for inventing the time machine.

I'd like to thank my parents. My mother, Shirley, has been supportive from the start and ever the embodiment of unconditional love. My father, Albert, was skeptical when I started my artistic ventures but enthusiastically supportive when they started to bear fruit. His analytical mind made him a problem-solver by nature and an engineer by trade. From him I learned to analyze the technical details of a story and rewrite the parts that didn't make sense. (Even if the Hulk weighs 500 pounds, how can he hold down a helicopter just by hanging onto the skid? How can the bionic man pick up a car engine if his back is flesh and blood? Why did Charlie's Angels throw away their guns and pelt the criminals with potatoes?) Don't blame my parentage for any technical or logical flaws that remain in the story.

I thank my brothers, Jay and Toby, and their families for their enthusiastic support of my first publishing venture. My aunts, uncles, and coworkers--many of them not science fiction fans--eagerly supported the venture as well. I included a glossary of science fiction terms for them and others like them who are new to the genre.

I spent the summer of 1992 in Hawaii serving as a summer missionary for the Baptist Student Union. The people of Waimea, Kona, Waikaloa, and Hilo, the students I served with, and the kind and patient adults who supervised us continue to inspire me, and I still dream about those rainforests and beaches. Readers will see traces of that summer in the early chapters of this book. Aloha, everyone.

You may also see traces of a trip to Panama City, Florida, I made with the youth of the First Baptist Church of Jonesboro back in the 1980s.

My classmates and teachers at Jonesboro-Hodge High School and Rundell Junior High were supportive of my writing efforts during the earliest stages of the Intrepid Force's creation. I loved seeing a number of them at my Jonesboro book signing and at my class reunion. Their kindness and support remain unchanged by the passage of time. I also appreciate the efforts of the fine staff of the Jonesboro public library.

My coworkers and students at Southern Arkansas University have encouraged me throughout the process of starting a publishing company and printing up books. It's great to have a job you enjoy going to, and people you enjoy working with.

There are others, of course, but I have to save some of my gratitude for the next book. Once again I'm reminded of the words of James 1:17, "Every good gift and every perfect gift is from above, and comes down from the Father of lights . . ."

THE COVER:

The cover was designed by author Timothy D. Wise. It features character and clothing figures created by DAZ Productions, Lourdes Mercado, and SanctumArt in addition to props designed by the author. Software packages used include Curious Labs' Poser, Procreate's Painter, Newtek's Lightwave, DAZ's Bryce, and Strata's StudioPro.

THE CAST:

The Members of Intrepid Force:

Pirate Eisman: An MBA student with training in team dynamics. He is trained in the use of mentally controlled armor.

Jared Thomas: Pirate's best friend, Jared is highly intuitive and has prophetic dreams. He specializes in stealth weapons.

Zapper Martin: His genetically engineered nervous system gives him the ability to generate electric shock. He is also trained in mechanical and electrical engineering.

Wendy Blake: Her mother, a member of an earlier team, died in the same attack that led to Wendy's bionic reconstruction.

Hal Wolfe: An officer in the Interplanetary Guard. Specializes in exo-weaponry.

Jaina Benedict: A teenage medical doctor. Her intelligence was artificially enhanced by scientist parents.

Michael Noguchi: His diseased nervous system was repaired by implants that give him superhuman speed and reflexes. He was trained in a variety of combat techniques.

Victoria "Tori" Sakai: She specializes in the construction and use of tiny robot probes that form a kind of "virtual body."

Ahadri Singh: (Deceased) An eight-foot-giant who was bred for combat but who rejected the philosophies of his "designers."

The Supporting Cast:

Neema: A biological replica of a young freedom fighter from the twenty-fourth century.

Balthazar: The intelligent computer on board Neema's starship.

Captain Nancy Butler: The commander of the *Intrepid*. Dr. Butler is the head of a team of researchers.

Chambers: The doctor aboard Cockrum's ship.

Jonas Cockrum: Acting chairman of DeFalco Space Industries and former member of the original Intrepid Force.

Lancing DeFalco: (Deceased) The reclusive trillionaire who founded DeFalco Space Industries. Leader of the original Intrepid Force.

Jolie Harrison: Preston's attorney.

Enoch Henry/Uncle Enoch: Pirate's 115-year-old honorary uncle. A former film producer who manages a museum in Crane Island, a Louisiana tourist town.

Lex Marston: A childhood friend of Enoch Henry's in the 1980s.

Richard Preston: A master of disguise. He was a member of the original Intrepid Force and a traitor to them.

Reverend Gene Sheppard: A former member of the original Intrepid Force. Sheppard left crime fighting and became a missionary after the original team disbanded, but reluctantly agreed to train the new team.

Echo Yazzi: Echo serves on the Intrepid. Her twin sister was executed by Gaith Corbalew.

Gaith Corbalew: An interplanetary crime lord. He was responsible for the deaths of most of the members of the original Intrepid Force.

Gogue: An ageless being of unknown origin. His first known contact with Earth was in the 1980s.

THE NEW SCIENCE FICTION READER'S GUIDE TO SCI-FI TERMINOLOGY:

Alternate Realities: "What if" universes where things that might have taken place are real.

Bionics: Electronic replacements for lost or injured body parts. They can be made to look completely human and to give the recipient superhuman abilities.

Cyborg: A human-robot combination. Either a person with bionic prosthetics or a robot covered with artificially grown human skin.

Deflection Field: An invisible field that pushes bullets, shrapnel, and other harmful forces away from the wearer.

Exobot: A robot that a user can climb inside of and wear like a suit of armor. The exobot can also move around without anyone inside.

Exoskeleton: A frame that is strapped onto a user's body to enhance his/her strength.

Microsingularities: Tiny holes in space and time caused by fields of intense gravity.

Nanites: Microscopic robots used in surgery or scientific exploration.

Nanoprobes/Nanobots: Microscopic probes or robots. In the novel, Tori Sakai uses a helmet and gloves to operate a swarm of nanoprobes.

Paragravitational Field: The author's term for a field that artificially simulates or negates gravity.

Recombinant: A person or animal whose genes have been rearranged to give him/her special abilities. (It comes from the term *recombinant DNA*.) The term is used as a proper noun in the 2080s.

Synthetic Reality: A more sophisticated version of virtual reality. A wearer puts on goggles, earphones, and other equipment that allow him/her to interact with an artificial environment.

Tachyons: Particles that move backwards in time and could theoretically be used to send messages back through time.

Wormholes: Tunnels through space and time that allow travelers to visit other times and universes or to travel great distances in a short time.

NEWSBYTES: A Retelling of Recent Events

INTERPLANETARY GUARD SHIPS DESTROYED
SUN TIMES: NEWS FROM AROUND THE SOLAR SYSTEM

September 11, 2084

Gaith Corbalew, the architect of the Tranquility Bay Massacre, has escaped confinement after serving nine years of a twenty lifetime sentence. The Interplanetary Guard had dispatched five Desolation-Class destroyers to transport the deposed crime lord to maximum security facilities on Ganymede, one of Jupiter's moons. The convoy was only hours from Earth when one of the cruisers reported engine trouble. A moment later, Vector station lost contact with the ships. Fragmentary messages indicated that the convoy was under attack. Later scans showed only a debris field. Rescue ships were dispatched to the site, but they found no survivors. Investigation into the exact nature of the attack continues. "Desolation class destroyers," according to General Henry Saunders, "are the biggest, meanest ships we have. Nothing we know of could have destroyed them so quickly and so completely." Sabotage has not been ruled out.

DEFALCO ANNOUNCES NEW INTREPID FORCE
MEGA-CORP REPORTS

September 30, 2084

Lancing DeFalco has begun recruitment of members for a prototype crisis intervention team comprised of young adults possessing a variety of skills, talents, and aptitudes. The team will include cyborgs and Recombinants as members but will not be limited to them. They will be trained in short-term combat, rescue operations, detective work, and exploration. They will be equipped with the latest weapons, protective clothing, and instrumentation developed by DeFalco Space Industries' various divisions. Dubbed "Intrepid Force" in honor of the previous group bearing that title, this team will participate in a three-month training program and will be assigned their first mission sometime this spring.

DeFalco neither affirms nor refutes allegations that the team is being formed in response to the escape of Gaith Corbalew whose forces killed eighteen members of the original Intrepid Force in 2074.

ASTROLOGY CULT UNDER INVESTIGATION
NEW ORLEANS TIMES-PICAYUNE
October 31, 2084

Eight young adults have been arrested in connection with a bizarre series of crimes including burglary, kidnapping, vandalism, and murder. Jared Thomas, 19, a part-time employee at DeFalco Bionics and a student at Louisiana University of New Orleans, reportedly found Dr. Craig Lindstrom, his supervisor, badly beaten and bound at his laboratory at the DeFalco Bionics Annex in Metarie. The lab itself had been vandalized and equipment stolen. Eight young men and women dressed in makeup and black opera capes apparently abducted Thomas.

Thomas's friends, fearing for his safety, reportedly drove to the DeFalco Annex, spotted a suspicious vehicle leaving the premises, and chased it through the New Orleans French Quarter. The chase ended when the van allegedly spun out of control and crashed through the fence of an historic cemetery. Police drones were quickly dispatched to the scene where they rendered the suspects unconscious with anesthetic gas.

The eight suspects, all children of prominent families from around the country, claim to have no memory of their crimes. All of them are undergoing psychiatric examinations at the Warner Krauss Institute in Panama City, Florida. Police have tentatively linked the crimes to a violent and little understood cult called Astrolus. The body of Dr. Craig Lindstrom has not been recovered.

MEMORANDUM
Subject: Jared Thomas' Psych Exam
From: Dr. Philip Lessig
To: Mr. Jonas Cockrum

Jonas,

The results of Dr. Cronin's hypnotic regression exam were interesting to say the least, but I'm staying with my original diagnosis. I believe this "dream woman from the future" is the product of an intelligent, creative, and highly intuitive mind coping with the loneliness of an unhappy home life and abusive classmates. So far (with the exception of the holographic face) this "Neema" has only appeared to him in dreams so I don't think we're dealing with any kind of psychotic condition--just a persistent fantasy and a case of adolescent wishful thinking. The appearance of the holographic face in the fortune teller's globe is corroborated by Jared's teammates, so we know it's not a fantasy. The resemblance of the hologram to the woman in Jared's dreams is intriguing but probably coincidental.

ASTROLUS RETURNS TO CRANE ISLAND
CRANE ISLAND MONITOR
December 27, 2083

One Crane Island teenager is hospitalized and catatonic as a result of brain trauma suffered at the hands of cultic kidnappers. Jared Thomas was abducted from a Crane Island parking lot on the night of December 26 by what is believed to be a giant robot in a black cloak. Jonathan Eisman, also from Crane Island, and Wendy Blake, an out-of-town guest, witnessed the abduction and tried to render assistance. They followed the kidnapper to the abandoned Crane Island Saltwerks, but were unable to rescue Thomas. Blake was also abducted. Thomas and Blake were transported to a hidden facility in the swampland beneath New Orleans and subjected to a form of virtual reality torture. The Intrepid Force, an interplanetary crisis intervention team formed by DeFalco Space Industries, joined local law enforcement officers in rescuing the two abductees. Jared Thomas remains comatose while

Wendy Blake is reported to be uninjured. Investigators believe the kidnappers are connected to Astrolus, a mysterious cult known to those familiar with Crane Island history. Known for practices of human sacrifice and brainwashing, the cult is said to have appeared in Crane Island in the year 1984. At least two accidental deaths and one unsolved missing persons case were linked to that incident.

VENUS COLONY ATTACKED
INTERPLANETARY NEWS SERVICE
March 15, 2084

Two hours ago, human colonists on the planet Venus were attacked by what appears to be a group of terrorists aboard a refitted asteroid mining ship. Planetary defenses have been obliterated. *Arcadia* station, the Venusian spaceport, has been destroyed and the sixty people on board are presumed dead. The manned space fighters, robot probes, and orbiting weapons platforms designed to protect the planet against invasions, piracy, and natural disasters have apparently been destroyed or neutralized as well. All of this seems to have been accomplished by a single ship armed with highly sophisticated weapons. Speculation continues about the identities of those aboard the ship and about a possible connection between this attack and the September destruction of the five ships transporting Gaith Corbalew to Ganymede.

CORBALEW SEIZES VENUS COLONY
INTERPLANETARY NEWS SERVICE
March 15, 2084

Venus Base DeFalco, the Venusian branch of DeFalco Space Industries, has been seized by an extremely well armed band of interplanetary terrorists. The leader of this group is now known for certain to be Gaith Corbalew, a deposed crime lord who once owned a substantial portion of what is now DeFalco Space Industries. His motive is believed to be revenge against DeFalco and his team for breaking the back of his interplanetary regime, for imprisoning him, and for assuming control of his former "empire." Corbalew has demanded that he be given the opportunity to speak to the entire solar system about the crimes perpetrated by the United System, the Interplanetary

Guard, and DeFalco Space Industries against his family. His request will be granted, but the time of the broadcast is still being discussed.

After being sentenced to twenty lifetimes in prison, Corbalew escaped from a convoy of Interplanetary Guard destroyers during a transfer to a maximum security facility on Ganymede last fall. Authorities have still not determined how his forces were able to neutralize five of the Interplanetary Guard's most powerful destroyers. Over five hundred members of the Interplanetary Guard perished in that incident.

WHO CONTROLS CORBALEW?
EDITORIAL, Nicholas Blessett
March 16, 2084

In spite of his obvious intelligence, Black Gaith Corbalew is clearly psychotic. He proved that much ten years ago when he seized control of the Tranquility Bay spaceport and took nearly 1,000 civilians hostage when the Intrepid Force was sent to arrest him. The question that concerns me, the question we should all be asking, is how Corbalew managed to escape from prison and amass so much power in so short a time. Who gave him those weapons? We know what Corbalew wants. He's made that clear enough. But what do his benefactors want? Who is really behind this?

CORBALEW CHALLENGES INTREPID FORCE TO REMATCH
MARTIAN TIMES
March 18, 2084

Gaith Corbalew has now challenged the Intrepid Force, a team of young men and women representing DeFalco Space Industries, to a fight to the death that he obviously plans to win. Ten years ago a different group by the same name brought an end to his empire. Since most of the first group is dead, he seems to want the new group as a kind of proxy sacrifice. Corbalew has more than twenty five thousand people hostage on Venus and has threatened to kill them if his demands are not met. What will DeFalco Space Industries do? Will they send nine young men and women into what is obviously a trap to save twenty five thousand others?

CORBALEW DEFEATED, DEFALCO DEAD
GOOD MORNING, SOLAR SYSTEM
March 22, 2084

Gaith Corbalew has been defeated and the twenty five thousand hostages on Venus have been released from his grip of terror. Sadly, however, reclusive trillionaire Lancing DeFalco has died. His death was not the result of the terrorist attack, however, but of a degenerative illness DeFalco has been fighting for nearly a year. Leadership of DeFalco's vast corporate empire has, in the interim, been assigned to a committee led by Jonas Cockrum, DeFalco's vice president of operations.

Also listed among the dead are Ahadri Singh, a member of the Intrepid Force, and around twenty civilians. Gaith Corbalew is believed to have died in an explosion. Twenty of his men are either dead or missing.

Ten years ago the original Intrepid Force battled Corbalew in his corporate stronghold on the moon. Their victory was marred by the deaths of nearly a hundred civilians and most of the members of the team itself. This Intrepid Force has managed to defeat Corbalew again with the loss of but a single member. Ahadri Singh sacrificed his life to prevent Corbalew from breaching the dome that protects the Venus colony from the planet's deadly atmosphere.

Questions remain, however, about Corbalew's ship, an asteroid mining vessel said to have been outfitted with unknown technology. Just over a week ago, this ship was able to annihilate the entire defensive system of Venus in a matter of moments. A saboteur from within Corbalew's own ranks disabled the ship's internal systems, freeing the Intrepid Force to battle and defeat Corbalew's ground troops. Is this the end to that threat or are there more of those ships out there?

INTERNAL MEMORANDUM,
DEFALCO SPACE INDUSTRIES
April 1, 2084

Gene Sheppard and the Intrepid Force have returned to Earth following the defeat of Black Gaith Corbalew on the planet Venus just over a week ago. Mr. Cockrum has sent the young men and women of the new Intrepid Force to somewhere "quiet and secluded" for some much-needed rest and relaxation.

"I'm afraid we can't take the credit for defeating that ship," Gene Sheppard told reporters. "We just got lucky."

Richard Preston, a member of the original Intrepid Force, was recruited by Corbalew and allowed access to his ship. Preston later used this knowledge to betray Corbalew in a stunning reversal of his alleged betrayal of his teammates to Corbalew ten years ago.

PROLOGUE I: Titan

The ringed majesty of Saturn filled nearly a quarter of Titan's tangerine sky. Far from home, a metal spider sat forlornly on a weathered plateau. Beneath it lay a rock-tattered sea of liquid methane. A ghostly shroud of fog hung over the sea like a ragged sheet. Pitted mountains half a kilometer east of the lander thrust themselves upward into the misty heavens. Benchley, encased in the bulk of his pressure suit, sat forlornly on the frosted steps of the lander and waited for his crewmates to return. He could hear their conversations through his helmet radio. The only other sound was the sound of his own breathing. The *Arthur Conan Doyle* circled overhead, a large star in a sea of orange mist.

Standing on the surface of Titan, Saturn's largest moon, was an explorer's dream. Being left behind while one's crewmates did the exploration was decidedly less. Benchley had argued with the commander. What point was there, after all, to anyone staying behind at the lander? No one was going to steal it--certainly not on Titan. The commander had pointed out that there were other dangers. The exploration party could be trapped by an avalanche, a cave-in, or some other planetary mishap. Someone needed to remain behind to assist or--if the worst happened--to at least let the people back on Earth know what had happened to the expedition. Benchley knew all of this. He had been trained. He still did not like being left behind.

The A.C. *Doyle* was an explorer ship. It was manned half by scientists and half by prospectors combing the solar system for valuable resources. DeFalco Space Industries, the sponsor of the project, had committed itself to preserving the natural order of the solar system as much as possible while trying to improve the quality of life for humankind. There were those, of course, who questioned the giant corporation's benevolence. The organization was, after all, in the process of terraforming Venus. Synthesizing massive explosives from substances found on the planet's surface, they had blown over half of the planet's soupy atmosphere into space and sped up the planet's rotation. Who gave them the right? The governments of Earth had given them permission, of course, but who gave them the right to transform an entire planet? It seemed blasphemous, they said.

What had brought the *Doyle* to the surface of Titan, however, was not the mere exploration of natural phenomena. Their probes had picked up a signal coming from the planet's surface. There were, according to databases, no probes or expeditions on the planet, so the source of the signal was a complete mystery. A probe was dispatched to the source of the signal and the images it had sent back were astonishing. Centuries ago something had crashed on Titan, plowing furrows hundreds of yards long. Debris was strewn across the surface of the planet. Several large pieces remained. The object that had crashed there had clearly been constructed by humans--or perhaps something humanoid--but it was an old wreck dating well before the manned exploration of the solar system, and it was too large to be one of the twentieth century space probes. If it turned out to be an alien artifact, the wreck would be the first substantial proof of nonhuman intelligence ever discovered. The captain had lost no time in sending messages to Earth, Mars, and the Jovian outposts. The expedition had been assembled and briefed in less than an hour. Benchley had been delighted to be chosen for the expedition. It was his first-- and what a first! If the wreck turned out to be an alien artifact,

3 / INTREPID FORCE

he would go down in history with the first astronauts to set foot on the moon. Now here he was babysitting the lander while the others made history. It did not seem fair.

"Nearing one of the larger pieces . . . ," one of the voices in Benchley's helmet said. It was Commander Yan.

"Some writing here," Dr. Futrell said. "I can just . . . ."

A burst of static drowned out the rest. Benchley stood up and tapped his helmet. The radio was out. Benchley looked out at the jagged horizon. This was just the excuse he needed to leave his post and join the others at the crash site. First things first, though. He had to contact the *A.C. Doyle* and let the captain know he'd lost contact with the others.

Benchley opened the heavy airlock door, slammed it shut behind him, and waited impatiently as the closet-sized compartment filled with warm oxygen-rich atmosphere. The process was almost complete when the lights in the airlock went out. He nearly panicked. His hands brushed the wall until they locked around the emergency escape lever. He pulled down hard and the door popped open. Benchley stumbled into the lander's dark interior. Red emergency lamps gave the small compartment a hellish cast. Benchley looked around wildly. What could have caused the ship to lose power? He was scanning the blank control screens when the power came back on. He breathed a sigh of relief and immediately put in a call to the *A.C. Doyle*. Lieutenant Garrison's face appeared on the flat screen. Captain Gillette leaned in behind her.

"What's going on down there?" the captain demanded.

"We just lost contact with the expedition."

"That's what I was calling to tell you," Benchley said. "Communications are out, and I just had a blink in power. Everything was dead for nearly a minute. Now it's back. So what do you want me to do? Do I stay with the lander or go try to find the others?"

The captain paused, thought it over.

"Give us a few minutes to scan the wreck site, and I'll get back to you," the captain said. "Stay with the lander."

"Yes, sir," Benchley said. He wasn't sure whether to be irritated or relieved. The power failure had panicked him, and his desire to make history was not as strong as it had been.

Benchley climbed back into the airlock, waited as the chamber filled with cold nitrogen, and stepped back out into Titan's frozen twilight. For a second time, he was struck by the breathtaking view of Saturn filling a quarter of the sky. The rings glistened in the glow of the distant sun. Benchley crept slowly down the steps. The gravity was light--about one-seventh that of Earth. The frozen ground crunched beneath his boots.

A blast of static slammed into Benchley's eardrums. He tried to cover his ears, but the helmet stopped him. Noise poured through the speakers of his helmet radio into his unprotected ears. Frantically, he fumbled with the volume controls on his wrist and turned down the noise. He thought he could make out voices. Someone was moaning or chanting behind the static. The radio fell silent.

Benchley stood in the dark with his pulse hammering. What was going on here? Something about the sounds he had just heard filled his lonely imagination with horror. Childhood nightmares and stories of hostile aliens crept up from the dark cellars of his memory. He looked up at the distant sun and suddenly wished he were on a sunny beach in Florida or in a quaint coffee shop on a busy morning. He thought he saw something moving around the back side of the lander and felt the hair on the back of his neck stand up.

Benchley knew his fear was irrational. If there was anyone there at all, it was probably one of the other explorers returning to the ship to check on the communications problems. That was all.

* * *

"No sign of anybody at the wreck site," Dr. Peeples reported.

5 / INTREPID FORCE

"Well, where are they?" Captain Gillette demanded.
"Contact the lander."

"I'm trying, sir," Communications Officer Anna Garrison
reported. "Nobody's answering."

"I am Gogue," a voice said suddenly. "This world has been
my prison for longer than you can possibly imagine. I have
called to you, and you have come. You have released me and
now you will serve me." The voice was inhuman.

Communications officer Anna Garrison looked at her
control panel like it had suddenly turned against her. The
other members of the A.C. Doyle's bridge crew glanced around
at each other.

"What station are you tuned into Garrison?"

Communications officer Garrison shrugged her shoulders.

"Did he say he was God?" Samuels asked.

"Gogue," Dr. Peeples said. "I think."

"As in demagogue?" Garrison asked.

"Or Gog from the Bible," Samuels said. "The leader of a
force prophesied to attack Jerusalem."

"All right," Captain Gillette said. "What's going on here?
This is starting to smell like a practical joke. Yan, is that you
down there?"

"The voice isn't human," Garrison said. "It sounds
computer generated."

"I have taken your shore party," the voice said. "They are
mine now as you will be."

"Who is this?" the captain demanded. "Identify yourself!"

"It sounds like an old horror show," Samuels said.

"Our TV transmissions have been traveling through space
for over a century," Peeples said. "If some other race
intercepted them . . ."

The ship's proximity alarms went off.

"There's something out here," Peeples said. "A fleet of
unidentified shapes. They came out of nowhere, and they're
swarming all around us."

"Well, what are they?" Captain Gilette demanded. "Metallic? Organic?"

"I'm reading metal," Peeples said. "Unknown alloy."

"Weapons," Gilette ordered.

"They just went down," Peeples said.

A concussion rocked the ship.

"Do you feel my power now?" the harsh voice on the radio said. "I have your ship."

The lights on the bridge went off. Green emergency lamps continued to glow giving the bridge an eerie, underwater appearance. The ship's rotating drum (which used centrifugal force to simulate gravity) slammed to a halt and gravity went out. Small objects began to float.

"Get the weapons back online!" Samuels ordered. His long hair was standing on end.

"It's no use," Garrison said. "Whatever it is, it's coming."

Something slammed against the outer hull of the ship. Airlocks were forced open and ghostly footsteps and the sound of something being dragged whispered through the ship's dark hallways. Then they heard laughter--cold and inhuman--coming through the speakers.

PROLOGUE II: Fever Dreams

He did not know where he was or how long he had been there. He was in a featureless concrete cell with a toilet and a drain hole in the floor. The floor was cold and the room smelled of mildew. There were hairline cracks around the drain. Most of the time he was kept in the dark, but he had seen the cell in those rare instances that his interrogators had dragged him out and beaten him.

He did not know who he was. He had murky and contradictory memories of some distant past life, but even those did not entirely make sense. Some of the memories, he was sure, were dreams but he could no longer tell dream from reality. Only hours before, he had found himself relaxing in some quiet desert oasis with a shallow, sandy pond, whispering palm branches overhead, and a dark red evening sky. A cool breeze rippled his clothing.

He did not eat. He could not recall eating or drinking anything for as far back as he could remember. Why he had not starved to death he did not know. Perhaps he had eaten and forgotten it. He didn't remember ever having used the toilet either, but that certainly didn't make sense.

Maybe I'm dead, he thought. *Maybe this is hell.* The thought sent a shiver through him. No. Surely he had eaten and used the toilet, and he simply could not remember. That had to be it.

He did not know if it was day or night if, indeed, such things really existed. Sunrises and open skies seemed as unreal as his fleeting visions of chrome robots with booming metallic voices and walking skeletons in tattered army uniforms.

He did not react the day he heard the noises in the hall and saw the orange light of a laser torch burning through the darkness. He was only dimly aware of the light pouring into his cell and the helmeted, uniformed figures that came running in. He could see the laces on their boots clearly, the metal clasps they wound through. He could see the corrugated soles. They were tan and rubbery.

"Stefan!" one of them yelled. "Stefan, can you hear me?"

He heard the words, but they did not make sense to him. The name Stefan seemed vaguely familiar, and he felt he should recognize it. It was a German name, wasn't it? European anyway.

Rough hands, in too much of a rush to be gentle, lifted him and carried him out into the hallway. Light burned his eyes. He squeezed them shut. The bulbs were in metal cages like birds. *Even the light bulbs are in cages here,* he thought and it struck him as funny. He started to laugh, but it came out as a cough.

"Are you all right?" someone asked him.

The floor was covered with bodies, men in black jumpsuits with steel-toed boots. He remembered the boots. He had lost several teeth to them. The tile in the hallway outside of his cell was a sickly green.

"They're coming! Back that way!"

9 / INTREPID FORCE

His consciousness faded to gray as they dragged him into a maze. The next thing he remembered, he was outside. It was dark. There were jagged mountains on the horizon. A huge, yellow full moon hung overhead. He was sure he must be dreaming again.

He felt himself strapped into a padded seat and got a distinct sensation of speed, of acceleration. A man leaned over him. He had a narrow, vulpine face, a black and gray beard and small, burning eyes. He looks like the devil, he thought. Then he struggled to remember who the devil was.

"My name is Gaith Corbalew," the man said. Language made sense for the first time. "I've come here to rescue you." The voice sounded far away. His world dilated into a small point of light.

His consciousness faded after that.

CHAPTER 1: No Rest

A modular beach house of glass and plastics stood on a cylindrical base overlooking a white strip of beach. Palm trees rustled in a gentle ocean breeze. Artificial tiki torches burned along a twisting trail of rounded stones that led from the beach house, through a gap in the plumaria bushes, to the beach. Waves rolled in and out in a steady, calming rhythm. The setting sun glistened on their writhing tips.

"I've got to get back to *Vector*," Reverend Gene Sheppard heard himself say. There was regret in his voice. Standing in the shadow of the house, he looked down the hill at the beach and found himself aching to spend the next few days, weeks-- maybe even months--lying in a hammock beneath two palm trees, strolling through the sands, sailing over crystal blue waters.

"You just got here," Wendy protested. "You need the rest as much as any of us. Maybe more. Can't you stay for a day or two?"

"I wish I could," Sheppard said, "but there are things I have to take care of. I hope it doesn't take long."

11 / INTREPID FORCE

"The preacher's leaving," Zapper Martin said. "Now we can have some real fun."

"There's a Bible verse that says to watch how you live because ye know not the day nor the hour of His return," Sheppard said. "It's talking about Jesus, but it goes for me too, Zapper. Invoke not the wrath of thy master."

"You know you don't have to worry about me, Rev," Zapper said. "It's the rest of these heathen you've got to watch out for. Especially these two."

Pirate and Wendy glanced across the picnic table at each other then quickly looked away. Wendy, with her shorts and bikini top and her damp, tangled hair, gleamed with careless youthful beauty.

"Looks like I hit a nerve," Zapper said.

"I'll hit your nerve," Pirate said.

If Jared Thomas had heard the exchange, he betrayed no outward sign. He was lying in a hammock listening to a book through hidden ear nodes. Mike, Hal, and Tori were down at the beach assembling a portable sailboat. Jaina was asleep on a beach towel.

In her computer-generated world, Neema stood--ghostlike-- among them, listened to the exchange, and smiled. She floated like an unborn child in a tube full of chemicals aboard a starship. Images from the world beneath her were piped directly into her brain. She saw, she heard, and she felt everything around her, but no one could see her. She was completely alone. Alone, that is, except for the comforting presence of Balthazar, her ship's computer. Balthazar was always there, always waiting over her shoulder for her to call upon him. He was, in many ways, the perfect parent, the perfect teacher, and the perfect friend, but he wasn't real. He was nothing more than a series of interactive, preprogrammed responses burned into a computer's artificial memory core by a group of scientists who would not even be born for nearly two hundred years. These were Neema's true parents if one such as she could be said to have parents. She had been artificially gestated--grown in a tube--and imprinted with the memories of a young woman from a future she had been sent to the past to prevent. Was such a paradox possible? Neema stroked Jared's brow and pretended he could feel her there. He stirred as though sensing something.

"At least stay for supper," Wendy told Sheppard. "We were about to grill burgers."

"I can't," Sheppard said.

"Lighten a little," Zapper said. "It's not like the fate of the world is riding on your shoulders."

Sheppard's face darkened.

"I'm not so sure it isn't." His eyes, Pirate knew, were focused on some scene of apocalyptic destruction that none of the others could see.

* * *

Captain Nancy Butler appeared on Sheppard's monitor screen. He had called her during the shuttle ride into orbit. Butler herself was in her quarters aboard the *Intrepid*, an interplanetary space cruiser that sat parked in high Earth orbit a stone's throw from *Vector* station. Butler was an attractive black woman in her mid-forties. Captain Butler was also Dr. Butler, a professor of biochemistry specializing in the study of the effects of space travel on the human body. At the time she had taken command of the *Intrepid*, it had been a scientific research vessel and a place for the testing of prototype equipment. Now it was more.

"How are the refits going?" Sheppard asked.

"About like they usually go," Butler told him. "Half the systems don't work, and we're having to relearn the ones that do. How are the kids?"

"Fine," Sheppard said. "They're fine"

"Did you tell them?" she asked.

"Not yet," he said. "Not until we know more."

"Be careful, Gene," she said.

"You too, Nancy. I'll see you in a couple of hours."

Sheppard broke communications. He looked around the shuttle's cabin. There were no other passengers. This was primarily a cargo run. Sheppard reached into his carry-on bag and pulled out a pair of synthetic reality goggles. The speaker plugs hung from cords on either end. Sheppard placed the goggles around his eyes, stuffed the plugs into his ears. He removed a data slide from a pocket inside his vest and inserted it into the viewer. Richard Preston, a former member of the original Intrepid Force, had given it to him after Ahadri's funeral.

"What is this?" Sheppard had asked.

"Just keep it," Preston had replied. "Don't let anything happen to it. It may be your only chance."

Sheppard had watched the slide repeatedly on the return flight from Venus. He had watched it over and over and had prayed constantly that what he had heard was wrong.

Using vocal commands, eye movements, and blinks, he paced through the onscreen menus. Finally the message began to play.

Richard Preston's pale, sweat-soaked face appeared. It was glaring wildly into the screen and so close that Sheppard found himself trying to pull away from it. Closing in around the figure were the tight walls of a crawlspace between a space ship's walls.

"Don't know how long I can hide here or if anyone will get this message," Preston whispered, "but I have to try. For the sake of humanity, I have to try." The picture faded to black and then returned. "Sorry. Thought I heard someone. Just the ship settling, I guess. You never know how many noises a ship can make until you're hiding in the walls to stay alive. If that filthy cyborg gets his hands on me, I'm finished. I'll make him pay dearly for it, though. I can promise you that." He laughed nervously, then placed his hand to his mouth and looked around. The picture faded and then returned. "There. I'm sure I'm alone now. There's so much I have to tell you and so little time. The Earth is in danger. The whole planet. I don't know exactly how, but Corbalew keeps talking to someone in his quarters about an armada. He says Earth's days are numbered. He has weapons--the same horrible weapons he just used on Venus. But that was just the beginning. That was just one ship.

"But that's not the worst of it. He keeps bragging about his agents, his inside men. He says he has connections in the governments of Earth, and inside DeFalco Space Industries.

"He even says he has someone inside of the Intrepid Force. One of them is a plant. Corbalew can see everything they do, and he says his agent could kill any of them at any time. I can't let that happen, but what can I do? How can I warn them? Even if I escape this ship, I don't know who to trust. His people are everywhere."

Preston paused, looked around.

"I've managed to download some data files from Corbalew's system. I'm putting those on here in the hope that someone can crack the encryption. I don't know of anything else that would help. I've heard Corbalew and that Gogue-thing talk about Titan. I think they mean the moon that orbits Saturn, the one with the atmosphere. And he's said something about Arthur Conan Doyle. He was the author of the Sherlock Holmes mysteries, but I have no idea what Doyle has to do with any of this."

The signal went black, then returned.

"I wish I knew more. I hope this makes it into the hands of someone who can make use of it. I don't know if I can ever make up for the things I've done or the people I've betrayed, but this is all I can do. Good luck."

Preston vanished. Sheppard removed the goggles, returned them to his carry-on bag. He did not know why he had watched the slide again. He had replayed the message so many times that he practically had it memorized. He could almost recite it word for word.

Sheppard sighed heavily and said a silent prayer for his young friends--especially for the one who was to betray them. He could not imagine who the traitor might be, but the mere thought of it depressed him. Sheppard thought back to the last moment before he left the team.

* * *

"Can we help you?" Pirate asked.

"No," Sheppard said. "No, not yet. I'll call you when the time is right, but there are some things I have to take care of first. On second thought, maybe there is something. Pirate, walk with me." Sheppard led Pirate down the beach a few meters. The others watched them and shrugged. Sheppard looked over his shoulder unzipped his shoulder pouch and pulled out a small sheet of glass, a data slide.

"Listen," Sheppard said. "I'm going to leave this with you. It could be important. There's another copy in my quarters on the *Intrepid*."

"You sound like you expect something to happen to you," Pirate said.

"I hope not," Sheppard said, "but this is too important to leave to chance. Just keep it, and if anything happens to me you'll have it."

Moments later Sheppard said goodbye to the rest of the team. He strapped into an airboat and soared off with his back to the setting sun. Blue water, still and smooth, rippled gently below him, but his mind had already left the island behind. His thoughts were as dark as the space he would soon be soaring into.

Wendy walked outside with a plate of hamburger patties and began to place them on a grill. Pirate and Zapper watched as Sheppard soared away.

"I wonder what the big emergency is," Zapper said. "Everybody's so uptight these days."

Sea gulls screamed overhead and a cool breeze blew in from the ocean. The sun was sinking beneath the horizon.

CHAPTER 2: Beachhead

Sheppard tried to sit still, to make himself relax, as the shuttle began its final approach to *Vector* station. He had a business meeting there. Sheppard hated meetings. When Cockrum had invited him to train and mentor the Intrepid Force, he had not mentioned meetings. Sheppard sighed. Cockrum was trying to turn him into a desk-bound bureaucrat. He had never had the patience for such things. Perhaps God was trying to teach him something.

Dark shapes drifted restlessly in orbit, running lights flashing like the rhythm of rapid heartbeats. Most of these were Interplanetary Guard ships. Earth had been on alert ever since the attack on Venus. Automated defense platforms floated past like rafts bristling with cannons.

As he left the airlock and walked through the crowded terminal, Sheppard passed families, children, teenagers, college students, and elderly sightseers. The station was supposed to be on alert. He had expected to find the station nearly empty, manned by a skeleton crew, but the place was filled to capacity. He could hardly get down the hall.

"I don't believe this," he mumbled under his breath. "What are you people doing?" Several people looked at him as he passed them. The sight of a huge, bearded man mumbling to himself like an Old Testament prophet having private conversations with God did not exactly reassure them. Ignoring the uneasy stares, Sheppard strolled down the hall to the executive offices, jabbed the lock button, and stepped into the lobby.

"Welcome back, Mr. Sheppard," Roxie, Jonas Cockrum's administrative assistant, said. She smiled nervously.

"Hi, Roxie," Sheppard said. He sighed, bottled his anger. He was not about to vent his frustration on this sweet child. Save it for someone who deserves it.

"They're having a meeting," Roxie said as she saw him start down the hall toward the main board room. "You might not want to go in there." She stirred restlessly in her seat. What was wrong with her today?

"They're expecting me," Sheppard said. "Cockrum asked me to represent him. Is everything all right?"

She looked down at her hands.

"Yes, sir."

"Are you okay, Roxie?"

"Yes, sir," she said. "Be careful."

Sheppard marched down the corridor, stabbed the lock button with his finger. The door slid aside, and Sheppard stalked into the room. Everyone turned and looked at him. No one spoke. Seated around the table were *Vector* station's chief of security, its assistant chief of operations, and twelve of the businesspeople--resort owners, restaurateurs, retailers, and research company heads--who leased facilities on the station. Seated at the head of the table was a tall man in a black suit.

"Reverend Sheppard," he said. "Join us." His face, Sheppard thought, seemed familiar though he could not immediately place him.

"What's going on out there?" Sheppard asked. "This station is supposed to be on alert. Cockrum ordered an evacuation."

"Those orders are no longer in effect," the man in black said. Sheppard was sure he had seen this man before but he could not, for the life of him, remember where.

"No longer in effect?" Sheppard gasped. "Don't you understand? Less than two weeks ago Venus was attacked by a single ship armed with a technology we have never seen before. It wiped out the colony's defense network, annihilated most of its navy, and sent its orbiting space station down in flames. One of our allies managed to disable that ship by sheer luck, but we have no idea where those weapons came from or who really sent the ship."

"We're perfectly aware of the facts, Mr. Sheppard," the man at the head of the table said, "but they no longer matter."

Sheppard looked uneasily at the others around the table. He expected cries of protest but no one said anything.

Suddenly Sheppard knew why the stranger looked so familiar. He looked exactly like Captain James Gillette, the captain of DeFalco's survey ships. What was the name of that ship?

The Arthur Conan Doyle. The name of the ship hit Sheppard like a fist in the stomach. The *Doyle* had vanished without a trace almost two years earlier--on an expedition to Titan, Saturn's large moon. Sheppard felt his mouth go dry.

"What's going on here?" Sheppard asked. He addressed Gillette directly. "What are you even doing here? Wasn't your ship declared missing?"

"Captain Gillette's ship was declared missing almost two years ago," the man said, "but I am not Captain Gillette. You may call me Gogue."

A rush of adrenaline slammed through Sheppard's body. The doors opened behind him.

"Don't move," a droning voice ordered.

* * *

Neema sat in the sand, her knees pulled up to her chest, as the waves washed in and out around her. Unaware of her watchful "presence," Jared and his friends laughed, talked, and played. Some of them sat around a picnic table beneath gently swaying palm trees. Others splashed through the surf.

Everything vanished. The shrieking of klaxons stabbed at Neema's eardrums. Neema found herself--with no warning or explanation--sitting in a raised captain's chair on the bridge of a starship. The lighting was blood red and alarms were going off all around her. She was dressed in a military uniform with boots and a banded collar. Her hair was pulled back into a tight ponytail.

"Balthazar," Neema said. "What's going on? Balthazar!"

"The Enemy has moved faster than we expected," Balthazar's gentle, computer voice replied. "I did not anticipate this."

Balthazar constantly monitored alternate futures transmitted to the past by his future self. How could he have missed anything?

"Why is this ship on alert?" Neema asked. "What's happening?"

"Watch," Balthazar told her. The wide screen that spanned the front wall rippled. Images burst to crystalline life.

"No," Neema gasped.

* * *

Roxanne Hanlon leaped to her feet as a figure in black body armor came hurtling through the air, struck a bulkhead, and dropped to the floor. A laser rifle clattered to the deck beside him.

"Stop him!" someone cried. "He must be stopped!"

A pile of tangled bodies burst into the room like a scene from a football game. Two black armored shapes clung to a shambling, disheveled man in a bloody uniform. *Sheppard?*

The heap of bodies slammed into the wall. Sheppard flung the black armored shapes from his body, slammed their helmeted heads together, and tossed them aside.

"Mr. Sheppard?" the young administrative assistant gasped.

Sheppard looked up at her. His face was a battered pulp. "Run," he said.

Sheppard scooped up the rifle that had been dropped by the first man--the one he had thrown across the room. He opened the door and Roxie ran through it. He bounded through after her, but ran in the opposite direction.

"Access *Intrepid* communications network," he shouted into his chronocomm. "Captain Nancy Butler."

"This communication is not authorized by Vectorcomm," a woman's voice replied.

"Security override," Sheppard said. "Authorization gamma gamma epsilon beta seventeen."

* * *

At first Captain Butler thought she was dreaming. She had stretched out for a nap and fallen fast asleep. Now, disoriented, she forced himself into a sitting position.

"Captain Butler!" She immediately recognized the voice of Charles Fairbanks, her communications specialist.

"Butler," she said. "What is it, Charles?"

"We just got a message from Colonel Sheppard," Fairbanks said. "I think you should see this."

"Show me."

Sheppard's face appeared on her screen. His left cheek was bleeding and his hair was askew.

"*Vector's* been taken over," he said. "Security compromised." He looked around wildly. The image spun. Butler got an instant's impression of several figures in black armor and helmets. They were upside down. Butler heard the rattle of weapon fire. "Those ships in orbit. . . *Xxxsssstttt.*" Lines of static formed on the image. Sheppard's face froze, pixelated, and broke apart. The screen blanked.

"What happened to that signal?" Butler demanded.

"Jammed at the source," Fairbanks said.

"Get me *Vector* station," Butler said. "Tell them I have to talk to Sheppard immediately."

"Planetary defense platforms have just armed themselves," Echo Yazzi, the tactical officer announced. "They're targeting us!"

"Evasive!" Butler cried. "Deploy all countermeasures."

Butler collided with the door--it opened too slowly--as she bounded out into the hall without even pulling on her boots. She'd stretched out on her bunk without ever changing into pajamas. At the moment she wouldn't have cared if she had been wearing a lace nightgown. She collided with several people as she fought her way to the bridge.

The doors parted. She rushed into the dark room with its giant screen and lumbered up to the captain's chair.

Butler's throat constricted when she saw the screen. Space was on fire. Red and yellow particle beams cut shimmering tracks through black fabric. These were, of course, false color images produced by the computer. The beams were really invisible in a vacuum. Silent flashes of exploding gas and brilliant bursts of plasma glowed in a swirling maelstrom of debris--debris from *Intrepid*'s hull. Hazy tracks of flaming metal plummeted down into Earth's atmosphere like burning tears.

One ship--an Interplanetary Guard battle cruiser judging by the shape--had leaped ahead of the others and was ripping *Intrepid* to pieces with torpedo bursts and particle beams.

"That's the *Dauntless*," Fairbanks said. "It's one of ours."

"Launch the drones!" Butler ordered. Yazzi deftly executed the order.

Defense drones swarmed from their launch bays, but most of them were taken down by the ship's flashing particle beams before they could clear the station. They blew apart like Fourth of July rockets and showered the Earth with fading sparks. The *Intrepid*'s main communications antennae had been sheared off. Torpedoes bit deep into the ship's armored hull. Chunks of debris spun through space on flaming axes--and were those bodies?

What am I going to do? That was her first thought. *I'm not a soldier. I'm a teacher, a scientist. This isn't what I trained for.*

"I'm getting distress calls from *Yosemite* station," Fairbanks said. "They've been attacked. They've got hull breaches all over the place."

"Captain?"

"What about *Vector*?" Butler asked.

"They're not bothering it," Fairbanks said.

Alarms went off. Trails of fire burned their way across space.

"Incoming!" Yazzi said. "Torpedoes."

"Shoot them down," Butler said. "Automatic firing."

"Initiating autofire sequence," Yazzi said. The forward cannon fired. The particle beams were dancing across space before she'd finished saying it.

This is insane, Butler thought. *What is going on here?* It was as if she had dropped off to sleep in her quarters only to wake up in some weird alternate reality.

"Particle beams engaged," Yazzi said.

The ship bucked. Klaxons hooted.

"We're hit!" Yazzi said. "It's the *Dauntless*. They've locked onto us."

"Keep the main cannon focused on those torpedoes," Captain Butler said. "Fire lateral guns at the *Dauntless*."

"Hull breach," the computer's voice said. "Decks 14 and 15. Emergency systems responding."

The ship rocked again. The klaxons continued to wail.

"Damage to starboard thrusters," the computer's voice said. "Emergency systems responding. Starboard weapons inoperative."

A flash lit the edge of the viewscreen. The ship rolled hard to one side.

"Hull breach," the computer's voice said. "Main shuttle port. Emergency systems inoperative."

"Evasive!" Butler yelled. "They're carving us up like a turkey."

A flash erupted over Earth's blue horizon.

"I just lost *Yosemite* station," Fairbanks said. "Getting distress calls from the Nagasaki."

"Captain," Yazzi said. "We've got two more ships closing on us. Asteroid smashers."

"Magnify!" the captain said.

The asteroid smashers moved in like sharks, pulling into formation around the *Dauntless*. Flashing ribbons of hellfire tore at the *Intrepid*'s hull.

"Evasive!" Butler said. "Fire everything we have."

"The controls aren't responding," Yazzi told her.

The big ships stopped moving. They hung still in space for several seconds, then turned back the way they had come.

"Looks like we got a reprieve," Yazzi said. "For the next thirty seconds anyway."

"There's another ship out there," Fairbanks said. The viewer zoomed in. "They're attacking it."

The new arrival was small and saucer-shaped with skid-like projections on each side, and the big asteroid smashers were firing at it as it darted, rolled, and dodged around them. It was stinging them, tearing into the asteroid smashers with some kind of concentrated beam weapons. The smashers were fighting back with compression bombs and particle beams. Most of them missed the target, but some of the bursts had struck home. The saucer's hull was damaged, but it would not be stopped. Space filled with bright flashes of weapons fire as it dodged like a bird darting through a pack of dogs.

"Emergency systems coming online," Yazzi said.

"What's going on here?" Captain Butler asked. "Scan that fourth ship. Can you identify it?"

"Checking, captain," Yazzi said. The image had been fed into the targeting scanners. It was instantly compared to every other ship in the *Intrepid*'s tactical files. "Completely unknown configuration," she finally said. "The maneuverability and the firepower. . . . We don't have anything that can do that."

"They've hit it," Fairbanks said. "It's spinning out of control. It looks like they've damaged it."

CHAPTER 3: Rude Awakening

"AAAAGGGHHH!"

Brightness. Pain.

Jerked suddenly, painfully, from her synthetic reality world, Neema Arita woke up in the dark, her skin burning, tingling as if from an electrical shock. She was floating in a tiny, underground sea. Murky emergency lights burned somewhere beyond a wall of heavy glass. The image of a starship's bridge had vanished. What had happened to the interface?

Neema was in a cryogenic tank aboard a starship orbiting late twenty first century Earth. This was no surprise to her, but she had never been awake while she was still in the tank. She wasn't supposed to be.

"Balthazar!" In her mind, she cried out for the ship's computer. "Balthazar!" For months--or decades, depending on your temporal frame of reference--the cybernetic interface that tied her active mind into the ship's computer system had been Neema's only link to the "real" world. Now it was completely silent.

Neema was alone. Her sluggish fingers brushed the crystalline fluid around her. She flexed her muscles and felt the harnesses around her. Electrical pads were stuck to her larger muscles. These had exercised them, kept them from atrophying during the months she floated in stasis. The harnesses had provided resistance.

The ship bucked. Neema fell against the glass. She was helpless, helpless as a fish in an aquarium. Beyond the ship's metal bulkheads were three asteroid smashers, and they were ripping the ship to pieces.

"Balthazar!" Neema cried out one last time. She tried to speak and found her mouth filled with fluid--something thicker than water, thinner than gelatin. She was breathing through a tube that plugged into a cybernetic interface in her belly--a kind of restored umbilical connection. Panic gave way to steely resolve.

She had to get out of the tank, had to find out what was happening. There was an emergency release lever mounted on the bar above her head. Neema pulled her hand out of the padded band that held her arm to the harness, reached up, and pulled against the lever. For an instant nothing happened. Then, suddenly she was sliding upward. The tank fell away and a heavy sheet of fluid fell away from Neema's body and splashed down into the tank beneath her. She blinked the fluid out of her eyes. The air of the ship was cold against her drying skin. Neema wasn't wearing much in the way of protective clothing. Her pelvis was encased in a waste removal unit. Even though the fluid pumped into her system through the umbilical interface had left little solid waste, the unit had still been necessary. Harnesses were attached to a brassiere made of rubbery, black neoprene and a jointed metal spine that was glued to Neema's backbone. Neema coughed up what seemed like gallons of fluid and finally found a vacuum hose and finished emptying her lungs that way.

A violent jolt threw the ship onto its side and tore Neema out of her harness. Artificial gravity blinked out and Neema found herself floating, surrounded by blobs and globules of floating green fluid. The dim lights played weirdly across them. Neema gently unplugged the life support tube from her navel. Folds of flesh closed around the spigot inside. She unplugged the wire mounted behind her right ear and disconnected the hose mounted on the back of her waste removal unit. Fortunately the unit was self sealing so she didn't have to add the dodging of flying urine to her list of troubles.

Neema swam through the air, grabbed a handrail, and dragged herself to an airlock that was roughly the size of a manhole. She pulled open the release lever and the heavy, pressurized door popped open. Neema dragged herself through and slammed the door behind her. The inside of the tube, unlike the rest of the ship, was brightly lit. It had an independent power source. Moments later Neema dropped through a second door into a closet-sized escape pod. She strapped herself into a heavily padded seat and tightened the belts. A couple of feet from her face was a device that looked like an earplug mounted on a roll of cable. It was a cerebral interface, a mental link to the escape pod's internal computer. Neema pulled the cable free, plugged it into the socket beneath her left ear, and found herself sitting in a large room surrounded by screens. On them, she could see the other ships firing on her own. One of the asteroid smashers had been damaged. The other two ships were hammering hers for all they were worth. The Earth hung in the background.

"Balthazar," she said. "Balthazar?"

"I am here," the soothing voice of the ship's computer replied.

"Damage report," Neema said. "How bad is it?"

"Engines damaged," Balthazar said. "The main computer is inoperative. I am a replica, a back-up."

"What do we do now?" Neema said.

"Recommendation," Balthazar said. "Eject escape pod and overload damaged engines."

"But I'll be trapped here," she said. "In this time."

"I'm afraid you already are," Balthazar said. "The engines are severely damaged. One more direct hit will disable them permanently. If I force an overload, however, we may be able to destroy the attacking ships."

Neema paused, considering it.

"Do it," she said.

The escape pod blasted free of the damaged ship and shot toward the sleeping Earth below.

* * *

"Something just ejected from the little ship," Yazzi said. "It's falling toward Earth."

The enemy ships tried to lock weapons, but ghost images confused their tactical systems.

Neema's ship exploded like the wrath of God and swallowed three of the attacking ships in a wall of silent fury.

Sizzling hunks of melting metal rained down into the Earth's atmosphere. Dust-sized chunks of debris pelted the Intrepid's hull.

Butler, Fairbanks, and the rest of the bridge crew watched the screen silently.

"Sir," Perez said. "I've got something on the long range scanners. They're coming into visual range now."

"They?" Butler asked.

Perez touched a button.

The screen rippled. An armada filled the screen. There were asteroid smashers, Interplanetary Guard ships, deep space survey vessels, automated factories that captured meteorites and processed the ore . . . .

"How many?" she heard herself ask. This was rapidly turning into a surrealistic out-of-body experience.

"Twenty," Perez said. "Maybe more."

Butler thought about *Vector* station sitting there in orbit. She thought of Sheppard and the other friends she had there, of all those shoppers, tourists, and station employees.

"Perez," Butler said. "Jose', get us out of here."

Perez turned to her. He opened his mouth, started to say something.

"We may be Earth's only chance," Butler said, her voice rough. "Get us out of here now."

"Yes, ma'am."

Perez returned the screen to forward view. Butler felt her stomach knot up as she looked at *Vector* hanging in orbit.

"Help them, God," she said.

CHAPTER 4: Splashdown

Discovered by Captain Cook in his exploration of the South Pacific, the island of Kele was only five miles long and two miles wide. Artifacts found in the island's caves showed that it had been inhabited once. It had briefly been home to a tropical resort that had gone bankrupt and to a billionaire's estate that had been wiped out by a hurricane. Gaith Corbalew's family had purchased the island as a place to "live it up" when their space mining regime had been in its heyday. They had also built a genetics research lab in an isolated area on the opposite end of the island from their private resort area. When Corbalew was arrested and his assets liquidated, reclusive trillionaire Lancing DeFalco had "inherited" the island along with Corbalew's company. He had used it as a research facility and retreat center. This was before he had moved to his secret base on Venus for some real seclusion. For Pirate, Jared, Wendy, and the others, it had truly been a paradise.

They had spent the past two days playing in the sand, swimming in the surf, snorkeling, or exploring the island's caves and waterfalls.

On the night of the explosion in orbit, Pirate Eisman and Wendy Blake were strolling down the beach in the moonlight. Their relationship, from Pirate's perspective, had been a strange one. They had started out as friends. Just as things seemed to be developing into something more, Wendy had pulled away from him, shut him out. Now here she was, looking great, playing with her damp ringlets of hair, and talking to him like they had been friends forever. They were walking back toward the beach house when they saw Jared standing in the shadow of a grove of palm trees gazing up into the heavens. Nobody else was anywhere around.

"Where are the others?" Pirate asked.

"I think we're the last ones," Jared said absently. His eyes never left the heavens.

"What is it?" Wendy asked.

"I just saw a shooting star," Jared said. "It was huge, crackling and exploding." He stopped. "I don't see it anymore." He looked at Pirate and Wendy. "Strange. It almost seemed familiar." He looked back up into the sky, shook his head. "I'm going in."

They watched him go.

"Did he have tears in his eyes?" Wendy asked.

"I think so," Pirate said. "It doesn't make any sense." He turned and gazed into the heavens. One of the overhead stars--he was never sure which--was *Vector* station. The yellow eye of Venus burned on the horizon.

Pirate walked over and took one last look at the face he, Tori, and Hal had carved in the sand earlier that day. By morning the image would be gone, but Pirate couldn't resist touching it up one last time. It seemed like a symbol of the fun they had had. Wendy stood beside him watching. It was cute how she dug into the sand with her curled toes. Wendy's toes, her feet, her entire legs were bionic. That didn't keep Pirate from sneaking peeks at them--and at Wendy in general.

She really looked beautiful in that swimsuit. Pirate stood up to examine his work.

"I've missed you," he said.

"I know," she said. "I've missed you too. I've missed a lot of things. At Christmas, when we were in Crane Island, I started to feel like myself again for the first time in years. It was almost like being nine years old again and having Mom, Bianca, and the first Intrepid Force still alive. For about three days, I could think about them without hurting. Then Jared and I were captured, Jared went into the hospital, and we nearly all died. Just when I started feeling like it was safe to be happy, we nearly died, and the old walls went right back up again.

"You and Zapper were both right about the things you said after the memorial service," she told him. "You don't have any idea how much you helped me." He gently stroked her cheek, smoothed her soggy bangs back from her forehead. "Coming here has helped me too. It's like Christmas in Crane Island. I can almost believe it's possible to really be happy."

"So what do we do now?" he asked.

"We take our time," she said. "Get to know each other better as friends and see what happens."

"I guess I can live with that," he said.

"I might let you kiss me if you want to," she said with a mischievous grin.

Pirate's mind was filled with questions. He knew that Wendy and Mike Noguchi, the team's martial arts expert, had dated each other once, and he had heard rumors that they were starting to rekindle their old relationship. Then suddenly Wendy and Mike were avoiding each other. What was really going on? Pirate was dying to know, but now was not the time to ask. This, he realized, might be the only chance he ever got to kiss Wendy, and he was not going to waste it.

"Well," he said. "Okay. If it will make you feel better." He turned around, took her face in his hands and gently lifted her delicate chin. His heart was pounding and his spirit was soaring. He couldn't--in his wildest dreams--believe this was really happening. *Dear God, don't let anything spoil this moment.*

"Oh, give it a rest," an alcohol-slurred voice said from behind them. Wendy pulled her face away, startled. Pirate and Wendy turned around and saw Zapper staggering up the beach in the moonlight. He had the shape of a bottle in his hand. He stumbled and fell headlong into the sand. His feet kicked the air as he crumpled to the ground like a broken kite. Pirate and Wendy ran to help him.

"Are you all right?" Pirate asked as he turned him over.

"Jim-spiffy," Zapper drawled. He had sand stuck to his face and matting his hair.

"Where have you been?" Wendy asked him.

"Just spendin' some quality time with myself," Zapper smiled crookedly. He clumsily brushed away the sand.

"Are you okay?" Wendy asked.

"You bet your bionic butt I am, sweet cheeks," Zapper said. He giggled wildly. He spent several colorful seconds telling Pirate and Wendy what a pathetic world it was, but how great he was feeling in spite of this fact.

"I think we better get you to bed," Wendy said.

"Don't you worry about me," Zapper said. "I'm a happy drunk in a sad world." He raised the bottle. "Here's to my buddy Ahadri who should be here with us, but he got himself blown to kingdom come saving our sorry butts." He raised the bottle to his lips, but it was empty. He rolled to his feet, a look of fury on his face, and smashed the empty bottle against a tree.

"Zapper!" Wendy grabbed him.

"Lemme go!" he yelled. He grabbed her and jolted her hard. Both of them fell to the sand. Wendy curled into a ball and lay still. Zapper lay on his back jerking and writhing, his eyes rolled up in his head. He was having a seizure. Other Recombinants of Zapper's "design" had died of a fatal form of *epilepsy.* Pirate reached for Zapper and jerked his hands back. Zapper was still discharging electricity. Pirate couldn't help him until the seizure died down.

Pirate knelt by Wendy and checked her pulse. Her heartbeat was strong. He gathered her into his arms, rested her head against his shoulder, and waited for Zapper's seizure to subside. His body continued to jerk.

"Help!" Pirate finally yelled. "Somebody help!"

The others, hearing the commotion, came running out and gathered around them.

"What happened?"

"He's having a seizure."

"What's wrong with Wendy?" Tori asked.

"He shocked her," Pirate said.

Hal reached for Zapper. "Don't touch him! He's still shooting off electricity!"

"He's coming out of it," Jaina said.

Zapper's trembling was beginning to subside. Finally his body relaxed. Jaina examined him.

"He's breathing normally," she said. "His heartbeat's regular. Let's get him inside. I'm going to call *Vector*."

A gust of wind rippled the palm leaves overhead. It had the threat of a coming storm hanging on its warm breath. The waves were crashing into the beach more violently now. Hal and Mike carried Zapper into the house. Jaina ran ahead. She snatched a chronocomm from the counter.

"Vectorcomm medical," she said. "Medical emergency."

"One moment please," the watch replied.

Jaina stood stiffly and patted her foot to alleviate the tension.

"Come on," she said.

"*Vector* Medical," a voice finally answered. "May I help you?"

"Dr. Garcia, please," Jaina said.

"One moment," the watch replied. "I'm sorry. Dr. Garcia is not available. Would you like to speak to Dr. Adams?"

"I've never heard of Dr. Adams," Jaina said. "Okay. Fine. Give me Dr. Adams."

"This is Dr. Adams," the voice of a stranger said. He had an odd accent. Jaina described Zapper's situation.

"Record his bioscans and send them to me," the doctor said. "I'll call you back after we've had the chance to analyze them."

"Okay," Jaina said. Moments later she scanned Zapper's body. The scanner indicated massive amounts of alcohol in his bloodstream and minor disruptions in his brain's electrical activity. Otherwise, he seemed to be normal.

Wendy was sitting up on the couch. Pirate sat beside her holding her hand.

"I think I'd better scan you too," Jaina said.

"Okay," Wendy answered sleepily. Jaina waved the scanner over her. Her brow furrowed.

"Something wrong?" Hal asked.

"I'm not sure," Jaina said. "I'm picking up something on your brain scans. The scanner can't identify it. I'd better send it to Dr. Adams."

Jaina uploaded the data immediately. Dr. Adams never called back.

* * *

About five miles away, Neema's head and shoulders broke the surface of the ocean. Her weakened body was wrapped around a floatation device. She gasped for breath. Somewhere in the dark void beneath her, a spent escape pod was sinking deep into the sunless depths. She could make out a strip of land on the horizon. There was a light. Gathering her strength, she began to kick herself toward it. The water near the surface felt like a warm bath.

Neema's heart pounded. The island ahead was the place where Jared and the others were resting, recovering from their fight on Venus. She was both excited and terrified by the thought of actually meeting them. They didn't know her, but she had watched them invisibly from the virtual reality world of her starship for months. She had stood beside them in New Orleans when they first met each other, had been with them on Vector space station when Reverend Sheppard had trained them, had spent Christmas break with Pirate, Jared, and Wendy in Crane Island, Louisiana. She had followed them to Venus and wept with them when giant, gentle Ahadri gave his life to stop Gaith Corbalew. She knew them like favorite characters in a video drama. No. More than that. They were real, and she had shared their lives with them. She had even helped them, sent them veiled messages through the empathic interface Balthazar had implanted in Jared's head years earlier. Surely they would accept her. Surely they would take her in and care for her in her weakened condition. Surely they wouldn't treat her like a stranger and shut her out.

But this wasn't just about her welfare. Neema clung to the floatation device with one hand and massaged a cramping thigh with the other. She had to warn them, had to save them from what was to come. This had been her purpose from the beginning. She just hadn't expected to be completing it without Balthazar's help. She choked back tears at the thought of Balthazar. He had only been a computer, an interactive device with no real feelings, with no real consciousness, but he had felt real to her. He had seemed as real as any friend she had ever known.

What friends had she really known? Neema was an artificially gestated being, a combination of a clone and a cyborg. Twenty third century technology did not allow biological beings to travel through time, only machinery. Her benefactors had been left with no choice but to clone her from genetically altered cells and to implant her with the memory imprints of a young woman who would not be born until the twenty-third century. That meant all of her childhood memories were really someone else's memories. Her memories of Jared, Pirate, and the others were real memories, but they were her memories only. The others had never even known she was there observing them, and might not have approved if they had known. The only real friends she had ever had were three boys and a girl who had lived in Crane Island, Louisiana in the late twentieth century--and their memories of her had been erased to protect their safety. Only months ago, she had said goodbye to them and frozen herself to wait for the late twenty first century to arrive. Two of them were dead and buried now, and Pirate Eisman was their great-grandson. It hardly seemed possible.

* * *

Pirate Eisman was reflective as he crept into the darkened bedroom the guys were sharing and slipped beneath the sheets of his bunk that night. He had kissed Wendy--well, almost. Things were actually all right between him and Wendy after all those months of uncertainty and rejection. What should have been unbridled joy was tarnished by his fear for Zapper's safety and the very real possibility that he would wake up the next morning, and Wendy would be cold shouldering him again--or making up with Mike. Beneath that was a darker, deeper fear that he couldn't even begin to name--a pervasive sense that something terrible was about to happen. Pirate sighed. He had been hanging around Jared too long.

Where was Jared? Pirate didn't see him. Zapper was snoring between the sheets as though he didn't have a care in the world. Mike and Hal were in the living room playing video games with Tori. Pirate could hear the occasional bursts of laughter and moans of defeat. Wendy and Jaina had already turned in.

The balcony's sliding glass door opened letting in the sound of rolling ocean waves and the salty smell of the ocean beyond. Pirate could see a lean, lanky shadow standing black against a field of stars.

"I saw you walking down the beach with Wendy," Jared said.

"Nothing happened," Pirate told him.

"I know," Jared said.

"You know?" Pirate said. "What does that mean? Are you saying I'm moral and chivalrous or that I'm not any good with women?"

"Exactly," Jared said.

"My friend."

They stood in silence for a moment.

"You feel it too, don't you?" Jared's voice said.

"Feel what?" Pirate asked.

Jared didn't answer.

"Yes," Pirate finally said. "I feel it."

* * *

Neema rested for a moment, floating in the warm ocean with her arms folded over the floatation device and her head resting on them. She kicked gently against the current, rose and fell with the waves.

A whirring insect sound brought Neema fully awake. She spun around, slipped off the floatation device, and swallowed a mouthful of warm salt water. She coughed and water came out of her nose. Her eyes watered. She fought to bring them into focus and saw a fleet of giant black insects sweeping over the face of the ocean. Spotlights skimmed the water beneath them.

Probes!

Panic flashed through Neema's body. Instantly she took a swallow of air and dove deep. Neema was about twenty-five feet below the surface of the water when she brushed against a sandbar. The white sand was like crushed diamond beneath her. She looked up and saw bright circles of light glowing against the surface of the water. She could make out eight discs of light dancing over the surface of the ocean in formation. There was a type of beauty in the dance. It looked like a kind of water ballet. The dance turned deadly. Neema heard the muffled sound of automatic weapons fire. Deadly needles of metal cut bubbling trails through the dark green waters. Neema pushed herself to the edge of the sandbar. She felt a burst of cold current sweep up from the dark abyss below. Something sliced across her thigh. Neema felt the sting of ocean water and realized she had been shot--nicked, at least--by one of the projectiles. She threw herself over the edge of the sandbar and embraced the darkness.

Neema held her breath for nearly five minutes. Her genetically engineered body, her superhuman stamina, allowed her to bluff the probes. She waited in the darkness until, one by one, the disks of light soared away.

Exhausted, starved for air, she kicked her way to the surface. In the moonlight she could see a dark cloud of blood floating from the nick on her thigh. She began to pray that there weren't any sharks around.

Neema's head broke the surface. She gulped in lungfuls of air and looked around for the probes. In the distance, she could see them headed toward the island. The island! Jared and the others were there. She had to warn them.

Neema found the pulverized bits of her floatation device. The largest piece was no bigger than a marble. She would have to make it to shore on her own--and she would have to get there fast. Neema stretched herself upon the water, kicking furiously, grabbing handfuls of water and shoving them behind her with tightly cupped fingers. She gulped air, put her head down, gulped more air. The island was still so far away, the lights so distant.

Neema saw something moving in the water about twenty feet away from her. A pectoral fin broke the surface. Sharks!

CHAPTER 5: Rain of Fire

Space was full of ships, so many ships. They hung over Earth; a dark and silent armada of gray metal dragons, mutant vessels possessed by a cold and calculating intelligence.

"My name is Ozymandias,King of Kings," the mysterious voice said, pulling a line from a poem by Percy Shelley. *"Look upon my works, ye mighty, and despair."*

The shattered remains of those who had dared to oppose the self-proclaimed emperor still floated in high orbit. They fell to Earth slowly, in burning trails, as their orbits decayed and gravity drew them, one by one, to fiery nonexistence.

There were no ships left to oppose the invading fleet. The planetary defense satellites, automated weapons of tremendous might, had turned their deadly cannons toward the fragile planet below. Humans lived on that world, a world like none other they had found. They clung to a thin layer of soil that could support their lives. Hate-filled mechanical eyes glared down through an ocean of oxygen, nitrogen, and water vapor onto their ant farm cities. Powerful generators began to churn out energy, to pour it into the waiting cannons.

The *Intrepid* was racing away from Earth at its top speed, its engines pushed to the limit. Captain Butler sat fused to her chair like a frozen corpse. She remembered a fragment of a story she had read about a ship full of dead men that had been found floating in some northern sea. The captain was still gripping the wheel, his body frozen solid. Captain Butler felt like that captain. Her mind was frozen. Her jaw was locked tight and her fingers gripped the arms of her chair. She had not spoken for nearly two hours.

"Captain," Fairbanks said. "Captain Butler?"

"Yes," she said. "Yes, Charles. What is it?"

"Something's been downloaded into our databanks," he said. "They're full. In fact, part of our library has been overwritten."

"That's impossible," Butler said. "There were over 70 astroquads of free space. It would take years to fill it up."

"See for yourself," Fairbanks said.

Captain Butler sighed and rose to her feet. She walked over and stood beside Fairbanks as he punched up readouts of the *Intrepid*'s databanks.

"Get ready to purge those new files," Butler said. "It's probably some kind of virus. It can't be anything good."

"I beg to differ, Captain," a man's voice said.

Captain Butler spun around.

"Who said that?" she demanded.

"I think it came from the speakers," Fairbanks said.

"Jonas warned us about this," Butler said. "They've taken over the ship's computer."

* * *

Sheppard woke up with a light shining in his face. He was in an empty room mounted on a frame that held his arms immobile. A bright spotlight was shining directly overhead making a circular pool of light on the floor around him. The rest of the room was dark. Sheppard felt like a museum exhibit. Most of the wall in front of him was taken up by a large viewscreen. Through the haze of the spotlight, Sheppard could make out an image of the planet Earth surrounded by its renegade defense platforms, asteroid smashers, Interplanetary Guard ships, and what was left of Earth's orbiting space stations. There was no furniture in the room--only gray carpet and white walls. Sheppard could only assume he was still aboard *Vector* station. He strained against his bonds. There were tight . . . and strong.

Sheppard felt the thrill of fear when he heard a rustle of fabric in the darkness outside of the spotlight's glare and realized there was someone else with him. He spun his head around a little too quickly--his head began to spin--and saw two red points of light hanging about six feet above the floor. They were moving closer.

"Who's there?" Sheppard growled into the darkness. His voice was rough. His throat, he realized, was raw and dry. How long had he been without water? Captain Gillette--or his image--entered. He wore a black turtleneck, black pants, and black boots. He stepped into the halo that surrounded Sheppard. His expression was calm, pleasant. Sheppard glared at him.

"Who are you?"

"Your enemy." The answer was calm, matter-of-fact.

"Should I know you?"

"I've gone by many names," the other said. "You may call me Gogue. That isn't my true name, of course, but you people are so hung up on names."

"What about Captain Gillette?" Sheppard fought to clear his throat. "Does that name mean anything to you?"

"Gillette?" He snorted dismissively. "The former occupant of this shell? He no longer matters. None of you do."

"Where are you from? You sound American."

The other one laughed.

"You people are so hung up on things like that. It's all you care about. Where are you from? Who are your parents? Trivia! Sheer trivia! My accent and language are for your benefit, Reverend Sheppard."

"You know who I am?"

"Of course I do. I know everything about you."

"Are you the one in charge of this fleet? The one responsible for these attacks?"

"Of course I am. I told you I was the enemy. Weren't you paying attention?"

"Why?" Sheppard asked. "Why have you done this?"

"Because that's who I am," the enemy answered. "I'm the son of Alexander, the stepchild of Genghis Khan, the nephew of Hitler, the grandchild of Napoleon, the disciple of Maltuvius. Their blood flows in my veins. I channel their ghosts. I'm going to take over this world, to establish my kingdom here. I think you and your kind have been expecting me for some time now--for over two millennia."

"Are you saying you're Christ?"

"Oh, no," Gillette's image laughed. "Of course not. That would be insane. I'm the other one. The yin to the yang. The shadow to the light. The dark reflection."

"The Antichrist?"

"Ah. You do understand. You're not as stupid as that heavy brow ridge makes you look."

"You are not the Antichrist."

"Oh? What makes you so sure?"

"Your methods are wrong." Sheppard strained against his bonds. They were tight.

"Wrong? How do you mean?"

"The Antichrist doesn't rule by military conquest. He rules by seduction. Evil appears as good. The flaws are hidden until the hook has been set and the victim no longer has the power to resist."

"Yes." Gogue seemed intrigued. "Go on."

"And what about Israel?" Sheppard continued. "Isn't the so-called man of lawlessness supposed to violate the temple or something like that?"

"Violate the temple. Total carnage! Delicious!" He clapped his hands together.

"Now, wait a minute."

"I'm really going to look forward to our exchanges. You tell me what the Antichrist is supposed to do, and I'll go do it."

"What about his defeat at the hands of Christ's army? Can you simulate that for me?"

"Don't ruin the fun."

"I don't know what kind of sick game you think you're playing . . ." Sheppard began.

"Have you ever heard of Risk?"

"The military strategy game?" The question took Sheppard off guard. "I used to play it in school."

"Didn't you ever want to play it for real?" the other asked. "Command armies. Drop bombs. Build monuments to yourself."

"'My name is Ozymandias, King of Kings,'" Sheppard countered. "'Look upon my works, ye mighty, and despair.'"

"Percy Bysshe Shelley." Gogue clapped his hands together.

"I heard you quoting it earlier," Sheppard said, "when you were blasting everything to pieces. I think you missed the point."

"Really? What point is that?"

"In the poem," Sheppard said, "those words were inscribed on a broken monument half buried in sand next to a statue whose head had been knocked off. That's how all despots eventually end up."

"Until now," Gogue said. He started toward the door. "I'd better go. I've got a world to conquer. I think I'm going to enjoy these discussions."

"I don't plan for it to be a lasting thing."

"You might as well enjoy it. You may be here for quite a while. That is up to you, of course."

"Why don't you just kill me now?"

"If I wanted you dead, I would have killed you already."

"Then what do you want? Information? Military secrets?"

Gogue laughed.

"From you? Hardly. Look around you. I control everything. There are no secrets from me. No one can keep any secrets from me."

"Then why am I here?"

"You're a lab rat. I want to see what it takes to break your primitive, outdated faith."

"If you push me hard enough and torture me long enough, you may coerce me into saying that I deny my faith--I'm only human--but you'll never make me deny it in my heart."

"Don't be so sure."

"How would you know what's in my heart?" Sheppard pulled at his bonds.

"Truth serums. Polygraphs. Synthetic reality simulations. I would know."

"What difference does it make to you what I believe?"

"As I said, you're an experiment. I have others, of course, but you are certainly one of the most colorful. A bionic killer turned missionary."

"I was never a killer. I was a soldier. Even before I found my faith, killing was a last resort."

"A last resort? Are you sure about that?"

The room aboard *Vector* vanished. Sheppard was still bound by his shackles and Gogue still stood in front of him, but everything else had changed. They were in a jungle at night. Tall grass whispered as the wind touched it. Crickets and cicadas sang. They were standing on the edge of a bog. Sheppard could smell the stagnant mud. A group of men in camouflaged body armor marched through the tall grass in front of them. Images of the jungle behind them moved across their bodies as they walked. Behind them was a "mule," a robot platform with tracks. It was piled with weapons and electronic gear. The men were carrying pulse rifles with heat and motion sensors on the scopes. Night vision scopes projected from their foreheads. They looked like aliens with cyclops eyes mounted on stems. In the midst of them were two barefoot men in ragged clothes.

"Take these prisoners to the detention center," the captain said. "Be back in ten minutes."

"But the detention center is two hours away," the younger man said. He was big and bearlike, but there was an honesty about his face. He looked like a big farm boy.

"I know that, sergeant," the lieutenant said. "We're surrounded by the enemy. I don't want to risk any more men than I have to."

"But sir . . ."

"These men have seen our camp," the lieutenant said. "They've seen our weapons and, thanks to that blabbermouth Kenrick, they know what we're planning to do. If we keep them with us, they'll give us away. If we drug them and leave them behind, they'll be found and revived. Then they'll give us away."

The young soldier looked down.

"Do you have a problem with this order, Sergeant Sheppard?"

A pause.

"No, sir."

The image froze, then broke apart.

"You killed those men." The accusation hung in the air for a moment.

"I didn't want to," Sheppard said, struggling to speak. "I didn't have a choice."

"Of course you had a choice," the other cried. "You could have refused to obey the order, let someone else do it."

"They would have given away our position." The words rang false as Sheppard said them. "We had to destroy their base and rescue the prisoners they had taken. It was too important."

"I'm sure that's what you tell yourself," Gogue said, "on those nights you can't sleep, those nights you see those men's faces in your mind."

Sheppard didn't answer.

"Your faith is nothing more than an illusion you cling to, a dream from which you are about to awaken."

"An Antichrist who doesn't believe in God? I find that ironic."

"What?"

"To break my faith," Sheppard said, "You have to convince me that there isn't a God, that the scriptures are wrong. To convince me that you're the Antichrist, you have to prove that you're a fulfillment of things written in the Bible. You can't have it both ways. Which is it going to be?"

"You argue well for your stupid ideas," Gogue said. "You could almost convince me that the Earth is flat--if we weren't in space. I can see I'm going to enjoy this,"

Gogue stepped out of the light and into the surrounding shadows. A door slid open across the room. It formed a gray rectangle against a field of black. Gogue's inky silhouette moved into the frame. As he reached the door, he turned around. His face was still hidden in the shadows, but the shape had changed. It looked twisted and deformed. The red glow had returned to his eyes.

"I'll see you later," he said, his voice rough and inhuman. "Enjoy the show." The door closed.

Enjoy the show? Sheppard thought. What had he meant by that?

A flash pulled his attention to the screen. One of the orbiting platforms had just engaged its cannons. It was firing on Earth. Flashes filled the heavens with a silent chorus of shining death.

"No," Sheppard said. "Dear God, no!"

CHAPTER 6: Riddles

Five ships--two long, angular Interplanetary Guard ships and three short, bulky DeFalco ships--orbited Venus's yellow eye like strange moons. Satellites were being dumped into orbit as engineers and technicians rushed to restore planetary defenses. Less than one month earlier, the planet's defenses had been destroyed and *Arcadia* station, its orbiting spaceport, had been sent plummeting through the planet's poisonous atmosphere like a falling star. When Intrepid Force liberated the planet, they believed the nightmare was over. Now it appeared history was about to repeat itself.

Venus Base DeFalco lay beneath an atmospheric dome on the planet's surface. The base was a man-made paradise, a modern Atlantis with interlocking circles of buildings and parkland. The dome lights had been dimmed to simulate night. Lamps glowed along the colony's streets and along the paths that twisted their way through the base's simulated rainforest. The shattered ruins of a great tower stood on a hilltop in the colony's center. Ahadri Singh, a member of the Intrepid Force, had willingly given his life there to save his friends. Repair crews--human and mechanical--were rapidly erasing the signs of the battle the Intrepid Force had fought there only weeks earlier.

"Thank you for joining me," Jonas Cockrum said as he fell in beside the others on a walkway between buildings. The station dome lights had been dimmed to simulate night, but the night was anything but peaceful. The air around them was thick with tension.

"Do you think he'll help us?" Lieutenant Bohl asked. He had quickened his pace to match Cockrum's.

"Yes," Attorney Jolie Harrison said with her characteristic drawl. "He's been very cooperative."

Bohl was young and athletically built. He had close-cut blond hair and muscular arms. Jolie Harrison was from a small town in Oklahoma. A softball uniform would have fit her personality better than the business suit she was wearing.

Bohl, Harrison, and Cockrum were flanked by armed security guards. They entered a square building with heavy, blast resistant walls and passed through several checkpoints. Many had accused Lancing DeFalco, the reclusive trillionaire who had designed the base, of paranoia. The buildings that housed his living quarters were fortresses. It had been easy enough to convert this one into a prison.

The men guarding the door rose to their feet. Skin samples were taken from each of the visitors and analyzed by machines. DNA patterns were matched and confirmed.

"Signal him," Cockrum said. "Let him know we're coming."

"Yes, sir."

One of them signaled the prisoner while the other keyed in the command to unlock the door. Servos whined and heavy bolts slid away. The door opened with a pneumatic hiss. Cockrum and the others stepped through a hallway and into a large, lavishly furnished room. The chamber inside was dark. A high-backed chair sat at the center of the room, but the figure sitting in it was swathed in darkness.

"Jolie," a nasal voice said. "Good ta see ya, kid. Ain't it good ta see 'er, boss?"

"Yeah," a deeper, raspier voice answered. "Good ta see ya, sweetheart. And Jonas, how are ya, pally? To what do I owe dis pleasure?"

"We don't have time for this," Cockrum said.

"What's he doing?" Bohl whispered.

"The implant in his throat allows him to alter his voice at will," Harrison explained.

"He's had it since we were in the original Intrepid Force together," Cockrum sighed.

"Preston?" Counselor Harrison asked. "Are you trying to cop an insanity plea?"

Preston laughed. It was a tired, joyless laugh.

"Just passing the time until my execution," a third voice--Preston's real voice--answered.

"You're not going to be executed," Harrison said. "You might even get a full pardon if we're lucky."

"It's not you I'm worried about," the shadowed figure in the armchair answered. "My old friends may have forgiven me, but Corbalew's people never will. They're going to kill me. It doesn't matter what you do, you'll never be able to stop them. You don't have any idea what they're capable of."

"You're wrong about that," said Cockrum. "Turn on your monitor."

"What?" Preston was suddenly taken aback. "What's going on?"

"Communicore," Cockrum said. "Show HNN, main desk."

Jonas Cockrum had treated Preston well and Preston didn't know whether to be grateful for the kindness or resentful of his old friend's condescension. His quarters were outfitted with a premium entertainment system. It had a holo-dioramic screen.

Three dimensional figures were projected onto a stage area in the front and the backgrounds were projected onto a large, curved screen that was over three meters across. He had never watched it.

The giant wall monitor obeyed Cockrum's command instantly. A holographic image of a man and woman at a news desk floated inches above a curved screen. Behind them was an image of Earth surrounded by burning debris and an armada of ships. On either side were menu buttons, lists of breaking stories that could be pulled up upon request.

"Access 'Burning of Rome,'" Cockrum said grimly.

The United System headquarters, what was left of it, lay in smoking ruins.

"Defensive systems were completely overwhelmed by the unexpected attack," a young Indian man commented. "The death toll continues to climb."

"Access '*Nagasaki* station.'"

A low-yield warhead struck *Nagasaki* station and sent it spinning off its axis.

"Access 'Gogue's Ultimatum.'"

A man's face, shrouded in shadow, appeared on the screen spouting boasts and blasphemies.

"No," Preston said. He squeezed his eyes shut and rubbed his face with his hands. "God, when will this nightmare ever be over?"

"Envirocon," Cockrum said suddenly. "Increase illumination to standard daylight levels."

The lights slowly came up on Preston's lavishly furnished prison. Preston didn't seem to notice. He just sat in his chair shaking his head. Preston was dressed in a dark suit. He was gaunt and blond, and he struck Bohl as faintly effeminate.

"I warned you," Preston said. "I told Sheppard and the rest of you what he was planning." Preston sighed again. It was a hopeless, world weary sigh. "Why didn't you listen? Why doesn't anyone ever listen?"

"We listened, Preston," Cockrum said.

"You didn't give us anything we could act on," Bohl cut in. "Just a lot of talk about what was going to happen to us."

"I told you everything I knew," Preston said.

"Corbalew is awake now," Cockrum said.

"You said you would talk to him," Harrison reminded him, "We have to know what he knows."

"I'll do what I can," Preston said. "I'm afraid it will be precious little."

One of the security men held out a pair of shackles.

"I don't think that will be necessary," Cockrum said.

"Thank you, Jonas" Preston told him. "You always were a good friend." Cockrum wasn't sure if Preston was sincere or not. Much of what he said dripped with cynical irony.

"Are you ready?" Harrison asked.

"Corbalew probably has the exits covered," he said. He pulled open his coat to expose his heart to an imaginary sniper. "Sure, I'm ready."

He rose to his feet.

"So long, Richie," a female voice with a Bronx-Brooklyn accent said. "Don't fahget to write."

Harrison looked around uneasily.

"He used to do a ventriloquist act," Cockrum said.

Preston followed them down the dark wood corridors of the improvised safe house. The security guards led him through several checkpoints and to an elevator cab.

The six of them rode an airboat--a flying police car--to the hospital complex, strode down the main hall, and took another elevator down into the bowels of the planet, to the older part of the city that had been built before the domed colony above. Black Gaith Corbalew, as far as the public and his own henchmen knew, was dead. In reality he was in Venus's subterranean depths floating in a REGEN tank and regrowing the skin he had lost in the explosion that had taken Ahadri's life.

A female medical technician in a teal blue jumpsuit led Cockrum, Preston, Harrison, Bohl, and the guards past a checkpoint guarded by six human guards and two twelve-foot tall robot drones with guns mounted on their sides. On either side were banks of scanners. Preston, the guards, and the technician stepped through an airlock. The heavy door slammed and latched behind them. A second door unlatched and opened with a pneumatic hiss. Cockrum, Preston, and the others stepped through.

Corbalew's charred body was suspended in a tank filled with blue green gel. He was covered in a thin mesh that formed lattices for his new skin. Tubes were connected to his throat, stomach, and groin areas.

"All of this trouble," Bohl said, "for a man who will very likely be sentenced to death by lethal injection. It seems like a waste of effort."

"He knows too much," Cockrum said quietly. "Ironic. That same reason has been used to justify so many murders, but it's our reason for keeping Corbalew alive."

"Tell him Preston's here," Harrison whispered to the technician on duty.

"Mr. Corbalew," the young technician said. "Mr. Preston is here to see you."

Corbalew made croaking noises and bubbles formed.

"I'm touched," a computer-enhanced voice said. It was coming from a speaker mounted on the wall of the tank. "Did he bring flowers?"

"Maybe next time," Preston said. "Earth has been attacked. I need some answers. What do you know about it?"

"Look at me," Corbalew said. "I've been in this tank since the explosion. You've monitored every word I've said. What could I possibly know about what's happening on Earth now?"

"I heard you talking on board your ship before the attack on Venus," Preston said. "I heard you and--and that--that Gogue planning everything."

"Really?" Corbalew said. "Then why ask me anything? You already know as much as I do."

"What have you done?" Preston said. "It was your planet too. If that thing destroys it . . ."

"Destroys it?" Corbalew said. "Oh, no. There's no future in that. He only wants to control the lives of every man, woman, and child on the planet. Destroying one's own empire would be pointless."

"It didn't keep Nero from burning Rome," Preston pointed out bitterly.

"True," Corbalew said. "Quite true. But Nero was mad."

"And this Gogue isn't?" Preston asked.

"I'm sure you think he is," Corbalew said. "Primitive intellects have little comprehension of their betters."

"You managed to free yourself from prison with weapons unlike any we've ever seen before," Preston said. "Where did you get them?"

"Gogue," Corbalew said. "You know that."

"But who is Gogue?" Preston finally asked. "What is Gogue?"

The question hung silently in the air between them.

"The devil," Corbalew said. He laughed, a rattling filthy sound. Then he closed his eyes.

"Corbalew," Preston said. "Corbalew?"

"It looks like he's asleep," the technician said. "That's the most he's spoken since the accident."

"If he regains consciousness, call me," Cockrum said.

"He's going to kill you, Cockrum," Corbalew said, suddenly awake. "And you too, Preston. And the rest of you." Then he laughed that filthy rattling laugh.

They all turned. He was still floating there with his eyes closed as though he had not spoken at all. He didn't say anything else.

"I'm sorry," Preston told Harrison, Cockrum, and the others as he was leaving. "I didn't think he would tell me anything. After what happened, I'm sure he hates me almost as much as he hated DeFalco."

"You were on his ship for nearly three months," Cockrum said. "Isn't there anything else you can tell us?"

"I've told you all I know," Preston said. "I'm sorry."

CHAPTER 7: Deadly Sunrise

Neema woke up to the sound of tropical birds and found herself curled up in the sand beneath a plumeria bush. Tall palm trees swayed gently overhead. She could hear the gentle sighing of the surf and the cry of sea gulls.

Neema pushed herself slowly, painfully into a sitting position and brushed the sand out of her hair. Neema was more uncomfortable than she had ever been in her life. There was sand in her bra and sand in the trunks of her waste removal unit. The tissue around the catheters in her removal unit was sore from all the kicking she had done. Her muscles were tired. She looked down at her leg and saw the long scab where the bullet had nicked her the night before. She was thankful that the "sharks" she had seen turned out to be dolphins. In the light of the morning sun, last night's events seemed distant and unreal.

The bullet! The probes! She had to warn Jared and the others before--before. Neema rolled to her feet. Her legs felt like rubber. She looked down at herself. She was wearing a rubber bra and a big, black diaper cover and had electric stimulators stuck in various places along her arms and legs. Some of them had pulled loose and fallen off. Her hair hung down in limp strings and was full of sand. The scab on her thigh was long and black. I'm going to make a great first impression, she thought.

Neema took a step. The nick in her leg had cut more deeply that she realized--or maybe it was badly bruised from the impact. She could barely move that leg. She stumbled through the wet sand, the surf washing up around her feet and washing back out. She stepped on something sharp, stumbled backwards, and fell rump first into the surf with a loud "splat." She pulled her foot around and saw blood flowing from a nasty cut.

"Hey!" someone yelled. "Are you all right?"

Zapper! Tears blurred Neema's vision. A young man with black hair, a round, boyish face, and a loud Hawaiian shirt and shorts that didn't match came running out into the surf without even taking off his shoes. Zapper looked every bit the clown he had always played, and Neema had never been more delighted to see him. She tried to get to her feet and stumbled.

"Hey," Zapper said. "Take it easy. Let me help you." He lifted her gently to her feet, put one arm around her, and half carried her up the path to the beach house. "You're gonna be okay," he kept telling her.

They stepped into the elevator tube beneath the house. The floor was lined with soggy, sandy carpet. Neema felt her stomach lurch as the elevator slid upward.

"So what happened?" Zapper asked. "Did you get in a ship wreck or something?"

The doors opened. Dr. Jaina Benedict was standing there in a robe. Her honey blonde hair was pulled back into a ponytail and her young, unlined face was dark with worry.

"Where have you been?" she asked. "Who is this?"

"Help me get her to the couch," Zapper said. "This is Jaina, she's a doctor."

Jaina moved an athletic bag and a heap of clothes off the couch and Zapper gently eased Neema over onto the cushions and set her down.

"What's going on here?" Jaina asked.

"Ya got me," Zapper said. "I was looking out the window, and I saw her stumbling along the beach."

Neema tried to say something. Her mouth was dry. She could barely make a sound. Jaina was already pulling a medical scanner from her bag in the corner.

"I'll get her some juice while you check her out," Zapper said. He walked over to the refrigerator and pulled out a half-empty jug of orange juice. Jaina frowned as she looked down at the readouts.

"I'm getting some pretty strange readings here," she said.

I bet you are, Neema thought.

Zapper held out a jug of orange juice.

"Hey, do you want some--?"

Neema snatched the pitcher from his hand, turned up the jug, and greedily gulped the juice down in shuddering gasps. Refreshment flooded her body. She realized she hadn't ingested real food or water for months. She'd eaten synthetic reality food and had been fed through her umbilical tube, but real food. . .

"Easy there, l'il girl," Zapper said. "You can have all you want."

She emptied the jug, lowered it from her lips. She sat gasping for air for several seconds. She wiped her mouth with the back of her arm then smoothed back her hair. She could feel the sand on her scalp. She looked down at her scantily clad body and felt embarrassed.

This is a beach house, she reminded herself. People wear swimwear here much of the time.

"I'm sorry about my manners," she said. "I was so thirsty . . . so weak. I just woke up . . . ." Woke up from stasis, she meant.

"I've got some questions about your bio-readings," Jaina said.

"There's no time," Neema said. "I've got to see Jared." She spoke English with an accent.

"I carry her in from the beach and give her juice, and she wants Jared," Zapper said. "There just ain't any justice in the world anymore."

"I'm not playing, Zapper," she said.

"Hey," Zapper said. "How'd you know . . .?"

"Where is he? Where are the others?"

"They're on the other side of the island," Jaina said. "We're meeting them for lunch in about two hours."

"There's no time," Neema insisted. "They're in danger. We've got to find them now. It may already be too late."

"Danger?" Zapper said. "From what?"

"Don't you know what's happening?" Neema said. "Don't you know anything?"

Zapper and Jaina looked at each other.

"Turn on your television monitor," Neema told them.

"Communicore," Jaina said. "Turn on the monitor."

"What program please?" the system asked.

"Live broadcast," Jaina said. "Breaking news events."

A young woman in a black suit stood against a wall of fire. The silhouette of a metal spire rose into the early morning sky behind her. The image broke apart and reassembled.

"Paris--*skkkt*-- in flames," she said. "Two hours ago the being known as Gogue began raining--*skkkkkkkkkkk*--deadly heat beams from Earth's orbiting defense platforms. The death toll is estimated to be in the hundreds of thousands."

"Good lord!" Zapper said. "Is that for real?"

"Scan breaking news," Jaina cried.

". . . live from Washington D.C. covering the latest in a series of deadly assaults by the being known as Gogue . . ."

". . . seems to have the power to override security codes. Police drones, unmanned artillery tanks, traffic control computers . . . ."

". . . United System headquarters in Rome destroyed. Over a hundred of the delegates assembled there are assumed to be dead. Further attacks . . ."

"Men and women take to the streets of Los Angeles pleading for their lives, waving white flags, and holding up signs proclaiming surrender. It is hoped that these messages, transmitted to the orbiting satellites . . . . "

A parade of nightmares continued to roll by.

"Stop," Neema said. "That's enough. Do you see how serious this is? Do you see why we have to hurry?"

"The whole world is in flames," Jaina said as tears began to flow. "And we slept through it."

"Do not feel guilty for surviving," Neema said. "The trouble will arrive here soon enough."

"The beam weapons?" Zapper asked.

"No," she said. "Probes." She pointed to the scab on her leg. "Fan powered flying drones with automatic weapons. They tried to kill me last night. They were headed here."

"We have to tell the others," Jaina said. She stepped over into the kitchen, into an alcove with a writing desk that served as the study. Neema heard her fumbling with something.

"Zapper," Jaina said. "I'm not getting anything."

Zapper stood up, patted Neema's arm, and walked over into the kitchen.

"What is it?" Neema asked.

"The comm unit may not be working," Zapper said.

"Have you still got your chronocomm?" Jaina asked.

"I left it on the table by my bed, I think," Zapper said. He ran back to the bedroom the guys were sharing and returned a moment later. "It's here," he announced. "But I'm not getting any answer from it either."

"Vectorcomm security," Jaina said, speaking to the communications console on the kitchen counter. "Come in, please."

"Vectorcomm security," a voice replied. "How may I help you?"

"What's happening up there?" Jaina demanded.

"Nothing," the voice replied calmly. "Everything is fine here."

Jaina was too stunned to respond.

"Thanks," she finally said. "Out." She broke the connection.

"That was not *Vector* security," Neema said.

"No kidding," Zapper said.

"I called the station last night," Jaina said. "I spoke to a doctor I'd never heard of. It wasn't really a doctor, was it?"

"Probably not," Neema said.

"But why the game?" Zapper asked. "Why pretend there was no problem?"

"They wanted to see what you knew," Neema said.

"About what?" Zapper asked.

"About me," Neema told him. "Come. We have to hurry."

* * *

The waterfall was over a hundred feet tall. It spilled down over the rocks from the rainforest above. There was a cave in the wall of the cliff behind the falls. Pirate, Jared, Wendy, Hal, Mike, and Tori had hiked into the rainforest, had found the dry entrance to the cave--an extinct lava tube--and had hiked through to the opening behind the falls. Shafts of sunlight filtered through sparkling sheets of water and threw rippling rainbows onto the walls of the tunnel. There was a narrow ledge at the mouth of the cave.

Wendy pulled off her tee shirt and shoes and set them on a rock. She walked over into the mouth of the cave and stood beneath the falls in her swimsuit. She closed her eyes, smoothed back her hair.

"Come on," Wendy said. "It feels great."

The rest of them stripped down to their swimwear and walked out onto the ledge. Pirate was careful and cautious. Tori bounded out onto the edge of the rocks with no fear at all. Pirate grabbed her by the arm.

"You're making me nervous," he said.

"Oh, Pirate," Tori said. "You're such a flower."

"Don't let her talk to you like that," Hal said. "Push her little butt off."

"If I fall," she said, "you're coming with me."

"I don't think so."

They all found comfortable places to sit along the rocky edges of the cliff and sat there enjoying the falls for over an hour.

"We better meet Jaina for lunch," Pirate finally said.

They dried off, pulled on shirts and shoes, and made their way back through the winding lava tube.

Pirate felt Wendy squeeze up beside him. She put her arm around his waist and smiled at him. He wrapped his own arm around her, felt her damp ringlets of hair against his arm. He wondered where his relationship with Wendy was going, how it would all turn out. He hoped for the best, but feared it was only a summer romance for her. As soon as they were back on *Vector*, it would be as if none of it had ever happened. Wendy would once again be out of his reach. Some people just didn't seem to form lasting attachments. Pirate tried not to think these thoughts, tried to just enjoy the moment. In the future, in darker days, it would be a bright time he could look back on.

The tunnel curved upward. Light shone down through a jagged hole, through twisted roots, thick vines, and heaps of rock. They climbed up through a hole in the floor of the rainforest and walked in the cool shadows of tall, tropical trees.

A mongoose scampered along the floor of the forest. They stepped through a gate in a rickety old fence and out into a clearing, a green, rolling field that ran down the slope of the mountain to the winding dirt path below.

They were strolling down the hill, nearing the road, when they heard the electric buzzing of a hoard of unholy locusts. Dark shadows swept across the grass. Pirate squinted as he peered directly into the sun and saw the black bird shapes overhead. No, they weren't birds. They were some kind of fan powered robot drones. There were cylinders mounted on their underbellies--gun ports.

Spat! Spat! Spat! Spat!

Clods of dirt and grass exploded from the ground at Pirate's feet.

"Run!" Pirate yelled. "There's a lava tube to the right!"

"Here we go again," Hal said.

The probes swarmed in around them and circled like buzzards. They blasted up a few chunks of sod.

"*Stop,*" one of the probes intoned. "*Stop and submit to analysis, and you will not be harmed. Try to escape and you will be destroyed. It is your choice.*"

Tori sprang forward. Hal grabbed her around the waist and spun her back. The ground in front of her exploded like a land mine. It left a smoking hole eighteen inches deep. Hal exhaled and shook his head. He was still clinging tightly to Tori. If he hadn't moved when he had . . . .

"Don't do that again," he told her.

"Okay," Tori said, too stunned for her usual mouthy retort.

"They can't hover," Mike said. "If we can keep them going in circles . . . . "

"Let's see what they want," Pirate said. "It doesn't look like we have much of a choice."

"He's right," Hal said. "We're sitting ducks."

The others looked around at each other uncertainly.

"*Stop and submit to analysis.*"

No one moved.

The probes' shadows made swirling ink prints on a canvas of grass. No one wanted to submit, but they *were* surrounded. All of them stopped. Scanning equipment unfolded from the underbellies of several of the probes. They carefully scanned the young men and women before them.

"Alert! Alert! Alert! Alert! Alert!"

The probes broke formation. Screaming jet engines, a blast of wind, and a roar of weapons fire engulfed the group.

"Get down!" Hal cried before the noise swallowed them.

They fell to the ground, hugged the earth. A dark shape blasted through the air overhead. It was so close it barely missed them. For an instant it blotted out the sun. Then it soared on past. Chunks of metal, plastic, and canvas tumbled in its wake and rained down into the tall grass below.

Pirate and Wendy were huddled together in the grass. The others were scattered around them. They looked up and saw a DeFalco airboat soaring toward the ocean--their airboat.

"Zapper," Hal said. "I'd recognize his driving anywhere."

"Yeah," Tori said. "He almost landed on us."

The DeFalco airboat spun about. The remaining probes pulled into formation around it. A gale of weapons fire ripped three of the probes to pieces. The rest of the swarm returned fire.

The airboat rolled onto its side and shot toward the place where the cloud of probes was thickest, weapons blazing as it went. Several more probes went down. The rest of the swarm spun about and fired onto the sides of the craft with cutting beams.

The vehicle strained to stay aloft as automatic weapons hammered its heat resistant sides with meteorites of super dense metal.

"He's got them distracted," Pirate said. "Head for the lava tube."

Particle cannons on the ship engaged. They blasted away at the probes. The probes returned fire. They scoured the sides of the airboat leaving wicked scrapes in the finish.

One more sweeping burst from the ship's particle cannons sent the last of the probes falling to the earth in smoking ruins.

The airboat hovered twenty feet above the clearing. Smoke was pouring from the turbines. Its engines howled as it fought to stay aloft. The last volley from the cannons seemed to have exhausted it. There was a loud pop and one of the engines spouted flame. The ship tumbled off its axis, rolled over onto one side, and slammed hard into the earth below.

"Zapper!" Tori yelled.

"How do you know it was Zapper?" Mike rasped as they ran toward the fallen ship.

"Because he nearly hit us," Tori said. "Nobody else drives that bad."

"Guess again," Zapper said as he climbed out of the upward-facing starboard hatch. "I was operating the guns. Blame the driving on our pretty young doctor-child."

Jaina lifted her head from the dashboard. The readouts on the instrument panels turned to gibberish--parts of letters, numbers, and scrambled symbols. Then they went dark.

"Are you all right?" Neema asked, her eyes wide.

"Yeah," Jaina said. "I think so." Her head ached.

A pool of dark and sticky syrup clung to the panel in front of her. More of it was dripping down into her face. Blood! It was blood!

"I'm bleeding!" she said. "I'm--I'm bleeding!" Jaina was about to unbuckle herself when she felt the vehicle lurch beneath her. Mechanical muscles slowly and deliberately righted the ship. The hatch opened.

"Jaina!" Pirate said. "Are you all right?"

"I'm bleeding!" Jaina said. She fumbled through her emergency kit with shaking hands.

"Easy," Pirate said. He took the kit from her.

"Clean the wound first," Jaina said. She forced herself to lean back. Every muscle in her body was rigid.

"I know," Pirate said. "Hold still." He unwrapped a sterile pad and dabbed her forehead. "It's okay. It doesn't look too bad." He looked back and saw Neema. Who was this?

"It burns," Jaina said.

"What a baby," Zapper said. "I guess it's true about doctors making bad patients."

"Shut up, Zapper!" Jaina snapped. Hal turned away so Jaina wouldn't see him chuckling.

"Wait a minute," Hal said as he saw Neema for the first time. "Who's this?"

Neema had been strapped into the seat behind Jaina. Still covered with sand and in need of a shower, she had hastily pulled on a black jumpsuit.

"Her name's Neema," Zapper said. "She says she knows Jared."

"Neema," Pirate gasped. "Jared's Neema?" He turned around. "JARED!"

Jared was already standing silently at his elbow. His expression was haunted and awestruck like a painting of Adam seeing Eve for the first time as she emerged, naked and perfect, from Eden's morning mists.

"Neema?" he gasped. "This can't be happening. It can't be real."

In his dreams, he'd stood in a clearing in a dark forest and watched her spaceship land. They had walked together down forgotten roads, stood on hilltops and gazed down on the green land below. She was that one perfect girl who understood everything, who looked past his shyness, his social clumsiness, and admired the person within. When he was with her, he could love himself and believe he was worthy of love. Yet she had always been a fantasy, no more than a projection, a fragment of his own consciousness--or so he had thought.

Neema stepped down. She looked younger and smaller than she had in Jared's dreams. Her hair was tangled and there were dark circles under her eyes. She looked afraid, but she still smiled when she saw him. It was a tired smile with a touch of sadness.

"Is it really you?" Jared asked. "The one from my dreams?"

"Yes," she said. "It's really me."

"But how?" he asked. "How is it possible?"

"It will take time to explain," she said. "And we don't have much time."

"Jared's seen her in dreams since we were fourteen or fifteen years old," Pirate explained to the others. "I never thought she was real."

"We don't have time for this!" Jaina wailed. "The whole planet is being ripped apart by heat beams. Paris and Washington and Rome are on fire. Millions dead in Beijing."

"What's she talking about?" Hal demanded.

"I just saw the news," Jaina said. She struggled to control her emotions. "Live broadcasts from all around the world. It was horrible, unbelievable."

"I believe you," Pirate said, his voice hushed. "But I still need to bandage your forehead."

She sat still as he gently smoothed the bandage into place.

"You're telling me the whole planet is being wiped out while we're just sitting here?" Hal said, his voice tight.

"We've been kind of busy," Tori said.

"We've been playing," Hal said. "Running around like a bunch of children while our planet was being destroyed."

"How could we have known?" Wendy asked.

"Sheppard knew," Pirate said. "I could see it in his eyes. He knew something like this was coming."

"We should have known the ship that attacked Venus wasn't the only one of its kind," Mike said.

"We've got to get back to civilization and find out what's going on," Hal said. "We've got to do something!"

"I don't think this airboat's going anywhere for a while," Zapper said. He had been examining the starboard engine. "Those probes carved it up pretty bad. This engine's completely burned up."

"I'm not getting anybody on my chrono," Tori said. "We can pick up news broadcasts, but we can't call for help."

"Let's get back to the cabin," Pirate said. He looked around at the wrecked ships, the ruined probes, and Hal's exoskeleton. "I think we'd better get as much of our equipment as we can carry."

"I want to know why those probes attacked us here," Zapper said. "I mean, they're burning down buildings everywhere else. Why probes?"

"There must be something here they wanted to find," Jared said. "Something they think we know."

"They were looking for me," Neema said. "I don't know if they scanned me or not, but if they did, they'll never let us off this island."

CHAPTER 8: Abominations

"Now," Gogue said. "Are you still going to tell me I'm not the Antichrist?"

"You," Sheppard snarled. He had been asleep when the mocking voice woke him. He woke up with a start and looked around. He could make out a dark shape standing in the glare of the monitor. The eyes glowed like red embers. Sheppard strained against the frame that was binding him. The straps were tight, and his back was really starting to hurt. His mouth was dry and pasty.

"What did you think of my show?" Gogue asked. "Fire from the sky. Burning cities. Impact craters."

"You're a monster," Sheppard said. "A murdering monster."

"The Antichrist," the shape said. "Do you believe I'm the Antichrist?"

"What if I say I don't?" Sheppard said. "How many more people will you kill?"

"As many as it takes."

"Fine. You're the Antichrist. You're the Beast. You're Satan."

"You don't believe me."

"It doesn't matter what I believe."

"But it does." Gogue stepped into the light. "You're my test subject. If I can't convince you, how will I convince the rest of my subjects?"

"That's not my problem." Sheppard turned away.

"You saw what I did to Jerusalem," Gogue said. "I entered the Holy of Holies, declared myself to be God."

"It's been done before."

"I beg your pardon?"

"Antiochus IV of Syria," Sheppard said. "He invaded Jerusalem, violated the temple, sacrificed a pig on the altar. His people were driven out eventually. You will be too."

"Don't be so sure. You saw what I did to that pathetic mosque too, didn't you? I couldn't let the Muslims off easy, could I?"

Sheppard didn't answer.

"I have some more massacres planned," Gogue said. "I'm thinking of making it a weekly event. Perhaps I'll stage one every Sunday morning in honor of your King."

Sheppard didn't answer.

"Perhaps I'll dress the people I kill in choir robes. Feed them poisoned bread and wine. Drown them in baptismal pools."

Sheppard said nothing.

"So," Gogue said. "What were you doing when I heaped my wrath upon the world? Did you pray for the people I was killing, for the cities I destroyed?"

"Yes."

"Did your God answer you?"

Sheppard didn't answer.

"No reply to that one, eh? The answer is obvious, of course. I killed millions, and your God was nowhere to be found. Thus I can only conclude that your God doesn't exist, doesn't care, or is incapable of stopping me. Perhaps he is huddled in a corner weeping."

"Other despots have said the same things," Sheppard said. "They're all dead."

"Perhaps," Gogue said. "But that hardly answers my question, does it?"

"God doesn't see things the way we do," Sheppard said. "For us, this world is all there is. For him, there's a better world the other side of death. This is all just a preparation for that, a kind of test."

"So your God doesn't care about what happens here?" Gogue said. "This world doesn't matter to him?"

"It matters," Sheppard said, "but for different reasons. We see this world as an end and want to enjoy this life as much as possible. For God, this is a place of teaching, a place where souls are shaped, developed, and tested. The things that happen here have a spiritual effect on our souls because of the ways we respond to them. Evil is allowed to exist because it helps in this process."

"Well," Gogue said. "I'm glad to be of service. Does that mean he won't punish me?"

"No," Sheppard said. "You're doing all of this for your own reasons, but God keeps you around for his. When you've served your purpose, you'll die with the other despots."

"I suppose prayer has no purpose then," Gogue said. "All of you little people pray for happy lives, and your God tells you to suck it up and suffer."

"He has compassion on us," Sheppard said, "and sometimes he takes away the danger because it's too much for us to bear. Sometimes he walks with us through the pain and teaches us to rely on him."

"So you still believe your God answers prayers?"

"Yes."

"I suppose you saw what I did to Rome. So much for the Eternal City, eh, Reverend?"

"I saw it."

"What did you think?"

"It was horrible."

"Are you afraid of me, Reverend?"

"More disgusted by you than anything else. A mixture of pity and disgust."

"Do you hate me?"

"I don't hate anyone."

"How nice. Do you forgive me for the things I've done?"

"It's not up to me."

"Of course it is. Do you think your God can forgive me?"

"That's not for me to decide either. I suppose he could if you repented, and asked forgiveness."

"Really? For carnage on this scale? I'll have to try it."

"You have to humble yourself, to sincerely mean it. That's where most people like you fail--why repentance is both so easy and so downright impossible. Once you become hardened, you lose your capacity for repentance, and only a hardened soul could kill so many."

"Do you believe I'm beyond hope then?"

"That's not up to me."

"Now you're starting to become tiresome."

"That brings me some small pleasure." Sheppard smiled faintly.

Gogue waved his arm. The wall-sized screen wavered. Then it filled with the image of several large and ancient buildings and an enormous bricked courtyard with a fountain. The spires and domed roofs were unmistakable.

"Is this place familiar to you?" Gogue asked.

"I recognize it."

"Saint Peter's Basilica. The Sistine Chapel."

"The Vatican. I know."

"A worldwide symbol of your faith, I believe."

"I'm not Roman Catholic."

"So this place means nothing to you?"

"I didn't say that. Of course it's special. There's a tradition that Peter died there. People come from around the world to visit the chapels. Yes, it's special."

"But not a universal symbol of the Christian faith?"

"You don't understand Christians at all. Our symbols aren't buildings or locations. They're events, beliefs, and relationships. You can burn a cross, but you can't destroy what Christ accomplished. You can burn a Bible, but you can't destroy the living Word of God."

"Don't be so sure. Do you believe I am a false God, Reverend Sheppard?"

"That would be giving you more credit than you're due."

"Are you familiar with the story of Elijah's confrontation with the prophets of Baal on Mount Carmel?"

"Yes."

"Two altars. One for your God. One for Baal. Elijah and the priests of Baal both called upon their respective deities. The true God, so the story goes, answered by sending fire upon the altar. Do you remember that story?"

"Yes."

"Do you believe your God still has that kind of power today?"

"Yes."

"Good. Shall we put it to a test then? Your God against me."

"No."

"I'm going to train weapons on Vatican City. You will pray to your God to spare it. It is, after all, a symbol for your beliefs. If I pulse blast the city and your God protects it, in answer to your prayers, we will know he is real. If the city is destroyed, we will know he is no more than an illusion you cling to."

"You're not supposed to test God. That's what Jesus told Satan when he tempted him in the desert."

"How convenient. Then you forfeit?"

"What? Forfeit? No."

"If your God is real, if he is the same as he was then, why will he not answer your prayers and protect his own honor? Why does he hide his face when his people are suffering?"

"I told you. Everything serves his purpose. Even suffering. He'll more than make up for it later. He's promised that."

"In some invisible, eternal kingdom that you have never seen."

"I've seen traces of it."

"And you maintain this fiction, this illusion of an all-powerful God?"

"Yes."

"Why?" Gogue raged. "Why? What good has it done you? What good will it do you?"

"I had wrecked my life. He gave it back to me. I couldn't face my own reflection in the mirror without him."

"A crutch. For an emotional cripple."

Sheppard smiled.

"We're all crippled."

"Speak for yourself. Don't insult the rest of us. How is your faith, Reverend Sheppard?"

"My faith is just fine, thank you."

"Do you believe your God will come for you? Do you think he will save you?"

"Yes. Maybe in this life, maybe in the next. To live is to serve Christ. Death is only a doorway to a better place."

"By the time you leave this room, you will be praying to me. You will renounce your worthless faith and pray to me."

"I'll die first."

"I believe Saint Peter made the same boast."

Sheppard shivered.

"Goodbye, Reverend Sheppard. I've enjoyed our exchange."

Gogue stepped into the shadows and vanished.

CHAPTER 9: Paradise Lost

An explosion shook the ground. Reverberations from the blast echoed out over the water. A twisted pillar of black smoke rose like a dark tribal spirit above the umbrella-shaped canopies of the palms.

"What was that?" Jaina asked. She and the others had pulled on their gear and were headed down the beach in a fast walk. Their weapons were armed. Neema, in her borrowed clothes, ran behind them.

"The cabin," Pirate growled with dark certainty. That was where they were going.

Tori was strapped into a hover chair she had taken from the wrecked airboat. A glistening swarm of nanoprobes--dust-sized robot probes--hovered in the air overhead. She had--moments before--released them from the honeycomb chambers of the cylinders that enclosed her forearms. Three dimensional images, reconstructed from their scans, were piped into the receptors in Tori's helmet and bodysuit. As her probes took to the air, she saw herself soaring above the trees. She felt the air whistling past her face, felt the sudden wall of heat, smelled the acrid scent of smoke. As she cleared the trees, she saw the twisted ruins of the elevated cabin blazing like a funeral pyre. The cylindrical trunk still stood, but the living quarters had been blasted away. It lay in charred and shattered pieces from the grassy hilltop to the sandy beach below. Two of the robot probes were still there. They circled the clearing like buzzards. Then, satisfied with their work, they soared off toward other parts of the island.

"What do you see?" Mike asked.

"They're leaving," Tori said. "The cabin's been destroyed."

Zapper cursed out loud and began to run. The others fell in behind him. Hal's giant exoskeleton/robot, powered by its cybernetic muscles, raced out ahead of the others. Its clawed mechanical feet left dinosaur footprints in the wet sand.

This beach, only hours before, had been a playground, a place of spiritual and emotional healing. Now it had become another battlefield. Dressed in body armor and bristling with weapons, the laughing group of young adults had been transformed, once again, into soldiers. They rounded a corner and ran up a twisting footpath with stepping stones and tiki torches. The path led through a gap in a wall of bushes.

"Is there anything waiting for us up here?" Pirate asked.

"No," Tori said. "They're gone."

They stepped out of the bushes into the clearing. The cabin was still burning like a sacrificial pyre. The plastic from the outer walls was cracked and brittle to the touch of their gloved hands. Shards of glass littered the sand beneath the house. The burned remains of the living room couch lay sadly against the trunk of a palm tree. Towels, articles of clothing, and someone's burned zebra print swim trunks were draped over bushes. A restless wind rippled through the leaves of the surrounding palms. The sky was overcast. No one said anything for several seconds. They just stood and watched the cabin burn.

"This doesn't make any sense," Mike said sadly. "It just doesn't make any sense."

"If they had meant to kill us, they could have killed us back at the clearing," Wendy said. She swallowed a lump in her throat. "Is that what you mean about it not making sense?"

"Yeah," Zapper said. "So why destroy an empty house?"

"No," Pirate said as a thought suddenly came to him. "Not that." He ran into the flaming heap and began throwing aside chunks of debris. His clothing protected him from the heat and he sifted through the fire. Finally he pulled out the smoldering remains of a backpack, threw it to the ground, and started pulling out charred clothing.

"If you're looking for clean underwear," Zapper said, "I'm afraid you're out of luck, man."

"No," Pirate said. "It's not here."

"What's not there?" Mike asked.

Pirate sighed.

"Sheppard gave me something," he said. "A data slide. He said it was important. Now it's missing. I should have taken it with me. I never should have let it out of my sight."

"Well," Zapper said. "There ain't nothing you can do about it now."

"I hate this," Wendy said. "Any time I start to feel safe or secure, something like this happens. I really, really hate this."

"At least nobody's been killed," Hal said. "Yet."

"So what do we do now?" Jaina asked. "Wait for Astrolus to come back?"

"They will be back," Neema said.

"Where did they go?" Pirate asked. "Tori, did you see the probes?"

"Yeah," Tori said. "They were heading inland."

"There are other people on this island," Pirate said. "Is that where they were headed? Toward the town? Toward Kele?"

"I don't know," Tori said.

"Send your probes toward town," he said. "Quickly!"

Tori's glistening cloud lifted itself above the clearing and followed the narrow, paved road as it wound out of sight toward Kele, the island's tiny collection of shops and condominiums. Hal raced after the nanoprobe swarm. The long, smooth strides of his exo-bot ate up twenty-foot stretches of road with every leaping step. Wendy's bionic legs, completely human in appearance, sent her hurtling along at superhuman speed. Pirate engaged his counter-gravity field and fired his boot jets. These were only designed to carry him for short distances. He fired them again and again in one successive leap after another. His froglike jumps could hardly match the grace of Wendy's fluid strides, but he did manage to keep up with her.

The winding mountain road led through a tropical jungle of exceptional beauty. Under other circumstances, the members of the team would have stopped to gaze at waterfalls, to walk through streams, or to gaze off high bluffs at the valleys below. There was no time. There were snakes in Eden that day, and they had to find them and root them out.

They came to a sharp twist in the road. There was a guardrail in the curve and beyond it was a steep cliff of jagged, volcanic rock that plunged down into a natural harbor. The harbor was, in actuality, a punch bowl crater left by volcanic activity. On the other side, built into the rocks, sand, and rainforest vegetation, was a cluster of buildings. Made mostly of dark wood and glass, the village of Kele had been designed to blend with the natural beauty of the setting. There was smoke coming from the village.

Pirate and Wendy plunged over the cliff. The jets on their boots, belts, and backs engaged. Pirate landed on a chunk of black, volcanic rock. Waves washed up on either side of him. Wendy dropped down beside him. Successive leaps carried them around the edges of the crater. Hal's exobot splashed up out of the crater behind them.

Tied to a wooden dock were the shattered remains of two large houseboats. Smoke poured from their shattered hulls. The air smelled of burning fuel and plastic.

"Do you think there was anybody inside?" Wendy asked.

"I don't see anybody," Pirate said. "And I don't smell any burned flesh." They had all smelled that horrible scent on Venus less than three weeks earlier. It was something they all hoped to forget but knew they never would.

Pirate, Hal, and Wendy ran along a narrow strip of beach and down a road between the buildings. They came out in a parklike mall area. Empty windows faced them. Tori's nanoprobes glistened overhead.

They had only been standing in the mall for a moment when a door opened. A man in his fifties with blond hair and a sun-weathered face stepped out of one of the buildings. He was dressed in a tropical shirt, shorts, and sandals and carrying a concussion pistol. In salty and acrid metaphors, he demanded to know what was going on. He had an Australian accent.

"We were attacked by a swarm of robot drones," Pirate said. "We thought they might have come this way."

"They were 'ere all roight," the Australian said. He lowered the pistol and sighed. "Nasty buggers. They sunk every boat we 'ad. Wrecked all the airboats too."

"Was anybody hurt?" Wendy asked.

"Not as I've 'eard," he said. "Not yet anyways."

"They wrecked our airship," Pirate said, "and blew up the cabin we were staying in."

"I take it you're all part of that new crisis intervention team," he said, "The Intrepid Force?"

"That's us," Pirate said. "I'm Pirate Eisman."

"Ernie Montgomery," the Australian said. He turned to the row of buildings behind him. "It's all roight," he yelled. Faces appeared in the window of a restaurant. "We've all been sittin' in there watchin' live news broadcasts all day. We 'eard the explosions outside and thought we were about to become news ourselves.

"Anyway, it's nice to meet all of you," Ernie said. He shook hands all around.

"Are you the mayor of this town?" Wendy asked.

Ernie smiled at the question.

"Never been called that before," he said. "I keep things runnin' around 'ere when I'm not out givin' boat tours, diving lessons, and the like. Mayor, eh? Sounds better than caretaker."

The rest of the team arrived a moment later. Tori scoured the area, but saw no sign of the flying probes. Some of the island's other residents came out of the restaurant. One of them was a blonde woman in her late twenties. She wore no make up and was heavily tanned.

"This is my niece, Shawna," Ernie said. "She lives 'ere and runs the restaurant and pub."

"Not bad," Zapper whispered.

"I'm with you, man" Mike agreed.

"You guys are so stupid," Tori said, disgusted. "Looking at girls at a time like this."

"Mike," Zapper said. "I think I see some green in those slanted little eyes."

"We didn't mean to make you jealous, Tori," Mike said.

"Keep dreaming, Mikey," Tori retorted.

Jaina shot all of them a withering glance.

"This is Harry Chan," Ernie said, introducing a heavyset Asian man. "He's an aeronautical engineer for DeFalco."

"Semi-retired," Harry said. He turned to the woman beside him. She was small and dark haired with a mixture of Asian and Polynesian features--probably Filipino. "This is my wife, Grace. She's a painter. We live in a condominium just over the hill."

"We can save the rest of the introductions for later," Hal said. "You say you've been watching the news. Do you know what's going on?"

"They've destroyed most of our orbital fighters," Harry said. "Wrecked them on the ground before they could even launch."

"They?" Jaina said. "You mean the ships in orbit?"

"The ships and the automated defense platforms," Harry said. "They've been taken over somehow."

"How much damage can those heat beams do from orbit?" Pirate asked.

"They were designed to be used in space against ships and asteroids," Harry explained. "Not to travel through hundreds of miles of atmosphere. That's the only thing that's saving the planet from complete destruction."

"I don't think he wants to destroy us outright," Shawna said. "He wants to rule us. He's said so himself."

"Who?" Pirate asked. "Who has said so?"

"Gogue," she answered.

The name hung heavy in the tropical air.

"Have you seen him?" Pirate asked.

"He's given a few speeches," Ernie said. "'Ow he's God, and he's going to take over the world. That sort of thing."

"I don't want to upset anybody," Hal said, "but we have warheads that can split an asteroid the size o' Texas."

"Yes," Harry said. "They were designed to protect the planet from killer asteroid strikes. They're disassembled and stored in secure locations until they're needed."

"There are no secure locations," Neema said.

"If he was able to arm himself with some of those . . ." Harry said. "Well, let's just hope Shawna's right, that he doesn't want to destroy everything."

"We've got to assume he does have them," Neema said. "He's managed to capture everything else."

"Let's get inside," Pirate said. "We need to try to get a handle on what's happening. Tori's probes can serve as an early warning system. The rest of us can take turns standing guard in case those probes return."

"They will return," Neema said.

* * *

Among the other visitors to the island were a couple on a honeymoon, a marine biologist, and half a dozen others. With Tori's probes and Hal's exobot standing guard, all of them met in Shawna's bistro. They sat staring in horror at the giant vidscreen as fire from the sky turned the planet's mightiest cities into funeral pyres. Police drones in several major cities had attacked civilians. Automated fighter jets and artillery tanks, their robot minds possessed by Gogue's demon intelligence, blew up buildings, attacked airports and train stations, and shelled civilians. There was no clear pattern to the attacks.

The whole thing seemed impossible. It could not be happening. The jaunty tropical atmosphere of the bistro seemed strangely inappropriate. The tables and booths had candles and drinks with little umbrellas. Neon signs lined the walls. The place was part of a happier, more innocent age.

"Turn it off," Ernie finally said. The video screen blanked. Ernie stood up.

"Right," he said. "You've all seen what's 'appenin' to the rest of the world. Meanwhile we'd better concern ourselves with what's 'appenin here."

"Is there any connection between the probes that attacked us here and the ships in orbit?" the marine biologist asked.

"That's what we're assuming," Pirate said.

"It is the same group," Neema said.

"Is it the same group that attacked Venus?" Harry Chan asked. "Gaith Corbalew's group?"

"Yes," Neema said. "Corbalew and the cult Astrolus also. But Corbalew was only a puppet. He was, as you say, the tip of the iceberg. It took only a single ship to take over Venus. There is a fleet of them in orbit now."

"I'm sorry," Tori said, "but this whole thing about an evil empire from the future sounds pretty far fetched to me. And you claim to be some kind of time traveling clone?"

"Wait a minute?" Ernie Montgomery said. "An evil empire from the future?"

"Gogue is from the future," Neema said. "By traveling into the past with technology that doesn't exist yet, he will be able to capture the entire Earth and turn it into a brutal police state that will last for three hundred years."

"Assumin' this is all true," Ernie said. "What 'appens next?"

"I don't know," Neema said. "This is how it all happened before, . . . yet it isn't."

"You want to tell us what you mean by that?" Hal said.

"It was supposed to be Corbalew who led the invasion," Neema said, "He almost destroyed the world, and Gogue was the savior that rose from the wreckage to rebuild it. That's what he seemed to be at first. People were willing to hand over their freedom just to have civilization back. It was only then that they realized Gogue's true nature."

"But we stopped Corbalew," Zapper said.

"I hoped you had stopped the invasion as well," Neema said. "But you didn't. Gogue simply changed his tactics."

"Just what is Gogue anyway?" Pirate asked.

"I don't know," Neema said. "In the twenty-third century, he controls Earth completely, but none of us know just what he is or where he came from. He claims to be the living fulfillment of all of Earth's ancient gods. According to those few of us who studied history from forbidden books, he suddenly appeared following Gaith Corbalew's military conquest of Earth."

"You mean he lives for over two hundred years?" Pirate asked.

"And never ages," Neema said. "He says he is immortal."

"So what happens next?" Mike asked. "What are we going to do about all of this?"

"I don't know," Neema said. "The computer on board my ship had the power to see alternate futures. Without Balthazar's abilities, I am blind."

"Are we safe here?" Grace, Ernie Chan's wife, asked.

"For the moment," Neema said. "For the moment, Gogue is more concerned with high profile targets. He is waging a war of terror on the Earth. His attention is on New York, Rome, Paris--the places that symbolize hopes and dreams."

"On the subject of dreams," Wendy said, "You said earlier that Jared has seen you in his dreams. Would you care to explain that?"

"It's not important right now," she said.

"Maybe you'd better let us be the judge of that," Wendy said.

Neema paused. She seemed to be searching for words. Should she tell him now or wait? She took a breath.

"Five years ago we implanted a device into Jared's mind," she said. "It's a kind of organic transmitter. I've got one in my head too. It formed a kind of empathic link between us. We share feelings, dreams, subconscious impressions."

Jared was jarred by the revelation.

"You put something in my head?" he asked.

"Yes," she said. "Yes, we . . . This is not coming out right."

"You implanted some kind of device in my head?" Jared asked again.

"Yes," Neema said.

"But who gave you the right?" he said. "You could at least have asked me."

"I did," she told him. "You said yes."

"But I don't remember," he said.

"I know," she said. "Those memories were erased for your own protection. Pirate's too."

"Wait a minute," Pirate said. "You mean I've met you too?"

"Yes," she said.

"Is there an implant in my head?" he asked.

"No," she said. "Jared was chosen because his mind already had unusual neural receptors."

"What kind of receptors?" Pirate asked.

"They're associated with extreme intuition," she said. "Flashes of insight."

"Telepathy?" Pirate asked. "Premonitions?"

"Yes," she said. "Those are your words for them."

"Are you saying you just picked me because of my brain chemistry?" Jared said, "That you've been manipulating me the whole time?"

"No," Neema said. "I mean, yes, you were chosen because of your brain chemistry, but I haven't been manipulating you. Our friendship--our bond--is real. You must believe that."

"I don't know what to believe," Jared said. "This is a lot to accept."

"You have always trusted your instincts," Neema said. "What does your intuition tell you now?"

"I don't know," Jared said. "I've never been able to trust it. You've already admitted you messed around in my head, and now you expect me to just accept you? I'm sorry, Neema. I'm going to have to have more than that."

"What would I have to do to make you believe me?" Neema asked.

"I don't know," Jared said. "I honestly don't know."

"Astrolus captured all of us last Christmas," Wendy said. "They probed our minds, laid our souls bare. If they wanted to manipulate Jared, copying a woman from his dreams would be the perfect way."

"No," Neema said. "It's not true. You can't believe that."

"It's about as believable as a living dream woman," Zapper shrugged. "I'm sorry, hon, but Wendy's got a point."

"It isn't true," Neema said. "I came to you for help, saved you from those probes. You have to believe me. You're all I've got left."

An awkward silence descended over the group for a moment. "It--uh-- may be a while before we can restock our supplies," Pirate said, changing the subject. "How much food do you have here?"

"Several months' supply," Shawna said. "Food's not a problem."

"What about power?" Pirate asked.

"Power?" Ernie said. "Everything's got internal power cells. We 'aven't had blackouts for decades."

"No," Pirate said, "but Corbalew's forces used a kind of power dampening field when they attacked us on Venus. It works like the old style electromagnetic pulses used to."

"Gogue is probably using it to shut down power in the world's population centers," Neema said. Her voice was quieter than before, more subdued. "Air travel will be disrupted and the distribution of food will be halted."

"So we're talkin' food riots?" Zapper said. "Mass starvation?"

"Yes," Neema said.

"This is ridiculous!" Hal said. "There has to be something we can do. DeFalco didn't pour all that money into our training so we could hide out on an island and let the rest of the world go to hell! Is this really a fighting team or is it just a publicity ploy?"

"Hal," Mike said. "Lighten up, man."

"Nobody's hiding out," Pirate said, his face dark with buried anger. "We can't do anything until we figure out what's going on here. Finding a way off this island might also be helpful."

"So we're just going to sit here and make excuses for letting them have everything without even putting up a fight?"

Hal asked. "Is this the kind of leadership you're going to provide for this team? No offense. You're all good people, but you're not soldiers. Soldiers don't just sit around while the world is being wrecked."

"Fine," Pirate said. "Why don't you tell us how you would fix this problem?"

"I don't know," Hal said. "All right? I don't know, but I can't stand to just sit here. It's driving me crazy." He sighed, shook his head, and stalked out into the night.

The town meeting broke up. Pirate shook his head in frustration. He sat down at a table with Wendy, Jared, and Zapper. Shawna, he suddenly noticed, was bringing out pizzas. He realized, in that instant, how hungry he was.

"Don't let Hal bother you," Wendy said. "He's just frustrated."

"Maybe he's right," Pirate sighed. "To tell the truth, I can't even begin to come up with a plan to deal with any of this. It's like one of those old horror movies."

"*War of the Worlds*," Zapper said.

"H.G. Wells," Pirate said.

"I was thinking about Orson Welles," Zapper said. "Back in 1938 he put on a radio show about an invasion from Mars. Based on the book, you know, but he made it sound like a real radio broadcast. Martians had landed in New Jersey. They shot down planes with heat beams. They'd attacked New York and the streets were full of poison gas. None of it was real, but people all over the United States panicked because they thought it was the end of the world. Then it turned out it was all just a joke."

"Jared," Pirate said. "You can profile criminals by studying a crime scene. How would you profile Gogue?"

"He's not real," Jared said. He seemed distant, distracted.

"What do you mean he's not real?" Pirate said. "Have you been watching the news? He's wrecked half of the planet!"

"He's not what he looks like," Jared said. "Or maybe he's exactly what he looks like. A facade. A sham."

"*The Wizard of Oz*," Zapper said. "'Pay no attention to the man behind the curtain.' Is that what you mean?"

"Yes," Jared said. "That's it. Exactly."

"Then what is he?" Pirate asked.

"I don't know," Jared said.

Shawna set a pizza on the table in front of him. Pirate, Wendy, and Zapper all pulled slices from the pan and set them on plates.

"Hey, Jared," Zapper said. "You better eat while you can. It smells pretty good."

"No," Jared said, his eyes far away. "I'm not hungry."

"Jared," Pirate said. "I know you've got a lot to think about."

"It's okay," Jared said. "It's okay." He clearly wasn't in the mood to discuss it.

"Sheppard used to talk about the end of the world," Zapper said. "Armageddon. The Antichrist. The Second Coming. I was never really sure if I believed any of it, but now you have to wonder. What if this is it?"

"The end of human history?" Pirate asked.

"No," Wendy said. "Not for us. Think about what it would be like to see the Second Coming of Christ."

"On a white horse with a knife coming out of his mouth?" Zapper said. His mouth was full of pizza. "Don't tell me you really believe that."

"The knife is symbolic," Pirate said. "Maybe the horse too." He took a bite of pizza. "Hey, that's hot." He grabbed his water glass, took a gulp.

"Maybe the whole book is symbolic," Zapper said. "So tell me this. If you decide this is the end of the age the Bible talks about, what are you going to do? Just hide out here until Jesus shows up?"

"No," Wendy said. "I don't think he would want us to do that. It would be cowardly, self-serving."

"And there's a chance this isn't the end of the age," Pirate said. "Unless we start getting visits from God, we can't assume anything. Back in the twentieth century some people thought Hitler was the Antichrist. Then there was Sarton in the thirties. He manipulated prophecy to make people think he was the Antichrist. Every generation thinks theirs is the last. We can't afford to assume it's all over and surrender."

"So what is our next move?" Zapper asked.

"I don't know," Pirate said. "Try to find some transportation. Get off the island."

"If those probes come back," Wendy said, "we might not get to choose what the next move will be."

* * *

Hal Wolfe strode out onto a porch overlooking the ocean. He could barely contain his frustration. What was the matter with all of them? His friends were back there ordering pizza while the world was being wrecked. He heard the door open and close behind him. He didn't turn around.

"Hal." He recognized the voice. It was Neema.

"Yeah," he said. "What is it?"

"You were hard on your friends," she said. "Don't underestimate them."

"Is that what you came out here to tell me?"

"No," she said. "I came because I need your help. There's something I have to do, but I don't want the others to know."

Hal turned around.

"The probes who attacked you were looking for me," she said. "If they scanned me earlier, they know I'm here, and they'll send an army for me. They will try to take me alive. I know things that may be of use to them. If nothing else, they will dissect me to learn what they can about the technology used in my design."

"What about the rest of us?" Hal asked. "Will they take us alive?"

"Once they are able to determine which one I am," she said, "they may consider you to be expendable if you get in their way. They will not kill you out of malice, but if you try to hinder their mission, they will remove you."

"That makes sense," Hal said. "So as long as you're with us, we're all in danger?"

"That is correct," Neema said.

"But if they want you that bad," he said, "that's a pretty good sign that we can't let them have you."

"I have secrets that they must not be allowed to learn," she said. "I will take my own life before I allow them to capture me."

"You said you needed my help," Hal said. "What do you want me to do?"

CHAPTER 10: In the Air

Enoch Henry was a hundred and sixteen years old, but he did not feel it the night he stepped out onto the porch of the Crane Island Saltwerks Museum into that spring night and looked up at the full moon. He had spent the entire day watching the news broadcasts about the planet's invasion. He could hardly believe the things he was seeing, yet he had waited decades for them. Everything was happening at last. He had known for years that this day would come and had hoped against hope that a way might be found to head it off.

He looked up and down the street at the sleeping shops and at the lights of Gentilly's, a popular sea food restaurant, that stayed open a long time after the other stores had closed down for the evening. Enoch had visited Crane Island as a teenager, had spent weekends and holidays there when he came home from college. Now, in an odd way, he felt like a teenager again as the haunting lyrics of a Phil Collins song from more than a century past replayed themselves in his mind over and over again:

I can feel it coming in the air tonight,
Oh, Lord.
I've been waiting for this moment for all my life.
Oh, Lord.

Something was coming for him. Something dangerous.
Enoch thought about his friends from that distant time, about
Ian and Joanie--Pirate Eisman's great-grandparents--and Lex
Marston, Joanie's brother. He almost felt them there with him,
halfway expected Lex's old Mustang to come roaring into town.
He thought of Emily, his one true love, who had showed up in
his life as he was approaching middle age. Like an unexpected
miracle of God, she had slain the specter of disappointment,
had annihilated the fear that he had wasted his life and had
only a lonely future ahead of him. Emily.

Somewhere, on some far green shore, they were waiting for
him to arrive. He would gladly join them in time but he had,
as poet Robert Frost had so eloquently put it, *"promises to keep,
and miles to go before I sleep."*

Enoch regretted that he had not been able to get in touch
with Pirate Eisman. He had so much to tell him. Now it would
have to wait. He only hoped they would both survive until he
had time to deliver the message.

A restless wind stirred the wind chimes that hung in front of
one of the shops. The sound, ordinarily peaceful, sounded
menacing and discordant. Something was coming. Enoch
gazed warily into the shadows beyond the street lamps, went
inside the museum, and locked the door behind him.

Enoch looked around the room at the lighted dioramas
there. In one scene was a replica of Lewis and Clark standing
beneath cypress trees as they explored the Louisiana purchase.
In another scene, two young Confederate soldiers stood around
a campfire and talked about home. The first mayor of Crane
Island, the founders of the Crane Island Saltwerks, and a much
younger Enoch Henry stood in their respective places around

the room. In another scene, mannequins wore the plastic sci-fi armor a group of actors had worn in one of Enoch's films. There were other props: a scale model of a salt mine, a 1966 Ford Mustang, a stuffed alligator . . . .

"They're coming, boys," Enoch said. "We better get ready."

They were only shadows at first, whispered movements in the inky fields of darkness that collected between the closed shops and empty stores. Slowly they emerged, their slinking bodies swathed in rippling waves of black fabric. Silver weapons gleamed coldly in their metal claws. They assembled on the empty street like an army of ghosts and marched with whispering steps to the porch of the Crane Island Saltwerks Museum.

A blast of weapon fire splintered the museum's front door. The black shapes, no longer slow and deliberate, swarmed through the ruined door like hungry crows.

The street was silent for nearly a full minute. Then the museum exploded. Windows, blown out by the force of the explosion, rained tinkling shards of glass onto the pavement up to a block away. Splintered fragments of burning lumber tumbled through the air. They lay dying in the street as silence returned.

Lights came on, and doors flew open. The people of Crane Island raced from their homes to find the museum, a structure that had stood for over a hundred years, now in ruins. The building had had a long life and a rich history. It had been a hotel, a police station, the town hall, and finally the town's museum. It was gone now. The dignified old structure had been blasted to rubble by who-knew-what evil and ungodly force.

"Enoch," Pirate Eisman's mother gasped as she stepped from the family's home. Alex, Pirate's younger brother, pulled on his pants as he ran down the main street of Crane Island.

With no shirt or shoes, he ran for the smoking ruins of the town's museum.

"UNCLE ENOCH!" he yelled. It took four men to hold him back. The local fire department arrived five minutes later.

CHAPTER 11: Laughter in the Dark

Wendy woke up to the sound of laughter. At least it had sounded like laughter. As her mind cleared, she wasn't so sure. Where was she anyway? The room was dark and she was lying on a small, rectangular bunk. A digital clock glowed blue from the face of an instrument panel.

"Lights," Wendy said. There was no response. "Lights," she said again. Slowly a single dim lighting panel began to glow. It flashed on and off and buzzed like a fly.

The room was completely unfamiliar. The walls were polished white. The ceiling was low--just over seven feet. One wall was filled by cabinets, shelves, and an alcove containing a communications system. The bed she was lying on converted into a couch. She pulled back the covers. She was wearing black exercise pants and a dark red tank top with an unfamiliar logo on it. Her arms looked pale. That was probably an effect of the lighting.

That's not what I wore to bed, she thought.

"Heh heh heh heh."

Wendy jumped out of bed. The floor was cold beneath her bare feet. She looked around wildly.

"Who's there?" the cried.

There was no one else in the room.

"Zapper," she said. "If this is one of your jokes, it's not funny."

No one answered. Where was she? The last thing Wendy remembered was going to sleep in a vacant store building on the island town of Kele. After their cabin had been destroyed, a man named Ernie had found them another place to stay. What had happened after that? She couldn't remember anything else.

Wendy walked to the door. She punched a button on a lighted control panel. A servo motor engaged with a hum and the door slid to the right and vanished into the wall. Wendy peered out at a long corridor lined with doors. The floor was covered with metal grating.

Still barefoot, Wendy stepped out into the hall. The grating left waffle impressions on the soles of her feet. She looked both ways but saw no one. The hall ended with a pair of heavy metal doors with a bank of control panels on the wall beside them. The word "AIRLOCK" glowed from a lighted sign above the doors.

Airlock? That would mean she was aboard a space station or a starship--or maybe a submarine. Wendy crept down the hall toward those doors.

"Heh heh heh."

She spun around. She could have sworn she had heard the strange laughter again, but there was no one to be seen. Wendy realized her heart was pounding. The whole situation was strange, frightening. What was she doing on a space ship? Who had brought her there? Out of habit, she ran her hands through her hair--and felt the back of her neck. Wendy gasped. Her ponytail was gone. Her hair had been chopped off to shoulder length. Her anger began to rise. Who was doing this to her?

She reached the airlock. The controls were almost identical to the ones she had used aboard *Vector* station and the *Intrepid*. Wendy keyed in the command to pressurize the chamber and open the door.

"*Please stand by,*" a distorted mechanical voice told her. The recording dragged, giving it a low, sinister sound.

She waited as she heard the whoosh of air filling the chamber on the other side of the door. Finally a green light flashed on the door panel. The locks disengaged and the heavy doors separated. There were two twisted bodies lying in the airlock's floor. One was a slender black man. The other was a blonde woman with a ponytail. Their panicked faces were gray and frozen. Their eyes were glazed with the pale film of death.

A roar of maniacal laughter erupted from the speakers in the airlock. Wendy screamed and stumbled. Her legs tangled around each other, and she went down. Her head struck the wall. Sparks flashed before her eyes. Her hip scraped against the metal floor grating. Wendy scrambled to her feet and ran back down the hall to the room she had come from. She punched the door panel. The servo engaged and the door was whisked aside. Wendy ran into the room, shut the door, and locked it. She sat in the dim room and gasped for breath. The lighting panel buzzed and flashed. She looked around the room. She had no idea where she was or who had brought her there, but there might be weapons. Wendy pulled open a drawer. It was full of undergarments, but they were not a style she wore. She slid open a closet door and found clothes hanging on hangers. She slid open another door. Inside was a small bathroom. She ran inside, turned on the water, and started to wash her face in it. Then she saw the mirror.

That was not her face.

Wendy stood and stared. Pale blue eyes stared back. Wendy's eyes were dark brown and her skin olive complexioned. The girl in the mirror had fair skin with freckles across the bridge of her nose and shoulder length brown hair. Wendy touched her face. The girl in the mirror did the same. She was young and pretty with soft, pale skin, and she did look a lot like Wendy. Wendy massaged her face and tried to rub away the make up, but nothing came off. There were other techniques for lightening skin though--and for changing eye color. There were other subtle differences. The shape of her ears was different. Her chest was flatter, and her feet were smaller. Her teeth were different. Who had done this to her? Why had they done it?

The laughter sounded in the room behind her. In the mirror, Wendy could see the room behind her. There was no one there. The laughter, she was sure, was coming from the speakers of her communication system.

Then a hand fell upon her shoulder.

Wendy screamed.

"Wendy?" she heard someone say. "Wendy, are you all right?" It was a male voice with a Japanese accent. *Mike.*

Wendy looked around. She was standing in a bathroom--a different bathroom--with the door closed. The face in the mirror--a different mirror--had dark brown eyes, olive skin, and a long ponytail. She recognized the long tee shirt and shorts as clothing Shawna Montgomery, Ernie's niece, had found for her. Her feet--bionic replicas covered with artificially grown human skin--were long and angular like they had always been.

"Wendy?" Mike said again. "Are you all right?" He knocked on the door.

"I'm okay," Wendy whispered. She looked down and saw blood on her fingers. She opened her fist. She was holding the crushed remains of a data slide. She had shattered it with her grip. She turned on the water, washed away the blood and the ruined fragments. The skin on her arms and legs had been grown over bionic limbs. She had spent a month in a REGEN tank growing skin over bionic prosthetics and scar tissue. Near panic, she examined the cuts on her fingers and palm. They were not serious. She breathed a sigh of relief. Then she began to wonder about the data slide. Where had it come from? She saw a pair of synthetic reality goggles sitting on the back of the toilet. Hadn't Pirate said something about a data slide?

"Wendy?"

"I'm okay," she repeated, louder this time. She opened the door. Mike was standing outside. He looked concerned.

"I thought I heard you screaming," Mike said. "What happened?"

In the light from the bathroom, she could see her friends camped out on the carpeted floor of an empty store building.

"Nothing," Wendy said. She looked down at her hand, at the cuts on her fingers and palm. "It was nothing."

"Are you sure?" Mike asked.

"Would you mind shutting the door?" Zapper moaned. "The light's in my eyes."

"They're here," Tori said suddenly.

* * *

"Pirate," Wendy said. "Pirate, wake up. They're here."

Pirate opened his eyes. For a moment he didn't know where he was. In the gray light he could see Wendy standing over him pulling on her gear. He was lying on an air mattress in a big, carpeted room. Then he remembered the vacant store beside Ernie's dive shop and tour company. The Chans had offered to put the Intrepid Force up for the night, but Pirate and the others decided it was too risky. They were targets. The empty store had seemed like a better idea. They could all sleep on palettes and take turns keeping watch.

"Zapper!" Jaina said in a loud whisper. "Zapper, get up!"

"Oh, Shawna," Zapper moaned. "You are such a minx."

"Stop!" Jaina hissed. "Gogue's people just landed."

"Where are they?" Pirate asked.

"On the beach," Tori said. She sounded like a prophetess describing visions of another world. She was plugged into her helmet and synthetic reality suit and receiving images from her probes. "There are about a hundred of them. They're wearing Astrolus robes and that black body armor like Corbalew's men had on Venus. And they've got six of those big robot drones."

Jared had been attacked by one of the drones the previous January.

"Armor up, everybody," Pirate said, hurrying into his own gear. Most of the others were already strapping on their gear. Zapper was still sitting on his blankets stretching.

"Hurry up!" Jaina yelled. She kicked him in the ribs.

"Yeow!" Zapper yelled. He leaped to his feet. "What's the matter with you?"

The door opened. Mike came running in.

"Where's Hal?" Wendy asked.

"He went back to the airship," Mike said. "He said he had an errand to run. Jared relieved him."

"Where's Jared?"

"He's warning Ernie and the Chans," Mike said. "He's wearing his invisibility armor."

"What about Neema?" Pirate asked.

They looked around.

"I don't see her," Jaina said.

"Maybe she's on the pot," Zapper said. "That pizza went right through me."

"She's not in the bathroom," Wendy said.

"They're coming," Tori said.

"We've got to try to lead them away from the village," Pirate said. "They could level this place. Let's go. You know the drill. Weapons armed. Power up deflection field emitters." The deflection field emitters worked on the same principle as the concussion guns in their gloves. They scanned the air for incoming weapons fire and automatically fired concussion bursts to scatter anything that was hurled in their direction. Bullets and projectiles were deflected. Concussion bursts were dissipated. Heat beams were refracted--partly, at least.

"Here we go, y'all," Zapper said.

Weapons raised, they crept out through the front door and moved out across the empty mall. The moon overhead was swathed in clouds. Everything looked normal. There was nothing out of place. The island was quiet. The only sounds were the sighing of wind and wave and a low hum. Just for a moment Pirate sheltered the wild hope that Tori's probes were sending back false images. They edged around the last building and into a pool of shadow beneath a grove of eucalyptus trees. From there they could see the beach.

They were there. The beach was choked with the black shapes of phantoms. Like a spectral army, they were pouring out of five big airships. One by one, each cloaked shape filed out of its airship and joined the others. Pirate zoomed in with his suit's viewfinder. He could see the black robes and the armor beneath. Their faces, this time, were hidden beneath heavy plastic masks. These were white with black eyeholes and a row of vents where the nose and mouth should be. They were moving in complete silence. There was no discussion among them. There were no shouted orders. They moved into place like pieces on a chessboard. They carried with them the same air of inhuman menace that Astrolus had always exuded before-- but they were much better armed this time.

"This is creepy," Zapper whispered. "Anybody bring any stakes and crosses?"

"Shh!" Jaina hissed. She was wringing her hands.

"Do you have any idea how far an 'S' sound carries?" Zapper whispered.

"Be quiet!"

The figures on the beach took no notice of them. They continued to file out of their ships and into formation.

"Jared," Pirate said. "Are you with us?"

"I'm here," Jared's voice replied from Pirate's helmet radio. "Ernie's getting everybody to safety."

"Good," Pirate said. "Do you know where Neema is?"

A pause.

"No."

"We don't either," Pirate said. "She said they were after her. Do you think they've already got her?"

"If they were after her, and they had already captured her," Mike said, "wouldn't they be leaving?"

"Just trying to cover the bases," Pirate said.

"I don't see her down there with them," Tori said. She was still inside the building and speaking to them through her helmet's microphone.

"Okay," Pirate said, "We've got two goals here. Number One: We've got to keep them from capturing Neema."

"Even though we don't know where she is," Zapper added.

"Even though we don't know where she is," Pirate acknowledged. "Number Two: We've got to defend the village."

"Do you suppose Neema ran away to protect the rest of us?" Zapper said.

"If they're after her," Jaina said, "they'll leave as soon as they find out she's gone."

"She may be depending on us to give her a good head start," Zapper said, "to cover her escape. Unless she's in the bathroom."

"She's not in the bathroom!" Wendy insisted. "I looked. Okay. I looked."

"Maybe she's in the pub getting a midnight snack," Zapper said. "Or at the bar getting herself a little hair o' the dog."

"Zapper!"

"What's going on?" Pirate said. "They've stopped."

It was true. Figures were no longer filing out of the airships. The dark shapes on the beach stood still. There was a mechanical whine followed by a pneumatic hiss. A set of metal doors had opened on the roof of one of the ships. Another of the ships opened its own doors.

Dark, batlike forms--hundreds of them--shot through those doors like bees from a hive.

"Probes," Mike said. "They're launching probes."

Most of them were about the size of sparrows. Some of them were larger, like the ones they had encountered in the clearing. Some of them were flying straight toward the place where they were hiding. Others were flying out in other directions, sweeping the island.

"Why didn't they do that in the first place?" Zapper asked. "Get the lay of the land?"

"Everybody down," Wendy said.

"They'll scan us regardless," Pirate said. "Prepare to shoot them down." They aimed skyward.

The probes filled the sky over the mall. Then they swarmed. Projectiles whistled through the air. Pirate fired into the sky over and over and over again. His deflector field emitters engaged. The waves of conconcussive force they threw off rippled the air in front of him like a heat mirage. Leaves and chunks of tree limbs rained down upon him.

Mike's superhuman reflexes made him an almost flawless marksman. He fired with both hands. The emitters on his gloves poured out a nearly continuous wave of concussive force.

"Five," Mike said, "Ten, fifteen, twenty. Thirty." Nearly every shot grazed one of the attacking probes.

"Quit showing out," Zapper said.

Jagged arcs of silver lightning erupted silently from the weapons on the backs of Zapper's forearms. Flashing electrical bursts from his generators chased pressurized streams of superconductive liquid through the dark gulf overhead. Zapper's bolts flash photographed the attacking probes, burned their blood red images into Pirate's retina as he watched. Several of the probes spouted flames and plummeted, burning, to earth. The air smelled like burnt plastic.

Tori's probes were smaller and more maneuverable than those of the attackers. They swarmed among them like bees, stinging and cutting. Shop windows around the mall shattered as the probes broke through. Swarms of them poured through the window of Shawna's bistro, through the window of the vacant store where the team had been sleeping.

Several of the probes swarmed around Jaina. Lights came on on their faces as they scanned her, but did not fire on her.

"They must think she's Neema," Mike said.

"They're both blonde and female," Pirate said, "and doesn't Jaina have brain implants?"

"Uh, oh," Zapper said. "Here come the troops."

The first squad of human attackers marched into the village. Two of the towering drones came with them. Pirate and Wendy hammered them with concussion bursts. Zapper fired on them with lightning.

Mike engaged the human troops hand to hand. He struck with blinding speed. His feet hardly seemed to touch the ground as his spiraling kicks and spinning thrusts and parries disarmed his foes and left them vulnerable to his bone-crushing blows. Even facing armored foes, he knew where the pressure points were, and his aim was flawless.

Tori's nanite probes swarmed one of the drones. Weapons bursts from some of her larger probes cut directly into the mechanical brain.

Jared fired gas pellets into the invading troops. Inky tentacles of smoke rose up and engulfed them. Zapper fired another arc into the cloud of probes overhead.

BOOM! A loud burst echoed through the treetops. A massive twelve-foot shape burst into the clearing. Cannon fire from the shoulders ripped one of the drones in half. Long mechanical arms swept through the black-clad army like a machete through grass. Hal Wolfe had returned. His exobot towered above the crowd as bodies were flung in all directions.

The Astrolus probes lifted into the air and scattered like crows. The human troops, dragging their wounded, turned and retreated toward the beach.

"Yeee-hah!" Zapper said. "We got 'em on the run."

The probes returned for one last barrage, buffeting the Intrepid Force with projectiles and concussion bursts while the human troops completed their evacuation. Finally they flew back to their hives. Almost silently the black airships lifted into the dark sky and vanished over the horizon.

Pirate Eisman surveyed the damage. The mall was littered with ruined probes and broken glass. One of the ruined robot drones lay in a twisted mass of black cloth and metal. Shop windows had been broken out. Leaves and limbs had been ripped from trees.

"Nice goin', Hal," Zapper said. "One look at you, and they all took off. Kinda like what the girls do when you show up at a party."

"Ha ha ha," Hal said. He had opened the canopy of the exobot so they could see him strapped into the cockpit. "They didn't leave on account of me, as much as I'd like to take credit for it."

"Then why did they leave?" Mike asked.

"Because Neema's gone," Jared said.

"Did they take her?" Zapper asked.

"No," Hal said. "Neema's not here. She's been gone for several hours."

"Gone?" Mike said. "Where did she go?"

"That's the beauty of it," Hal said. "I don't know. It was better if she didn't tell me."

"Is she--like--hiding in a lava tube?" Zapper asked. "Underwater breathing through a straw?"

"No," Hal said. "She's nowhere on the island. I used my exobot to recover the escape pod she came down in. I welded some thrusters onto it and added a few spare exobot parts from the airship. It was a pretty good job if I do say so myself. She could be anywhere by now, and there's enough life support on board to keep her alive for months."

"So we were covering her escape?" Zapper asked.

"That was the idea," Hal said, "but somehow they must have figured out she wasn't with you and sent out those probes to look for her."

"Are you sure they didn't find her?" Mike asked. "Are you sure she got away from them?"

"Yeah," Hal said. "I'm sure." He paused for a moment, suddenly uneasy. "Listen," he said. "I'm sorry for the things I said earlier. I was frustrated. It didn't have anything to do with you."

"It's all right," Zapper said. "We never listen to you anyway."

Some of the others laughed. Jared didn't notice. He just sat staring out at the ocean.

"She's gone," he said. "I didn't even get to say goodbye to her."

"What about the bond you have with Neema?" Mike asked Jared. "Do you sense anything now?"

"No," he said. "But it wasn't like constant, clear communication anyway. I would see her in dreams or suddenly know things I couldn't have known. But no, I don't sense anything. I hope she's all right. I didn't really treat her very well. I didn't trust her."

"No one could blame you for that," Hal said. "Not after what we've been through with Astrolus, Corbalew, and all the rest. All of these things happen, then suddenly your dream woman from the future is here to help us."

"It was too good to be true," Jared said. "I mean, face it. I'm a techno-geek, a lab rat. I fabricated this perfect woman in my mind because it was easier to face than rejection. Then when she showed up in real life, it scared me. You can control your fantasies, but what do you do when they suddenly become real, when they take on a life of their own? As long as she was a fantasy, she could never disappoint me, never reject me. Then when she showed up for real. . . . I never even gave her a chance."

"She left you a note," Hal said. There was a park bench a few meters away. "You might want to go over there and read it."

Jared's heart was pounding as he took the letter. He walked over to the bench and sank heavily onto the wooden slats. Before him was a scene of flawless tropical beauty, but he barely even saw it. His world shrank down to a tiny bubble where he sat reading from Neema's flowing script.

Dear Jared,

I know my arrival was unexpected and a bit unsettling for you. You didn't know I was real. Suddenly here is this person from your dreams, and you do not know whether to love her or be afraid of her. This is not the way I wanted our reunion to go.

I know you do not remember the weekend I met you and Pirate as you were walking in the woods or the times I met you at night in the alleyway behind your house, but I will always treasure those times in my heart. I have had a strange life and very few friends, and you always understood what it was like. Erasing your memories of me was one of the most painful things I ever had to do. I cried for several days afterwards and felt more alone than I have ever felt.

I am so glad I finally got to meet your friends. Zapper, Jaina, and Hal have been so kind to me. You are lucky to have such friends. I understand if you do not trust me, but please do not be angry with me. I could not bear it.

I am sorry we had to meet in this way. I do not know if either of us will survive the days ahead, but I pray that God will be merciful to us and will let us meet again. I have so much I want to tell you.

Goodbye, my love
Neema

CHAPTER 11: Solace

Sheppard woke up. He had no idea how long he had been sleeping. He looked around at the wall panels, the recessed lighting, the bookcases. Disbelief suffused his features. This was a dream. It had to be. He was lying in a double bed in his own quarters on *Vector*. The mattress was soft and deep beneath him. The lights were dim, but the room was unmistakable. His pictures of the Intrepid Force--both teams-- hung on the wall. A hand drawn sketch of Christ healing a leper hung over a desk with a computer dock. The time, in blue digital numbers, glowed in the corner of a blank monitor screen.

3:00 A.M.

Sheppard had once heard the 3:00 a.m. hour referred to as the witches' midnight. He shoved the thought aside as he looked down at his wrists and saw that they had been bandaged. He pulled back one of the bandages and saw the damage to his bionic flesh. The artificial skin had been torn away from the cables and servos that served as his muscles, from the synthetic bones. He wiggled his figures, opened and closed his hands. The cables slid back and forth on tiny pulleys. Cosmetic damage aside, everything still worked.

Sheppard remembered the last round of torture--the boiling pain, the psychological torment. He had been burned alive, buried alive, covered with snakes, dismembered . . . . None of it was real, of course, but knowing that didn't seem to help. Gogue's illusions, whatever they were, seemed to be pumped directly into his nervous system and no amount of concentration could make them go away.

"Good," a woman's voice said. "You're awake." A young woman, possibly thirty years old, stepped through the door and stood at the end of Sheppard's bed. She had shoulder length black hair and olive skin. She was wearing a sleeveless black top and white pants that looked like part of a medical uniform.

"Who are you?" Sheppard asked.

"My name is Maive," she said. "Maive Collins. I've been looking after you. You've been sleeping for nearly three days."

Sheppard noticed the tubes attached to his body.

"You were dehydrated," she said. "And completely exhausted." She stepped into the room and stood beside his bed. She pulled a medical scanner from her pocket and switched it on.

"Who are you?" Sheppard said. "I mean, how do you fit in to all of this?"

"I'm a prisoner," she said, "same as you. Gogue kept some of the medical staff on to treat his own wounded." She waved the scanner over Sheppard's body.

"I don't remember you," he said. "I think I would have remembered you."

She smiled a lovely smile.

"That's sweet of you to say," she said. She studied the readings on her instrument. "You're doing much better."

"Why am I here?" Sheppard asked. "Why did he let me go?"

"You would have died if he hadn't released you when he did," she said.

Sheppard rolled onto one elbow and slowly pushed himself into a sitting position. The human parts of his body sent spasms of pain through him. He clenched his teeth.

"So what's he going to do with me now?" he asked.

"You're under house arrest," she said. "You can't leave your quarters, but at least you're not being tortured."

"Thank God for the small blessings," Sheppard said. It almost seemed to be a vain use of his Creator's name, a sarcastic jab at a God who would make him endure such torture.

"I understand you were a minister," Maive said, "a missionary?"

"Yes," Sheppard said.

"I gave up on religious faith a long time ago," Maive said. "It just seemed pointless. I respect someone who can still have faith, but I'm not one of those people."

"I lost my faith sometime in my early teens," Sheppard said, "and found it again about ten years ago. It has made so much difference in my life."

"That's good," she said. "But how do you know it's not just wishful thinking?"

"I can't prove it isn't," Sheppard said. "I mean, there are some smart people who can make a good intellectual argument. I'm all for that, but my beliefs are more than just the sum of those arguments. One of the Christian philosophers--Pascal, I think--said 'The heart has reasons that reason can not know.' I know what he means."

"Willing suspension of disbelief," Maive said.

"A man of La Mancha," Sheppard said. "That's what you think I am? Don Quixote tilting at windmills."

"What?" she said.

"That's what Preston used to say about DeFalco and the rest of us," Sheppard said.

"Who's Preston?"

"He was a member of the first Intrepid Force," Sheppard said. "An actor. He always used to talk about a play called *Man of La Mancha*. It was a musical about a Spanish nobleman who lost his mind. He rode around the countryside fighting windmills because he thought he was a knight fighting dragons."

"It sounds like a funny play," she said.

"No," he said. "I mean, there were funny parts, but the Don Quixote character wasn't just a fool you could laugh at and dismiss. His dragons weren't real, but his nobility was. In that sense, he really was a noble knight. He could see the beauty in others that they couldn't see in themselves, and they started to see it too."

"Yes," she said.

"Preston said the Intrepid Force was an army of Don Quixotes tilting at windmills," Sheppard said. "The resurrected knights of King Arthur. He never could completely buy into DeFalco's ideals, and he ended up being the one who betrayed us."

"I'm sorry," she said.

"I know my faith may look like nothing more than windmill tilting to you," Sheppard said, "but I still believe it's more than that. There's just enough evidence to believe if you want to or to deny it if you don't."

"But what about the atrocities?" she asked. "The Inquisition? The Crusades? The Salem Witch Hunts? Surely you can't believe God was a part of that?"

"No," he said. "What about the hospitals, orphanages, and schools? The record hasn't all been bad." He sighed. "Can we talk about something else? I've been arguing religion with that monster for weeks. I'm tired of defending my religion. I just want to go on believing it and be left alone."

"Okay," Maive said. "I'm--I'm sorry. Maybe I should go now."

"No," Sheppard said. "No, that's okay. I'm glad you're here. Tell me about yourself. Where are you from? Are you married?"

"I'm from Cincinnati," she said. She smiled. "I'm not married. Does that make you happy?"

"I don't know," Sheppard said. He shrugged, smiled sheepishly. "I don't guess it matters. I was just making conversation."

"You're teasing me, Reverend," she said.

"Don't call me that," Sheppard said. "Gogue threw it in my face every chance he could."

"I'm sorry," Maive said. She sat down on the bed beside him and took his hand between hers. Sheppard looked uneasy. "Does it bother you for me to hold your hand?"

"No," Sheppard said. He was lying, of course, but it was a lie of compassion. God would understand.

"I've been so afraid these past few weeks," she said, "So alone. Caring for you has been the only bright spot in my life since Gogue took over." Tears came into her eyes. She held Sheppard's hand to her face. "I'd better go now," she said.

She rose to her feet and left the room. Sheppard started to follow but realized he was only wearing rubber underpants with tubes attached to them. He sighed and lay back down.

CHAPTER 12: Of Escape Plans and Dreamwatching

Preston sat in the dark, listening to sultry jazz music, and wondering what form his death would take. On the tray beside him sat a small tumbler. Inside it was an amber liquid, a synthetic Scotch substitute that would never give him more than a slight buzz. It was at times like this that he really missed the solace of his old drug habit. He was clean and sober now. He supposed he should be proud, but all sobriety offered him was fear and death. He wished Corbalew's henchmen would just kill him and get it over with. Why did they keep prolonging his life? The buzzer's insect thrum disturbed his thoughts. The lights slowly came up. The locks disengaged and the heavy doors parted.

Jonas Cockrum came rushing in. Jolie Harrison and two security guards were with him.

"Preston," Cockrum said. "We have to talk to you now."

"Are we disturbing you?" Harrison asked.

"My dear," Preston said in W.C. Fields' voice, "If you're not here to kill me, you're a better surprise than I deserve." He sat up and slowly opened his eyes.

"We're not here to kill you," Harrison said.

"It wasn't you I was thinking about," Preston said, his voice normal again. "Any word from Earth?"

"We have to get out of here," Cockrum said. "Preparations are underway now. You're going with us."

"Going where?" Preston asked.

"We're still deciding that," Cockrum said.

"What's happened?" Preston asked.

"Gogue's ships are headed this way," Cockrum said. "They're only four days away."

"I knew he would come here eventually," Preston said. "It was only a matter of time."

"Meanwhile there's another reason I wanted to see you," Cockrum said. "I need to know about the boy we found on the *Vanguard.*"

"The what?"

"Corbalew's ship, the one in the sleeper unit."

"I told you," Preston said. "I don't know who he is."

"I know that," Cockrum said. "We just wanted to show you something. We'll need to use the comm system. Do you mind?"

"No," Preston said. "Not at all."

"Communicore," Cockrum said. "Access the synthetic reality unit in Medical Center Lab H-15. Override security lockouts based on visual scans."

The holo-dioramic monitor hummed to life. A gray sky came up in the background. Ragged heaps of clouds covered the entire face of the heavens. Beneath them were the remains of a city, a dusty post-apocalyptic ruin. Most of the windows had been blown out of the buildings. The street was lined with the dusty hulks of wrecked aircars. Scrawny leafless trees and scrub brush were growing up through cracks in the street. Two men stood in the foreground. One of them was a teenage boy dressed in baggy pants and a ragged sweater. The other was a middle-aged man in an olive military uniform. He had black hair and a satanic goatee.

"Corbalew?" Preston asked. Harrison nodded. "What is this?"

"We don't know," Cockrum said, "but this is what is being projected into that boy's mind. We're seeing it from a bystander's point of view, but he sees it as though he's experiencing it."

"Does he know it's a simulation?" Preston asked.

"No," Cockrum said. "This simulation plays twenty-four hours a day. This is his world."

"And Corbalew's a part of it?" Preston asked.

"Yes," Cockrum said. "He's one of the main characters. Corbalew's counterpart here is a general in some kind of war. So you have no idea what this is?"

"No," Preston said. "I've never seen it before."

"We've scanned the boy's brain," Cockrum said. "There are clear signs that he experienced some kind of trauma to the brain."

"Trauma?" Preston said. "How serious?"

"Without modern nanosurgical techniques," Cockrum said, "it would have killed him."

"Is he still in danger?" Preston asked.

"Not from the brain trauma," Cockrum said. "That's been completely repaired. Our problem now is that we can't end the simulation. Corbalew's got it wired directly into his nervous system--some kind of nanofibers. If we try to disconnect it, there's a good chance we'll destroy his mind."

"Have you asked Corbalew about it?" Preston asked.

"Yes," Cockrum admitted. "He's not saying much. He just keeps repeating the part where the devil has taken over Earth, and we're all going to die horribly."

"At least he's consistent," Preston said, smiling for the first time. "How much of the simulation have you watched?"

"Enough of it to get an idea of what's going on," Cockrum said, "He's obviously got that boy convinced he's living in this world, but why would he want to do that?"

"I don't know," Preston said. "He may be trying to extract some kind of information from him, but what could a teenage boy know that would even matter to him?"

"He may have seen something," Cockrum said. "Something of some kind of strategic importance to Corbalew's people."

"Maybe," Preston said. "But if it's simple information he wants, why didn't he just torture him for it?"

"I don't know," Cockrum said.

"Could you leave this on," Preston said. "I'll monitor their conversations and look for clues. It's not like I've got anything else to do."

"You'd better start packing," Cockrum said.

"Leave me here," Preston said. "The boy too. If you value your lives, you'll turn both of us over to Gogue's forces when they come. They might just take us and leave."

"I can't do that," Cockrum said. "That boy may hold some kind of key to what's happening on Earth. I'm not surrendering you either."

"What about Corbalew?" Preston asked. "What are you going to do with him?"

"He's the most valuable asset of all," Cockrum said.

"Because of what he knows," Preston said, "or as a bargaining chip?"

"Either one," Cockrum said. "Take your pick."

Preston nodded.

"If Gogue finds out all of us have left the planet," Cockrum continued. "do you think he'll leave everybody else alone?"

"It's possible," Preston said. "Do you have enough ships to evacuate the whole colony?"

"No," Cockrum said. "The food supply is also a problem. It's not like we can go back to Earth and replenish our supplies. Most of the people voted to go underground. There's still a network of tunnels from the days before the dome. They should have enough food to last a couple of years."

Preston turned toward the image of the boy on the screen. Corbalew--the image of Corbalew--smiled and nodded at something he had said. Preston remembered a time when he had trusted Corbalew too. It had ruined his life.

"I'd better go now," Cockrum said. "Get packed. I'll be back for you in about an hour."

Preston nodded and looked back at the screen.

"Goodbye, Preston," Jolie Harrison said.

Preston didn't seem to hear.

CHAPTER 13: Roughing It

The sun was setting and the beach was deserted. The water was still a little too cool for swimming. Airboats skated above the surface of the highway that ran between Santa Monica, California and Ventura. Neema shivered as she stumbled through the surf, but she wasn't sure if she was shivering from the cold or from exhaustion. She wore a black wetsuit she had borrowed from Ernie's dive shop. The pack on her back weighed less than twenty pounds, but it seemed unbearably heavy now. Waves washed in and out around her legs. The water was only shin deep. She was only a few ponderous steps from the shore.

Neema stopped and took a breath. Palm trees lined the beach. On the other side of the highway was a noble stand of fir trees and a suburban neighborhood. Through the trees, she could see mountains. Was this the Diablo Range or was that further north? She couldn't be sure.

Neema stumbled to the shore, crossed the highway, and kept walking. She passed a young man, about college age, on the sidewalk.

"Hey, surfer girl," the guy said. "Where's your board?"

Neema smiled but didn't say anything. She trudged through a neighborhood and into the forest behind it. She walked until she was safely hidden in the shadows of the forest. Exhausted, she slung off her backpack and dropped it at the gnarled foot of an enormous tree. She sank to the floor of the forest and felt the needles and leaves crunch beneath her. She opened the pack, pulled out a bottle of water, and drank greedily. She felt around the pack for a power bar and finally found it. Fingers trembling, she peeled away the wrapper and bit away half of the bar with her first bite.

Neema had been squeezed into the escape module for nearly two days. She had, so far as she knew, managed to avoid detection. Ditching the module five miles offshore had seemed like a sensible precaution, but it had forced her to swim so far. She had wondered, more than once, if she would meet her death by drowning somewhere off the coast of California.

She missed Jared. More than his physical presence, she missed the connection they had shared. The implants had kept them empathetically linked for so long. Now the link was gone. Neema had severed it by taking a drug that suppressed the link. The organic transmitter in her brain slept now. This was, she supposed, what Jared had wanted. He had been so angry about the invasion of his mind. Neema had felt his resentment, the cold distrust that struck her like a sudden slap across the face.

Strengthened by the short pause in her journey, Neema stood up, pulled on the pack, and started toward the mountains. The place she was going was still about two days away, and she had to get there quickly. There was no time to be weak.

Neema emerged from the forest and stepped across a split rail fence into an empty parking lot. The lot was rugged, covered with white rocks. It ran along the edge of a wide, rocky stream. There was a steep bluff on the other side. Slabs of rock guarded the stream. Needle leaf trees covered the hills beyond. Beside the stream was a rough wood shack. A hand painted sign told of kayak rentals, ice, food, and beer. The place looked deserted.

Neema felt a twinge of guilt about breaking into the empty store, but she had few options. Perhaps she could pay them back later. The store was better than its word. Neema found food, drinks, a refrigerated chest, and a pair of well used hiking shoes that fit almost perfectly. She also took some soap and deodorant. She was beginning to need a bath--and a hairbrush. She packed her supplies into a backpack--also borrowed--and broke into the shed where the kayaks were kept.

Nightfall found Neema skirting a clear mountain stream and feeling like a new woman. She had taken a quick bath in the icy water and pulled on some clean clothes.

This part of California was a place of rugged beauty, a place with nature trails, biking paths, camp grounds, and fishing streams.

Neema saw an old fire tower standing on the top of a ridge. It towered over the tops of the pine and fir trees that shrouded much of the landscape around her. She had no idea how far she had traveled or how far she was from civilization. She thought of the tracking equipment she'd left on the starship and sighed.

She paddled to the edge of the stream, climbed out on the rocks, and pulled the kayak up onto shore. The tough plastic surface rasped against the rocks. Neema stowed the kayak in some bushes. She pulled out a bottle of water and some power bars, and started through the forest toward the ridge. She had only taken a few steps when she came out on a narrow mountain road. Gravel had been poured onto the path to limit erosion, but it was not paved. Neema found two broken limbs and laid them at the base of a tree to mark the place where she had emerged from the forest. This would enable her to find the kayak again later.

Neema trudged up the hill toward the tower. It took her twenty minutes to reach it. The tower was even older than she had realized, but it looked solid and well maintained. The old structure was made mostly of rickety metal. The steps were wooden slats.

Neema started up. After swimming five miles and hiking through the forest and up the hill, her legs felt like they would collapse beneath her at any moment. She slowed her pace and kept going. The tower squeaked beneath her as she climbed. By the time she was halfway up, Neema could already see over the tops of the trees around her. By the time she reached the trap door on the bottom of the tower's observation compartment, she could see the lights of several cities in the distance. To the east was Bakersfield. Los Angeles ran along the south.

The trap door was held shut by a lock. Neema picked it in a matter of seconds, moved it aside, and opened the hatch. She climbed up into the tower's observation compartment. The place was sparsely furnished. Inside were a table, two chairs, a cot, and a miniature refrigerator. The cot's mattress looked dirty and lumpy. Neema decided to stretch out for a moment, to rest her eyes.

* * *

"Jared?" Pirate said. There was no answer.

A rock, large and black, lay in the surf. A single still figure sat perched upon it. It faced out into the rolling waves, into the starry sky, like a statue on the prow of a ship. It did not move. Pirate squinted through the darkness. Just for a moment he wondered if the still figure was really a part of the rock, if its human appearance was only his imagination playing tricks on him. When Jared finally did move, it startled him.

"What are you doing out here?" Jared asked suddenly.

"That's what I was about to ask you," Pirate said.

"I don't want to talk about it," Jared said.

Pirate nodded.

"I keep thinking about what Hal said," he told Jared. "You know, about how the whole team being a publicity stunt, us not being soldiers."

"We're not soldiers," Jared said. "Not the kind he is, at least. That's not why we were formed."

"Still," Pirate said. "It wasn't something I wanted to hear. It's like he thought we were all sheep, and he was the only real man among us."

"What he said didn't have anything to do with us," Jared said. "There's something wrong, something he's not telling us."

"How do you know?" Pirate asked.

"I just do," Jared said.

Pirate didn't say anything for a moment.

"Neema came to me for help," Jared said, his voice desolate. "She came to me for help, and I turned her away."

"No one could blame you for being suspicious," Pirate said. "It's not every day that your dreams come to life."

"It is for me," Jared said. "I've had premonitions for almost as long as I can remember--especially since I started dreaming about Neema."

Pirate climbed onto the rock and seated himself. It was smooth, scoured by the waves. It was also warm from the heat its black color had absorbed.

"She says we've both met her before," Pirate said. "To tell the truth, she did seem familiar. Wasn't there a blonde girl who used to live in your neighborhood? She was from Norway, Sweden, or somewhere like that."

"I think you're right," Jared said.

"We never saw her at school," Pirate said.

"No," Jared said. "Maybe it was during the summer."

"Maybe," Pirate said, "but I think I've got this mental picture of us playing in the snow."

"She was wearing a parka," Jared said.

"With a fur collar," Pirate said. "And a hood."

"She loved the snow," Jared said. "She acted like she was seeing it for the first time."

"Which wouldn't make sense if she was really from one of the Scandinavian countries," Pirate said.

"You're right," Jared said. "Come to think of it."

They sat without talking for a while.

"I was such a fool," Jared said. "Why didn't I believe her? Why did I get angry at her?"

"Defense mechanism," Pirate said. "A way to keep from being disappointed again."

"I know," Jared said. "I know. I was such a fool."

"Do you think she's all right?" Pirate asked.

"I don't know," Jared said.

"What do you feel?" Pirate asked.

"Nothing," Jared said. "I don't feel anything."

They sat and stared at the distant horizon as the waves washed in and out. Jared prayed silently for Neema. He prayed for a second chance. Jared was grateful for the darkness, grateful that his friend couldn't see his silent tears.

* * *

Neema woke up suddenly. Silvery shafts of moonlight poured through the tower's windows. The sky outside was gray. Neema could hear the cadence of footfalls on the tower's steps. She could feel the tower shaking. Someone was coming.

Neema ran to the window and looked out. Two black airboats were sitting at the tower's base. Neema could see several figures moving in the shadows beneath the tower. They were wearing black body armor and helmets.

They've found me! she thought. She felt her panic beginning to rise and fought it down.

Neema threw open the trap door and started town. Five of the black clad figures were already on the steps. The first of them was nearly halfway up.

Neema looked back at the empty tower. She thought about trying to hide. She thought about locking the door and pretending no one was home, but didn't think it would work. Her only chance was to get a little closer to the ground and jump into the canopy of one of the nearby trees. Were they really as close as they looked?

Neema started down.

"Stop!" the nearest figure yelled. Neema jumped, cleared a flight of stairs, and slammed into him. His gun went tumbling into darkness. Neema heard it hit the ground below.

She climbed upon the guardrail and prepared to jump.

"Freeze," the second figure cried.

A red dot, a laser site, showed up on Neema's side. Other red dots appeared on her body. They covered her head and torso. There was no way she could escape--except maybe one. Neema leaped into the air. She heard projectiles zipping past as she fell. Neema tumbled through space, ripped through a tree canopy, and hit the ground with bone-jarring impact.

The wind was knocked out of her. She gasped for breath, but her throat seemed locked. She felt straw stuck to her face and in her hair, but didn't care. She gasped and struggled to get to her feet. A stab of pain tore through her ankle. She had broken it in the fall.

A red dot appeared on her chest. Two more appeared on her torso. The black armored figures moved in around her. She couldn't make out their faces. They were only silhouettes against the gray sky. Their heavy boots made crunching noises in the straw.

"We won't hurt you," one of them said. "But you have to come with us."

"Gyyyaaah!" one of them cried. Concussion beams tore through the group of them, knocked them to the ground.

Neema tried to get up, tried to run. A concussion beam grazed her shoulder, threw her to the ground.

"No."

"Neema," a young man's voice said. "Stay down. Stay down."

The shadows around her rippled and shifted as a barrage of concussion bursts sent her foes falling this way and that. Finally there were none left. Six figures in bulky, brightly colored body armor stepped into the light.

"Who are you?" Neema asked.

The first five had removed their helmets. Four young men and one young woman stood looking down a her with hauntingly familiar faces. Neema had never actually seen them, but the original Neema, the girl from the future whose memories she carried, had known and loved them all. The sixth figure, a young woman, removed her helmet. Neema found herself staring mutely at her own dark reflection. This young woman, this phantom from a post apocalyptic nightmare, wore Neema's face but her hair was raggedly cut and there was a wicked scar across one of her cheeks and one of her earlobes had been sliced away.

"It can't be you," Neema said. "You're dead. You're all dead."

"They're not dead," an older man's voice said. "They've haven't even been born yet. It's good to see you, Nina."

Neema studied the old man's face for a moment. He knelt down beside her and smoothed back her pale hair. Recognition dawned, and she threw her arms around him. He gently embraced her.

"Let's get you somewhere safe," he said.

CHAPTER 14: Burial Ground

"Neema must have been right about Astrolus," Hal said. "They left and haven't come back." He slid a window pane into its slot and snapped it into place.

"I guess they weren't interested in us after all," Mike said. He wiped his hands with a towel.

"Ya know," Zapper said. "That's really insultin' if you think about it."

"Maybe they'll come back and kick our butts so Zapper can feel better about himself," Hal said as he snapped another pane into place. The three of them were replacing the front windows of Shawna's bistro. The team had spent most of the previous day trying to salvage parts from wrecked airboats and cobble them together. Their efforts had ended in failure. They had gone to bed angry and frustrated, but the light of a new day had brightened the collective mood of the group. Even Hal, who had spent the previous day pacing like a caged lion, was smiling and making jokes as he had done before the attacks.

Pirate, Jared, Wendy, Tori, and Ernie Montgomery walked up as they were working. Pirate, Jared, and Wendy were dressed in their uniforms and gear and carrying their helmets. Tori wasn't wearing her usual synthetic reality gear, but she was wearing bulletproof mesh and carrying a tool chest.

"'Ow's it goin'?" Ernie asked.

"Great," Mike said. "We're almost finished."

"Anybody seen the news this morning?" Hal asked.

"I watched for a little while," Ernie said. "Things had quieted down some."

"That's good news anyway," Mike said.

"For however long it lasts," Zapper added.

"What are you guys doing anyway?" Hal asked.

"Actually," Pirate said. "We were about to take a stroll across the island to Corbalew's old lab."

"For what?" Zapper asked.

"To look for transportation," Pirate said. "Ernie says there used to be some high speed submersible vehicles over there. They'll probably need some maintenance, but some of them might still be seaworthy. We're going to need Zapper and Hal to go with us since they're our top mechanics."

"What about me?" Tori asked. "I'm not a top mechanic?"

"You're a Jill of all trades," Pirate said. "But Hal and Zapper still know more about transportation equipment."

"Things like putting oil in a car," Zapper said.

"I'm a mechanic," Tori protested, "not an archaeologist. You keep bringing that up."

"How are the repairs going?" Wendy asked.

"Fine," Hal said. "It was mostly broken glass."

"And doors," Mike said. "They really broke a lot of doors."

"It's funny how they targeted this place," Pirate said. "There's more damage to this pub than all the other buildings combined."

"Yeah," Mike said. "This place and the girls' bathroom in the store. It's like they nearly tore the place apart getting to it."

"That's weird," Pirate said.

"Maybe there was a name on the wall they wanted," Zapper said.

"So why are you guys wearing your gear?" Mike asked. "Are you expecting another fight?"

"Because that old lab is a dangerous place," Ernie said. "DeFalco's men disarmed all of the booby traps they could find when they took over the island, but they still warned those of us who set up here to stay away from the place. With a guy like Corbalew, you can always expect a few nasty surprises. There's a network of tunnels built in the lava tubes under the mountain. The men who explored those tunnels wouldn't even talk about the things they found there. I think they may have been under orders to keep it all quiet, but there was something about the way they acted when they came back from searching through those tunnels. It was like they'd just walked through a graveyard. If I was to make a bet about what they found down there, my money'd be on genetics experiments."

"Genetics experiments?" Mike said. "On people?"

"That's what I think anyway," Ernie said. "I didn't see what those men saw, but I've found a few things of my own that convinced me that's what was going on. Bodies, y'know. I found one of 'em in the woods. Another one washed up on the beach."

"Did you tell anybody?" Pirate asked.

"Yeah," he said. "DeFalco's got his own security people, of course. I mean, you guys should know, right? I called 'em about it. They came and bagged 'em up. Never 'eard anything else about it."

"What did they look like?" Hal asked.

"There wasn't much left of the skeleton I found in the woods," he said. "Skull was shaped funny--fangs and all. The one that washed up on the beach still had some flesh on it. It was like some kind of a human fish with webbed hands and gills. It was chewed up pretty bad. Poor thing looked like it might have picked a fight with a shark and got the bad end of the deal."

Pirate and Wendy looked at each other. Both of them wondered if Ernie was telling them one of the fish stories he used to entertain tourists. Zapper, Mike, and Hal finished up their repairs and pulled on their gear. They debated about bringing along Hal's exobot but decided to leave it back in the village. Hand held sensors would be able to detect land mines, laser beams, and most other conventional weapons. With Corbalew, however, it was always the unexpected that one had to worry about.

The first part of the hike across the island was pleasant. Even Hal and Jared seemed to enjoy it. The weather was warm but there was a nice breeze. Brightly-colored flowers grew at the bases of tall trees. Tropical birds filled the rainforests with their exotic cries. The peaceful sounds of rolling ocean waves were always in the background. They followed a paved road along the edge of a high bluff. Guardrails protected them from an eighty-foot plunge onto the jagged volcanic rocks in the shallow stream below. The road led into a forest and divided into two forks. Ernie led the group down the left path. They had only gone a few meters when they came to a gate. There was a sign:

DANGER
KEEP OUT

Beyond a metal crossbar the road was shady and overgrown with brush. The grass on the shoulders of the road was tall and was slowly pushing its way into the road itself as the edges eroded and broke away in crusty, rock-filled chunks. Leaves and limbs and whole trees had fallen into the path and no one had removed them. The tops of trees had grown together overhead. They had turned the road into a tunnel.

"This is it," Ernie said. He bent over and slid under the crossbar. Pirate noticed he had a concussion pistol strapped to his belt, but didn't comment on it. The others followed. No one said much. Even in bright daylight, the shady path still held an air of supernatural menace. It felt haunted, cursed. Walking through that stretch of forest was like walking through a tribal burial ground with angry spirits behind every bush. Finally they emerged into broad daylight once again. The road in front of them was blocked by a crossbar and an empty guard's shack. Tall hurricane fences stood on either side of the road. They were overgrown with vines. The tops curved inward. They were lined with sharpened spikes and twisted spirals of razor wire. The lawn on the other side of the fence was hip deep in tall grass and weeds. Along the coast was a sprawling compound of flat-roofed brick buildings with bars on every window. There were guard towers overlooking the grounds. On the far right the buildings were built right into the wall of a cliff.

"After you," Ernie said.

"Let's go," Pirate said.

"I've got to go back," Zapper said. "I left my crosses and holy water back at the village. Too bad Hal's mama's not here to scare away the evil spirits."

"You leave my mama out of this," Hal warned. "Yours may be waiting up in here somewhere."

"You guys be quiet," Tori said.

"Why?" Zapper said. "There ain't supposed to be anything in here."

"You're still getting on my nerves," she said.

"Moody moody moody," Zapper said. "Shock her on the booty."

"Try it and you'll get a toolbox on your head," Tori warned.

"Give it up, man," Mike said. "You're no match for her."

"Yeah, yeah, yeah," Zapper said. "Like you could handle her."

"You don't handle a girl like Tori," Mike said. "She's like surfing on a typhoon. You know you're going to drown, but it's fun while it lasts."

They all moved past the crossbar and into the compound. Even inside the gate there were tall fences on either side of the road that separated it from the overgrown yard. These fences, like the ones outside, were topped with spikes and razor wire. Who or what had been held prisoner within those fences? Who had tried to climb the fence only to be dragged, screaming, to the ground or slashed to bloody ribbons on the spikes and razor wire above? What rough beasts had been bred into existence by arcane sciences and sent back to hell by guns, hypodermics, and electric jolts?

They reached the main entrance and found it chained shut. Two heavy metal doors were bound by chains that encircled the latch handles. Padlocks held the chains in place. There was another sign:

ABSOLUTELY NO ENTRY

VIOLATORS WILL BE **EX**ECUTED

Someone had scratched through the first part of the word prosecuted and written the 'exe' in red paint. It was a joke of course--graveyard humor--but it was too believable in that setting to be very funny.

"I don't feel right about disturbing this place," Jared said.

"If the whole planet's in danger," Hal said, "I don't think we have to worry too much about breaking and entering charges."

"That's not what I meant," Jared said. "This place has a feel to it, a kind of aura. I don't know what happened here, but I can still feel it. It's like the whole area is charged with evil."

"Charged with evil," Zapper mocked. "Hah."

"Don't laugh," Mike said. "There are places like that. Haunted places."

"And white people never know when to leave them alone," Hal said.

"If you guys don't want to go in," Ernie said. "That's up to you."

"No," Pirate said. "We've come this far. Our weapons should protect us from anything human or animal. We'll just have to count on our prayers to protect us from anything supernatural." He engaged the concussion field emitters on the backs of his gloves and sliced through the chains. Another burst tore through the locking mechanisms inside the door itself. He pulled the door open, and they all stepped inside.

There was a bank of switches inside the door. Pirate reached over and flipped on the lights. The power cells still worked. Pale lights came up on a dingy corridor lined with heavy metal doors. Beneath the musty building smell was a scent of chemicals and the faint odor of something dead. Pirate kept his concussion field emitters engaged. Anything that tried to attack him would find a hole the size of a basketball driven through its belly. He could not fully explain the heaviness of spirit that descended on him as he walked through the gloom of that empty building. Perhaps it was just a result of Ernie's stories and Jared's pronouncement about the place being charged with evil. He could not be sure. He felt something brush against him and spun around with a start. Wendy had taken him by the arm.

"Oh my gosh," he said. "I nearly shot you."

"I'm sorry," she said. She pulled away. "I didn't mean to startle you."

"No," he said. "It's okay. This place is making me jumpy." He brushed her cheek with his glove. She bristled slightly. Pirate cursed himself inwardly. Wendy had almost completely avoided him since the night of the attack. This was the first time she had even tried to touch him, and he had driven her away. "It's okay," he said again.

"I know," she said. She forced a smile, but stayed at arm's length.

They walked about a hundred yards further into the building. Their footsteps echoed in the empty corridor.

"Be careful," Mike whispered to Pirate as he walked past him.

"Of what?" Pirate asked.

"Wendy," Mike said. "She's nice, but you can't get close to her."

Pirate looked back. Wendy was several meters behind them and distracted by her surroundings.

"I know you two had a relationship once," Pirate said.

"Only for a little while," Mike said. "It didn't last long. Wendy has a low outer wall. She's easy to talk to, easy to be friends with. She hugs people." He shook his head. "But once you get past that, she shuts you out. It's like walking in a maze full of mirrors and trap doors that just keeps going on forever."

"She's been through a lot in her life," Pirate said.

"I know," Mike said. "But she won't let anybody help her. I care a lot about her, but I don't want to be hurt anymore. I'd rather just be her friend."

"Thanks for telling me," Pirate said.

Pirate wondered if Mike was warning him out of friendship or just trying to discourage his competition for Wendy's affections. No, he decided. Mike was honest and genuine--a real friend. Even so, his words stung Pirate. He looked around at Wendy walking alone through that hallway and everything about her drew him to her. The physical attraction was strong-- there was no denying that--but the emotional hunger ran even deeper. At times he felt he was only moments away from the emotional breakthrough that would bond them for life. At other times he was sure that Mike was right. Wendy's heart was buried so deep within a maze of mirrors and trap doors that no one would ever find it--especially not Pirate Eisman. Why did he even bother to try? There were, after all, other women in the world. Some of them might even allow him to get close to them. Why did he keep wasting his time with this one? At times he wished he had never joined the Intrepid Force in the first place.

They explored Corbalew's empty complex for nearly an hour. They found examining rooms, autopsy tables, and whole wings of empty cages and cells. They found storerooms full of chemicals. Dusty bottles lined the shelves and the walls were stacked with unopened boxes.

Finally they stepped through a set of sliding electric doors and found themselves staring over a rail into rippling water. The flashing surface cast flickering caustic reflections on the rock walls overhead.

"We're in some kind of a cave," Hal said.

"It's a lava tube," Ernie said. "Full of sea water. It's moving pretty fast."

"I wonder how far this thing goes," Hal said. They followed the tunnel as it led deeper into the hillside.

Pirate put on his helmet and used the digital targeting system to zoom down the tunnel.

"I can't make anything out," he said. "But the roar seems to be getting louder."

A few meters ahead, the tunnel widened out and the water poured over a shelf of gray rock into a pool below. Stairs led down to a lower level. They followed them. The tunnel narrowed to half its former width and bent to the right. They followed it for several minutes.

Wendy heard a tone like the buzz of the communication system in her quarters on *Vector*. She saw a greenish glow coming from a smaller side tunnel they had just passed and dropped back to investigate. Suddenly Wendy was back on the starship she had seen in the dream on the night of the attack. The corridors were metallic, dimly lit, and lined with doors.

The floor was covered with metal grating. She touched the nape of her neck. Her hair was shoulder length and her ponytail was gone. She was wearing a blue pant suit. It looked like a uniform. She saw her reflection in the glass of a control panel. She had become the blue-eyed girl again.

"No," she said. "NO! Pirate! Hal! Help me!"

SCCCHHHLIPPP!

One of the doors had opened. Wendy started to go inside, but drew back.

"Are you coming in or not?" a young man's voice said from inside the room.

Wendy stepped into the room. It was small and compact like the room she had seen earlier, but much less spartan. It looked like the tomb of an Egyptian king. The walls and shelves were covered with Egyptian, Aztec, Hindu, and Hebrew relics. A statue of Anubis stood in one corner. An Aztec sundial hung over the bed, the face of Quetzalcoatl glaring from the center. A bronze statue of Kali, the six-armed Hindu goddess, sat on a nightstand. Mirror image bookends, cast in the shape of Solomon's temple, sat on a bookshelf. Between them were volumes on ancient civilizations, computer programming, and artificial intelligence.

Seated in front of a console, his hair uncombed and his clothing rumpled, sat a young man in his late teens.

Darnell. The name sprang up suddenly in Wendy's mind. His name was Darnell.

"Darnell," Wendy gasped.

The young man sighed, shook his head.

"Arwen," he said. "I have told you repeatedly to call me Dokanuchu."

"I'm sorry Daku--"

"Dokanuchu," he repeated. "Doh-kan-ooh-chooooo. Say it for me, angel?"

"Dokanuchu," Wendy said.

"Perfect," Darnell/Dokanuchu said. "So what can I do for you?"

"I don't know," Wendy said. "I don't know what I'm doing here. I don't even know where I am."

"Being in my room often has that effect on women," Dokanuchu said. He laughed at his own joke. "Well, you came at a good time. I've got something to show you."

"What is it?" she asked.

"Come over here," he said. "Come on. I don't bite. Not very hard anyway." He reached out and took her by the hand.

Wendy felt terror starting to rise within her. Her skin felt icy cold and her heart began to pound. She struggled to pull away, but Dokanuchu didn't seem to notice.

"Here," he said. "Look at this."

He turned the desktop screen toward Wendy. She focused on the image and screamed.

* * *

"She's coming out of it now."

Wendy sat up with a start and wrapped her arms tightly around her body.

"Are you all right?" Mike asked.

"I don't know," she said. She began to cry. "It was horrible."

"What is it?" Pirate asked. "What's wrong?" He knelt down beside her, tried to hold her. She pulled away.

"Please," she said. "Everybody just leave me alone."

Pirate sighed. *So we're back to that again,* he thought. *Pretty much the story of our whole relationship.*

"Don't move," Jaina said. She was digging wildly through her medical bag. "I want to run some scans."

"I don't need any scans," Wendy said.

"You were having a seizure," Jaina said. "I'm going to scan you if I have to wrestle you down and sit on you."

"Okay," Wendy said.

Pirate started to help her to her feet, but thought better of it. Wendy had crawled back into her secret fortress and pulled up the drawbridge. It would be a long time before she came out of it again. She sat still as Jaina scanned her brain for abnormalities. The scans revealed nothing out of the ordinary. Wendy hardly spoke to anyone for the rest of the time they were in the compound, but she seemed more afraid of the eerie place than she had been before.

The team searched for another forty-five minutes and finally found three four-passenger submersibles docked in a boathouse at the edge of the ocean. Someone had blasted holes through the canopies and ballast tanks and the passenger compartments were full of water. Ten years of residue coated the seats and control panels. Even if they could not escape from the authorities, Corbalew's men apparently had not wanted to leave anything usable behind.

"They don't look very seaworthy," Mike said. "I don't think I'd want to cross the ocean in them."

"If the parts are mostly plastics and alloys that don't rust, I may be able to get 'em working," Zapper said. "Getting the smell out of them is another matter."

"I better get my exobot," Hal said.

CHAPTER 15: Confessions of a Traitor

The corridor was nearly a quarter of a mile long. It ran on either side of the *Vanguard*'s main cannon. The heavy blast shutters were open and Preston could look out through thick glass windows at the endless expanse of space. The planet Venus was now two days away.

Jolie Harrison's magnetic boots gripped and released the metal hull plating as she approached. This part of the ship did not have artificial gravity. Without the spin of a drum or a low-pressure repulsor field to simulate gravity, the crew had to rely on magnetism to hold them to the deck. Harrison's boots thumped along in a steady cadence. That sound, for Preston, brought back a flood of unpleasant memories. He had walked this corridor before under very different circumstances.

"Ironic," he said.

"What?" Harrison asked.

"This," he said. He held out his hands, indicating the ship around them. The *Vanguard* was an asteroid smasher. It was over twenty years old and built from a solid, utilitarian design. It was homely yet reliable. Charred pieces of cyber-organic cable hung from brackets along the wall. Less than one month earlier the mutant fibers had clung to machinery throughout the ship like parasites. Now they lay lifeless and burned. Preston himself was to thank for that.

"Oh, right," she said. "Because this is Corbalew's ship, the one he used to attack Venus Base."

"The one I sabotaged," Preston said.

"And now we're escaping in it," she said. "And hoping the damage you did wasn't as extensive as it seemed. Like you said: ironic."

"It still seems haunted," Preston said. "Corbalew has a way of cursing everything he touches. Bringing him with us was a very bad idea."

"He's in a REGEN tank," Harrison said. "What can he do?"

"I don't know," Preston said. "With voice-activated controls, machines that respond to brain waves and gestures. . . Basically he just scares me. I don't think any of you understand just how cunning and evil he is."

"He's only a man," Harrison said.

"That's what DeFalco used to say about him," Preston said. "I believed it once. I thought maybe we were wrong about Corbalew, that he wasn't that bad. Underestimating Corbalew was the biggest mistake I ever made."

"When was this?" Harrison said.

"Oh," Preston said. "About eleven years ago. They used to say I was the world's greatest master of disguise. After working for several years as an actor, I got rich and bored and started looking for new challenges. I started going on secret missions, using my equipment and my natural acting abilities to infiltrate drug rings, genetics engineering operations, interplanetary terrorist groups. It was all very cloak and dagger. I became quite the master.

"So what happened?" Harrison asked.

Preston sighed, shook his head.

"Don't bury yourself in the part," Preston said. "Back when I was an actor that's what my friends used to tell me. Not my actor friends, of course. They understood the importance of becoming the character. The others didn't understand, but they provided a kind of balance to my life. They reminded me that regardless of what Shakespeare said, the world isn't all a stage. I should have listened to them. I should have listened."

He didn't say anything for a while. Harrison turned and looked at him. Preston's eyes were focused on some far away vision. Finally he spoke again.

"I was part of a deep cover operation," he said. "An actor's ultimate test. My job was to infiltrate Corbalew's operations and find out what was really happening there behind the facades, behind the smoke and the mirrors. I thought I had. I lived among Corbalew and his people for over a year and something unexpected happened. Corbalew and I became friends."

He stopped for a moment and thought of it.

"He trusted me, told me things. I began to understand him. He was flamboyant, a bit machiavellian. Some of his methods went beyond what was legal, but I came to understand that life in space has rules of its own. Mind-altering drugs make the long, dark months tolerable. When you're a million miles from home, you deal with your own problems. The police are weeks away. I did a few small jobs for him. DeFalco knew about that. It was something I would have to do to earn Corbalew's trust, to keep from raising suspicion. It worked.

"After spending so much time with Corbalew, becoming friends with him, when the time came to give him up to the authorities, I found that I couldn't bring myself to betray him. He considered me a friend. He had trusted me, confided in me.

"I told DeFalco we'd been wrong about Corbalew, that the raid was a mistake. He wouldn't listen. He always thought he knew better than everybody else. Superior, genetically-engineered intelligence. He was so arrogant. When I couldn't convince him, I went to Corbalew, told him who I was, and warned him about the coming raid. It wasn't until then that I saw his true face. I had thought of myself as an actor performing before an audience and fooling them all only to find out that the audience was me. He had known who I was all along, had shown me the things he wanted me to see and hidden the rest.

"Corbalew promised to reward me for my loyalty. In a strange way, I think he actually felt indebted to me. He mobilized his secret army and launched a raid on Tranquility Bay Spaceport. I begged him not to do it. I told him my daughter was there. He promised me she would be safe and sent Brunkert to fetch her. He murdered the woman who was taking care of her and ended up using her as a hostage to cover his own escape. Sheppard tried to rescue her, but the attempt went bad. She was horribly maimed in an accidental explosion. Corbalew almost managed to escape, but was captured in orbit. Eighteen of my friends, my own teammates died that day including my beloved Karen. I soon found that I couldn't face the day without the mind-numbing effects of alcohol and other stronger substances. The nine years that followed are all a blur to me now, a murky haze of disjointed events. I used my gifts for imitation and misdirection in female impersonator acts and magic shows.

"I never told my friends--the ones who survived--what happened, but I could see in their eyes that they suspected I had betrayed them. I was too cowardly to confess what I'd done and turn myself in. Now I wish I had. I don't know what they would have done to me, but it couldn't have been any more degrading or humiliating than the punishment I chose for myself."

"Does your daughter know you're alive?" Harrison asked.

"No," Preston said. "She doesn't even know my name."

"And she's disfigured?" she asked. "Horribly maimed."

"No," Preston said. "Not anymore. DeFalco saw to that. He was a far better father to her than I ever was. He paid for years of reconstructive surgery. Now, thanks to him, she's a beautiful and healthy young woman--at least she was until this invasion started. Who knows if anyone is alive on Earth now?"

They stood in silence for a moment.

"Jonas just got a message from Venus," Harrison said. "Gogue's ships turned back when they found out you, Corbalew, and that freezing unit were gone."

"That's good," Preston said.

"Now they're looking for us," Harrison said.

"Gee, toots," Preston said, reverting to one of his gangster voices. "You're just full of good news, ain'tcha. Ain't she full o' good news, Lefty?"

"Yeah, boss," another voice answered. "She's a card."

Harrison supposed Preston's voices had been funny once, that they had been used to entertain an audience. Now they just seemed pathetic and a little unsettling.

CHAPTER 16: Last Night in Paradise

It was to be their last night on the island. The Intrepid Force, along with Ernie Montgomery, Harry and Grace Chan, the honeymooners, the marine biologist, and the island's other residents, gathered in Shawna's bar and grill for a luau. All of the damage from the attack had been repaired. Broken glass had been replaced. Pictures and artifacts from other parts of the island had been brought in to replace those things that had been destroyed. Candles burned on every table.

"We don't know what we've got ahead of us," Pirate told everyone during one of the quieter moments. "We've all seen the news. We know what's happening in the world.

"If this Gogue is the Beast and the book of Revelation is being fulfilled, there's nothing we can do but wait out this conflict and hope the return of Christ isn't too far behind. I guess we could just wait here on this island and hope Gogue doesn't notice us. I'll admit that option has a certain appeal."

Pirate looked around the dark room at the sad and serious faces of his friends and those who had shared the island with them for the past three days. He searched his heart for some word of assurance.

"But there's also a possibility that this being isn't the Beast written about in the Bible. He may be an imposter deliberately fulfilling Biblical prophecies. He may be counting on fear to keep anyone from opposing his rule. Neema told us she was sent back by a group of freedom fighters from nearly two hundred years in the future. I did some reading. The Beast in the Bible isn't supposed to reign but seven years before his rule is overthrown by the return of the Messiah, so there's a chance this isn't the Biblical Beast at all. On the other hand, Revelation is full of symbolism and the number seven may stand for something. We're not really that sure of anything.

"We don't know what Gogue is, but we do know that Lancing DeFalco formed this group to protect innocent lives. Prophecy will take care of itself, but we've got a job to do."

"What are you going to do?" the marine biologist asked.

"DeFalco Space Industries has offices in L.A.," Pirate said. "We're going to start there. We're hoping we can rearm ourselves, maybe get a better sense of what's going on and what we can do about it. After that, we're not sure."

He looked around the room at the cheerful decorations, the band, and the Hawaiian girls' print dresses.

"Look around you now," he said. "This is the life our group was formed to protect. I want us to enjoy this last night together. I want us to be able to think back on it in the days ahead and get some comfort from the memory. That's all I have to say." He sat down.

A musical combo stood beside the bar. They began to play. Ernie strummed on a ukulele, Grace Chan played a keyboard, and Hal played a Hawaiian guitar. Wendy and Tori had borrowed Hawaiian print sundresses and flower leis and entertained everyone with a hula. Wendy also sang some of the songs she had sung during the EXPO '84 tour.

"Do you know *Amazing Grace*?" Harry Chan asked the rest of the group as they paused between songs.

"Sure," Ernie said, "but I thought you were Buddhist?"

"Yeah," Harry smiled. "But I think Buddha would understand."

Wendy stood up in her sundress and lei and sang. Her young, soulful voice swelled within her, and filled the darkened room with its gentle force.

> Amazing grace, how sweet the sound,
> That saved a wretch like me,
> I once was lost, but now I'm found,
> Was blind, but now I see.

She and Tori improvised graceful hand and body movements to accompany the song. Tears were beginning to form in the eyes of those who watched them.

> Through many dangers, toils, and snares,
> I have already come.
> 'Twas grace that led me safe thus far,
> And grace will lead me home.

The others softly joined in on the last verse. Harry Chan wiped away a tear. Shawna Montgomery wiped her eyes with her apron.

> When we've been there ten thousand years,
> Bright shining as the sun,
> We've no less days to sing God's praise,
> Than when we first begun.

A hush fell over the room.

"Well," Zapper said softly. "I guess the drunken orgy I'd been planning is a no-go."

* * *

The submersibles were already loaded. Ernie Montgomery and Harry Chan met the team early the next morning. Everyone was dressed in zip-up wetsuit tops--short sleeved or sleeveless--, black swimpants, and rubber soled socks. A red sun was just rising over the waves. The island was still and peaceful.

Shawna prepared a pancake breakfast for the travelers. The room smelled of brewing kona blend coffee and sizzling bacon and sausage.

"So this trip will probably take us about eighteen hours," Zapper said. "There's very little land between here and the mainland, and those subs don't have a bathroom. Does anybody besides me see a problem here?"

"Everybody go before you get on board," Hal said.

"Every three hours or so, we'll bring the subs to the surface," Ernie said. "Everybody can get out for a little swim and stretch their legs."

"And hide behind a tree," Hal said.

"No," Tori said. "You wet your pants, and it soaks out into the ocean."

"That's nasty," Zapper said. "We'll be swimming in each other's urine."

"The ocean's full of fish poop," Hal said.

"Yeah," Zapper said, "I know that, but it's still nasty. I mean, urine's bad enough, but it's the floaters I'm worried about."

"Oooh!" Tori recoiled from the image in her mind.

"Be quiet, man," Mike said.

"Do you mind?" Jaina snapped. "I'm trying to eat!"

"Everybody go before you get on board," Hal repeated.

"What do you talk about on dates, Zapper?" Mike asked, laughing. The others laughed when he said it.

"You'll never know, candy man," Zapper said. "At least I didn't ask Shawna if she wanted to see me break a board with my face."

"I was talking about what you can do when you put your mind to things," Mike said.

"Put your mind to things," Zapper said, "or beat your brains out?"

Pirate finished eating before the others and slipped outside without saying anything to anyone. He stood alone in the courtyard between buildings and looked around at the dark wood and glass of the buildings, the palm trees, the plumaria bushes, and the shells along the paths. It had only been a week since they had come to the island, but it seemed like much longer. So much had happened. The isle, with its beaches and palm trees, had been a place of quiet sanity in a world gone mad. He hoped he would be able to return one day, but had no way of knowing if he ever would.

"What are you doing out here?" Wendy asked. Pirate turned around.

"Just saying goodbye to the place, I guess."

"I know," she said. "It's hard to leave--especially with what we're heading into."

"I want to find my family," Pirate said, "I'd at least like to see them one last time."

"I may get to see mine pretty soon," Wendy said. Wendy's mother had died ten years earlier.

"You keep hoping, don't you?" Pirate said. He put his arm around her shoulders. She didn't pull away.

"I don't want to die," she said, "but I'm not afraid to either. I know it's coming, and sometimes it seems like it would be a relief to go ahead and get it over with."

"I would miss you," Pirate said.

"Not if we all go out together," she said. "One last big adventure, the biggest of all, and we'd make it together. That doesn't sound so bad."

"Until you two realize there's no guy-girl stuff up there," Zapper said. He had slipped up on them unnoticed. "Just harp playing and camp songs."

"You've got a warped view of heaven, Zapper," Pirate said. "Assuming you make it there."

"Hey," Zapper said. "I got friends in both places--that is assuming we don't just vanish forever or get reincarnated. There's other views of the afterlife you know. I may come back as a dolphin or a swan or a beautiful woman."

Wendy laughed.

"Or a fish," Pirate said. "Swimming in an ocean full of poop."

"With my karma," Zapper said, "you're probably right. Maybe harps ain't such a bad alternative after all."

"Let's go, ladies" Hal said, grandly exiting the bar and grill. "Anchors away! A day in the service is like a Sunday on the farm. We're burnin' daylight here."

"I don't know what they put in his oxygen tank when he was on space patrol," Zapper said, "but I can see why the Interplanetary Guard loaned him to DeFalco."

"Stow that attitude, soldier," Hal said. "Or you'll be digging latrines in zero gravity."

Hal and Zapper continued their banter all the way out to the submersibles. Pirate wondered if either of them had planned their exchange deliberately as a way to soften the sadness they all felt leaving the island. Intentional or not, it was a brilliant strategy.

Hal's exobot, a submersible in its own right, clung to the back of one of the subs. It had its own ballast tanks, thrusters, and oxygen supply. The thrusters would add additional speed and, in the event they encountered any kind of hostility, Hal could disengage the giant robot and use its powerful weapons to defend the less maneuverable subs.

Hal had been confined to the inside of an exobot for longer than fourteen hours during his days with the Interplanetary

Guard, but it was not something he looked forward to. The exoskeleton/robot suit had internal heating and air conditioning, of course, but being confined for fourteen hours was still no picnic.

"Cali-forny, here we come," Zapper said.

"I guess this is goodbye," Wendy said. "Thanks for everything, Ernie."

· "You're quite welcome, princess," Ernie said. "So long, Jared." He and Jared soberly shook hands. "I hope you find Neema soon. Don't give up hope."

"I won't," Jared said. "Thanks."

"Goodbye, Shawna," Zapper said.

"Goodbye, Zapper," Shawna said, kissing him on the cheek.

"I know I'm your favorite," he whispered. "But I won't tell anybody."

"You wish," Hal's voice said from the radio. He was climbing onto the back of a sub.

"It's been an honor," Mike said, hugging Shawna. "Don't forget about us."

"Never," Shawna said. "Cross my heart. You blokes take care of yourselves, now."

"Goodbye, Harry," Jaina said.

"Aloha, guys," Harry said.

Pirate, Jared, Wendy, and Zapper climbed into one submersible. Tori, Jaina, and Mike climbed into another. Hal's exobot had latched itself to the back.

Ballast tanks gulped water and the subs dropped down into the misty blue depths.

CHAPTER 17: The Choice

Sheppard had been under house arrest in his quarters for what seemed like weeks. He had no concept of time's passage. His communicore was not connected to any of the world's news networks--if they still existed--and the clock on the wall always insisted it was 3:00 a.m. There were armed guards stationed outside his door. Alarms went off every time he got too close or if he touched the control panel beside the door.

Maive had been Sheppard's only friend, but she had been faithful. During the first few days after he had regained consciousness, she had actually slept in his living room. He was not sure how she kept track of time, but she still seemed to have a sense of it.

Sheppard had spent much of his recovery time reading. He had reread St. Augustine's *The City of God*, C.S. Lewis's *Mere Christianity*, and about half of the Bible. He had also reread Tolkein's *Lord of the Rings* series. He had soaked up the vivid imagery of that fantasy universe like a thirsty man gulping down water so fast that it nearly strangled him.

One day Maive arrived later than usual. Sheppard could tell she had been crying.

"What is it?" he asked. He set down the reading pad, stood up from the living room couch. "What's wrong?"

"I can't do this anymore," she said. "It's so wrong. It's so evil."

"What are you talking about?" Sheppard asked. "What have you done?"

"If I tell you, you'll hate me," she said. Tears sprang into her eyes.

"No," he said. He put his hands on her shoulders. "No, I won't hate you. I promise I won't hate you."

"Gogue sent me here," she said. "He sent me here to convince you to give up your faith and swear allegiance to him."

"You were afraid of what he would do to you," Sheppard said. "I understand, Maive. I don't judge you for that."

"Gogue's never going to let you go," she said. "You know that. But I was going to offer to stay here with you."

"Stay here?" Sheppard asked, "In--you mean, in a love relationship?"

"Yes," she said.

He sighed, shook his head.

"You know my faith," he said. "We would have to be married."

"Gogue would never allow that," she told him.

"Wait," Sheppard said. "Let me see if I understand this. If I deny my faith, he'll let us stay here together."

"Yes."

"And if I don't?"

"He'll kill us both," she said. "You for defying him. Me for failing to convince you."

"No," Sheppard said. "There's got to be another way."

"I've been honest with you," Maive said. "I've told you the truth. Will you do something for me now?"

"What is it?" Sheppard asked.

"At least consider the offer," she said.

"Maive, I--"

"I know," she said. "You can't deny your faith. Your God would never forgive you, and your soul would be damned."

Sheppard turned away from her and shook his head.

"He's a merciful God," he said. "A God of grace and forgiveness."

"Then He will forgive you?" she asked.

"That's not the point," he said.

"Isn't it?" she said. "You're willing to sacrifice both of our lives for a God who may or may not even exist, for a heaven that may not even be real. We could be happy here and now. That's all we really have, all we can really be sure of."

"It's not enough," Sheppard said.

"I'm sorry," Maive said. "I wish I had more to offer you."

"You've given me more than you'll ever know," Sheppard said. "If anyone could make me happy, it would be you, but you can't take the place of God. You weren't meant to. It's a paradox. The more I love God, the more I can love you, but if I try to make you God, I'll only end up destroying anything we might have had."

"You and your God," she sighed.

"I wish you could believe," Sheppard said. "I wish there was some way I could convince you."

"Look at me," she said. "Doesn't sharing what's left of your life with me sound better than torture or death?"

Maive looked achingly beautiful. Sheppard had never married. There had been women in his life before his conversion, but no one since. The picture of sharing his small and comfortable suite of rooms with this beautiful young woman pulled at him. All he had to do was deny his faith verbally--not in his heart--and seek God's forgiveness later. God would understand, wouldn't He?

But whosoever shall deny me before men, him will I also deny before my Father which is in heaven.
~Matthew 10:33

The verse sprang into his mind with bracing clarity. The words stung him with their stark directness. Gogue, he knew, was watching him, baiting him.

"It won't work," he said. He rose to his feet. "It won't work, Gogue. I'm not falling for it."

"That is too bad," Gogue's voice said. Sheppard started when he heard it. He had not really expected an answer, had hoped he was wrong. The door of the quarters opened. Gogue stepped inside. He was still speaking through Captain Gillette's body. Black cloaked henchmen stood on either side of him. Their faces were painted with the black and white greasepaint of Astrolus. Both of them were armed with pulse rifles.

"I made you a good offer," Gogue said. "Comfortable quarters. A good-looking woman. You can't say I didn't try." He gestured to his henchmen. "Take her away."

"No!" Maive cried. "Please!" The two men started toward her. Sheppard sprang forward. He tore the rifle from one man's hands and smashed it into the other man's temple. He fell back, struck the wall, bounced off, and tumbled to the floor. Sheppard turned on the other man, aimed the rifle at him.

"You're not taking her anywhere," Sheppard said.

"So predictable," Gogue said. "So stupid."

"I'm warning you," Sheppard said.

Electricity leaped out of the rifle's stock and into Sheppard's hands. Sheppard fell, convulsing, to the floor as spasms of electricity burned through his body. The trigger, it seemed, had locked itself. Sheppard lay jerking on the floor for what seemed like an eternity. Finally the assault ended. Gogue pulled the rifle from Sheppard's trembling hands. His palms smoked. The imprint of the stock's texture was burned into his flesh. Sheppard lay gasping on the carpet. The overhead lights burned into his tearing eyes.

"That would have killed anyone else," Gogue said, "Your bionic limbs must have saved you. Too bad." He aimed the rifle at Maive. The girl lay sobbing in a corner.

"Leave her alone," Sheppard said. "If you want to kill somebody, just kill me and be done with it."

"I haven't broken you yet," Gogue said. "I want to hear you deny your faith."

"Don't punish her for my choices," Sheppard said.

"This is your last chance," Gogue said. "Deny your faith or I will kill her."

Sheppard waited for a long moment. His pulse hammered. A lump formed in his throat and tears filled his eyes.

"Gene," she said. "Please."

"All right," Sheppard said. He looked at the floor. "I-- deny my faith."

"What?" Gogue said. "I want to hear it again."

"I deny my faith," Sheppard said. He felt the tears starting to flow. "I'm sorry," he whispered.

"Gogue is my only lord and master," Gogue said. "Say it."

Sheppard didn't answer.

Oh, God, he silently prayed. *I can't just let her die. Help me. Help me. Help me.*

"Say it or she dies."

"Gogue is. . . ," he hesitated. "Gogue is. . . who he says he is." He felt his stomach rising into his throat. He was about to throw up.

"No," Gogue said. "Say the rest or she dies."

He spoke the dreaded words.

The room vanished.

Sheppard was still in the monitor room, still strapped to a frame there. He had never left. His quarters, Maive, and the guards had all been simulations. Like the tortures he had endured earlier, they had all been computer-generated hallucinations. How could he have been so easily fooled? How could he have been so stupid?

"No," Sheppard gasped. "What have I done?"

"Well done, my good and faithful servant," Gogue, still in Captain Gillette's body, mocked. He clapped his hands.

Fury flooded Sheppard's consciousness. Adrenaline poured into his veins. Rage hammered his temples, his eardrums. Bellowing with rage, he bent his body onto the straps that bound him and pushed with everything he had.

The straps broke. They broke. Sheppard's arms were free. He looked down in disbelief then tore his feet out of their bindings.

No longer laughing, Gogue backed away. His figure stood silently at the edge of the screen. Sheppard charged across the floor like an angry bull. He drew back his fist and slammed it hard into the arrogant shape before him. His fist connected with flesh. The figure collapsed and lay still. In the glare of the screen, Sheppard could make out the face of Captain Gillette. His eyes were open, but he was not moving.

"Oh, my," Gogue's voice said from some hidden speaker in the wall. "I think you killed him."

Sheppard checked the throat for a pulse. There was none.

"No," he said. "No, that's impossible."

"You killed him," Gogue said again.

"No," Sheppard said. "You lie! I didn't hit him that hard. He was already dead. He was already dead."

"You murdered him," Gogue said. "Murdered an innocent man." He began to laugh. "And you denied your faith." He laughed even harder.

"No," Sheppard said. "Liar!" He stormed around the room punching and kicking the walls, searching for doors. "I didn't kill him! I didn't kill anybody!"

"Lie to me," Gogue said. "Lie to yourself. We both know the truth, *Reverend* Sheppard. We both know who and what you are. Murderer. Blasphemer."

"Liar!" he cried again. He fell to the floor. "It wasn't real. It was only a dream. You can't blame a man for something he does in a dream." His voice collapsed into a sob.

"No salvation for murderers and blasphemers," Gogue said. "Tricked by a woman, Reverend? Humph, humph, humph. You should have known better. Didn't you read in your own Bible about Adam and Eve? Samson and Delilah? You can't trust any of them."

"Oh, God," Sheppard said. "I'm so sorry. I'm so sorry. Please forgive me."

"I forgive you, my son," Gogue said.

A hypersonic concussion slammed into Sheppard's eardrums and sent him sprawling to the deck. Merciful darkness engulfed his tortured spirit, and he slept without dreaming.

CHAPTER 18: Plague of Locusts

"There it is," Jared said.

It was after three in the morning when two high-speed mini-subs surfaced off the coast of California. The dark skin of the ocean rolled gently beneath them. The inky shadows of buildings lay dark against the horizon. Lights still glowed in some of them. Pirate felt a rush of relief. It had seemed, for a time, like the dark journey through the ocean's depths would go on forever. He could envision a version of hell where he and his friends spent all of eternity trapped in the hot, tight confines of a minisub navigating their way through the ocean's endless depths.

"I've got to get some air," Pirate said.

He twisted a handle. Locks disengaged and the submersible's transparent canopy popped open with a pneumatic hiss. The door moved outward and then slid backwards along the side of the craft. Pontoons along the sides of the vehicle held it just above water level. Jared Thomas sat at the control panel beside him, his face illuminated by glowing instrument panels. Wendy and Zapper were asleep in the back. Pirate noticed how they were draped across each other and fought down a pang of jealousy. It was the only way they had of stretching their legs in such a tight place, he told himself. Purely platonic. Hah!

Without satellites to guide them, Tori had used her nanite swarm to lead them unfalteringly to the coast of California. The ancient sailors had relied on the stars, but Tori had her own glowing constellation.

"You did it," Jaina said. "We're here."

Tori didn't answer. Her mouth, the only part of her face that Jaina could see beneath the bulky control helmet, was tight with unvoiced urgency.

"What is it?" Jaina asked. "What's wrong?"

Tori held up her hand, signalling for silence. Then she breathed a sigh of relief.

"I lost contact with my nanoprobe swarm for a few seconds there," Tori said. "There's some kind of jamming field along the coast."

"Did you regain contact with your probes?" Pirate asked.

"Yeah," Tori said. "The swarm's programmed to turn around and come back if it passes out of contact with home base. The jamming field's about a mile off the coast. I'm picking up something else too."

"I see them," Hal said, the lenses on his exobot instantly zooming out over the water, adjusting for darkness and distance. "Police drones. Saucer shaped with guns mounted on their bellies."

"Like the ones that gassed us in New Orleans," Pirate said. "Nasty brutes."

"We can try going under them," Hal said. "I'll disengage and stand guard."

"We'll try it," Pirate said. "Everybody look sharp." He slammed the canopy shut and locked it into place.

"What's going on?" Wendy asked sleepily from the back seat.

"We've got police drones guarding the coast," Pirate said. "We're going to try to go under them and hope they don't sink us."

"Lovely," Zapper said.

Tori opened the canopy of the other sub long enough to draw her glistening nanoprobe swarm back into the honeycomb compartments on her armbands. When she had finished, she slammed the canopy and nodded to Pirate

"Take us down," Pirate told Jared.

The ballast tanks inhaled water and the submersible plunged back into the ocean's cold embrace. Darkness almost completely swallowed them. Pirate could see the murky glare of the other sub's running lights a few meters away.

"We better kill those lights," he said. "The drones might see them."

"Our engine noises could be a problem too," Jared said. "We'll have to go deep and cut back our speed."

They rode in near-silence for several minutes.

"Hey," Hal's voice spoke crisply through the speaker grid. "Look down beneath us on the right. Do you see that?"

Two hazy lights glowed through the water like the eyes of a giant frog. They were ahead of the craft and to the right, as Hal had said, and about fifty feet beneath them.

"What is that?" Pirate asked. "Some kind of submersible drone?"

"Hang on," Hal said. "I'm scanning it. Aw, man."

"What is it?" Wendy asked from the back seat.

"It's a car," Hal said. "An airboat."

"What's it doing down there?" Zapper asked.

"It must have lost power and crashed into the water," Pirate said.

"The headlights are still burning," Wendy said. "Somebody may still be alive in there."

"The power cells could burn for weeks," Jared said.

"I'm going down to check it out," Hal said.

"Be careful," Jaina told him.

Hal released the back of the submersible and dropped farther down into blackness. The others waited in silence as he moved toward the waiting wreck. Moments later a big, dark shape blotted out the glow of the distant headlamps. Something was moving toward them.

"Hal," Pirate said. "Is that you?"

"Yeah," Hal's voice said. "Don't panic." He moved around to the back of the submersible Jaina was piloting.

"Well?" Zapper said. "Anybody in there?"

"Yeah," Hal said. "Woman and her kid. About the same age as mine."

Hal's got a family? Pirate thought. He filed the question back in his mind.

"Were they dead?" Mike asked.

"Yeah," Hal said. He gripped the back of the minisub. "Something had shot holes through the canopy. Let's get out of here."

"Are we just gonna leave 'em out here?" Zapper asked.

"I flagged the car," Hal said. "The ocean patrol can pick 'em up later--provided the ocean patrol still exists."

The pale floor of the ocean grew nearer as they moved toward shore. They passed beneath the police drones without incident.

As they hummed through shallow water, they dodged around a tangle of palm trees, an orange plastic trash container, and a sign from *Cafe Laguna*, a beach-side coffee shop.

"This isn't looking good," Zapper said. "It looks like a hurricane hit the place and blew everything out to sea."

"Look out!" Pirate said.

Jared jerked the controls, swerved to one side. A bulky rectangular object that had been floating on the surface smacked against the canopy and spun off to one side.

"What was that?" Pirate yelled.

"Hey," Zapper said. "That was a porta-pot. I don't believe it! That was a porta-pot, man! Look at that!" He stared out the side window in disbelief as the object receded in the distance.

"I thought you said there weren't any bathrooms out here," Mike said.

"Guess I'z wrong," Zapper said.

The rest of the team laughed.

"I hope there's nobody in there," Hal said. The laughter died.

* * *

The pod surfaced in a harbor full of sunken boats and floating aircars. These cars were empty. They had apparently been blown out of a parking lot. Some sat upright while others lay on their backs like turtles unable to right themselves. Pieces of a wrecked boardwalk lay in the water like wooden river rafts from a Tom Sawyer novel. Warped, twisted street lamps hung their glowing dinosaur heads above the water's cluttered surface. Jared maneuvered his minisub to the edge of a shattered wooden dock. Pirate popped open the canopy, stepped carefully over the dark waters onto the dock's treated wood. The wooden structure felt solid beneath his feet. He had halfway expected it to spill him into the ocean. Pirate tethered the craft to a heavy piling. Jared switched off the engines. The second sub popped to the surface a few meters away. Hal's exobot was no longer attached.

Jared, Zapper, and Wendy climbed out of the minisub and stood beside Pirate on the dock. The city of Los Angeles was a haunted ruin. Buildings lay in battered stacks like toppled heaps of dominoes, as though giant hands had pushed them over onto their sides. The blast patterns were irregular. The damage had not been done by a single explosion but by many smaller bursts.

"This wasn't done by those satellite lasers," Pirate said. "The city looks like it's been shelled."

"Concussion bombs," Mike said, stepping from the second sub. "This city's been flattened by concussion bombs,"

"Yeah," Jared agreed. "They work on the same principles as the concussion wave emitters on our gloves and deflection systems, but the bursts are larger, more concentrated."

"Thanks for the scientific analysis, Mr. Einstein," Jaina said. "Any idea how many people died here?"

"Easy, pudd'n," Zapper said. "Scientific objectivity may be the only thing holding us together right now."

"Don't call me pudding," Jaina mumbled.

"Sorry, precious," Zapper whispered.

"Remember what I said about surfing on a typhoon," Mike whispered.

"More like a blizzard," Zapper muttered.

"I think I just lost my objectivity," Tori said. "Look."

A small figure in a brightly colored swimsuit lay face down in the water by the dock. Nobody spoke for a moment. Jaina pulled out her medical scanner, let out a sigh, and walked over to the edge of the dock. She picked up a piece of planking, moved the floating figure toward the dock, and flipped it over. Wide eyes and a plastic smile stood out in eerie contrast to the grim surroundings.

"She's a dummy," Tori said. The group released a collective sigh of relief.

"You should talk," Zapper snorted.

A loud splash broke the ocean's surface. A big, metal shape slogged through the water and stepped into the lights that burned along a deserted strip of beach.

"Hal," Zapper said. "That better be you over there, man."

"It's me," Hal's amplified voice replied. His voice was hushed, subdued. "This is bad," he said. "Looks like they were shelled by concussion bombs."

"Yeah," Zapper said. "We noticed."

The team moved carefully along the dock. Hal joined them on the beach beneath a broken stand of palm trees.

"Jaina," Pirate said. "Scan for life readings--movement, heat patterns . . . ."

"I know," Jaina said. "So far I'm not getting anything."

"Hal," Zapper said. "I didn't know you had a family, man."

"*Had* is right," Hal said. "The marriage didn't work out."

"And you had a kid?" Zapper asked.

"Yeah," Hal said. "He's five years old now. I haven't seen him since I joined the Intrepid Force."

"Where are they?" Mike asked.

"They were in Washington D.C.," Hal said. "That was one of the first places to be hit."

"Why didn't you tell us?" Tori asked.

"I don't know," he said. "Didn't want to talk about it, I guess. And didn't want you to ask. If none of you knew anything was wrong, I could pretend it wasn't happening."

The lights still burned in seaside shops. Windows had been blown out and the streets were strewn with merchandise, but the lights were still on. Upbeat music played on recessed speakers. Without shoppers and traffic, it seemed eerie, out of place.

"Hey," Zapper said. "Look at that." He was peering through the window of a ruined ice cream shop. The others gathered around. The lights inside the shop still burned, music still played, and four human skeletons lay huddled on the floor beside the counter. The metal bistro chairs and tables were overturned. Colorful candy, used for toppings, lay in the floor.

"What happened here?" Pirate asked. "Their bones are picked clean. Jared, you've been trained in crime scene analysis. What do you think happened here?"

"The clothes are completely eaten away," Jared said. "That and the signs of a struggle would rule out a flesh eating virus."

"Some kind of acid?" Wendy asked.

"A corrosive spray would have eaten through the candy on the floor," Jared said. "Intense heat would have melted the candy and charred the bones."

"What does that leave?" Tori asked.

Jared turned around, saw the honeycomb housings on her arms.

"I think we better suit up," he said. "Quickly! Lock down the helmets and go to internal oxygen supply."

"Why?" Wendy asked. "What is it?"

"Quickly!" Jared said. "Hal, get the bins open. We've got to hurry."

Hal had been carrying their gear on the back of his exobot. He dropped to his knees, swung the bins down from his back, and popped them open with his exobot's chisel-shaped metal fingers.

With Jared driving them, the team hurriedly pulled on their bulletproof mesh, breastplates, boots, gloves, and helmets.

"All right," Zapper finally said. "Why all the rush?"

About a block away somebody screamed. There were two voices. Their piercing screams sounded like animal howls. There was another sound too, a low thrum.

"Arm weapons," Pirate said. "Deflection systems active." He ran toward the screams. The others fell in behind him. They ran down an alley, turned down a side street, and stopped.

About fifty feet ahead of them was a shimmering metal tornado. It stood in a column almost thirty feet high. Trapped in the center were two human figures--a young man and woman, both in their late teens. Swarms of metallic insects clung to their bodies.

"Good lord!" Mike said. "What is that?"

"Nanites," Jared said. "That's what I was afraid of."

The twisting, shimmering cloud of microscopic robots was more than a hundred times the size of Tori's benign swarm. It swarmed the young couple like a cloud of killer bees, like a school of piranhas. In moments there would be nothing left of them but well-scoured bones.

"Fire at will!" Pirate cried. "Try to scatter the swarm." He unleashed a volley of concussion bursts from the ports on the backs of his gloves. Holes formed in the swarm and quickly filled back in. It was like shooting through a column of falling water. Wendy, Jaina, and Mike joined him. Hal blasted away with his shoulder cannons. The swarm scattered, flew apart, and reassembled every time it was hit. They swarmed over the team, covered their face masks, crowded into every visible crack searching for a way inside.

Tori opened the honeycomb housings on her forearms and released her own modest swarm.

"NO!" she cried out. She watched in horror as her own nanobot cloud flew away and joined the larger swarm.

"I've lost control of them!" she cried. "They've overridden me!"

The young man had thrown himself onto the body of the girl and was trying to shield her with his own body. His features were completely covered by the silver-gray dust of a million stinging metal insects. He fought to brush them away.

Zapper activated the generators on the backs of his wrists. Jagged bolts of electricity leaped along trails of superconductive vapor. They struck the swarm and leaped through the metal fragments. The metallic thrum of the swarm grew higher and louder. It was almost like a collective shriek of surprise, a cry of insect pain. The swarm began to back away.

"That's it!" Pirate said. "Electricity!"

Zapper carefully adjusted the voltage and amperage of his generators and fired directly at the struggling figures at the center of the storm. Lightning flashed over their bodies and the metal locusts began to withdraw.

"Hang on!" Hal said as his consciousness fought through the mental controls of his exobot. "I'll give you some back up." Hal switched on the generator nodes in his armor and fired off electrical bursts of his own.

The swarm began to pull back.

"Drive them over to the right," Hal said. He continued to shoot off electricity with both clawed hands while his brain clicked through the menus of a mentally-activated control panel. Zapper poured electricity onto the struggling couple like a fireman dousing burning people with water. The amperage, at that setting, was not deadly to humans but it threw the nanites' internal control systems into electronic disarray. Connections broke. Nanoprocessors crashed and reset themselves, only to crash and reset again.

The shimmering cloud spun away and left the victims lying in a tattered heap. They took to the air, dodged the bolts Zapper and Hal were sending out, and started to withdraw. Just then a volley of shells erupted from Hal's forearms with a sound like a string of firecrackers exploding. Metal pellets fell into the middle of the cloud and ignited into a ball of fire. A blast of searing heat rolled through the air. Drops of molten metal rained down onto an empty street.

"Are they gone?" Zapper asked.

"We got most of them," Hal said. "That may not be the only one of those swarms floating around."

"Somebody did this on purpose," Tori said. "Somebody programmed that swarm to kill people, to strip away their flesh and leave the bones. This was an act of terrorism."

Jaina was scanning the bodies of the young man and woman with her medical scanner. They looked like plague victims from Edgar Allen Poe's "Masque of the Red Death." The young man was bleeding from nearly every pore. His face was a swollen, bloody pulp. The young woman was a mass of bruises and blood blisters. Her face, though swollen, was still recognizably human. Her long, blonde hair was sliced raggedly away in places.

"The boy's dead," Jaina said. "The girl may have a chance, but we've got to get her to a hospital."

The young woman cried softly. She was in searing pain, but had little strength left to cry out.

"Can you hear me?" Wendy told the girl.

"Can't--can't see," the girl said. "My eyes. Can't see. Hurt--hurting all over."

"Can you stabilize her?" Pirate asked.

"Ordinarily," Jaina said, "I'd inject her with medical nanobots. They could repair the ruptured veins and arteries. After what happened to Tori's swarm, I'm afraid to try it. I can treat her for shock, give her drugs to lower her blood pressure, try to increase clotting."

"She needs something for the pain," Wendy said.

The girl tried to sit up, but fell back to the street.

"My eyes."

"You've got a lot of broken blood vessels," Wendy told her. "It will take them a while to heal."

"Marco. Where's Marco?"

Marco was the name of her boyfriend, the one they had just pronounced dead. She didn't seem to have heard them.

"We'll--," Wendy choked on her reply. "We'll take care of him."

"What's your name?" Mike asked her.

"Ch--China."

"That's a beautiful name," Mike said. "Where are you from, China?"

"Do what you can for her," Pirate told Jaina. "Hal, have you still got that portable stretcher you used to carry Mike that time?"

When Mike had been injured during the battle on Venus, Hal had strapped him to the back of his exobot and carried him through the jungle.

"Yeah," Hal said. "I've still got it. Zapper, could you give me a hand?"

"Sure," Zapper said.

With as much care as they could, the team packed China onto Hal's portable stretcher. Lifting her had been heart-rendingly difficult. Nearly every inch of her small body was covered with blisters and contusions. Jaina's injections were taking an edge off the pain.

Past the rows of wrecked buildings and debris, other buildings still stood. Part of the city, it seemed, was still intact. The team was moving toward that part of the city when they heard the whistle of airboat engines. Two heavy police transports, red lights flashing over their armored surfaces, glided over the sheared-off tops of office buildings and dropped down into the manmade canyon of city streets. Bright lights engulfed Pirate, Jared, and the rest of the Intrepid Force like a scene from an alien encounter. Amplified voices echoed from behind the light.

"This area is restricted," a man's voice said. "By order of the Los Angeles Police Department, you are to power down your weapons."

"It's the cops," Zapper said.

"It's about time," Pirate said. "Power down." He switched off his weapons array. The others did the same.

The armored airboats lowered themselves to the street. Their engines fell silent and their doors popped out and slid aside. Men and women, all of them clad in segmented body armor and helmets, burst through the hatches with impact rifles raised. Pirate and the others stood and waited as they approached.

"They don't look too friendly," Zapper said.

"I don't like the look of this," Jared whispered. Pirate looked around and noticed Jared was gone. He had switched on his armor's virtual invisibility field.

"So," one of the armored figures said. He was a big man with sergeant's bars on his shoulder and a gravelly voice. "Who are you people?"

"Intrepid Force," Pirate said. "We work for DeFalco Space Industries."

"Take off your helmets and gloves," the sergeant said. "Submit to cranial scans."

They obeyed. The sergeant motioned for some of his officers to move among them with hand held scanning devices.

"Hold out your hands," a female officer ordered. Her voice was cold, tense.

Pirate held still as the device was passed over his head and his hands. He saw his own bones glowing through on a scope.

"I'm getting some strange readings here," a young Asian man told the female officer who seemed to be in charge. "The scan is almost a perfect match, but it isn't."

Jaina stood still as they scanned her.

"Who are you?" the female officer asked.

"Jaina Benedict," Jaina answered coldly.

"Patrice Benedict's daughter," the woman said with a sarcastic kind of satisfaction. "I might have known."

Moments later Pirate and the others watched as the female officer consulted with the sergeant.

"None of them are authorized," she said. "One of the women has bionic prosthetics. I'm also reading neuro-muscular and cortical implants. These people are packing."

"Of course they're packing," the sergeant said. "Didn't you hear them? They're the Intrepid Force. You know. Venus Base and all of that."

The woman shook her head.

"Don't you watch the news, Prentice?" the sergeant asked her.

"Not much, sir."

The sergeant waved his hand dismissively.

"What about the girl on the stretcher?" he asked.

"Unauthorized," the woman said. "Probably from here."

The sergeant nodded.

"Oh, yes," the female officer added. "One of the women is Patrice Benedict's daughter."

"This just keeps getting better," the sergeant said. "All right. Go back to the ship and call Damiano for instructions."

"Yes, sir."

"Something's wrong here," Mike said. "This doesn't look good at all."

"I know," Pirate said.

Moments later the female officer--the sergeant had called her Prentice--returned. She and the sergeant spoke for a moment.

"Okay," the sergeant said after deliberating with Prentice for a time. "Here's what we'll do. We'll collect your weapons and take you to Patrice and Nigel Benedict."

"Who?" Zapper said.

"My parents," Jaina said. "This just keeps getting worse."

Pirate eyed her curiously.

"Listen," the sergeant said. "We'll take your gauntlets and store them. Then you can board the airboats, and we'll take you out of here."

"What are you going to do about the girl on the stretcher?" Pirate asked. "She was attacked by a swarm of bone-stripping nanites. She's in shock and needs a hospital now."

"I'm afraid that's impossible," the sergeant said. "This area is quarantined. She doesn't have authorization to leave."

"What?" Pirate said. "What are you going to do with her?"

"That's not your concern," the sergeant said.

"I'm afraid it is," Jaina said, stepping forward. "If she doesn't go, we don't go. You can convey that message to my parents if you like."

The sergeant sighed, shook his head in frustration.

"Call Damiano again," he told Prentice, the female officer.

"Yes, sir," she said.

She returned moments later.

"He says we can bring the girl," Prentice said. Her tone betrayed her irritation.

"There's no need," Jaina said, her eyes bright with unshed tears. "She's dead."

"Just get in the ship," they were told. "Leave the robot here."

"What do we do?" Zapper whispered.

"I'll find you later," Hal whispered.

Mike looked back at the girl's body.

"Goodbye, China," he said, his voice rough. "Have a good trip." His eyes were bright with tears.

"Okay," Pirate said. "Let's go. Maybe we can find some answers to all of this. Jared?"

"Still here," Jared whispered.

Pirate nodded. He climbed through the open hatch into the waiting airboat. Jump seats lined the walls and faced the center. The upholstery inside was all black. So was the carpet on the floor. The driver was protected by a thick glass shield in the front of the compartment. Pirate sank into one of the waiting chairs and strapped himself in. The others followed. The car lifted off. High rise buildings blew past.

"Why didn't you tell us your folks were here?" Zapper asked.

"Quiet," Jaina said. "They might be monitoring us."

CHAPTER 19: Ninety-Nine Red Balloons

"Do you know what this is?" Cockrum asked. Jolie Harrison stood silently at his elbow.

"He ain't much on small talk, is he, Georgie?" a woman's voice asked.

"No, Gracie," a gravelly man's voice answered. "He ain't."

"Stop doing that," Cockrum said. He pulled a chair from beneath a desk that sat in the corner of Preston's quarters and sat down. Preston's own seat was reclined. The sultry jazz music he constantly listened to was starting to annoy Cockrum. Preston opened his eyes and studied the small, silver disk Cockrum was holding up.

"Optical disk," Preston said. "Early twentieth century vintage. Is this some kind of test, Jonas?"

"No," Cockrum said. "You really don't know what it is?"

"Sorry," Preston said. "I don't think I understand the question. Is this a riddle?"

"Yes," Cockrum said. "I think it is. We found it in a vault close to where we found that freezer unit with the boy inside. Childress and his men spent the whole day breaking through encryptions and booby traps. When they opened the vault, this is all they found."

"But that doesn't make any sense," Harrison said as she studied the disk. "That format hasn't been used in five decades. There's nothing to play it on."

"Actually there is," Cockrum said. He pulled out a small metal box and patted it. "Corbalew had adapted this scanner to read old style optical disks. We found it in his quarters."

"If he had it locked in a vault, it must have been important to him," she said.

"I know," Cockrum said. "I wish I knew why."

"Have you watched it already?" Preston asked.

"Yes," he said. "It's an unfinished movie. The story is all there, but the editing is still rough in spots. Some of the scenes don't have backgrounds. I checked our archives, and there's no indication that this movie was ever released."

"I don't know anything about it," Preston said. "I'm sorry."

"I'd like you to watch it," Cockrum said. "See if any of it connects with anything you've seen."

"A flick!" one of Preston's gangster voices said. "I want some popcohn and a sody. Lotsa ice, see."

"Preston!" Cockrum snapped.

"Sorry," Preston said. "The communications console is over here."

The scanner Cockrum had found had a jack that plugged directly into the communications console. Cockrum touched a button. An image formed on the screen. There was a gray sky, a howling wind, and a ruined city filled with burned out buildings, dusty heaps of ruined automobiles, cracked streets filled with debris. The camera panned through the scene. Theme music began to play.

"That's the scene from the simulation," Preston said. "The one the boy in the freezer is living in. That's the same gray sky, the same buildings."

ESCAPE

The words formed on the screen in huge yellow letters.

An Enoch Henry Film

Who was Enoch Henry? Cockrum thought the name sounded faintly familiar.

"It *is* the same place," Harrison said. "But why did Corbalew base the simulation on this place? There has to be a reason."

They sat for nearly two hours and watched the footage. The film was, as Cockrum had warned, not quite complete. In places there was no background--only the green or blue walls of studio sound stages. In other places the audio was rough. Voices had not been dubbed. Sound effects had not been added. The film had never been completely finished, but the story was there.

Escape was an old style science fiction film about a young group of freedom fighters in a hard, cruel world dominated by a merciless overlord and his cybernetic police force. The young men and women wore ragged haircuts and threadbare clothes and lived in the ruins of an ancient city. Their mentor, a renegade scientist, wore gloves with the fingers cut out and had arcane gadgetry hanging from his belt, his backpack, and his boots. His eyewear was equipped with scanning equipment.

The film ended sadly, hauntingly. The Overlord had found the refuge of the scientist and his young disciples. In a fire fight between the cybercops and the dissidents, the scientist and all but one of his young charges were slain.

A single young woman crawled out of an overturned trash barrel. Her tattered clothes were black. So was her short, raggedly cropped hair. She wore no make up or adornment, but still had a pretty young face. There were pale freckles across the bridge of her nose. She was bleeding from a cut on her cheek. Slowly and silently she moved among the bodies of her fallen friends. A music track began to play. A young woman began to sing in a voice both sad and sweet.

> You and I, in a little toy shop,
> Buy a bag of balloons with the money we've got,
> Set them free at the break of dawn,
> 'Til, one by one, they were gone.

As the music played and the ragged girl moved among the fallen bodies of her friends, faded flashbacks showed her playing chess with them and laughing, showed her walking with her beloved Ishmael in a park they had found, showed her listening to the scientist as he talked about the stars, the universe, and the mysteries of faith. Tears formed on her face as she walked among the bodies. Finally she made her way to the ruins of a building, an old planetarium. In the center of the room was an amazing contraption assembled from spare parts seemingly by the hands of a mad sculptor. Throbbing generators pumped power into its sleeping mechanisms.

"If we can go back through time," the scientist-teacher explained, "We might be able to prevent all of this from ever taking place. It's a mad gamble, but it may be our only hope."

The song continued;

> Ninety-nine dreams I have had,
> And every one a red balloon.
> It's all over and I'm standin' pretty
> In this dust that was a city.
> If I could find a souvenir
> Just to prove the world was here.

She threw a switch. Power flashed like lightning through the spokes of the machine. A red sphere of energy surrounded the girl. She smiled.

And here is a red balloon.
I think of you and let it go.

She threw one final switch. The girl, the machine, and the glowing sphere of light vanished. The film ended.

Preston, Harrison, Cockrum, and the rest of the group sat silent. Preston and Harrison wiped away tears.

"Okay," Cockrum said. "What does this all mean?"

"I don't know," Preston said. "I don't fully understand it, but this film was clearly the basis for the artificial reality that Corbalew has that boy trapped in. He thinks he's living in that time, that he's one of those freedom fighters."

"And he's been using his knowledge to help Corbalew," Harrison said, "because he thinks they're both fighting together against this Overlord."

"Okay," Cockrum said. "So he's got information Corbalew needs, some kind of technological secrets maybe, and Corbalew's using this artificial reality as a way to get them out of him. Maybe he's the kind of person that can't be bought. Torture won't work if you actually need the person's cooperation to pull something off."

"But if he thought he was saving the world from the Overlord," Harrison said, "and that Corbalew was an ally, he'd help him in every way he could."

"He has to know the truth," Cockrum said.

"But we don't know how to free him from the machine," Harrison said.

"No," Cockrum said. "But we can go in with him--enter his dream. That should be possible."

"I'd like to go," Preston said.

Cockrum hesitated.

"I know you don't completely trust me," Preston said, "and I can understand why."

"Why do you want to go in, Richard?" Harrison asked.

"I've spent hours watching those simulations," Preston said. "I feel like I know him enough to talk to him. He's completely alone, and he needs a friend. I understand what that's like."

"I'll see what I can do," Cockrum said.

"Okay," Preston said. He sighed. "Okay. Whatever you decide."

* * *

"You'll feel some disorientation at first," Dr. Chambers warned. Preston was lying on his back. His body and most of his head were encased in a black sensation suit. He was lying back in a padded metal chair. His legs were strapped in place and his arms were held by elastic bands.

"I've been in synthetic reality simulations before," Preston said. "I know how it works."

Cockrum and Harrison stood at his side.

"Whenever you're ready then," Dr. Chambers said.

"Let's get this show on the road, Doc," one of Preston's voices answered. Cockrum sighed. Preston closed his eyes. Sensory input poured into his brain through neural filament connections.

Preston heard the sound of wind and felt it rustle through his hair and clothes. The gray sky came into focus first. Then the rest of the landscape took shape. Preston was standing in what was left of a park. The grass was tall. Crisp brown leaves rattled on some of the trees. A young man stood staring from a concrete park bench.

"Who are you?" Stefan asked.

"My name's Richard Preston," Preston told him.

"Where did you come from?" Stefan asked.

"From the real world," Preston told him. "The world outside this simulation."

"Get out of here!" the computer simulation of Corbalew snapped. He had suddenly appeared from behind a battered brick wall. "You'll spoil the whole plan."

"That's what I'm trying to," Preston said, "but it's not the plan he thinks you're talking about."

"Quiet, you fool," Corbalew whispered. "They're coming. *His* people are coming."

"Let them come," Preston said.

The cadence of heavy boots on pavement grew louder. Five black-clad lawkeepers burst around a corner. With mechanically synchronized movements, they raised their weapons and trained them on Preston.

"You do not belong here," one of them said. His voice had a droning, trance-like quality.

"You can't hurt me," Preston said. "None of this is real."

The weapons roared, spat fire. Preston stood his ground. Bullets ripped up chunks of pavement, punched holes in the skin of a wrecked car, turned over a dumpster, shattered several windows, cracked bricks. Preston stood uninjured.

"Freeze lawkeeper characters," he said.

The lawkeepers stopped and stood frozen.

"Remove lawkeeper characters from simulation," Preston ordered.

The lawkeepers were gone.

The young man called Stefan watched intently.

"It's not real," Preston said. "All of this is a simulation. You're lying in a hospital plugged into a machine, and we're trying to find a way to get you out of here."

"You lie!" the Corbalew character raged. He brought up his gun.

"Remove Corbalew character," Preston said.

Corbalew was gone too.

"He was part of the simulation too," Preston said. "You and I are the only real people here."

"I don't know what to believe anymore," the boy sighed.

"I know," Preston said. "I'm sorry."

"Where am I really?" he asked.

"You're in the year 2085," Preston said. "We're--Well, we're aboard a spaceship. What's the last thing you remember?"

"I don't know," the young man said. "I remember waking up, being tortured. At first I thought I was Lex Marston from Crane Island, Louisiana . . . in 1984. They told me it couldn't be true, that Crane Island doesn't exist."

"There is a Crane Island, Louisiana," Preston told him, "And I'll bet your name really is Lex Marston."

"But how did I get here?" Lex asked.

"Honestly," Preston said. "I have no idea. They found you on board a spaceship. We don't know where the people from the ship found you or how long they had been keeping you."

"I remember being Lex Marston from Crane Island," he said, "but I remember being Stefan too. Those memories aren't as clear. There are gaps in them, but I do remember them."

"And I think those were the memories Corbalew was interested in," Preston said as the truth came to him. "He didn't need Lex Marston from Crane Island, but Stefan had secrets he was trying to access." He shook his head. "This world, the one you see around you, doesn't exist. It never has. We believe Corbalew copied it from a movie."

"But where did I get the memories?" Lex asked.

"The answer to that question is probably the key to everything," Preston said. "The only one who knows for sure is Corbalew, and he isn't talking."

"You say you're real," Lex said, "that you're here to help me. Why should I believe you?"

"After all you've been through," Preston said. "I can't think of a single reason why you should, but I promise I'll get you out of this place. It's just a matter of time."

CHAPTER 20: House of Light

Pirate woke up and realized he had been sleeping. Jared was sitting on the floor beside him, his invisibility armor still active. Pirate looked out the canopy at a gray sky filled with knotted strips of cotton. A bloated moon--just short of full-- glared down on a patchwork quilt of glistening miniature cityscapes separated by inky black patches of darkness.

The airboat had stopped. It hovered for a moment and then began to sink down into the darkness below. In pools of light, Pirate could make out ghostly images from another time, a fantasy world pulled directly from the pages of a gothic mystery novel.

On the top of a hill sat a sprawling mansion made of dressed stone. It had shingles that looked like reptile scales. There were tall, pointed spires, leaded windows, and a courtyard in the center. Beneath a dome of glass panes and metal framework was a greenhouse filled with tropical plants. Behind the mansion were a guest house, riding stables, and an Olympic-sized swimming pool surrounded by Greek statues.

Tall palm trees stood on either side of a lighted path. Off to one side was a hedge maze.

Beneath the hill on which the mansion sat lay a sprawling complex of multi-story, flat-roofed buildings connected by sidewalks and breezeways. Twisting paths threaded their way beneath tall, stately palm trees. Surrounding the complex was a high stone wall.

The airboat touched down on a helipad in the courtyard behind the mansion. Carved from stone, surrounded by shrubbery, and outfitted with marble rails and granite stairs, the modern structure blended with the nineteenth century architecture of the mansion itself. The hatch popped open, blowing its seal, and rose on humming servos until it was completely extended.

Jaina sighed. She shook her head and unbuckled her seat belt.

"You don't look very happy to be home," Mike said.

"Let's get this over with," Jaina said. She rose to her feet and stepped out of the ship, across the smooth helipad, and down the stairs onto a weathered brick courtyard. The others followed.

"This is mag," Wendy said softly. The others nodded and looked at the amazing buildings surrounding them. They stared up at an imposing nineteenth century castle with balconies and towers. A lavishly dressed man in his early sixties emerged from the shadows of a covered porch and walked down the path toward them.

"Well," he said as he approached. "This is a surprise. Quite a surprise indeed." His accent was English.

"This is Dr. Nigel Benedict," Jaina said. "My father. Father, I'd like to present Wendy, Victoria, Jonathan, Michael, and Zapp--Aaron." Nicknames, obviously, were frowned upon in the Benedict home.

"It is a pleasure to finally meet all of you," Benedict said. "If you'll follow me, please."

"What do we do with their gear?" Prentice, the female officer, asked.

"Where is it?" Benedict asked.

"We've got it in the cargo area," she said. "In a storage container."

"Leave the container beside the helipad," Benedict said. "I'll have someone pick it up later."

"If it's all the same," Pirate said. "We'd like to have our equipment back."

Benedict paused, covered his mouth with one hand as he thought about it.

"Don't you trust us?" Jaina asked. "Don't you trust your own daughter?"

"Yes, darling," Benedict said. "Of course I trust you, but you know how I've always felt about weapons. This place is a sanctuary of life. Your mother and I have dedicated ourselves to saving lives, not to taking them."

"That was DeFalco's philosophy too," Pirate said. "He developed most of the non-lethal weapons used today by military peacekeepers."

"He believed in using deadly force only as a last resort," Mike added. "That's how we were trained."

"But why would you want those weapons here?" Benedict said. "Why would you want them if you don't plan to use them?"

"Why would you not want us to have them," Jaina replied, "if we're not going to need them?"

"*Touche'*," Benedict sighed. "I will admit that I'm completely mystified by your lack of trust. What danger could you possibly encounter here?"

"Sir," Prentice said. "We've got another call. What do you want me to do?"

"Let them have their equipment," Benedict said. "Of course."

"Yes, sir."

The officers removed a plastic cargo container from the rear compartment of their airboat and carefully placed it on the ground beside the helipad. The vehicle lifted off, running lights flashing, and shot out over the dark city below.

Pirate and the others opened the cargo container, took out their gauntlets, and rearmed themselves. Benedict watched with obvious distaste but said nothing.

"Shall we go," he finally said.

Benedict led them across the courtyard and through a pair of French doors into a cavernous great room with marble flooring, expensive throw rugs, bookshelves, a large fireplace, a staircase, and a balcony. An attractive blonde woman in business attire stood at the foot of the stairs. She looked like an older version of Jaina.

"Jaina," the woman said. "Oh, baby." She ran up to the younger woman, threw her arms around her, and kissed her. Finally she pulled away, still holding Jaina's face in her hands.

"Hi, Patrice," Jaina said. She seemed embarrassed by the older woman's display of affection. "It's good to see you."

"Where have you been?" the woman demanded. "How did you end up here?"

"We were just passing through," Jaina said casually.

"Passing through?" the woman said. "Nigel said they found all of you wandering around in the Red Zone. What were you doing there?"

"We were on an island when the attacks took place," Pirate said. "We just made it back to the mainland. Could you tell us what's going on here? We were told the area along the coast is under some kind of quarantine."

"Yes," Ms. Benedict said. "Yes, I'm afraid it is."

"What kind of quarantine?" Pirate asked.

"I'm afraid the answer to that question is a complicated one," Ms. Benedict said. "You all look so tired. Why don't you rest for a while? I'll be happy to answer all of your questions later. We've prepared quarters for you in the guest house out back. We thought you might want your privacy. Jaina, I suppose you'll want to stay with your friends?"

"Yes," Jaina said.

"You can leave your laundry outside the front door," Patrice said. "One of my housekeepers will pick it up and clean it for you."

"Our laundry's still in the Red Zone, as you call it," Pirate said.

"We have some spare clothes in the guest house," Ms. Benedict said. "Mostly sportswear for golf, tennis, and swimming. Maybe you can make do with that until we can send someone for your clothes."

"That should be fine," Pirate said. "Thanks."

"I'll have breakfast prepared for you," Jaina's father said. "Lynch will bring it to you after you've had time to settle in."

"Thank you," Jaina said.

"Yeah," Zapper said. "Thanks."

"*Arigato*," Mike said, bowing slightly.

"Listen," Pirate said. "We really appreciate all of this, but I was wondering if you could do us one more favor."

"I'll certainly try," Patrice said. "What is it, dear?"

"Well," Pirate said. "We were hoping we could talk to someone from DeFalco Space Industries."

"Provided they still exist," Zapper said.

"Is there any way you could contact them for us?" Pirate asked.

"I think I might be able to help you there," Jaina's father said. "Our organization has worked with DeFalco on a number of projects. I'll try to set up a meeting with one of my contacts there sometime later today if that will be acceptable."

"That would be great," Pirate said.

Nigel Benedict led them back through the courtyard, and through a tall, wrought iron gate. They followed him down a brick path surrounded on either side by waist high hedges and tall palm trees. Lights were mounted on tall poles at even intervals along the path. Night insects sang in the darkness beyond. The group passed tennis courts, riding stables, and an ornate swimming pool surrounded by vine-encrusted pillars and marble statues of Greek gods.

"What is this place?" Pirate asked. "What's its history?"

"This mansion was built in 1898 by Dr. Raymond Leighton," Benedict explained. "Leighton was something of a renaissance man, if you're familiar with that expression. He was a psychiatrist by profession, something of a pioneer in the treatment of mental illness. He also dabbled in botany, astronomy, and the breeding of race horses. Mrs. Leighton was an actress in silent films."

"What's all that down below us?" Wendy asked. "All those buildings?"

"Those are part of the Leighton Institute," Benedict said. "It is one of the world's leading mental health research facilities."

"Mental health research?" Mike asked. "Like treating people with mental problems?"

"Yes," Benedict said. "In part."

"I don't feel too good about this," Zapper said. "Bunch of crazy people running around down there."

"Your compassion astounds me," Benedict said. "What you perceive as insanity is often simply an adaptive response to painful stimuli in the patient's life. Would you blame a man who was dying of thirst if he saw a mirage of water in a desert? Would you consider him weak, an object of scorn? I think not. Then why do you look down upon a man who is emotionally thirsty when his senses begin to deceive him? We do not look down upon those who suffer from these things."

"Sorry," Zapper said. "I was just running my mouth. Don't pay any attention to me. Nobody else does."

"We also use artificial means to enhance the mental ability of healthy patients," Benedict said, changing the subject.

"Gene therapy and cortical implants to increase intelligence. That sort of thing."

"Is that why Jaina's such a brain?" Tori asked.

"Precisely," Benedict said.

"My daughter the experiment," Jaina said, her expression sour.

They reached the guest house. It was a single-story structure constructed of the same dark red brick as the surrounding buildings. It was shaded by trees and surrounded by neatly manicured shrubbery. The guest house had large windows and heavy shutters. Benedict led the group up wide stairs to a large porch. His feet thumped across wooden floorboards. Light from artificial gas lamps on either side of the front door brushed across the surfaces of rocking chairs, thickly padded couches, and a wooden porch swing. Puddles of inky darkness gathered in the places the light did not reach.

Benedict opened the front door and led the team inside. They passed through a short entry hall into a large, open room with a high ceiling. Bookcases lined two walls. Couches and recliners formed a U-shape around an elaborate holo-dioramic video system. The kitchen and dining area were in the back and there were bedrooms on either side. Jaina's father showed them where they might find towels, washcloths, and spare clothing.

"Well," he finally said. "I'm sure you would all like to freshen up and get a bit of rest." He hugged Jaina somewhat stiffly and excused himself.

Zapper pushed aside the curtain and watched him go.

"They're not so bad," Tori said.

"Your dad's a little uptight," Zapper said, "but he seems decent."

"He's on his best behavior," Jaina said. "Believe me. Don't say anything else until I tell you." She went to a touchtronic panel beside the door and punched through lighted menus there. "There," she finally said. "I just shut off the guest house security cameras."

"You don't trust your own parents?" Mike said.

"Not exactly," Jaina said. "We haven't had the best relationship over the years. I was always their little experiment."

"I was taught to honor my parents," Mike said.

· "It's an Asian thing," Zapper said.

"You call your mother Patrice?" Wendy asked.

"She's not exactly my mother," Jaina said. "We have an odd relationship."

"Not your mother?" Pirate said. "But she looks just like you."

"You're a clone," Jared said, suddenly materializing. He removed his helmet.

"Don't do that," Zapper said, startled by Jared's sudden appearance.

"You're a clone of Patrice Benedict," Jared said. "Aren't you?"

Jaina didn't answer. Her shoulders dropped and she looked at the floor.

"You don't have to answer that," Pirate said. "It's none of our business. Not that there's anything wrong with being a clone."

"It's true," Jaina said. "I'm a clone."

"I thought human cloning was illegal here," Mike said.

"They had it done in a lab in Singapore," Jaina said.

"They found me in an illegal genetics lab," Zapper said. "A raid. Be glad you're just a copy. They played around with my nervous system. It's been screwed up ever since."

"That's for sure," Tori said.

"Can we talk about something else?" Jaina said.

They stood in uncomfortable silence for several seconds.

"Let's get some rest," Pirate said. "We can talk tomorrow."

A knock sounded at the door. Jared dropped his helmet into place and faded into the shadows. Mike, who was closest, went to the door and opened it. A tall, gaunt man in a black suit stood behind a wheeled cart. On the cart were plates containing pancakes, french toast, scrambled eggs, and sliced fruit. Pots of cocoa and hot coffee filled the air with their rich aroma. There was also a pitcher of orange juice and a big bowl of cream of wheat.

"Your breakfast," the man in black said. His voice sounded vaguely English.

"Thanks, Jeeves," Zapper said. "Bring it on in."

With no change of expression, the gaunt man pushed the cart into the room. The wheels squeaked and shimmied as he walked past the group without acknowledging them and went directly to the dining area. In slow, measured movements, he emptied the cart of its contents and methodically arranged everything on the table. He turned.

"I will return for the dishes later," he said. "Enjoy your breakfast." He bowed, walked to the door, and left.

"Who was *that*?" Mike asked.

"One of the butlers," Jaina said. "I think his name is Lynch."

Zapper burst out laughing. Jaina glared at him.

"I'm glad my family is so funny to you," she said.

"Look," he said. "I'm sorry. It's just that it's all so--you know--gothic."

"Come on, Jaina," Mike said. "It looks good." He hugged her from the side and winked at Zapper. Zapper sighed.

"Blizzard," he mumbled.

They all seated themselves around tables and began to eat.

* * *

Hal Wolfe stood statue-still inside the twelve-foot exobot as the airboat lifted off--running lights flashing--and glided through the darkness of early morning toward the mountains outside the city. He waited, counting silently to himself, as the craft vanished. When he was sure no one was watching, he exhaled and took a step. He glanced around for any sign of the flesh-stripping nanoclouds.

The police had mistaken his armored form for a drone, never realizing there was a man inside. Pirate and the others, for whatever reason, had decided not to correct the mistake. Hal's instincts told him the decision made good tactical sense. Something was clearly amiss, but Hal had no idea what it was.

The digital lenses in Hal's helmet locked in on the police craft and watched as it landed on a hill at the edge of town. He saw the old style mansion and the sprawling complex of buildings below. He recorded the location in his suit's internal database. That way he could catch up with his friends at leisure.

Hal had already activated the heat, noise, and motion sensors in his exobot before stepping ashore. Before catching up to the others, he decided to scan the blasted cityscape for trapped survivors and help anyone he could find.

Hal walked beneath the cell-powered lights of debris-littered street, turned right at the corner, and continued to walk. He stepped through broken glass fragments, waded through a pool of muddy water that flowed from the shattered remains of a hydrant.

He picked up a blip on his sensors. They were picking up movement and heat signatures ahead. Hal moved toward them. He amplified the auditory sensors on his helmet and zeroed in on the area ahead.

"Maybe it didn't see us," someone whispered.

"Shhh."

He could hear the rapid heartbeats, the heavy breathing.

"It's coming this way."

"I'm getting out of here."

"Stay still! You can't outrun it."

He heard the sound of running feet.

"O'Neal. O'Neal!"

"Maybe he'll lead it away from us."

"That's a terrible . . ."

"Shhhh!"

Hal moved toward a parking garage. These people, he knew, were right above him. The concrete blocked his visual scans, but he could hear them.

"Come on out," he said, his voice magnified to a reverberating mechanical rumble. "I'm not here to hurt you."

A shadow moved. A human shape sprang up over the balcony. A flash lit the darkness. His suit's deflection system activated. Shockwaves radiated from the concussion field emitters on his shoulders. Something exploded about thirty feet in front of him. A wall of yellow fire engulfed him. A blast of heated air swept over him. A shockwave, partly deflected by his own emitters, threw him onto his back.

Hal rolled onto his side. His suit was covered with black carbon, but everything still functioned. He looked up at the fourth floor balcony and saw a man reloading a hand held cannon.

"Drop it!" he yelled. "I said, DROP IT!"

The man fumbled the shell he was holding in his shaking hands. He cried out as it hit the rail and finally rolled out of the garage and tumbled four floors to the street.

The shell landed between a shrub and a garbage can. It detonated on impact, raining Hal with leaf fragments and smelly chunks of brightly burning garbage.

Hal ran toward the parking garage, leaped into the air, and grabbed the rail with giant robot hands. His wedge-shaped fingers dug in as he scaled the building and squeezed over the balcony onto the fourth floor.

A ragged cluster of men and women in plastic hazard suits and diving gear huddled in the dark.

"Beast!" someone yelled. "Antichrist!"

A thin man with a reedy voice came running toward Hal. He was swinging a twisted piece of metal, using it as a club.

"Everybody run!" he said. "I'll distract it."

The man came in swinging. He slammed the club into the side of Hal's exobot, drew back, and hit it again. Hal sat still as the man struck the armored plating over and over again. Finally he stopped, gasped for breath, and stuck him again.

"Run!" he gasped. "He'll kill us all."

"I think you better calm down and tell me what this is all about," Hal said.

"Filthy servant of darkness!" the man wheezed. "How dare you feign ignorance."

"Whoa, there," Hal said. "Who you callin' a servant of darkness?"

"Justin," a woman's voice said. "Calm down. If he wanted to kill us, he'd have done it by now." A figure in a wetsuit moved forward.

"Thanks," Hal said. "It's about time somebody started talking some sense here."

"My name is Abigail," the woman asked. "Who are you?"

"Lieutenant Hal Wolfe," Hal said. "From the Interplanetary Guard."

"He's a sell-out," the man called Justin said. "The Antichrist executed the ones that wouldn't go along with his tyranny."

"You don't know that," Abigail said.

"I'm not working for Gogue," Hal said. "I'm here with the Intrepid Force. We're an independent crisis intervention team sponsored by DeFalco Space Industries. We were on an island when all of this happened."

"It's a trick," Justin said. "He's one of them. An agent of the Beast."

"Who are you people?" Hal asked.

"We refused the implant," Abigail told him.

"The mark of the Beast," the man called Justin said.

"You've been goin' to too many revival services," Hal said.

"No one would listen to me before," Justin said. "They're going to have to listen now."

"You may question his terminology," another man said, joining the group. "But he's telling the truth." This man was wearing a yellow environmental hazard suit with a mirrored faceplate. Hal saw his exobot's menacing features reflected there. He did look like a servant of darkness.

"We're trapped here," the woman, Abigail, explained. "We're chased by droids and flesh-eating nanoclouds."

"Do the police know about this?" Hal asked.

"They work for him," Justin said. "The ones who refused are dead or imprisoned."

"That's crazy," Hal said. "You're telling me the police trapped all of you here?"

"There is a brain in that armor somewhere," Justin said.

"What is this implant you keep talking about?" Hal asked.

"It's a subcutaneous transponder," Justin said. "It's tied into the nervous system. They can use it to track every move you make, every word you say. If you're disobedient, they can kill you with the touch of a button."

"In order to receive it," Abigail explained, "you have to renounce all nationalistic and religious ties."

"Why would anybody go along with that?" Hal asked.

"If you don't," she said, "you end up here."

"I've got to tell my friends," Hal said. "We've got to do something about this."

"You can't do anything about it," Justin said. "It's all been foretold."

"That may be true," Hal said, "but I'd still rather go down fighting that just let it all happen. Do you know where those implants are being made?"

"At the Leighton Institute," Abigail said. "They specialize in cerebral interface technology."

"Who's in charge of it?" Hal asked.

"A married couple," Justin said. "Patrice and Nigel Benedict. They run the whole thing."

* * *

Wendy closed her eyes as hot water scoured her body. The walls of the shower stall closed in around her like the walls of a glass coffin. Steam clouded them, distorted the world beyond. Wendy heard a faint buzzing noise, a sound like the handset of her communications system as *Vector* used to make.

No, Wendy thought. *Not now. Not again.* Even with hot water coursing down her body, she still felt a chill. She had heard the buzzing noise before. The sound, she now realized, had preceded every one of the ghastly hallucinations, every one of the eerie waking dreams she had experienced.

Wendy didn't move, didn't open her eyes.

Heh heh heh.

She heard the eerie laughter and cringed.

"I can see you through the keyhole, Wendy," a familiar voice said. "Lookin' good."

Zapper! she thought. *I'm going to kill him.* She shut off the water, threw open the shower door, grabbed a towel, and wrapped it tightly around her dripping torso. The water from the shower spigot dripped behind her as she stepped out onto the cool tile.

She opened the door and gasped. Outside of the bathroom was an airlock--the same one she had seen earlier. Lying in the floor were the bodies of two dead people, two mummified corpses.

"What's up, hot stuff?" one of them said.

Wendy sprang backwards and hit something solid. She spun around and found herself staring into a massive chest. She looked up into the plastic face of Lars Brunkert. His face was dark against the bathroom light.

Brunkert had taken her hostage as a child, murdered her baby sitter. He had fought the Intrepid Force on Venus and died there. He had died.

In the gray light, Brunkert's face flexed into a wrinkled imitation of a smile.

Wendy screamed. She found herself standing in the hall, dripping wet, with the towel still tied around her. In her bloody hand was a shard of glass, a pointed wedge from a broken mirror. Pirate, Zapper, Jaina, and the others stood staring in total shock. Wendy saw her own ashen face in the shard she was holding. She released it, watched it tumble to the floor, and shatter. Then she began to cry.

"What's happening to me?" she said as the others gathered in around her. "What's happening to me?"

CHAPTER 21: Return to Crane Island

"It's a match all right," Dr. Chambers said. He looked around the lab at Cockrum, Preston, and Harrison. The screen on the desktop before her showed a black and white picture of a young man with long, light brown hair and high cheekbones. This was aligned with an image of the sleeping patient's face. Inset windows indicated matches of dental records and fingerprints. Retina and DNA scans were not widely used in the 1980s.

"So he is Lex Marston?" Cockrum said.

"Or a cloned replica," Chambers said.

"But why would they replicate Lex Marston and try to convince him he's not Lex Marston?" Preston asked.

Chambers shrugged.

"Just trying to cover all the possibilities."

"But if he *is* Lex Marston," Harrison said, "where has he been for the past century and what was he doing aboard Corbalew's ship?"

"I don't know," Preston said. "I don't think he knows. There's only one person who can answer that question."

* * *

"Tell me about Lex Marston," Cockrum said.

Eerie croaking noises came from the mummy in the tank. Corbalew's swollen eyelids, surrounded by webbing, opened slowly. He peered through the misty liquid around him.

"I'm sorry," Corbalew's mechanically reproduced voice said from a speaker. "I'm not familiar with that name."

"Drop the act," Cockrum snapped. "We found him aboard your ship. We know you've been using him to design your weapons. I doubt you'll get any more out of him now that he knows you're an interplanetary terrorist."

Corbalew coughed up a laugh.

"I've gotten quite enough from him already," he said. "It might be time for him to join his friends and family now."

"Where did you find him?" Preston asked.

"Grave robbery is simple if you know where to dig," Corbalew said.

"Is he really Lex Marston?" Cockrum asked.

"I told you," Corbalew said. "I'm not familiar with that name."

"Tell me about Stefan then," Cockrum said.

"Ah," Corbalew said. "A remarkable mind and a useful tool. He had known almost everything we needed to know. Almost everything. Too bad he has to die," Corbalew whispered. "Quite a shame. Quite a shame."

"But that future doesn't exist," Cockrum said. "It's a fabrication based on a film. Surely you know that. We found the film in your quarters."

"You still haven't figured it out, have you?" Corbalew said. "I can't help you if you can't see the obvious."

"We don't have your intelligence," Preston said, suddenly trying to appeal to Corbalew's egotistical view of himself. "Could you at least give us a hint?"

"I'm afraid not," Corbalew said. "Good day, Mr. Preston. Mr. Cockrum. I so enjoy your visits, but I'm quite fatigued."

He closed his eyes. Preston knew there was no point in continuing the conversation.

* * *

Lex Marston was sitting on a park bench in a dusty, burned out town when Preston appeared. He looked up but didn't say anything.

"Hello, Lex," Preston said.

"I was starting to wonder if you were ever coming back," the boy said.

"I'm not going to desert you," Preston told him. "We're still trying to find a way to sever the connection, to free you from the machine."

He nodded.

"We found a missing persons report in our archives," Preston said. "It was a positive match. You are Lex Marston."

"I told you."

"We still don't know how you ended up on Corbalew's ship in suspended animation," Preston said, "Or why you've got the memories of a freedom fighter from a future that never existed."

"Sorry I can't help you," he said.

"Maybe I can help you," Preston said. "Would you like to go home?"

"I thought you said you couldn't get me out of here," Lex said.

"We can't yet," Preston said. "But there's something else we can do. Computer, run Crane Island Christmas Festival."

The world grew dark and cool and crowded with people in winter clothes. Lex and Preston were sitting on a park bench in front of a gazebo. The ironwork on the frame and the wooden slats were cool beneath them. Their clothes, Preston noticed, had changed to fit the weather. Warm lights burned in the windows of the shops that lined the street. Shop canopies, shrubs, and the iron posts of gas lamps were wrapped in strings of colored lights.

Lex gasped and rose to his feet. The air around them was cool. It smelled like cider and cinnamon, like pine and cedar boughs. The sky overhead was the purple of late dusk. Fireworks exploded with muffled pops and shrill whistling sounds across the face of the heavens. Carolers stood on the steps of a church and sang "O Holy Night." Airboats glided down the streets and docked in brightly lighted parking areas. Lex watched them intently for a moment. A horse drawn carriage rolled by, the horses' hooves striking their crisp, hollow cadence against brick streets. The driver wore a top hat. A young couple snuggled beneath a blanket in the seat behind him.

Desperately, wordlessly, Lex began to walk. Preston strolled behind him with his hands in his pockets as he walked down the sidewalk, moved among the crowd, looked through shop windows. They came to a gap in the buildings and walked down a narrow and brightly lit alley that led to the road behind the buildings, the path that wound along the riverfront. Lighted displays across the river reflected in misty watercolor paintings on the dark face of the water. Lex stopped and stared. There were tears on his face.

"I'm back," he said. "It's changed. So much has changed, but it's still the same."

Preston nodded.

"I want to go back here," he said. "As soon as you can free me from the machine, I want to go back."

"I know some young men who live here," Preston said. "I think they would be glad to take you."

Preston thought of Pirate Eisman and Jared Thomas and wondered, not for the first time, if there was any connection between them and this stranger from the past.

"This is wonderful," Lex said. "It's like really being back."

His shell of studied indifference, sarcasm, and cynicism had melted away in a flood of computer generated tears born of true emotion. In his heart he had finally come home.

CHAPTER 22: Brain Anomalies and Tennis

"I am detecting a few cortical anomalies," Patrice Benedict said. Wendy sat on a couch in the Benedicts' den while Patrice circled her head with a hand-held scanner.

"I already scanned her," Jaina said. "I didn't detect anything."

"Neurochemistry isn't your specialty, honey," Jaina's mother said. Jaina bristled, but didn't respond.

"That scanner is programmed to detect irregularities most machines would miss," Nigel Benedict explained. "It's state-of-the-art."

Jaina's father and the other members of the team stood around the couch. Wendy sat silently in a white robe and pajamas and submitted to the scans. Her eyes were swollen from crying and her hand was bandaged. She always worried about damaging the living flesh that had been grafted over her bionic endoskeleton.

"When did you begin to experience these delusions?" Jaina's father asked.

"Last spring," Wendy said. "They were just short flashes at first. Lately they've gotten longer, more terrifying."

"What do you see?" Mike asked. "Are they visions? Do they try to show you anything?"

"I saw Corbalew once," she said, "and Brunkert. "There's a space ship full of dead people. I've seen that one several times."

"Who are the people?" Pirate asked. "Is it anybody you know?"

"No," Wendy said. "They're mummies in an airlock. There's a girl who looks like me, but isn't. She has blue eyes and short hair. She's pretty--I mean, I think I'm pretty. I know I shouldn't say that."

"It's okay," Jaina's mother said. She stroked Wendy's hair. "And I think you're very pretty."

"Why didn't you tell us, Wendy?" Pirate asked.

"I was afraid to," she said. "I was afraid I was going insane. I thought I'd be kicked off the team if I said anything. You wouldn't have let me go to Venus."

"No," Pirate said. "We wouldn't have."

"What's happening to me?" Wendy asked. "You said there were cortical anomalies?"

"It's something we sometimes encounter in young people who are addicted to synthetic reality simulations," Ms. Benedict said. "We're only beginning to see the effects of long-term exposure."

"Can you help her?" Mike asked.

"We'll take her down to the clinic for a few tests," Ms. Benedict said. "The rest of you need to get some sleep."

"Could I go with her?" Pirate asked.

"It would be better if you didn't," Jaina's mother said. "She will be asleep through most of the tests anyway."

"Thanks, though," Wendy said. Pirate hugged her. Jaina's mother took Wendy by the hand and led her down walnut paneled walls to an elevator. The others followed.

"Wait a minute," Zapper said. "You can get to the clinic from here?"

"There's an underground tram system," Jaina's father explained.

"Recognize Patrice Benedict," the elevator's computer voice said. The doors opened.

"We have a security protocol in place to keep out intruders," Nigel Benedict explained.

Patrice Benedict led Wendy into the elevator. Wendy, Pirate noticed, was still barefoot. She raised her hand to the group as the doors closed.

* * *

"This isn't fair," Mike Noguchi said. He stood on one side of the net with his tennis racquet raised like a samurai sword.

"So you finally admit you're outnumbered," Zapper said. Zapper, Pirate, and Tori stood on the other side of the net. Jaina sat on the sidelines pouting. Tori held the ball in her hand and was about to serve.

"No," Mike said. "I meant it wasn't fair to all of you. You might as well give up."

"Three against one," Pirate said, "and still he worries about us."

"Serve the ball, Tori," Zapper said. "It's time for us to put this guy in his place."

"I tried to warn you," Mike said.

Tori served the ball. The ball cleared the net, hit the court, bounced, . . . and vanished.

"What?" Zapper said. "Where's the--?" He turned around and saw the ball wedged in the crack at the bottom of the fence.

"All right, show off," Tori said. "How do we know it landed inside the boundaries?"

"Because you know I'm a man of honor," Mike said. "Samurai code. My serve." He held up the ball.

Thwok! The ball hit the court between Pirate and Tori, bounced, and struck the fence behind them.

"He's too fast for us," Pirate said.

"I say he's cheating," Zapper said.

"It doesn't seem right," Tori said, "Us here playing and the rest of the world is falling apart."

"We offered our help," Pirate said. "The police obviously didn't want it. Besides, we've got to find out if Wendy's okay."

"She doesn't have a brain anomaly," Jaina said. "Not the kind they say she does anyway."

"Why are you so suspicious of your own parents?" Mike said. "They seem like nice people."

"You don't know them like I do," Jaina said.

"I think you're winged because they shot down your diagnosis," Zapper said.

Jaina kicked over a can of tennis balls and stomped off.

"I've never seen Jaina act this way," Mike said softly. "She's so angry."

"Acts like she's in kindergarten," Zapper said as he gathered tennis balls. "I'm surprised she's not wetting her pants by now."

"Coming home can be like that sometimes," Pirate said. "You fall back into the old roles, the old habits."

Pirate looked around at the palm trees, the perfectly manicured lawns, and the swimming pool.

"Anybody seen Jared?" Zapper asked.

"Let's play some more tennis," Pirate said.

"Would you guys like a handicap?" Mike said. "Maybe I could hop on one foot."

"Keep talking," Tori said. "Everybody has a weakness, and we'll find yours."

"Hey," Zapper said. "It's Wendy."

Pirate and the others spun around. Wendy was walking slowly up the sidewalk from the mansion. She had just passed the swimming pool. Wendy was wearing surgical scrubs and had her hair drawn back into a ponytail. Pirate lay down his racket and went to her. The others followed.

"Wendy," Pirate said. "How are you?"

"I'm fine," she said.

Pirate and Mike both hugged her. She accepted their embraces a little awkwardly. She seemed embarrassed by the attention.

"What did they do to your hair?" Zapper said.

"They greased it," Wendy said. "Some of the scanners are thrown off by static electricity."

"You look great," Mike said. "What did they say is wrong with you?"

"They're treating me for Landers' Syndrome," Wendy said. "Some people get it after spending too much time in synthetic reality simulations. They think it could have been caused by all of the simulations Sheppard used in our training. We used to spend twelve-hour days in SR immersion suits."

"How long do they think it will take to clear up?" Zapper asked.

"With medication," Wendy said, "it should clear up immediately, but I'll have to stay away from synthetic reality simulations for about six months, and I'll have to stay on the drug for three."

"That's good news," Pirate said. "You scared all of us half to death."

"Yeah," Zapper said, "coming out of the bathroom looking like something from a horror film."

Wendy didn't say anything.

"I mean, you didn't look like a monster or anything," Zapper said. "You know, just the blood and all that."

"I think I'll get some lunch," Wendy said.

"It's still on the table," Tori said.

Wendy walked back toward the guest house.

"It's not Landers' Syndrome."

Pirate and the others turned around to see Jaina standing beside the swimming pool. She had been sitting on the diving board listening.

"What makes you so sure?" Pirate asked. "I mean, your parents study brains for a living."

"I know about Landers' Syndrome," Jaina said hotly. "I tested all of you for it in the spring when we were spending so much time in those simulations."

"Maybe you made a mistake," Pirate said.

"No," she said. "I didn't make a mistake. Wendy does not have Landers' Syndrome."

Jaina turned around and stalked away.

"Moody," Zapper whispered.

"Shut up," Jaina said without turning around.

"That's enough of this," Pirate said. "Jaina, come back here!"

Jaina kept walking.

"Jaina," Pirate yelled. "Are you going to act like a doctor or are you going to pout?"

* * *

"I don't believe this," Jaina said as she stared down at her medical scanner. "This can't be happening."

They were in the guest house, in the bedroom the girls had chosen to sleep in. Wendy was sitting on the bed in the scrubs Jaina's parents had given her. Jaina was sitting beside her in a chair. Pirate, Zapper, Tori, and Mike were standing around them.

"What is it?" Pirate asked. "What's wrong?"

"Landers' syndrome," Jaina said, her face downcast. "It says she's got Lander's syndrome."

"Well, that's good," Zapper said. "Isn't it? I mean, at least we know what's wrong with her."

"I tested all of you for Landers' when we were training," Jaina said. "Nobody had it."

"Some medical conditions don't show up on scans until you've had them for a while," Pirate said.

"I've made a fool of myself," Jaina said. "Acted like a spoiled adolescent brat. I'm sorry."

"It's okay, Jaina," Mike said. "We understand."

She stood up and walked out of the guest house without saying anything else.

CHAPTER 23: Ultimatum

Warning klaxons went off all over the ship. Lights flashed in their metal cages and wall-mounted horns hooted through raspy throats. The four bridge officers scrambled to their stations. The *Vanguard's* bridge was divided into booths and cages and painted in flat industrial colors.

"There's a security alert in the ventral cargo bay," Jim Halloran said. Cockrum punched a rocker switch on the console before him and dropped into his chair.

"Get me Security Chief Childress," he said.

A short pause.

"Childress," a tense voice replied.

"What's going on?" Cockrum asked.

"It's Preston," Childress said. "He's locked himself into the cargo bay with Corbalew and reset the lock codes."

Cockrum cursed inwardly. That lunatic! What was he trying to do?

"Can you override them?" Cockrum asked.

"That's not the problem," Childress said. "He says he'll blow the hatch if anyone tries to come in there."

"What does he want?" Cockrum asked.

"Nothing from us," Childress said. "His problem's with Corbalew."

"I'll be right there," Cockrum said.

* * *

Preston had blackened the air with every curse, every obscenity he could think of. Corbalew sat quietly floating in his chamber and smiled through the webbing that covered his face.

"I've had it with your arrogance," Preston said when he was too tired to yell anymore. "I've had it with the smug way you play with people's lives. If you don't tell me what I need to know, you'll be dead in less than one minute."

"I believe you're drunk, Mr. Preston," Corbalew said. "Where did you find alcohol on board a starship?"

"I mean it!" Preston said. "You've ruined my life, murdered hundreds of people, betrayed your whole planet. You're a waste of air. It's obscene that you're still alive."

Corbalew's chest rattled with laughter.

"Where's your pressure suit?" Corbalew asked. "I heard you threaten to breach the cargo bay hatch. If I die, you die with me."

"I'm ready to die," Preston said. "Especially if the last thing I see is your filthy body falling through space."

Corbalew didn't answer.

"But I don't have to die to take you out," Preston said. "All I've got to do is cut off your oxygen supply and let you choke on that green slime they've packed you in. Or I could detonate the charge they've attached to the base of your REGEN tank. The last time anyone tried to transport you, five hundred people died, and you escaped. If anybody even attempts to free you from this place, we'll detonate that charge and blow you straight to hell. But talk is cheap."

Preston touched a button on the control panel of the life support unit. A musical tone sounded. He touched two other buttons and an alarm began to sound.

"That was me shutting off your air supply," Preston said.

"You're bluffing," Corbalew said.

"Actually," Preston said. "I've got a better idea." He restored life support and touched off another sequence. "That was me shutting off your pain killers."

Corbalew didn't respond.

"And I could introduce a few antiseptics into that delicate mixture of chemicals you're swimming in," he said. He touched off another sequence.

Corbalew began to squirm.

"It burns, doesn't it?"

Corbalew didn't answer.

"You know," Preston said. "The nanites in that chemical mixture are programmed to eat away the dead skin cells without harming the new skin growth. I could reprogram them." He placed his hand on the control panel. "With a few simple commands, I could set them to eat away every inch of skin on your body over a period of five or six minutes. Or sixty seconds." He touched a button.

"Wait!" Corbalew said.

"I'm listening," Preston said.

* * *

Childress and his security team led Preston out of the cargo bay in handcuffs. He was smiling. Jonas Cockrum and Jolie Harrison were standing in the corridor as they led him past.

"Stop," Cockrum said. "Bring him to me."

The guards, one on each side, escorted Preston into Cockrum's presence.

"Did he tell you anything?" Cockrum asked.

"I know how to release him," Preston said.

"Can you tell Dr. Chambers?" Cockrum asked.

"There's a safe in the dispensary. Inside you'll find a secret medical log that tells how to dissolve those nanofilaments in his brain. It's on a data slide. I have the password."

"What is it?" Cockrum asked.

Preston hesitated. Was he going to try to cut a deal, to bargain for his release?

"*Azrael*," Preston said. "The password is *Azrael*."

"Thank you," Cockrum said.

"What should we do with him?" Childress asked.

"Take him to his quarters," Cockrum said, "He's had a stressful day."

"Do you want us to post a guard?" Childress asked.

"I don't think I'll need to," Cockrum said, "Will I, Preston?"

"No," Preston said. "I'll behave myself from now on, Jonas. I did it to help the boy. You've got to believe that."

"I do," Cockrum said. "I'll come by your quarters to talk to you later. I expect you to be there."

"I will be," Preston said. "I'll be waiting."

CHAPTER 24: Shades of Usher

The day had been quiet. Pirate and the others had spent the afternoon playing tennis and swimming in the pool. Wendy fell asleep on her towel, but the others woke her before she could burn. No one turned on the communicore. After so much chaos, they silently had agreed to spend one day pretending life was normal again, that things were like they used to be. They knew better. Behind the smiles and laughter, lurked a dark sense of menace. The leaded windows of the brooding mansion glared darkly down at them from the high walls. Gargoyles skulked silently along the rooftops and around corners.

That night Jaina's parents invited them to the mansion to meet Dr. Arno Simpson, the DeFalco scientist they had worked with on so many projects. The group of them sat around a long, marble-topped table in a spacious dining hall. The roof was domed and painted with stars. The floors were hewn of white marble and the walls were dark oak. Jaina sat sullenly picking at her food while the others ate.

Dr. Simpson spoke at length about the things that had happened since the night of the attack. He talked at length about the occupation of *Vector* station and the closing of the DeFalco lab in Los Angeles.

"Thanks for clearing things up, Dr. Simpson," Pirate said at the conclusion of the meal.

"It was my pleasure, Pirate," Dr. Simpson said. "I'm glad I got the chance to meet all of you. DeFalco and Cockrum are old friends of mine." Simpson stood up. He looked around the den at the youthful faces of the Intrepid Force, at Jaina's parents.

"And you're sure about *Vector* station?" Tori asked.

"Yes," he said grimly. "The station was one of the first places they occupied; a beachhead, if you will."

"And they've got Venus Base too," Pirate said.

"I'm afraid so."

"And you're sure there's no word from Reverend Sheppard?" Mike asked.

"Nothing that I'm aware of," Simpson said, "but I'll keep checking. You can be sure I'll notify you if I find anything."

Pirate and the others rose from their places around the table. Jaina sat and looked at her plate.

"Thank you for coming on such short notice, Dr. Simpson," Patrice Benedict said. "I know you've been quite overwhelmed with everything that has happened."

"It's been difficult," Simpson said. "Frankly, it was a relief to get away from the lab."

Simpson walked to the door. Lynch, the butler, opened it for him.

"Thanks again, Dr. Simpson," Wendy said.

"You're welcome, Wendy," Simpson said. "Good night."

"Good night, Dr. Simpson," several voices said at once.

Dr. Simpson stepped out into the waiting darkness. The butler closed the door behind him.

"I hope that cleared things up for you," Nigel Benedict said.

"Maybe we can finally relax a little bit," Pirate said. "At least until we figure out where to go next."

"You're not going stay for a while?" Patrice asked.

"We'll stay for a few days," Pirate said. "But I've got to check on my family."

"Old style radio communications are being restored around the country," Benedict said. "If you'll be patient, we should be able to contact them for you."

"That would be great," Pirate said.

Nigel and Patrice Benedict walked their guests back across the courtyard to the guest quarters. They stayed and talked to their young guests for a while before finally turning in.

* * *

The clock struck eleven. Its low, mournful chimes echoed down the mansion's empty halls. Nigel and Patrice Benedict sat beside a tall, empty fireplace that looked like the mouth of a cave. Their glasses were filled with red wine. It glistened weirdly in the feeble light of a crystal chandelier.

"The drugs in their food should have rendered them all unconscious an hour ago," Nigel Benedict said sadly.

"I wish we hadn't had to do this," Patrice said. "I wish we could have told them everything."

"They never would have gone along with it," Benedict said. "They're young, idealistic, and foolish--our daughter most of all. This is the only way, Patrice. You must believe that."

A gaunt, black-clad shape came crashing through the French doors that separated the den from the courtyard. Wooden timbers split asunder and crystalline panes of highest quality glass burst from their ruined frames and shattered on a stone floor.

Nigel Benedict stared, aghast, at the still figure of his butler.

"Lynch," he gasped.

The skin of the butler's face was melted away to reveal the steel smile of an android skull. His charred servos popped, smoked, and whirred as he struggled to rise.

Wide awake and fully armored, the Intrepid Force stormed into the room. Opaque visors shrouded their faces.

"You snake in the grass!" Zapper Martin's voice reverberated through the speakers on his helmet. "You fed us drugged food--even your own daughter."

"And sent your butler after us with a shock rifle," Tori said.

"Calm down," Pirate said. "Let them talk. We want the truth this time."

"You have no idea what's happening here," Nigel Benedict cried, indignant. "How dare you come in here with those ghastly instruments of violence and judge me for my methods."

"Nice try," Pirate said. "One of our members happens to have an invisibility suit. He followed you when you took Wendy down to the clinic. While we were up here relaxing, he took a stroll to the complex down the hill to see what you were doing there." Pirate turned. "Jared, do you want to show them what you saw?"

Jared's gray shape materialized at Pirate's elbow.

"Replay from time index 02:03," Jared said. His body transformed itself into a screen, a man-shaped portal through time and space as digital images flashed across the surface of his invisibility armor.

Men in black armor, the same armor that Corbalew's men wore, stood talking to Nigel Benedict. The images raced by. Men and women, strapped to tables, writhed in pain. Nigel implanted devices into their bodies. He administered drugs to them, studied scans of their brains and nervous systems.

"We saw Gogue's men down there," Pirate said. "We saw the people you had captured, tortured, and brainwashed."

"We never tortured anyone," Patrice protested.

"What's really going on here?" Mike demanded. "You're both respected doctors. Why are you doing these things?"

"I wish there had been another way," Benedict said.

"I was beginning to think I'd been wrong about you," Jaina said. "I was beginning to think you really had changed. Then I saw Jared's pictures. I thought I was being foolish when I scanned my food for poisons. After all, what kind of parents would drug their own daughter? Then the scans showed positive. You drugged us. You drugged me. If I hadn't had a medical kit . . . ."

"You brave, foolish children!" Patrice said. She shook her head. "You have no idea what you're talking about. You don't know what's really going on."

"Then educate us, Mother," Jaina said. "You always wanted to educate me."

"What were you going to do to us?" Pirate said. "What would you have done after you'd drugged us and disarmed us?"

"Saved your lives," Nigel Benedict said bitterly.

"Saved us?" Pirate said. "But how?"

"Those forces you saw in orbit are only the beginning," Patrice said. "We've been invaded by something more powerful than you can possibly imagine. You can't fight it and hope to win. You can't defeat it. The only hope of humanity is to surrender to it, to cooperate with it."

"Is that what you're doing here?" Pirate asked. "Cooperating?"

"That's why the police recognized your name so quickly," Jared said.

"But what are you doing for them?" Mike asked. "Medical research?"

"Cerebral implants," Pirate said. "Isn't that what you specialize in?"

"Cerebral implants?" Zapper said. "Chips that go into the brain?"

"Mind control," Pirate said. "That's what it's about, isn't it?"

"It was a compromise we made with them," Nigel Benedict explained. "As long as we are free to resist them, they have no choice but to destroy us. With implants in our brains, they no longer need their ships in orbit. They will disarm them and allow us to go on living."

"Living?" Mike said. "Living as zombies? As slaves to others? You would condemn your own daughter to that?"

"Humanity will go on," Patrice said.

"Tell me about this quarantine," Pirate said. "Tell us about the place we were walking through when the police found us."

"Some people refuse to cooperate," Patrice said. "They resist the re-orientation process and refuse the implants because of religious superstition."

"The mark of the Beast," Pirate said.

"Exactly," Patrice said. "We can't simply allow them to go free. Gogue won't permit it."

"So you confine them to a ghetto?" Jaina said. "And fill it with bone-stripping nanoclouds?"

"Like feeding Christians to the lions," Zapper said. "I've seen those vids."

"They made their choice," Nigel said. "But you still have time to make yours."

Black armored forms poured through the second floor doorways and took positions along the balcony. There were twenty-five--possibly thirty--of them. They were armed with high impact concussion rifles.

"Please," Nigel Benedict pleaded. "We don't want them to kill you."

"Reorientation isn't pleasant," Patrice told them, "but it's better than death."

"Don't expect any help from your robot," Nigel said. "It's not coming."

"Hal?" Tori gasped.

"What are you saying?" Pirate asked.

"It was causing problems in the Red Zone," Nigel said. "They destroyed it."

"Destroyed?" Mike said. "You killed him?"

"Not me," Nigel said. "The police. It had taken out five of their drones and a police saucer."

"There was a man in there you--," Zapper sprang forward.

"Zapper!" Mike yelled. "Look out!" His blurred form knocked Zapper to the floor just as a concussion wave rippled the air over them and a heavy marble vase behind them exploded.

"Deflection fields," Pirate yelled.

Black armored forms poured through the second floor doorways and took positions along the balcony.

"Please," Nigel Benedict pleaded. "Surrender to them. We don't want them to kill you, but we don't have any choice."

"Neither do we," Pirate said.

Electric arcs erupted from the generators on Zapper's wrists. They chased trails of superconductive spray through the dry air. Jagged blue flashes burned through the air. Concussion bursts exploded from the gunports on the backs of Pirate's wrists. They blasted chunks of varnished wood from the overhead balcony. Wendy and Jaina joined him. The balcony sagged, broke apart, and dumped its armed occupants into the floor.

"Let's get outta here," Zapper yelled.

With concussion bursts raining behind them, they charged through arched doorways into a long hallway. They cut left into a greenhouse filled with tropical plants. Concussion bursts from across the room tore into the plants overhead and pelted them with green debris.

A leaded window exploded into the night. Pirate Eisman, Wendy Blake, and the rest of Intrepid Force poured out onto the lawn in front of the mansion. Their enemies came out of doors, appeared on the roof and on balconies. Ripples of concussion fire slammed against the counter-concussion fields put off by their suits' deflector systems.

Pirate shuddered as century-old balconies crumbled to the ground, as stained glass windows wailed and died, as gargoyles burst apart. The mansion was a priceless relic, a monument, perhaps, to a more graceful time. One of the tallest spires tore off and fell. As Pirate watched it crumble and rip a jagged gash down the middle of the mansion's face, he thought about the end of an Edgar Allen Poe tale:

> While I gazed, this fissure rapidly widened--
> There came a fierce breath of the whirlwind--
> The entire orb of the satellite burst at once
> Upon my sight--
> My brain reeled as I saw the mighty walls
> Rushing asunder--
> There was a long tumultuous shouting
> Like the voice of a thousand waters--
> And the deep and dank tarn at my feet
> Closed sullenly and silently over the fragments
> Of the "House of Usher."

CHAPTER 25: Ghost Towns and Glitter

It was two in the morning. Pirate Eisman woke up and found himself sitting in the dark on the gritty concrete floor of an abandoned warehouse.

Hal. Sorrow twisted Pirate's stomach as bitter reality settled in around him. He was hiding in a abandoned building, running from the police, and it was very possible that Hal Wolfe had been killed. It was true that Hal's exobot could operate independently of his body, but had he gotten out in time? Would they ever know?

The place had a musty smell and the roof was falling in on one end. The night air was cool, but not unbearably so. Pirate's friends lay sleeping around him. He heard someone sobbing softly in the dark.

"Jaina?" he whispered. "Is that you?"

She took a breath, tried to stifle her sobs. Pirate crawled through the dark, carefully avoiding the arms and legs of his sleeping friends. Jaina was sitting in a corner by herself, away from the others. Pirate sat down beside her.

"Are you all right?" he asked.

"Physically," she said, "I'm fine, but I don't think I'll ever be all right again."

"I'm sorry about your parents," he said. "I'm sure they thought they were doing the right thing. They weren't evil, just frightened."

"Cowards, you mean," Jaina said, sniffing.

"I didn't say that," Pirate said. "They seemed like good people. Sometimes smart people can become too sure of their own intelligence. They don't think they can be fooled. Then they end up making some of the worst choices."

"I guess you don't think I've got a soul," Jaina said.

"Don't have a soul?" Pirate said. "Because of your parents? That's not your fault."

"Because I'm a clone," Jaina said. "I know what your religion says about clones."

"My religion is divided over the issue," Pirate said.

"What do you think?" Jaina asked.

"I'm not an expert on souls," Pirate said, "but I think you've got as much of one as any of us. Now you've got to decide what you're going to do with it."

"So you think I've got a soul, but I'm going to hell?"

"I just meant that if there are souls, then there's probably a God. Then the next question becomes 'who is God?' What is he like and what does he want from us?"

"But how could you answer something like that?"

"It's a question we all have to wrestle with and answer as best we can--and hope that God is out there to lead us to the answers. Otherwise there's not much hope of us finding them."

"But what about hell? You do believe in it, don't you?"

"It's part of the package," he said, "but probably not the best place to start a conversation about God."

"I imagine not," she said. "'Believe what I tell you or I'll send you to this horrible place.' So tell me something: How is that any different from what Gogue did to those people back there? From what my parents helped him to do?"

Pirate froze.

"No answer for that one, huh?"

"I guess . . . I didn't think about that."

He stopped.

"I do have an answer though."

"What?"

"The difference is that Gogue didn't die to keep people out of that place."

"Still," she said. "Why does he have to punish them at all? Why can't he just leave them alone?"

"That's what hell is," Pirate said. "God leaving them alone."

She nodded, thought about it.

"I'm am glad you think I've got a soul," she finally said. "And if you're right about God, I hope he has a sense of humor."

"Me too," Pirate said.

"I'm going to try to sleep now," she told him. "Would you stay here next to me until I fall asleep? It doesn't feel quite as lonely that way."

"Sure," he said. "Sure I'll stay."

"Thank you." She squeezed his hand and then pulled herself into a ball and squeezed up against his side. Pirate sat in the dark beside her and tried to sleep. He looked around nervously. Jaina needed a friend now, but what would Wendy think if she saw them sitting close like this? He sighed, closed his eyes.

* * *

"Pirate. Hey, Pirate."

Pirate opened his eyes. He did not remember falling asleep, but clearly he had. He squinted and peered through the darkness. Jared was gripping his shoulder and shaking him.

"I'm awake," he whispered. "What is it?"

"I just dreamed about your uncle's old movie studio," he said. "How far is that from here?"

"I don't know," Pirate said. "Twenty miles or so."

"We've got to go there," Jared said.

"For what?" Pirate asked.

"I think Neema's there," Jared said, "and I think she's trying to call me. Come on. We've got to get going."

"Now?" Pirate said.

"We've still got about three hours before daylight," Jared said. "It will be easier to travel in the dark."

Jaina was leaning against Pirate's side. He gently rolled her into the corner and rose to his feet. He felt terrible. His tongue was pasty, and his hair was greasy and disheveled.

"What's going on with you and Jaina?" Jared asked.

"Nothing," Pirate said, embarrassed. "She was upset about her parents. We talked for a while."

"Come on," Jared said. "We've got to wake everybody up and get going. I always wanted to see that place."

He actually sounded excited. Pirate found himself looking forward to visiting the old studio again himself. It had been a special place to him during his childhood. He hoped some of the old magic still remained.

* * *

The old studio turned out to be closer than Pirate had expected. After almost three hours of creeping through empty streets and dark alleys, they found themselves in a rundown neighborhood on the edge of a desert. Across the street was a tall adobe fence topped with barbed wire. On one corner sat a gate with an empty guardhouse. Above the gate was a sign:

HERITAGE PRODUCTIONS

"So this is it?" Mike asked. "Your uncle's studio?"

"That's it," Pirate said.

"Well, let's go then," Zapper said. "What are we waiting around for?"

"It might be safer to take the long way around," Pirate said. They crossed the street and walked down a dirt and gravel road that ran between Heritage Studios and the Jones Salvage Yard.

"A movie studio next door to a junk yard?" Zapper said.

"Times change," Pirate said.

"How far down this road are we going to walk before we climb the fence?" Tori asked.

"Just a little farther," Pirate said. They walked in silence for about five minutes. Finally they came to a door in the wall. Pirate stopped.

"Wait here," he said.

Pirate leaped into the air. Paragravity generators confused the pull of gravity and jets guided his trajectory.. He flew over the wall and landed inside.

He found himself standing at the end of a dirt street beside a stone well with a shingled roof and a bucket that could be lowered by cranking a wooden handle. In the light of a nearly-full moon, he could see that he was standing on the main street of a western frontier town. He felt the ache of nostalgia. He and his brothers and cousins had played here as children.

There were no lights or sounds. In the dark of night, the place looked real and a little bit menacing. On the right side of the street was a saloon with a hitching post and a horse trough out front. On the left was a two-story hotel with a balcony. Just past that was the undertaker's place of business. Two coffins were propped in the alley between the buildings. Along the street were a general store, a livery stable, the sheriff's office, a blacksmith shop, and a bank. A white church stood beneath a large oak tree at the end of the street. The dirt main street was empty but well swept. The sidewalks were made of wooden timbers.

"Yeah," Pirate thought. "Almost exactly the way I remember it." He had forgotten how much he had loved the old studio, how much those memories had meant to him.

"Hey, Pirate," Tori said. "We're waiting."

Pirate turned around. A large bolt secured a door in the wall. He twisted it, pushed it aside, and pushed open the old door. It creaked on its hinges. Jared, Wendy, Mike, Zapper, Tori, and Jaina entered.

"What is this place?" Tori asked.

"A backlot set," Pirate said.

"This was a movie set?" Wendy said.

"One of the few remaining," Pirate said. "Most of the modern studios use virtual sets, virtual lighting, virtual effects. Even after this studio switched to the new technology, Uncle Enoch couldn't stand to tear down the old backlot sets. He always said they were a part of Hollywood history, and that walking down these streets was like taking a walk through time."

"Of course it's like a walk through time," Tori said. "That's what it's supposed to be like."

"That's not what he meant," Pirate said. "He used to talk about people like Lon Chaney, John Wayne, and Lucille Ball."

"And the stunt men," Mike said with unhidden reverence. "They didn't have computer generated actors then. They did their own stunts, risked their lives."

"But this isn't a real place," Jaina protested. "It's all a representation."

"Of the old west," Mike said, "but, like Pirate said, that's not the point. This place is part of the old Hollywood, the days of the big studios, big stars, and big budgets, the stunt men. It's part of history."

"There's somebody else here," Jared said.

The conversation fell silent. They looked up and down the dark western street.

The saloon door creaked open.

"Is anybody there?" Pirate called.

A dark shape in a western style hat emerged from the shadow. Another emerged from the sheriff's office. Other spectral figures came out of the bank, the general store, and the livery stable. Another appeared on the balcony of the hotel. All of them were armed with old style western firearms. Silent and menacing, they raised their weapons. Pistols cocked as their hammers were drawn back. Shotguns were aimed. Their shells slammed into place.

"I'm not getting human readings from them," Jaina said. She was looking down at her medical scanner. "These readings are mechanical. They're androids."

"What are you people doing here?" a gravelly voice yelled from somewhere in the shadows, from some hidden nook. "Don't try anything. Those cowboys may not be real, but their guns are. I don't want to hurt anybody, but I'm not letting anybody cause any trouble around here either."

"He's human," Jaina whispered.

"Where is he?" Pirate asked, his voice a whisper.

"In the alley," Jaina said, "between the livery stable and the sheriff's office."

"We're not here to cause trouble," Pirate answered the studio's hidden guardian. "We're friends of Enoch Henry."

"Say again?"

"We're friends of Enoch Henry," Pirate repeated.

"What's Enoch's middle name?" the figure in the shadows asked.

"Enoch," Pirate said. The others looked at him. "His first name's John."

For a moment there was no answer. Finally a slim, elderly black man stepped out of the alley. He was wearing an old fashioned suit with a pocket watch tucked into the vest pocket.

"You said the magic words," he said. "Anybody that's friends with Enoch Henry is welcome here any time. I'm Andre Hayden."

"Who are you?" Jaina asked.

"An-dre Hay-den," he repeated slowly.

"I know," Jaina said. "That's not what I meant. What's your place here? What's your position? Who are you?"

"A ghost," he said. "Ghost towns are full of them. That's what this old studio is, a ghost town. Don't worry, though. I'm a friendly ghost. Stand down, boys."

The android specters holstered their pistols and lowered their rifles. They turned around and walked back into their buildings.

"So what are you all doing here?" Andre asked.

"Just looking for a place we can stay," Pirate said, "until we figure out what to do next."

"Stray cats!" Andre said. "Enoch always did have a soft spot in his heart for stray cats."

"Excuse me!" Tori said. "You're comparing us to a bunch of mangy cats?"

"No offense intended, madame," Andre said. "I'm a member of the stray cat union myself. Enoch brought me here and gave me another chance after I nearly ruined myself with drugs. He was always helping people out like that. Best friend I ever had."

"That sounds like him," Pirate said. "Have you seen him?"

Andre hesitated.

"Not since sometime before satellite communication went down," he said. "It's been about three months now. Last time I talked to him, he was beside himself with worry."

"What was he worried about?" Wendy asked.

"He'd had a break-in," Andre said. "Somebody broke in and stole some things from him. Important things."

"He never told me," Pirate said. "Not directly anyway. He kept saying something was wrong, that he needed to talk to me. I should have listened."

"You're Ian and Joanie's great-grandson?" Andre said. "Johnny?"

"They call me Pirate," Pirate told him. "But you're right. That's who I am."

"Ian and Joanie were good people," Andre said. "So they call you Pirate, huh. Well, shiver me timbers." He cackled at his own humor. The others laughed at his self-induced merriment. "Come with me now. We got things to see."

Andre chattered away as they followed him down a dark alleyway and through a gate. They came out on another dirt street facing a high wall of dressed stone. They turned to the left and found themselves staring into the open gate of a castle. A rough-hewn drawbridge lay across a dry moat filled with cracked mud. Heavy chains linked the bridge to a pair of turrets--one on either side. The entrance to the castle was arched. The spiked grating of the portcullis hung down from the top of the arch like metal teeth.

The hollow sound of hoofbeats against bare earth sounded inside the gate. With almost no warning, a massive figure on horseback thundered out onto the drawbridge. His powerful form was encased in gleaming armor. He carried a lance. The horse, also armored, snorted menacingly. Andre had already pulled a control pad from his pocket. Nonchalantly, he punched in a few commands. The knight galloped past him and vanished from sight.

"Another android?" Wendy asked.

"That's Sir Rudolph," Andre said. "Don't nobody want to mess with him."

Following Andre through the old studio grounds was like strolling through holes in time. Around the corner from the castle was a haunted mansion with a cemetery. Red eyes glowed through the open door of a mausoleum.

"That's Wolfgang," Andre said. "Don't nobody want to mess with him either."

They stepped through a hole in a hedge and came out on a paved street that led between a row of buildings and finally to a gate with a guard shack. Three of the buildings ahead of them looked like old style aircraft hangars. The buildings, according to the signs mounted on them, were Stage 4, Stage 5, and Stage 6.

"Sound stages," Zapper said.

"A student of film," Andre said. "That's good."

"Do you ever use them anymore?" Pirate asked.

"We've got some of them fitted to be used as virtual sets," Andre said. "We still rent those out from time to time. The others we just keep up as parts of the historic studio tour."

"Where are we going?" Wendy asked.

"The main office," Andre said. "We're almost there, but I wanted you to see something first."

Andre walked up to the side door of the nearest set. A light flashed as a hidden scanner identified him and released the lock. "Come with me," he said as he opened the door.

They walked through into a lobby. Six armored figures stood in an alcove. Their weapons were aimed.

"Ambush!" Wendy yelled. She armed her gauntlets and dodged behind a large post. Most of the others had pulled out weapons of their own.

The six figures remained frozen in place.

"Stand down," Pirate said. "They're not real. They're characters from one of Uncle Enoch's movies."

Wendy lowered her gauntlets.

"Hah," Zapper said. "I knew they weren't real."

"I know," Jaina said. "You knew it all the time."

"That's right," Zapper said.

Pirate stared at the six figures in the display. He had seen them years before as a child. One of the women, he noticed, looked almost exactly like Neema. Her hair was short, and she had a scar on one cheek, but the resemblance was definite.

"Pretty good reflexes," Andre said. He did not seem alarmed that his guests were armed. "But what else would I expect from Lancing DeFalco's best?"

"You know who we are?" Tori asked.

"He's known all along," Jared said. "Haven't you, Mr. Hayden?"

"Please," he said. "You can call me Andre."

A door swung open behind him. A tall black man stepped through. It was Hal Wolfe.

"Hal," Zapper said. "Look, it's Hal."

The others ran to him and surrounded him. Tori leaped into Hal's arms and nearly knocked him down.

"Easy," Hal said. "I'm pretty sore." One side of his face, they noticed, was swollen. His right hand was swathed in bandages.

"What happened to you?" Tori asked.

"I got into a scrap with the police," Hal said, "or whoever's wearing their uniforms now. I managed to take out some of their drones and a helicopter, but they kept sending in reinforcements until they had me outgunned. I managed to get out of the suit before they blew it up, but I almost didn't make it."

"Ya look pretty good for a dead guy," Zapper said.

"You guys look pretty good yourselves," Hal said. "I didn't know if I would ever see you again. I heard some pretty bad things about the place where they took you."

"We made it through all right," Pirate said.

"You okay, doc?" Hal asked.

Jaina was brushing away tears. She took a breath and nodded, but didn't trust herself to speak. Zapper put his arm around her and patted her. For once she didn't push him away.

"What about the people in the Red Zone?" Wendy asked.

"That's what they call the place you were in," Zapper said.

"Do we need to go back there?" Wendy asked. "Finish liberating the people?"

"They're pretty much liberated," Hal said.

"Not bad for a bottlehead," Zapper said. Interplanetary Guardsmen--space rangers--like Hal had been nicknamed *bottleheads* because of the space helmets. Hal wore the title with pride.

"Have you seen Neema?" Jared asked.

"You just missed her," Hal said.

"She's gone?" Jared asked, his voice betraying the depths of his disappointment.

"I'm afraid so," Hal said. "She sends her love to all of you though."

"These dummies sure look real," Zapper said as he gazed at the armored freedom fighters from Uncle Enoch's movie. He reached out to the woman who looked like Neema and touched her scarred cheek.

"Stay behind the ropes," the girl ordered. She pivoted, aimed her rifle at Zapper. Zapper yelped, leaped backwards, and fell into Tori.

"Hey!" Tori cried.

"At ease!" Andre yelled.

For a long moment nobody moved.

"What is this?" Jaina asked. "What's going on here?"

"They're androids," Pirate said. "Like the others we saw."

"This place is crawling with them," Zapper said.

"We're pretty well protected," Andre said. "But these six are special. They've got more personality than most of the others."

"Why does that one look like Neema?" Jared asked.

"That, my friend, is a long story," Andre said. "Oh, my. The sun's starting to come up outside. We better get you some breakfast. Pancakes. Bacon and eggs."

"Ooh," Tori said. "That's nasty."

"Tori's a vegetarian," Hal said.

"Well," Andre said. "I may have some fruitcake left over from Christmas." He turned to Pirate and winked.

"I hate fruitcake," Tori whispered.

"The cafeteria is across the way here," Andre said. They followed him through the doors and into the narrow street that led through the complex. Andre opened the cafeteria door and held it as they went inside. Pirate caught a flash of motion out of the corner of his eye. He shifted his gaze and saw an inky shadow gliding across the asphalt. Panic seized him. He whirled around and scanned the sky just in time to see the batlike shape vanish over the wall. *A probe!* He had just seen a probe. It was identical to the ones that had attacked them back on the island.

Her turned back around and saw Andre scanning the skies, his dark eyes narrowed.

"They been watchin' us ever since Gogue took over," he said. "I reckon they know you're here now. Y'all be careful."

Pirate followed Andre into the studio's cafeteria. His friends were laughing as Zapper and Mike bantered with each other. As he tried to fight down panic, his eyes scanned the walls, the photographs. Framed black and white photographs showed Uncle Enoch with the stars he had met during his years as a producer. There were also pictures of his wife Emily, of Pirate's great-grandparents, and of the friends who worked with him at the studio. One of them was a black man with a cane and top hat.

"Jared," Pirate said. "Jared. Come over here."

Pirate looked around. Andre had vanished into the kitchen.

"Yeah," Jared said. "What is it?"

"I just remembered something," Pirate said. He looked back at the kitchen.

"What is it?" Jared asked again.

"Andre Hayden," Pirate said. He pointed to the black man in the picture. "Uncle Enoch used to talk about him. He died about five years ago."

CHAPTER 26: Rude Awakening

Jolie Harrison looked at the simulated world around her. A street lamp hummed as it came on beside her. The day was ending in a glorious sunset. Jolie had "tuned in" on the synthetic reality system and found herself in the late twentieth century standing on a sidewalk in Crane Island, Louisiana. The name of the street, according to a green and white metal sign, was Oak Street. Jolie was standing in front of a white frame house. There was a water tower on the corner and a convenience store with old style gas pumps across the street. Big, combustion powered cars roared by on the street. Everything was vintage. Jolie climbed the front steps of the little frame house and knocked on the door.

Lex Marston opened the door. He looked carefully through the screen door at Jolie before speaking.

"Good evening, Lex," the strange woman said. "I'm Jolie Harrison. I'm a friend of Mr. Preston's."

"Oh," Lex said. "I thought you might be a part of the simulation. Come in." He pushed the screen door open. The spring sang out as it stretched.

Jolie followed Lex into a small, twentieth century home with varnished wooden floors and walls of painted sheetrock. A rumpled recliner and a couch faced an old style television set. The set was big and bulky. It had a wooden cabinet and rollers on the bottom and a pair of metal antennae sitting on top. Characters in black pants and tunics of orange, blue, and red moved about on the screen.

"What are you watching?" Jolie asked.

"*Star Trek*," Lex said. "The first *Star Trek*. Did you know there were seven *Star Trek* shows?"

"No," Jolie said. "I never heard of it. I'm sorry."

"There were seven series," Lex said. "I only saw the first one. They canceled it after three seasons. The reruns used to come on right after I came in from school. It was my favorite show."

"I guess entertainment technology has changed some since your day," Jolie said.

"Yeah, it has," Lex said. "I love these controls--the way you can access any program, stop, go back, go forward. We never had anything like this."

"I can't imagine that," Jolie said. "Why don't you tell me about this house."

"I used to live in one like it," Lex explained. "Almost like it, anyway. The one thing that's really different is the smell. It's not the same."

"What's different about it?" Jolie asked.

"It's hard to say exactly," Lex said. "It just smells wrong, and I don't know how to describe the right smell. Maybe it's a mixture of dust and old paint. I don't know."

"That makes sense," Jolie said. "My grandma's house always had a certain smell to it. I couldn't describe that smell either."

"So where *is* Preston?" Lex asked suddenly.

"He's . . . ," Jolie started. "Well, he's gotten himself confined to quarters for the moment, but I imagine that will be worked out soon."

"What's going on?" Lex asked. Suspicion clouded his eyes.

"He went to bat for you," Jolie said. "The man who imprisoned you in this simulation is in a life support tank in our cargo bay. He wouldn't tell us how to get you out of there and Preston got a little rough with him. It needed to be done, but he did it without talking to anybody else."

"Did he tell you how to get me out?" Lex asked.

"He told us how to get into some medical files," Jolie said. "Those files had some information on how to disable the nano-neural links that are holding you here."

"When are you going to let me out?" Lex asked.

"The doctor's ready to start now," Jolie said, "but we didn't want to do it without talking to you first. I wanted you to know what was happening, and I wanted to ask your permission before they attempted it."

"Are you a doctor?" Lex asked.

"No," she said. "I'm a lawyer. Taking care of people's rights is what I do best, and you have a right to know as much about this surgery as we can tell you."

"Is it risky?" Lex asked.

"Yes," Jolie said. "The doctor says he's never encountered the technology before. It isn't from this century. He thinks he's got a pretty good grasp of how things are supposed to work, but there's no substitute for actual experience. Unfortunately there isn't anybody around who has had that kind of experience."

Lex nodded.

"We'll all understand if you want to wait, Lex" Jolie said. "There may be someone on Earth who understands the technology better than we do, but Earth's under siege right now, and we can't go back there just yet. We can wait if you want to, but it may be a while."

"No," Lex said. "Let's do it now. I give you my permission. I'll take the risk."

"We appreciate your faith in us," Jolie said. "I'm sure Dr. Chambers will do his best to be worthy of it."

"Thank you," Lex said.

Jolie turned to go.

"I'll see you on the other side," Lex said.

Jolie removed the helmet and sat up slowly. Dr. Chambers helped her out of the gloves and the stirrups that held her legs in place.

"Let's go," Chambers said. "He's given us permission to proceed."

* * *

The top of Lex's chamber had been removed. Lex lay on his back, his eyes twitching behind closed lids. The rest of his body was still.

"It looks like all of the nanofilaments have been disconnected from his nervous system," Chambers said. "Shut off the simulation."

"Yes, sir."

A technician punched in a command code on the keypad of Lex's life support unit. Lights, one by one, began to go out. Chambers started to breath a sigh of relief.

Alarms went off. All of the systems monitoring Lex's vital signs shifted into alert mode. Lex's body began to jerk.

"He's having some kind of seizure," one of the nurses said suddenly. "His vital signs are crashing."

Lex began to convulse wildly. Spittle ran from his mouth. His eyes rolled back. The seizure stopped suddenly, and Lex fell back onto the bed. He lay quiet and still as the monitors around him wailed.

"We've lost him," the nurse said.

"Get him back!" Chambers said. "Begin cardio stimulation. Everybody clear."

Bolts of electricity lifted Lex's body from the bed. Slowly his heartbeat returned.

"What happened?" Chambers asked. "Why did that happen?"

"It's happening again!" the nurse cried.

Lex's body jerked. His arms and legs contorted in wild spasms. Then, as before, his vital signs plummeted, and his heart stopped.

Five hours later, Dr. Chambers emerged, ashen-faced and exhausted, from the operating room. He walked into a small waiting area and sank heavily down into a thickly-padded easy chair. Cockrum, Preston, and Harrison were waiting there.

"What happened?" Cockrum asked.

"Is he alive?" Preston asked.

"Yes," Chambers said. "Yes, he's alive, and he should make a full recovery. We lost him seven times, but we managed to drag him back."

"What happened?" Harrison asked.

"I don't know exactly," Chambers said. "Some kind of block, maybe. Something to keep him from regaining consciousness and sharing anything with anyone."

"But that's crazy," Preston said. "We could already access his dreams."

"That may be so," Chambers said. "But I don't think Corbalew ever intended for him to wake up."

CHAPTER 27: Memories

"I think you boys better come with me," Andre Hayden told Pirate and Jared. "I have to show you something."

Pirate blinked, looked around. Wendy, Tori, Jaina, Zapper, Mike, and Hal were all eating breakfast.

"Just you two," Andre insisted, his voice low.

"You're not Andre Hayden," Pirate whispered.

"No," he said. "But I am a friend. You're all safe here, as safe as you can be anywhere these days."

Andre led them back across the street to the sound stage they had visited earlier. They passed the place where the armored android sentries had stood earlier and noticed they were missing.

Andre led them to a set of double doors. He went to a control panel and disarmed the security system. Locks disengaged and the doors opened inward.

"Come on in," Andre said.

Pirate and Jared followed him through into the sound stage. They were standing on a dusty, demolished street: the ruins of some futuristic civilization. Debris littered the broken streets and sidewalks. Scattered aircars lay on their sides and backs like they had been knocked from the sky by explosions. Small trees, bushes, and vines grew up through cracks in the pavement. The buildings were burned and twisted. Most of the windows were missing.

"Who's there!" a voice yelled from one of the buildings. "Identify yourselves!"

"At ease," Andre yelled. "It's just us. Come on out."

The five armored sentries stepped through broken windows and out of alleys. Their weapons were raised and their eyes were narrowed with suspicion. Neema's scar-faced twin moved among them.

"I built this set for my first movie," Andre said, his voice suddenly different. "I never finished that movie, but a lot of life-changing things happened to me while I was making it. That's how life is sometimes."

"Your voice . . . ," Pirate said. "Uncle Enoch?"

Jared nodded.

"Yes, Pirate," Andre/Enoch said. "It's me."

"I can't believe you're here," Pirate said. "Why didn't you tell us who you were?"

"I had to be careful," Enoch said. "Those things have been watching the studio."

"What are you doing here?" Pirate asked. "How did you get here? This is . . . ," he shook his head. "I've got to tell the others."

"You can't," he said. "You can't tell anybody you've seen me. There's too much at stake here."

"What do you mean?" Pirate asked. "What's going on?"

"It's time you knew the rest of the story," Enoch said. "This is more than just a movie set. Much more."

"This is where I came from," the armored, scar-faced Neema figure said. "This is my world." Her hair, Pirate noticed, was no longer shorn and ragged as it had been earlier. It was tied back in a curt ponytail on the back of her head.

"Neema," Jared said.

"Hello, Jared," she said. She was smiling but her manner was sad and subdued. Jared seized her in a sudden hug and held on.

"This is quite a masquerade party we've stumbled into," Pirate said.

"I'm sorry we had to mislead you," Enoch said. "These are dangerous times."

"Jared," Pirate said. "Let her go before she passes out."

"I'm sorry," Jared said. He relaxed his grip. "I didn't think I'd ever see you again."

"It's all right," Neema said. "I understand."

"What's going on here?" Pirate said. "I'm glad to see you, but why are you here?"

"Sit down," Neema said. "Both of you."

Pirate and Jared seated themselves on a park bench. It looked rusty, but the rust had been painted on. Neema sat down between them and took their hands.

"Now," Neema said. "Relax yourselves. Close your eyes."

What was going on here?

"I want you to picture a metal box with a combination lock on it. Do you see the box?"

"Yes," Pirate and Jared said.

"The lock does not have numbers on it," Neema said. "It has pictograms, pictures of objects and animals. You start to turn the lock. You turn clockwise to a snowflake, counterclockwise a rocket, and clockwise to a dove. The lock clicks. The box opens."

Pirate saw the box open. Light surged out.

"Remember everything," Neema said.

Pirate felt like he had just been dropped into an arctic lake. He gasped and trembled as spasms of memory burned through his mind on electrically charged pathways.

Pirate was back in Crane Island. He was fourteen years old and Jared was with him. The sun was going down, burning low on the horizon and pouring shimmering cobwebs of light through the skeletal limbs of winter oaks and the black shadows of pines. The two friends were walking through the ruins of the Crane Island Saltwerks. The abandoned factory was off limits to them, of course, but it was irresistible. Tall clumps of yellow grass and a few scrawny trees grew up through cracks in the street. The buildings scowled at them through empty windows. The rusted out conveyor belts looked like the collapsing spines of dinosaur skeletons.

"What is that?" Pirate asked. A movement in the sky had caught his attention. A big, dark shape flashed by overhead.

"It looks like a ship," Jared said. "Some kind of airship." The phantom shape was dropping from the sky.

"But it's not making any sound," Pirate said. He watched it go down, falling from sight behind the ruins of the old factory.

They ran for all they were worth down debris-strewn alleys between empty buildings, but by the time they came to the other side, there was no craft to be seen. The long, sloping hillside was empty all the way to the muddy, twisting river that lay a hundred meters down the hill. Disappointed, they started home. That was when they saw the girl. She was tall and blonde with icy white hair and crystalline blue eyes. She wore a long, black coat with a high collar.

"Hello," she said. "My name is Neema."

Suddenly tongue-tied, Pirate and Jared fumbled their way through introductions. This girl, they realized, was only a couple of years older than they were. She had a slight accent-- Swedish, maybe.

That night was the beginning of their friendship with Neema. They saw her dozens of times after that. She was always out walking, always alone, and always seemed glad to see them.

"I think I'm in love with her," Jared blurted out one day when he and Pirate were out for one of their hikes. "Do you think I should tell her?"

"I don't know," Pirate said. "She's a little older than we are."

"Maybe I'll write her a poem," Jared said, and that is what he did. He gave the poem to Neema in an envelope and asked her to read it after he had gone. The next time they saw her, she told him it was "very sweet" and kissed him on the cheek. Jared hardly slept for a week after that.

"I have something to tell you," she told them one evening as they were walking through the Saltwerks. "It is very important. Can I trust you?"

"Of course you can," Jared said.

Pirate wasn't so sure.

"What is it?" he asked. He never made promises without knowing what was being asked of him.

"Come with me."

They followed her through the grounds to one of the rickety elevators that led down into the abandoned salt mines. Those mines, Pirate had been told, were enormous underground rooms with eighty-foot ceilings supported by pillars of salt. The mines had been closed nearly a hundred years earlier after a cave-in that had killed several people. Stories of ghosts haunting the mines circulated among the children of Crane Island. Pirate had once asked his Uncle Enoch if they were true, if the Saltwerks were really haunted.

"They're haunted," Uncle Enoch had told him, "but not by the ghosts you're thinking of." Pirate had always wondered what he meant by that. On that dark evening when he and Jared followed Neema down into the mine, he found out.

The elevator platform had a floor of corrugated metal and walls and a gate made of metal grating. A control panel was mounted beside the gate. The ride down into the musty earth seemed to take forever. Pirate could hear rumbling echoes traveling up and down the shaft as the platform dropped deeper and deeper into the Earth's sunless depths. Finally Neema pushed back on a lever and the platform squeaked to a halt. Neema shoved down a brake, slid aside a bolt, and threw the gate open. She stepped out into a dimly lit chamber. Pirate and Jared followed. The floors were made of damp earth. The ceiling was high above them and shrouded in darkness. They could only guess at the height of the room.

Neema took Pirate and Jared by the hands like a mother leading her children across the street. They would not have appreciated the analogy, of course, and Pirate was a little embarrassed by the way she sometimes treated them like baby brothers and not the mighty men of adventure they believed themselves to be. Jared never complained. Holding Neema's hand, under any conditions, was too heavenly to complain about.

Neema led them through near darkness for about fifteen minutes. Finally they arrived at a smaller cave that had been hewn into the walls of the larger one. This room was lighted and filled with machinery. An elderly man sat at a desk pecking at an old style computer keyboard. Pirate recognized him immediately. It was Uncle Enoch.

"Uncle Enoch!" he had sputtered. "What are you doing here?"

"Waiting for you," he said. He rose to his feet. Neema hugged him. Enoch embraced her fondly, stroking her hair and patting her.

"You two know each other?" Pirate had asked, stunned.

"For almost a hundred years," Enoch had told him.

"You're a hundred years old?" Jared had squeaked.

"Actually" she had said, "I skipped most of it and spent the rest in cryogenic sleep. You call it suspended animation, I think. I am a time traveler."

"From the past," Pirate asked, "or the future?"

"Both," she said. "In a way. About two hundred years in the future, a group of scientists will find a way to open doors to the past. Unfortunately living beings can not survive the trip, so they can only send robots or they can store the memories of living people, grow biological replicas of them in the past, and implant the memories."

"Or implant the memories into living hosts," Uncle Enoch said.

"Yes," Neema said. "We can also do that. I am one of the biological replicas, a copy of a girl from the future."

"A clone?" Pirate asked.

"Not precisely as you understand cloning," she said, "but the process is close enough. I will not argue over the exact meanings of words."

"So you showed up in Uncle Enoch's time," Pirate said. "Then they froze you and sent you to our time."

"Yes," she said.

"But what were you doing back in the past?" Jared asked. "Why Uncle Enoch's time?"

"I have an enemy who is timeless," Neema said. "He has appeared at different points in history. We do not know exactly what he is or where he comes from. We only know that he has appeared, and that trouble always follows him."

"This enemy," Pirate said. "Is he here? Now?"

"Not yet," Neema said. "His appearance in this era is still about five years in the future, but we must begin preparations now if we are to be ready for him. I need you to help me prepare."

"What can we do?" Pirate asked.

"The greatest risk will be to Jared," she said. "He will be my link to this world, my eyes and my ears. Jared has a very special mind with unusual neural receptors. He has uncommon powers of observation and intuition. If Jared will allow it, I will implant a device into his head that will allow me to communicate directly with his subconscious mind."

"But why his subconscious?" Pirate asked.

"Because the enemy, when he arrives, will be watching for signs of interference from the future," Neema said. "He must not find them. By linking with Jared's subconscious, I can send information directly into his brain, but he will not know where it came from."

"You want to do brain surgery on me?" Jared asked, shocked.

"Not surgery as you know it," she said. "Just an injection of tiny devices into your blood stream. It will not hurt at all."

"Okay," Jared said. "Okay, if that's what you need me to do. I'd do anything for you. You know that."

"I do know that," she said. "You are a very brave young man, Jared. The most painful part is what I must do next."

"I'm afraid to ask," Pirate said.

"I'm going to have to erase your memories of me," Neema said. "Neither of you must remember ever having met me."

"No," Jared said. "You don't have to do that. What if we promise not to tell anybody?"

"Yeah," Pirate said. "We won't tell anybody."

"I know you would never willingly betray me," Neema said, "but I have to do this. I'm very sorry."   .

"Don't do this, Neema," Jared told her. "You're all I've got. My dad ran out on us, and I've never been close to my mother. My teachers don't like me. They all think I'm strange. There's nobody else like you in my life."

"You're special to me too, Jared," Neema said. There were tears in her eyes. "I don't have any choice about erasing your memories, but I promise you we will be together in your dreams. Every night when you close your eyes, I'll be there waiting for you."

The cave was filled with strange and wondrous devices. Neema had stored them there years before, and Enoch had served as a kind of caretaker. One of the machines was a chair with straps around the armrests and a band that fit around the user's head. This was used to hold the user in place while memories were either injected or suppressed. Pirate and Jared took turns sitting in the chair. Two hours later they returned, each to his own home, with no memory of Neema or her mission.

Pirate shook his head, massaged his temples, and found himself back in the cafeteria at Uncle Enoch's studio. He realized there were tears on his face. He looked across the table at Jared and saw the same gleaming tracks on his cheeks.

"I'm glad Hal's not here to see us," Pirate said. Jared smiled slightly. Both of them turned to Neema.

"You have no idea how much I've missed you both," she told them. They both hugged her, one on each side.

"Neema," Pirate said. "You've shrunk. You used to be taller."

"I know," she said, smiling. "Being frozen will do that to you."

"Neema and I go back about a hundred years," Enoch said. He was sitting on a wrecked aircar in front of them. "She and Balthazar, her ship's computer, showed up in Crane Island back in the 1980s. I was fifteen years old at the time."

"You told us about it," Pirate said. "That night in the cave."

"Dangerous people had come to my time," Enoch said. "people with weapons from the future and a plan to change history. Neema needed a team to stop them, a team like your Intrepid Force. Unfortunately there wasn't anybody in that time who had the weapons or knowledge to stop them.

"Neema here used technology from her time to inject the memories and knowledge of her friends from the future into my friends and me. It was like they had possessed us, like we had become them. She outfitted us with the weapons we needed to stop Gogue's forces cold. Then, when it was all over, she erased our memories of the whole thing. A little over twenty years later, the year I started this studio, those memories started to come back. That's a story for another time."

"They don't know about Lex," Neema said. Enoch nodded.

"Lex Marston," Enoch said, "was your great-grandmother's brother, was one of the friends Neema had injected with memories from her own time. Unlike the rest of us who came through fine, Lex--well, it's a long story. Neema had to put him into suspended animation and hid him in the abandoned salt mine beneath Crane Island. None of us knew what had happened to him until years later. After I found out, I kept watch over him and kept his location secret."

"Is he still there?" Jared asked.

"No," Enoch said. "That's the problem. I don't know where he is. Last Christmas, the night Wendy and Jared were captured by Astrolus, they also found the cryogenic freezer unit where Lex was stored. They stole it. I was frantic to get it back. Lex is my friend, but there's more to it than that. He also has memories of technology from Neema's time."

"Somehow Gogue tapped into those memories," Neema said. "That's how he was able to shoot down my ship. His technology was never more advanced than the early twenty second century before. Suddenly he was using twenty-fourth century technology, technology from my time."

"Where is he now?" Pirate asked.

"We don't know," Enoch said. "But we've got to get him back. And they can't know about me. They can't be allowed to find out what I know."

"What's happening in Crane Island?" Pirate asked. "Is my family all right?"

"They were when I left," Enoch said, "but that was the night after the invasion. You might say I left rather hurriedly."

"What happened?" Pirate asked.

"I knew Gogue's forces would come for me," he said. "Since they found Lex hidden out in that salt mine, I knew it was only a matter of time until they traced him to me. Sure enough I was right. Gogue sent Astrolus for me. There were about twenty people and some of those robot drones they use. They thought they'd taken me by surprise, but I was ready for them.

"You remember when Wendy asked me if I was scared to live in the museum with all of those wax figures?"

"Yeah," Pirate said. "I remember. You said they guarded the place."

"That wasn't a figure of speech or a sentimental fantasy," Enoch said. "When those people came into the museum after me, I had a little surprise waiting for them. Those weren't wax figures. They were androids like the figures here. Every last one of them was armed. As soon as those goons came in there, all of them came to life, and they started shooting at each other.

"I didn't expect for them to blow the place up, but it worked out to my advantage. Those people had come to capture me. They needed the memories Neema had left buried in my subconscious, and they would stay after me as long as they thought they could get them. If they thought I was dead, they would leave me alone. I hated to leave your family thinking I'd been killed, but I didn't really have a choice."

"They blew up the museum?" Pirate asked incredulously.

Enoch nodded.

"I loved that place," Pirate said.

"I'll rebuild it," Enoch said, "If we come out of this alive. Meanwhile we've got other things to worry about."

"I need to get to *Vector* station," Neema said, "and I need the Intrepid Force to help me."

"How can we even get near the place without Gogue knowing about it?" Pirate asked.

"He will know," Neema said. "That's what I'm counting on. He has tried to capture me at every turn, but I've managed to escape."

"But if you deliver yourself right to him," Pirate said, "he'll leave the door open for you."

"Exactly," she said.

"What if you can't stop him?" Jared said. "What if he captures you?"

"That," she said, "would be most unfortunate."

"What do you want the rest of us to do?" Pirate said.

"You will try to infiltrate the station," Neema said. "Gogue will probably catch you."

"So we're decoys?" Pirate said.

"Yes," Neema told him. "The others must not know this. The attack on the station must be believable."

"What will he do to us?" Pirate asked.

"Interrogate you," Neema said. "Possibly torture you."

"Is there any chance of us coming out of this alive?" Pirate asked.

"There is always a chance," Neema said. "After all, you are the Intrepid Force."

"Like that means anything," Pirate said.

"After Gogue took control of the world," Neema said, "he destroyed most of the historical records from this time. One of the few records that remained was a handwritten document about a legendary group of young men and women called the Intrepid Force. My friends and I discovered that book, read those stories, and tried to model ourselves after those noble people."

"Hal says we're nothing but a publicity stunt," Pirate said.

"Hal is wrong," Neema said.

"I can't lie to the team," Pirate said. "Even if I can't tell them about you, our efforts to infiltrate the station have to be genuine. There has to be some chance of success. Can you tell us anything that might be helpful?"

"I'll tell you what I can," she said.

Pirate and Jared spoke with Neema and Enoch for over an hour. Finally, under the cover of darkness, they returned to their beds.

* * *

"We're going to do what?" Zapper said. The team was gathered in a meeting room in the studio's front office. Donuts and cinnamon rolls sat, uneaten, on the table. Uncle Enoch, still disguised as Andre Hayden, silently watched the exchange from the kitchen door.

"*Vector*'s Gogue's base of operations," Pirate said. "We're going to hit it."

"That's what I thought you said," Zapper said. "How are we going to get in?"

"Neema thinks she can get us in," Jared said. "The rest is up to us."

"Where's Neema now?" Tori asked.

"Someplace safe," Pirate said.

"She better be," Hal said. "Gogue wants her bad."

"I'm not afraid to risk my life if I have to," Mike said, "Some of my ancestors used to crash planes into ships, but are you sure this is the best way?"

"It's suicide," Jaina said. "Are you all insane?"

"So far," Pirate said, "Gogue hasn't shown much interest in us."

"That's for sure," Zapper said. "Once Neema had left the island, he didn't even bother with us."

"How are we going to get in?" Hal asked.

"By breaking into DeFalco's computer network," Jared said. "Gogue seems to be using it to control the flow of supplies and personnel to and from *Vector* station. We'll create false identities for ourselves, assign ourselves to duty on board *Vector*, and show up at one of the spaceports."

"Just like that?" Zapper said.

"It won't be easy," Pirate said, "but we *are* the Intrepid Force."

The others sat silently as Pirate outlined the plan for them. After the meeting broke up, they all went to gather their gear.

"Pirate," Hal said as the rest of the team was leaving. "I want to say something to you."

"Okay," Pirate said. He watched as the others left, then turned back to Hal.

"I understand why Cockrum and DeFalco made you the leader," Hal told him. "I know I said some things earlier about the team, things I shouldn't have said."

"It's okay," Pirate said. "You were worried about your family."

"Partly," Hal said. "But mostly I kept comparing the team to the Interplanetary Guard, wishing I was back in space on board one of those war ships. It's what I'm used to. I realize though that DeFalco didn't want this team to be another Interplanetary Guard. There's already an Interplanetary Guard. There wasn't any need for another one. They wanted a team that was creative and idealistic. That's what they saw in you, and it's why they put you in charge and not me."

"That doesn't mean I don't need you," Pirate said. "Your military experience, your knowledge of tactics."

Hal didn't answer for a moment.

"Back on the island," he said, "I was mouthing off about how we weren't doing anything but sitting on our butts while our planet was being destroyed. You looked at all of this and said, 'What can we do?' You didn't think there was anything we could do but go out and get ourselves killed."

"That's not what I said," Pirate said. "I said I didn't know what to do, but that if you had any ideas I'd like to hear them."

"And I didn't have any ideas either," Hal said. "I remember now. Well, I'm sorry about what I said earlier."

"Thanks," Pirate said.

"So," Hal said. "Do you really think there's a chance we can save the planet?"

"A chance," Pirate said.

"Because of Neema?" Hal asked.

"Mainly," Pirate said.

"You trust her?" Hal asked him.

"Yeah," Pirate said. "Actually I do."

Hal nodded.

"Let's do it then."

* * *

Sheppard pulled against the frame that bound him, but it was no use. The bands that held his wrists and ankles now were far stronger than the leather he had torn through earlier. The position they held him in sent spasms of pain through his body.

A door opened across the room. A man in black stepped into the room. His back was to the light. The door closed behind him and the shadows swallowed him. Sheppard saw red eyes gleaming into the dark. Finally the man stepped into the circle of light beneath him. He looked Hispanic or Mediterranean, but his dark features were unfamiliar.

"Well, Reverend," he said. "I see you haven't died yet. Too bad."

"Gogue," Sheppard said. "I should have known. How many bodies have you taken over?"

"As many as I want," he said. "My hands and eyes are everywhere. I'm omnipresent."

Sheppard snorted with contempt but said nothing.

"You'd better show me some respect," Gogue told him. "After all, I am your lord and master."

"No," Sheppard said. "You're not. You never were."

"Has God forgiven you for denying Him?" Gogue asked. "Do you feel loved and accepted?"

"I don't know," Sheppard said bleakly. "Why don't you just leave me alone? If you're going to kill me, just do it. This game of cat and mouse has gone on long enough."

"I have something to show you," Gogue told him. "Behold." He gestured and the big screen across the room swirled with liquid color and resolved itself into a meeting room. Zapper Martin was sitting at a table with a steaming mug and a donut in front of him. Pirate Eisman, Sheppard saw, was sitting directly to the right of him.

"We're going to do what?" Zapper said.

"Vector's Gogue's base of operations," Pirate said. "We're going to hit it."

"That's what I thought you said," Zapper said. "How are we going to get in?"

"Neema thinks she can get us in," Jared said. "The rest is up to us."

"Where's Neema now?" Tori asked.

"Someplace safe," Pirate said.

"She better be," Hal said. "Gogue wants her bad."

"I'm not afraid to risk my life if I have to," Mike said, "Some of my ancestors used to crash planes into ships, but are you sure this is the best way?"

"It's suicide," Jaina said. "Are you all insane?"

"So far," Pirate said, "Gogue hasn't shown much interest in us."

"That's for sure," Zapper said. "Once Neema had left the island, he didn't even bother with us."

"How are we going to get in?" Hal asked.

"By breaking into DeFalco's computer network," Jared said. "Gogue seems to be using it to control the flow of supplies and personnel to and from Vector station. We'll create false identities for ourselves, assign ourselves to duty on board Vector, and show up at one of the spaceports."

"Just like that?" Zapper said.

"It won't be easy," Pirate said, "but we are the Intrepid Force."

The last line repeated itself.

"It won't be easy, but we are the Intrepid Force."

"It won't be easy, but we are the Intrepid Force."

"So sure of themselves," Gogue said. "I love it!"

No, Sheppard thought. Dear God, no.

"So," Gogue said. "It looks like you'll be seeing your young friends soon. Dead or alive."

"You've been monitoring them the whole time?" Sheppard asked.

"Of course," Gogue said.

"But how?" Sheppard said. "We turned off our communications links, scanned for listening devices."

"Do you remember that night in the swamp?" Gogue said. "The night Astrolus captured you and plugged you into their machines."

"Yes," Sheppard said.

"We implanted devices into each of you," Gogue told him. "Devices that would allow me to watch you, to control you."

"That's impossible," Sheppard said. "All of us went through extensive medical scans. Something like that would have been detected."

"No," Gogue said. "It would not have. It doesn't really matter though. Unfortunately, you see, those stupid cops rescued you before the integration process was complete. Only two people were in the pylon long enough to complete the process."

"Wendy," Sheppard sighed. "And Jared."

"Yes," Gogue said. "Unfortunately Jared turned out to be immune. Somehow his mind shut itself down before we could complete the process. We still don't know why. Maybe I'll have the people in the lab do an autopsy on his brain after we execute him."

"So Wendy is the spy," Sheppard said, "The traitor. Only she doesn't know it."

"Well, that's not my fault," Gogue said. "I've given her plenty of clues. She's not very smart, is she? The pretty ones never are. The ugly ones are bright, but who would want them? It's so unfair. How can you believe in a loving God in such an unfair universe?"

"Let's stay on the first subject," Sheppard said. "If Wendy had some kind of transmitter in her head, she'd have to be sending out some kind of signals."

"She's a cyborg," Gogue said. "The neural links at the base of her skull are always sending and receiving signals from her prosthetics."

"And she's got internal batteries," Sheppard said. "Plenty of power to send out carrier waves."

"You really are smart for a cave man," Gogue said.

"You said you didn't have any interest in the Intrepid Force," Sheppard said. "Why do you care about them now?"

"I don't," Gogue said. "Not exactly, anyway. You really are behind on recent events. They've made a new friend. She claims to be from the future, and I'm inclined to believe her. The night we attacked your planet, a small ship appeared. It destroyed several of my warships before we finally brought it down, but, at the last second, it jettisoned an escape pod. We tracked the pod to the South Pacific, to the island where your young friends were staying. The young woman appeared shortly after that. So far she has managed to elude us. Now, for whatever reason, she has decided to bring herself to me."

"What do you want with her?" Sheppard asked.

"Secrets," Gogue said. "Technology. If she really is from the future--even farther into the future than the time I came from--she may have technologies that have escaped me. Secrets like time travel."

"But you already know how to travel through time," Sheppard said. "Your presence here is proof of that."

"Yes," Gogue said. "You're right. But I can't let other people have that secret, can I?"

"No," Sheppard said. "Of course you can't. They might find a way to stop you, to stop this whole sick plan of yours."

"I've had about all of your insults I can take," Gogue said. "I'm going to enjoy watching you die. Have a nice day." He gestured toward the screen. "And enjoy the show."

CHAPTER 28: Idol of Clay

"How are you feeling, Lex?" Dr. Chambers asked.

"Weak," Lex said. He held up his arms. "My arms are so thin." He was sitting in a reclining bed in the ship's hospital area.

"You'll get your strength back before you know it," Chambers told him. "While you were unconscious, your muscles were receiving electrical stimulation. It kept them from atrophying. We'll begin your rehabilitation later today. In the meanwhile, you've got visitors."

Chambers went to the door.

"Come on in."

Cockrum, Preston, and Harrison entered.

"Preston?" Lex said. "You look different."

"Older and wearier," Preston said. "How do you feel, Lex?"

"That's what everybody keeps asking me," Lex said. "I feel okay. I keep wondering if any of this is real, or if I'll wake up from it too."

"That's perfectly understandable," Dr. Chambers said.

"Are we really on a spaceship?" Lex asked.

"Yes, we are," Preston said.

"Would you like for us to take you on a tour?" Cockrum asked.

"Yeah," Lex said. "I think I would."

"I'll get a chair," Chambers said. "The gravity on this ship is lighter than on Earth, but your muscles still need some time to recuperate."

* * *

Preston pushed the wheelchair up and down the corridors of the space station. Jolie Harrison walked beside Lex and talked with him. He seemed to like her. Cockrum had returned to the bridge.

"I still can't believe we're on a spaceship," Lex said.

"Would you like to look out a window?" Harrison asked him.

"Sure," he said.

"We'll have to go to the zero gravity part of the ship," she told him. "It's the only part that doesn't spin."

"If you looked out the window here," Preston said, "it would be like looking through the door of an old style clothes dryer and realizing you were being tumbled dry."

"The magnetic bands in the wheels of your chair will keep you from floating away," Jolie explained. "Preston and I have magnetic grippers in the soles of our boots."

They rode an elevator car to the zero gravity level. As the car slowed down, they could feel their hair and clothes starting to float.

Jolie's shirt tail drifted up, showing her pale midriff. She let out a squeak of embarrassment and stuffed it into her waistband.

"It's a good thing I'm not wearing a dress," she said.

"I am," Lex said. He stuffed the loose folds of his hospital gown beneath his legs.

The elevator doors opened. Lex rolled out into one of the long hallways that ran along either side of the ship's asteroid cannon. The blast shutters were open. Preston pushed Lex over to the nearest window. He placed his hands on the cold, thick glass and peered out into the void beyond.

"Where are we?" he asked.

"That's Mars to the left," Preston said.

"Will we be passing any closer?" Lex asked.

"On the way back maybe," Jolie said. "We're headed for Saturn now."

"It's unreal," Lex said. "This whole thing is so unreal."

He didn't say anything for a moment.

"Is there anything else we can show you?" Jolie asked.

"I understand General Corbalew is a real person," Lex said, "and that he's somewhere on this ship."

"Yes," Preston said. "I'm afraid he's not the person you thought he was."

"I know that," Lex said. "You told me. I'd still like to meet him."

"Are you sure you want to?" Jolie asked. "It could be upsetting."

"I want to meet him," Lex said.

"I'll okay it with Cockrum," Jolie said.

* * *

Preston waited out in the hall with a security guard as Jolie Harrison pushed Lex's chair into the cargo bay. Heavy boxes, all of them secured by netting, were piled against the walls. Corbalew's life support chamber sat by itself in a corner. Power systems, scrubbers, and control panels were linked to it by snaking hoses and wiring conduits.

"Mr. Corbalew," Harrison said. "You have a visitor."

The mummified figure opened its filmy eyes and peered through the heavy glass of the REGEN tank.

"I see you managed to revive him," he said. The croaking noises inside the tank were translated into words.

"No thanks to you," Harrison said. "He nearly died."

"Too bad," Corbalew said.

"Bad that he nearly died," Harrison said, "or that we saved him?"

"It doesn't matter," Corbalew said. "We got everything we wanted from him. Almost everything anyway."

"You were using me," Lex said, "using me to get information."

"I'm afraid so," Corbalew said. "No hard feelings, I'm sure."

"Where did those memories come from?" Lex asked. "Who was Stefan?"

"He doesn't exist, I'm afraid," Corbalew said. "But he might one day--about three hundred years from now, I think."

"Where did the memories come from?" Lex asked again.

"The only person who can answer that question is a young woman called Nina," he said. "Or is it Neema? That would depend upon who you ask."

"Where is she?" Lex asked.

"Ah," Corbalew said. "Where, indeed? Somewhere on Earth, I think. She has managed to elude us so far. As soon as we find her, you'll be the first to know. Or maybe you won't. If you like, I'll try to get them to preserve her body for you when they're finished with her. She's quite attractive."

"Thanks for bringing me," Lex told Harrison. "Let's get out of here."

"Are you leaving so soon?" Corbalew said. "Does my presence upset you?"

"Your existence upsets me," Harrison said. "Maybe we ought to let Preston pay you another visit."

"My body has almost completely regenerated," Corbalew said. "What are you going to do when I'm no longer helpless, Miss Harrison?"

"Let's go, Lex."

Corbalew made a choking, wheezing noise Harrison recognized as laughter. When the doors of the cargo bay closed and the locks thumped into place, Harrison noticed that Lex had tears on his cheeks.

"I thought he was a good man," he said. "Even when you told me he was a criminal, I didn't really believe it. I thought he might be a good man fighting for a bad cause, but he's not. He's just plain evil."

"I understand," Preston said. "He fooled me once too. He tricked me into betraying the best friends I ever had."

"He tricked me into betraying my whole planet," Lex said. "I told him everything Stefan knew."

CHAPTER 29: Farewell to Earth

Even with a light rain falling, Pirate was sweating as he crossed the airfield. The humidity was oppressive. So was everything else about the transfer station. Every inch of ground was overlaid with concrete. The complex was surrounded by twelve-foot high walls, also concrete. These were guarded by beam weapons mounted on spinning turrets.

The men and women of the base, all dressed in identical gray coveralls, marched around the field like drones. Their faces looked tired, blank, and devoid of emotion. Pirate wondered what had been done to them. Had their minds been dulled with drugs or had they been tortured into submission? Whatever had happened to them, he knew, would happen to him too if Gogue's people caught him and identified him as an infiltrator, a saboteur. The sky overhead was gray and menacing. Pirate saw one of the walking mannequins staring at him and tried not to stare back.

Pirate made his way across the airfield to Terminal C and stood in line with nearly fifty other gray-clad puppets. He saw

Tori and Zapper standing in line in front of him but gave no sign that he recognized them. They passed through a checkpoint. Pirate tried to look nonchalant as invisible beams peeled away his skin to scan his cranial contours, scanned his retinas, analyzed body heat patterns. Pirate felt his pulse starting to race, and wondered if the machines scanned for physiological changes. *Not a bad idea,* he grudgingly admitted to himself.

Pirate made it through that first checkpoint unchallenged and unscathed. He was given a badge and directed to a monotram loading platform. He climbed the platform steps and saw Wendy and Zapper both standing against the rail. They, like the others, pretended to be strangers.

A tram arrived, and its doors whispered open. Pirate and the others climbed inside. He sat down in a padded seat. Wendy sat down beside him but pretended not to notice him. It was, he thought, a lot like their relationship. They were only inches away from each other, but he was forbidden to say anything, to do anything. One misspoken word would bring disaster. The tram whined softly and shifted into motion. Gray concrete walls washed past the windows. As the tram picked up speed, they became a gray blur.

The tram had already stopped five times before it finally arrived at the area printed on Pirate's badge. He climbed out of the tram and into a waiting hallway. So did Wendy and the rest of the Intrepid Force. Hal and Jaina were waiting there. They were dressed in pilots' uniforms. There was no sign of Neema or Jared. The tram pulled into motion and rolled away. Zapper sighed and shook his head. He started to say something but thought better of it.

Looking as gray and depressed as the rest of the bizarre shadow realm they had found themselves in, Pirate and the others walked down the corridor and stepped through a hatch, through an open airlock, and into the passenger compartment of a waiting shuttle. The heavy airlock door slammed shut behind them.

"Everybody take your seats," Hal said. "I'll check the cargo hold." Jaina stepped through a hatch into the pilot's compartment.

Pirate, Wendy, and the others sank into heavily padded black seats. They pulled down heavy shoulder harnesses and strapped them into place. Hal disappeared through a hatch in the rear of the passenger compartment. Pirate looked out through thick glass at the gray, gloomy world beyond. Drops of rain left distorted snail tracks on the window. Pirate felt Wendy touch his hand briefly. He turned and looked at her. She smiled for an instant and then looked away. Hal returned a moment later. He stepped into the pilot's compartment with Jaina and the door closed behind him.

Twenty minutes later, the spaceplane shot down the runway and lifted into a gray sky. The concrete world receded below it. Finally a wall of fog blotted it out altogether.

Powerful thrusters hurled the plane skyward. It punched through the clouds into a serene blue sky. The dark world beneath the clouds seemed unreal. The craft climbed higher and higher, and the blue of the sky faded to cold, inky black. The weight of gravity slowly lifted as the unnatural weightlessness of space descended. Bright objects filled the dark gulf over Earth's blue expanse. Space was full of steel daggers. They were ready to drop through the clouds and plunge themselves into the planet's living heart. The reality of the ships in orbit, of the corrupted defense platforms, sank in as Pirate saw the steely armada hanging in orbit. He noticed the others gazing grimly through their windows.

Vector station loomed ahead. The place seemed both hauntingly familiar and strangely alien. Pirate felt his pulse quicken as the space plane engaged braking thrusters and glided slowly toward the docking platform.

Dear God, he prayed. *Don't let us die here. Not now. Not with so much depending on us.*

Heavy doors closed around the craft and shut out the cold void of open space. Tethered by cables, the spaceplane glided down a long passageway and latched itself to a waiting dock. Then it sat still. Several minutes passed. Zapper unbuckled his harness and rose to his feet.

"Please stay in your seats," Jaina's voice said through hidden speakers. "We're awaiting security clearance."

"What's going on here?" Zapper whispered.

Hal and Jaina emerged from the pilots' cabin.

"Is everything all right?" Mike asked.

"I think so," Hal said. "Just a little delay."

The outer airlock door hissed open. They heard footsteps in the airlock's narrow passage. The inner door opened. Five security guards stepped into the passenger compartment. All of them were wearing black jumpsuits and helmets and carrying rifles. One of them wore a gold armband.

"Don't move," the one with the armband instructed. "Your attempt to infiltrate this base has failed. You will accompany us to holding cells until the security chief can decide what to do with you."

"There must be some kind of mistake," Hal said. "We were sent here."

"You manipulated the crew assignments," the guard said. "Gave yourselves false identities. Did you think we wouldn't recognize the Intrepid Force?"

"I don't know what you're talking about," Hal said. He didn't sound very convincing.

"Hassim," the man with the armband ordered. "You and Corbin check the cargo hold."

"Yes, sir."

Two of the men vanished into the hatch in the back of the ship. They looked around the narrow room at the pile of boxes there. From inside of one of them, they heard a loud thump.

"Corbin," Hassim ordered. "Open it. There's someone inside."

Corbin nodded. He stepped over to the box. The words "Danger: Explosive Hazard" were printed on the box in red letters. Corbin carefully released the straps that held the lid in place. He opened the lid.

An explosion slammed Corbin and Hassim to the deck and a swarm of silvery nanite dust flew out of the box and filled the cargo hold.

"Arm band" and the others spun around at the sound of the explosion. Mike ripped the gun from Arm band's hand and knocked a second man to the deck with a mighty kick. The third man backed toward the airlock. Tori's replenished swarm engulfed him. Tiny needles injected him with anesthetic gel. He fell to the deck.

"Let's get out of here," Pirate said. "Get the guns."

"Where's Neema?" Hal asked.

"Neema!" Tori yelled.

"Check the hold," Hal said. "She may have been hurt."

"Got it," Zapper said. He ran back into the cargo hold. A moment later his head popped through the door. "I don't see her," he said. "But I got us some more guns."

"She's not in there?" Hal asked. He ran back into the hold. "What about Jared?"

"I don't see either of them," Zapper said.

"We've got to get out of here," Jaina said.

They rushed through the airlock into the narrow tunnel beyond. By the time they emerged into the familiar gray corridors of *Vector* station, alarms were going off all around them.

Intruder alert. Intruder alert. Terminal C-5. Terminal C-5.

"Welcome home," Zapper said.

Armed guards swarmed into the hallway.

"Fire at will," Pirate said.

The air rippled with concussion bursts. Silver nanites swarmed the guards like angry hornets. Pirate and Wendy dodged through a doorway into a side corridor. A concussion burst slammed Zapper to the deck. He lay still. Pirate turned back. "Come on!" Wendy yelled. Pirate turned and ran. Wendy pulled a piece of grating from the lower part of the corridor wall. She and Pirate dropped through into the dark, narrow crawlspace beyond. Pirate pulled the grating back into place. He watched as booted feet ran past. He saw Zapper, Jaina, Hal, and Mike dragged along the floor. Who knew if they were unconscious or dead?

Pirate ducked back into the shadows. He and Wendy held each other as they watched their friends disappear down the corridor. They had warned each other that it might be like this.

Pirate heard movement in the tunnel. He started to turn. A flash from a shock pistol flared in the darkness. Wendy slumped against a wall and fell to the floor. Pirate watched in horror as a familiar figure emerged from the darkness into the gray light. He raised his pistol, started to fire.

* * *

Twenty guards, all of them dressed in black body armor and helmets, trained their weapons on their five captives. Hal, Zapper, Mike, Tori, and Jaina trudged warily though *Vector's* spaceport. A man in a black, hooded cowl and a silver pendant, led the patrol.

"This way, please," he ordered. He marched the captives up to the station's two security gates. A second group of men in black waited on the other side. A man in a lab coat sat at a console with a bank of monitors.

"Now," the man with the cloak said. "You will each remove your clothing and step through."

"Now wait a minute," Zapper said. Pistols were pointed at him.

"You will then dress yourselves in the clothing provided on the other side," the man continued. "If you have pretensions of modesty or chivalry, the men may turn their backs as the women go through first."

"The men will go through first," Hal said.

"If that is your wish," the man shrugged.

The men stepped forward.

"No peekin'," Zapper whispered to Jaina as he walked past her. Jaina didn't seem to hear. She just stood chewing nervously on her right index finger.

Hal, Mike, and Zapper stripped away their clothing. Zapper and Mike hurried through the scanners. Hal moved with the slow dignity of a man who refused to be humiliated. When Mike stepped through, the machine sent off warnings.

"I've got cybernetic implants," Mike sighed.

"Two guards will watch him at all times," the man in black ordered. "Let him pass. If he tries to resist, kill him immediately."

Zapper and Hal both set off the scanner also.

"Do all of you have implants?" a man in a medical uniform asked.

"Pretty much," Zapper said.

Finally the men were all standing on the other side dressed in disposable black jumpsuits and rubber-soled socks.

"Now, ladies," the guard ordered.

Hal and Mike looked away as the girls undressed and stepped through. Hal thought he saw Zapper taking a sideways glance.

"Zapper!" he whispered.

The guards' faces were hidden behind their tinted masks, but Hal was sure that they were smiling, enjoying the humiliation they were putting them through. His soldier's soul burned with anger. He was an officer in the Interplanetary Guard. Nobody was going to treat him like this and get away with it. The scanners went off when Jaina stepped through.

Zapper started involuntarily, turned, and saw her standing there beneath the arch with her arms covering her chest. He quickly looked away and felt his face grow hot. She had seen him. Their eyes had met.

"Brain implants," one of the men said.

"Two guards will watch her also," the leader ordered.

Moments later the women were standing fully clothed alongside the men. No one seemed to want to look at anyone else. Even clothed, Jaina still kept her arms folded tightly against her chest. She was crying silently. Tori, on the other hand, seemed to be fighting a case of the giggles.

A second group of guards and robots took over the "tour." The leader of this group had an Australian accent. The humbled group was herded into a spacious lobby with restaurants, shops, and a baggage claim area. It was a place all of them had visited before. During their training for the team, they had eaten in the restaurants, bought gifts for friends in the shops, and played in the arcades. Those days seemed so far away.

Tori giggled.

"Quit it, Tori," Zapper growled.

She pinched him on the behind and he shoved her. The others looked on in total disbelief. Tori shoved back. Guns pointed at them.

"Try anything like that again, and I'll kill you," one of the guards said coldly. They reached a bank of elevators.

"Now," the Australian ordered. "Step into these elevators."

Three large elevator cabs stood open and waiting for them. Guards stepped in ahead of them and pointed weapons at them. More guards motioned them inside.

Tori shoved Zapper hard. He lost his balance and fell into two of the guards. Then, suddenly, he grabbed them both and shocked them unconscious. Tori threw her ninety-pound frame into one of the men and knocked him off his feet. Zapper grabbed a pistol and the others started to leap into action.

"Seal the room!" the man in the robe cried.

"Kill them!" one of the guards yelled.

"No!" the man in the robe said. "Gas! Use the gas!"

Mike flung Zapper to the floor as the wall behind him collapsed. He rolled to his feet, sprang into the air, and took down three guards with kicks, elbow smashes, and lightning fast punches.

Zapper fired into a knot of guards. A shockwave flattened them like a tidal wave of energy.

"The gas!" the man in the robe kept yelling. "The gas! The gas!"

"Blow the hatch!" Hal yelled. "Shoot out the hatch!"

Zapper started to raise the rifle and realized his arms were no longer responding. He tried to step forward and found himself free falling a thousand feet toward a tangled forest of gray carpet. His jet pack had failed him. He was falling fast, but he still felt a sense of peace as the floor rushed up to meet him. Finally someone smacked him across the face with a pillow made of dirty carpet and the lights went out.

* * *

Pirate had dragged Wendy's limp body through what seemed like miles of labyrinthine crawl spaces. Pallid splinters of light poured through the occasional vent, but most of the tunnel was completely dark.

"Are we about there?" Pirate whispered.

"Quiet," Jared's voice answered from ahead of him. "Almost."

Five minutes later Jared lifted aside a loose square of sheet metal. Pirate watched as the gray shape of his invisibility armor dropped through a narrow hatch and into the dimly lit chamber below. He lowered Wendy feet first through the hole. Jared caught her and lowered her to the deck. Pirate dropped through behind him. He found himself in a small, gray room little larger than a walk-in closet.

Neema sat cross-legged in a corner. On her lap was a touchtronic computer console not much thicker than a sheet of paper. A thin filament of cable ran from the device to a hole in the wall.

"Now," Pirate said, anger rising in his voice, "I suppose you're going to tell me why you shot Wendy."

"She will be all right," Neema said, not looking up from her work. "Her brain has been modified. Gogue was using signals from her neural linkages to spy on us."

"What?" Pirate said.

"Gogue's been watching us the whole time," Jared said, "through Wendy. Neema knew about it."

Pirate was too stunned to say anything at first. He folded a piece of packing material into a makeshift pillow and slipped in beneath Wendy's head.

"Why didn't you tell me?" he asked.

"To keep you from giving anything away," Neema said.

"So you tricked us," Pirate said, "like we tricked the rest of the group?"

"I only told you what you needed to know," Neema said.

"So that's what's been wrong with Wendy?" Pirate said. "Not Landers' Syndrome?"

"It happened the night Astrolus captured us," Jared said.

"What about you?" Pirate asked. "They captured you too."

"The implant I placed in his head acted as a kind of circuit breaker," Neema said. "It shut down his brain to protect him."

"How did you two get here?" Pirate asked. "You weren't on the shuttle."

"That was part of the plan too," Jared said. "We used Wendy's implant to send Gogue false information. Then we took an earlier flight."

"And what are you doing now?" Pirate asked.

"Tying into the station's computers," Neema said. "Please be quiet now. This is not as easy as it looks."

"Sorry."

* * *

The detention cell was icy cold and completely dark. The walls and floor were made of metal.

"What's this around my ankles?" Zapper groaned.

"So you're awake now," Hal said.

"I've been awake," Zapper said. "I just didn't have anything to say. What's this around my ankles?"

"Shackles," Hal said. "We've all got them."

"It's cold in here," Zapper said.

"At least they gave us these jumpsuits," Jaina's voice said in the darkness. Her teeth were chattering.

"They don't offer much warmth," Tori said.

"That's not what I meant," Jaina said. "That search was so humiliating."

"Hey," Zapper said. "You ain't got anything to be ashamed of. Not that I looked."

"Always digging a deeper hole," Mike said.

"We've got worse things to worry about than our modesty," Hal said.

"At least the gas didn't make me sick this time," Zapper said.

"What you did out there was crazy," Hal said.

"It was my fault," Tori said. "Zapper just went along with it. And Mike. Did you see those moves?"

"Thanks," Mike said. "You did pretty well yourself."

"It was crazy," Hal said. "I couldn't have done it better myself. You guys should have been in the Interplanetary Guard."

"What do you think they'll do to us now?" Tori asked.

"That depends on whether they've caught Neema or not," Hal said. "If they catch her, they'll probably kill us. If they don't, they'll keep us alive for questioning."

"Do you think they're monitoring us?" Mike asked.

"Oh, yeah," Hal said. "You can count on it."

"This floor is so cold," Tori said. "I keep changing feet, but now I can't feel either one."

"Stand on my feet," Hal said. "Maybe it will warm both of us up some."

"I think we ought to hug together," Zapper said.

"You would," Tori said.

"It's a good idea," Jaina said. "I'll hug with Mike."

"I've got Hal," Tori said.

"No," Zapper said. "Wait a minute! This isn't a couples thing! I meant all of us together."

No one said anything.

"So how come nobody wants to hug me?" Zapper asked.

"Quiet!" Tori said. "Somebody's coming."

CHAPTER 30: The Fight to Be Free

Sheppard had been pushing against his shackles for--for how long? Twelve hours? Two days? A week? He had pulled every human muscle he had left. He had torn muscles, snapped tendons, shredded ligaments. His body trembled with every feverish, shuddering breath. He cried out to God, begged His master for help. Nothing came.

It was hopeless. The leather straps had been strong, but he had been able to rip them free. The frame that held him now was practically indestructible. Even after an eternity of struggling against it, the heavy metal bands showed no sign of give, no sign of fatigue.

Sheppard cried out in rage. It sounded like the howl of a lost spirit, a beaten animal. It ended in a sobbing whimper. So this was what he had been reduced to.

The ghosts started to form. A parade of mocking phantoms poured through the feverish miasma of his consciousness. He had no way of knowing if they were real, products of Gogue's synthetic reality devices, or simple hallucinations. A figure in a black Astrolus robe stood in the shadows and stared at him. It never spoke, but its eerie stare made his skin feel like ice.

"Stop it, Gogue," Sheppard snarled. "Stop it. It won't work." He heard Wendy crying, begging someone to stop torturing her.

"Look what they did to me," she sobbed. "Look what they did to me." She stumbled into the room in a shredded hospital gown. Her brown hair had been completely shorn. Half of her face was horribly bruised. The skin coverings had been peeled away from her bionic arms and legs. A hulking figure grabbed her from behind, forced her good arm behind her back. He grabbed her by the chin and twisted her head around. Then he turned and smiled at Sheppard. His face was rubbery, an artificial representation of life.

"Brunkert," Sheppard gasped. "Stop it!" he cried. "Stop it! Stop it! Stop it! I can't take it anymore. Leave me alone. Just leave me alone."

"They're not really here," someone said. "You're only dreaming." The voice was deep. The accent sounded Indian. Sheppard knew that voice.

"Ahadri?" he gasped. Brunkert and Wendy had vanished, and Ahadri was standing in front of him in the dim light of his cell. "I'm so sorry about what happened to you," Sheppard sobbed. "If I'd only left you in India."

"You saved me," Ahadri said. "You gave me dignity and friends--and helped me find God."

The giant pulled at Sheppard's shackles.

"We have to get you out of here," Ahadri said. "The others need you."

"I can't," Sheppard said. "I've been trying for days to get out of here, but I can't."

"You have to," Ahadri said. "Come on. I can help you."

"You're not really here," Sheppard said. "You're dead. This is a dream, another one of Gogue's illusions."

"One last time," Ahadri told him. "Like you told us in training when we were too tired to take another step. One last time. Come on."

Sheppard started to strain against his bonds. They were as immovable as ever.

"I can't," he said. "They're too strong."

"Come on," Ahadri said. "You have to. Come on."

Sheppard took a deep, shuddering breath. Squeezing his eyes shut and biting down hard, he bent himself with all his might against the manacles that were holding his arms. He opened his eyes for an instant. Ahadri, he noticed, had grabbed them and was twisting against them. He felt the bands starting to give. He closed his eyes and pushed with all that he had. Sparks and flashes of red exploded through the darkness behind his closed eyelids. He thought his arms would rip from their sockets, but he kept right on pushing. He felt something snap, felt the manacles twist open. He pulled his arms free.

"Good," Ahadri said. "Very good. Now your feet. We've got to get them free. I'll help you."

The bands around his ankles were not nearly as strong as the ones that had bound his wrists. They twisted apart as he strained against them. He pulled his feet free. His legs felt like lead. He could hardly move them.

"Now," Ahadri said. "We have to get out of here quickly. There is only one guard. You must hurry."

Sheppard stumbled into the next room. There was a man in body armor. He was bent over tying one of his boots. His rifle was sitting on a control panel beside him. Sheppard lunged into the room. The guard looked up, his eyes wide with surprise. He sprang for his rifle. Sheppard's punch took him down like a sledge hammer.

"Take his rifle," Ahadri said. "Hurry."

Sheppard grabbed the rifle. He checked the pulse of the man he had struck. He was still alive. Sheppard punched a button on the control panel, and the cell door opened.

Sheppard lumbered out into the corridor. It was empty. Sheppard recognized the hallway. It was two decks below the security offices. He turned around and looked back. Through the open door he could see the security guard lying unconscious.

"Ahadri?"

Sheppard looked around. The giant was nowhere to be seen.

"Ahadri?" he said again.

Silence answered him. Ahadri was gone. He had never been there. The weight of his friend's death settled on him once again. In the distance, Sheppard could hear footsteps. He looked down at his ragged jumpsuit, at the rifle in his hand, and wondered if he was still in his cell. No, he decided. No. This was real. He was not dreaming. He really was free of his bonds and standing in the hallway outside of his cell with a rifle.

The others need you. That was what Ahadri had told him. He thought about his hideous vision of Wendy being tortured and abused, crying for him to help her. The memory of that helpless frustration still burned within him. Every system in his body begged for rest, but that vision drove him on.

I'm coming, Wendy. Just hang on, sweetheart. Tell the others I'm coming for them too.

He lumbered on down the hall.

* * *

A heavy boot kicked Zapper's feet out from under him. He tried to catch himself but his hands were bound. He slammed hard against a bulkhead and slid down onto the deck.

"Get up," the guard said. "Get up!" Zapper started to rise. The guard kicked Zapper hard in the ribs. He fell back against the bulkhead and lay there gasping.

"Stop it!" Jaina cried.

Hal, Tori, and Mike started to surge forward. The other guard raised his concussion rifle.

"Stay where you are," he ordered.

Zapper braced himself against the wall and slowly pushed himself upright. He gasped for breath.

"Now keep up," the guard who had kicked him said, "Or you'll get some more."

"I'd walk faster," Zapper said. "But some idiot chained my legs together."

"Zapper," Mike said. "Shut up, man. He just wants an excuse to kill you."

An elevator door opened beside them. Inside was a big, wild-eyed man with a ragged beard.

"What the--?" one of the guards started to say. A concussion blast rippled the air and slammed him hard against the wall. He sagged to the floor like a bag of laundry. The other guard spun around, his rifle aimed. Mike, still bound, threw himself into the man's path and knocked his rifle aside. The guard took a concussion burst to the head. His helmet flew off and rolled down the hall like a severed head. The man toppled to the floor.

"Hey, guys," Mike said. "It's Reverend Sheppard."

"Sheppard?" Tori said, suddenly recognizing the wild man with the rifle.

"Sheppard?" Zapper said. "Good gravy, Preacher! You look horrible."

"Thank you," Sheppard said. He managed a smile. "I don't feel so great either. Are you guys okay?"

"Fine," Zapper said. "Just like a vacation on the beach only with torture chambers."

"I know what you mean," Sheppard said. His voice was thick. He was staying on his feet by force of will. "Where are the others?"

"Pirate and Wendy got away," Zapper said.

"What about Jared?"

"Jared wasn't on board the shuttle," Hal said. "Neither was Neema. We haven't seen them since we got here."

Sheppard nodded. He bent over and panted for a moment. "Are you all right?" Mike asked.

"No," he said. "But I think I can hold together long enough to rescue the girls." He stopped and caught his breath. "Do you remember when I was training you," he stopped and gasped, " I told you how to get around the station without being seen."

"You mean the cra--," Zapper started to say.

"No," Sheppard said. "Don't say it. Don't say anything in front of me."

"What's wrong?" Hal asked.

"There's an implant in my head," Sheppard said. "Gogue can see and hear everything that goes on around me. You've got them too, but yours are dormant."

"How did this happen?" Mike asked. "When did they do it?"

"Last Christmas," Sheppard said. "Wendy and Jared were captured by Astrolus. We went to rescue them and ended up being captured ourselves, wired into their machines."

"Yeah," Hal said. "Everybody but Tori and Jaina. They were outside."

"Wendy and Jared were in there the longest," Sheppard said. "Astrolus had time to complete the process with them. The police broke in before they could finish with the rest of us."

"So we can't say anything in front of Wendy either?" Mike said.

"You have to knock her out," Sheppard said. "If you don't, she'll give you away."

"What about Jared?" Zapper asked.

"He's immune," Sheppard said. "When they tried to actuate the implant, something took over and shut down his brain until he could fight it off."

"Why?" Hal asked.

"I don't know," Sheppard said. "Neither does Gogue."

"So that's why he was in that coma," Zapper said. "Makes sense. You know, Neema said. . . "

"No," Hal said. "Don't talk about it."

"So what do we do with you?" Tori said.

"Leave me behind," Sheppard said.

"No, sir," Hal said. "I'll carry you if I have to, but we're not leaving you here. Can Gogue read your mind or just see and hear through you?"

"He can't read my mind," Sheppard said.

"All right," Hal said. "Close your eyes. We're going to take you somewhere safe. We'll come back for you later. Meanwhile don't look at anything that might give you away."

"I understand," Sheppard said.

"It's good to see ya, Preacher," Zapper said. "Things haven't been the same without you."

* * *

Pirate shifted uneasily from one foot to the other as Neema worked feverishly in the corner of the tiny chamber. The room was hot and tight and it did not have a bathroom. Pirate could hear Neema talking to herself in some other language--Russian maybe--as she tapped away on the wafer-thin console on the floor in front of her. Jared knelt down behind her and massaged her shoulders but didn't say anything.

"How's it coming?" Pirate finally asked.

"We have a problem," Neema said. "I was afraid of this. Gogue is not on board this station. He's somewhere else. Somewhere far away. I was afraid of this."

"So what do we do now?" Pirate asked.

"We have to get off this station," Neema said.

"Get off the station?" Pirate said, fighting down his urge to shout. "We lost most of the team getting on. And what about all those ships out there?"

"I have a plan," Neema said.

"Great," Pirate said. "I can hardly wait to hear it."

* * *

"Technical review," Hal said. "There are crawlspaces on this station that don't show up on any of the monitors. They were put there in case of something like this. Only a few of us know where they are."

Hal, Zapper, Mike, and Tori were squeezing their way through a narrow access tunnel that ran beside one of the bulkheads. The passage was choked with air pipes and power conduits. Jaina had stayed behind with Sheppard.

"Where are we going?" Zapper asked.

"I thought we might just pay a little visit to the old armory," Hal said. "Pick up a few things that might be useful to us."

"Body armor," Zapper said. "Robot suits. Sonic grenades. Just like your neighborhood grocer used to carry."

"Let's go, then," Mike said.

"It's a good idea," a wry voice said. "Too bad Gogue thought of it first."

Jared appeared in the corridor ahead of them.

"Jared!" Hal said. "Man, I nearly shot you!"

"We've got to get off this station," Jared said. "Neema came here to find Gogue, but he's not here."

"What did you say about our equipment?" Tori said.

"There's nothing left in the armory," Jared said. "I've already been there."

"So where are we going?" Tori asked.

"One of the shuttle bays," Jared said. "Follow me."

"We've got to get Jaina and Reverend Sheppard," Mike said.

"Sheppard?" Jared said. "He's here?"

"Yeah," Hal said. "Poor guy looks like he's been through hell."

"Lead the way then," Jared said.

Then they heard the alarms.

CHAPTER 31: Fire in the Hole

A screaming wall of sound assaulted Neema's senses as she crawled through the metal rabbit's hole on her knees and elbows. Alarms were going off all over the station. Droning voices called for security teams.

Neema's heart hammered in her chest. She only had a few seconds to make it to the shuttle port or her friends would be forced to leave without her. If she had taken a wrong tunnel, missed a turn, she would be trapped on the station and abandoned to Gogue's inhuman torture. Neema had seen bodies in the station's sick bay, horrors she would revisit in nightmares for the rest of her life.

Neema squirmed to the right, kicked open an access panel, and dropped through space to the floor of a metal cavern.

"Neema," Zapper said. "Good to see ya, darlin'."

A sleek silver craft filled most of the chamber. This was a mid-range exploratory cruiser. It was larger than a shuttle but not quite large enough for comfortable journeys between planets. It could reach Mars in about six months, but the trip would not have been a pleasant one. Mike and Tori were welding the shuttle bay doors shut. Cutting beams were already starting to burn through from the other side. Hal, in his exobot armor, was inserting explosive charges around the hinges of the main hatchway, the giant gate to outer space. Blasting out the doors with the ship's particle weapons was too dangerous.

"Everybody inside," Hal said. "I'm about to blow the seal."

Neema, Zapper, Tori, and Mike hurried through the airlock and slammed the inner door shut behind them. Neema lurched down a short hallway. Electric doors parted. She stepped onto the ship's bridge.

Pirate was sitting at the captain's workstation, punching madly away on a console. Jared spun around as Neema entered. He ran to her and embraced her a little self-consciously.

Jaina sat strapped into a chair. She was wringing her hands. A giant viewscreen showed the massive space doors in front of them.

"Where are Wendy and Sheppard?" Neema asked as she sat down beside Jaina..

"In medical," Jaina said. "I've got them both under heavy sedation."

"Stations," Pirate said. "Everyone take your stations."

"Hal's blown the space doors," Jaina said.

The doors began to open. Hal's exobot dodged away from the doors. Its magnetized hands and feet gripped the floor of the shuttle port as he fought the rush of escaping air.

Hal pounded his way to the airlock. The outer doors closed behind him.

"Hal's in," Jared said.

"Engines powered up for launch," Pirate said.

A flash of fire grazed the ship's outer hull. It had come from outside. The space doors parted like giant curtains. An asteroid smasher hung in space outside the station. It's weapons ports were burning hot.

"He can't really open up on us until we're clear of the station," Zapper said. "I hope."

"Neema," Pirate said. "Didn't you say something about a diversion?"

Musical tones sounded as Neema's fingers drummed the control panel in front of her.

* * *

Twenty-four automated defense platforms hung in Earth's orbit like sleeping beasts. Their particle cannons were inactive, but their sites were set on the planet's population centers. They and the ships that surrounded them had held the planet under siege for weeks. Suddenly those sleeping beasts awoke. In a deadly ballet, their thrusters spun them about. Power flowed into their deadly cannons. Their sites locked onto the invading ships.

"Chief!" one of the operations technicians cried. "CHIEF!"

Operations Chief Harker spun around. He saw the automated platforms targeting Gogue's ships, but there was no time to react. Jets of invisible flame leaped across the void and slashed into the orbiting armada. The ships were big and well-shielded, but the attack had taken them completely by surprise. His life, he knew, would be over in minutes if he could not find a way to salvage this situation.

"What's happened?" Harker demanded. "What's happened?"

"Something's taken control of those platforms," the technician cried.

"Get it back," Harker cried. "Get it back now!"

Technicians and engineers punched furiously at the panels before them.

* * *

The ship outside the space doors spun aside as an energy beam ripped a chunk out of its hull.

"Let's go!" Hal yelled as he burst into the bridge.

Pirate keyed in the final command and the *Viking* burst free of its moorings and fell out into space. The ship looped around *Vector* and shot out toward the moon. Giant asteroid smashers and warships bucked, pitched, and unleashed their deadly energies as the automated platforms heaped their mindless wrath upon them. The *Viking* dodged through them in an erratic pattern.

"That's your diversion?" Mike said.

"You took control of the automated defenses," Pirate said, "turned them on Gogue's fleet."

"She's gonna wipe out the whole fleet," Zapper said.

"One little lady saves the planet," Hal said.

"It won't stop them," Neema said. "This will only buy us a moment's time. The ships are too powerful."

A flash erupted and one of the defense platforms spun out of its orbit. Burning pieces broke away as it plunged down through the Earth's atmosphere.

"One of the ships is firing on us," Jaina said.

"Time for Stage Two," Zapper said.

An energy beam sliced through the ship's hull. The craft bucked. Another beam struck home and a flash of cosmic fire lit up the eternal night like a nova. Chunks of debris rained down on the attacking ship's hull.

* * *

The *Viking* had been drifting in space for nearly eight hours. Thruster bursts had pushed it out of the search area and around the rim of the moon.

"You think they fell for it?" Zapper asked. "Pirate?"

"What?" Pirate raised his head from the console. He had fallen asleep there.

"Do you think we got away with it?" Zapper asked.

"Who knows?" Pirate said. "You can't count on anything when it comes to enemies like them."

"It was a good plan though," Tori said, her voice tired. "Filling the cargo bay with explosives and dumping it just at the right time."

"Yeah," Pirate said. "It was a good plan. Jared and Neema are the best."

"I just wish we could have finished the job," Zapper said. "We had them on the ropes, and then we ran away."

"We never had them 'on the ropes' as you say," Neema said. She had come through the door just in time to hear

Zapper's comment. "Those defense platforms were a diversion. Nothing more."

"We managed to damage six of their ships," Mike said, "and take out all twenty-four of those platforms that used to be pointed at Earth. Not bad."

"They still have the planet under siege," Neema said. "And they have more ships being refitted somewhere out in space."

"Did you find out where?" Pirate asked.

"No," Neema said. "I'm sorry."

"Don't be sorry," Pirate said. "Did you think you could save the planet by yourself?"

Her chin trembled.

"Yes," she said. "I thought I could." She began to weep. Jared and the others moved to comfort her.

"You used us as a diversion," Hal said. "We were decoys?"

"Yes," Neema said.

"Quack, quack," Zapper said.

"What did you think you would find on *Vector?*" Pirate asked.

"Gogue," Neema said. "I thought, 'If I can find him, I can destroy him.' Even if I had to destroy *Vector* station and all of us, I was going to destroy him."

"Why didn't you?" Mike asked.

"He wasn't there," Neema said. "He has simulations--computer-generated replicas of himself--on every ship and station, but he was not there."

"So where is he?" Zapper asked.

"I don't know," she said.

"So where do we go from here?" Pirate asked.

"Titan," Neema said.

"Titan?" Hal said. "You mean the moon Titan? The one that orbits Saturn?"

"Yes," Neema said.

"What's on Titan?" Tori asked.

"I'm not sure," Neema said. "While I was still on board my ship, I monitored Corbalew's conversations with one of Gogue's computer-generated replicas. They spoke of an expedition to Titan and of a ship, the *Arthur Conan Doyle*."

"Arthur Conan Doyle?" Zapper said. "The author of Sherlock Holmes?"

"It fits," Pirate said. "A mystery author for a mysterious situation. We'll check the database, see if there's a reference to it."

"I already did," Neema said. "It's one of DeFalco's ships. It disappeared during a survey expedition two years ago."

"An expedition to where?" Tori asked.

"Saturn," Neema said. "That's why we have to go there."

"Saturn's a long way from here," Hal said. "Earth's ninety-three million miles from the sun. Saturn's over eight hundred million. We're going to need something faster than this little ship to get us there."

"I know," Neema said. "That's something I can help us with."

"What do you plan to do?" Zapper asked. "Just whistle us up a starship?"

"Yes," Neema said. "Exactly."

* * *

It was night shift aboard the *Intrepid*. Captain Nancy Butler raised her mug to her lips. The tea was cold. It had been cold for hours.

"Captain Butler," Fairbanks said suddenly.

"Yes, Charles."

"I just got a signal from Neema," Fairbanks said. "They're putting some distance between themselves and the fleet. They're going to rendezvous with us in about twelve hours."

"Thank you, Charles," Captain Nancy Butler said. She set down her mug. "That *is* good news. Echo, set a course."

"Yes, ma'am," Echo Yazzi said.

"Wright," the captain said into the microphone on the arm of her chair. "Wright?"

"Yes, ma'am, Captain. What is it?" Wright sounded out of breath.

"What are you doing down there?" Butler asked.

"A little toilet time if you want to know the truth," Wright said. "That pizza last night was more than I could handle."

"Sigmund," Butler said. "That's already more than I want to know. How's that stealth technology coming along?"

"It's passed all the preliminary tests," Wright said.

"Are we ready to use it for real?" she asked.

"What did you have in mind?" Wright asked.

"We need to swing within a million miles of Earth and pick up a few friends," Butler told him. "How's that?"

Silence answered the question.

"Sigmund?" the captain said. "You there?"

"Maybe I better do a couple more tests," Wright said.

"Make it quick," Butler told him.

"Yes, ma'am."

Moments later, the *Intrepid* engaged thrusters and shot back toward Earth.

* * *

The *Intrepid* looked huge as it hung in space above the *Viking*. Hal coaxed the smaller ship toward the open doors of the shuttle bay and, with the chime of a button, released the thrusters to the precise control of the ship's computers.

"The Hotel Claustrophobia," Zapper said. "I never thought I'd be glad to see that hulk again. Neema, darlin', you did okay."

"Thank you, Zapper," Neema said.

"Captain Butler," Pirate said. "You're a sight for sore eyes, as the saying goes."

"Thanks," Captain Butler said. "You all are looking pretty good yourselves."

Moments later Pirate and the others stepped through an airlock and out into the *Intrepid*'s familiar halls. Only weeks before, this ship had taken them to Venus. Now they were back on board and headed for Saturn. Only God Himself knew what was ahead for them now, but it felt good to be back.

CHAPTER 32: The Watchers

Sheppard was groggy. The drugs Dr. Sanchez had used to neutralize the implant had left him with a splitting headache and a drunken clumsiness. Wendy lay sleeping in sickbay, her mind pumped full of drugs. Her implants had been growing for months. They were more deeply embedded into her brain than Sheppard's had been and were taking longer to deaden. At Sheppard's request, Captain Butler had summoned the Intrepid Force to a small lounge across from the sickbay. The group was playful, almost giddy. Zapper traded barbs with Hal, Mike, and Tori and made remarks about Jared and Neema who were cuddled together in the same chair. Pirate and Jaina looked worried.

"The good news," Sheppard told the group, "is that Wendy's going to be all right."

"And the bad news is that Gogue has watched everything we've done since Christmas?" Zapper asked, incredulous.

"Yes," Sheppard said, his voice still rough from sleep. "Everything Wendy saw or heard."

"The implants mimic the host's DNA," Jaina said. "They're almost undetectable, even when you're looking for them."

"Unless you hit 'em with an electric charge," Zapper said.

"Right," Jaina said. "I noticed anomalies in Wendy's brain scans that night on the beach when Zapper jolted her."

"I'm sorry about that," Zapper said. "I made a fool of myself."

"It's all right, man," Mike said. "What Jaina is saying is that some good actually came out of it."

"Right," Jaina said. "Whenever I hit Wendy with a low-level electric charge, the implants react to it. That's how I'm able to detect them."

"But how could she get a signal out without us detecting it?" Jared asked.

"Wendy, Mike, and I all have brain stem implants," Sheppard said. "Wendy and I have bionic prosthetics. Mike has neuro-muscular implants. The stem implants allow our brains to communicate with our bodies. They're putting out signals constantly. A transmission could easily be broken into code and hidden in the signals our brains send to the artificial parts of our bodies."

"So everything you do or see would be transmitted," Pirate said. "Can they read your thoughts?"

"Yes and no," Neema said. "That technology will not come until later, and I do not believe he has been able to develop it yet. Some of you have equipment that you can control by sending signals directly from your brains. You think about firing a weapon or activating night vision, and your equipment responds. However the scanners that allow you to direct your equipment can not be used to scan your memories. They don't work that way. They're only keyed to recognize and respond to the changes in your brain scans created by certain specific thoughts."

"Like the way synthetic reality works," Jared offered.

"Yes," Neema said. "With synthetic reality, your brain's signals to your body are intercepted by scanners in an immersion suit and sent to an artificial body that exists inside cyberspace. In turn, signals from that artificial body are sent to your brain while the signals from your real body are minimized by chemicals similar to the ones that keep us from running in place when we're asleep."

"Jaina's parents were working with DeFalco's entertainment division to develop the next generation of synthetic reality," Jared said. "Synthetic reality without the immersion suit. All you'd need was nanofilaments injected into the bloodstream. They would intertwine with the user's nervous system and the signals could be sent directly from the brain into cyberspace."

"So people would have to undergo brain surgery to play computer games?" Mike said. "Seems like that would limit your market."

"They wouldn't call it surgery," Jaina said. "It would really only be an injection. Once inside, the nanofilaments would find their way to the right part of the brain and lodge there."

"And once almost everybody had those nanofilaments implanted in their brains," Pirate said, "it would only be a short jump to mind control. The cables are in place and all you need is the transmitter."

"But isn't that illegal?" Tori asked.

"Implanting full fledged synthetic reality transmitters is illegal," Pirate said. "Theoretically these nanofilaments wouldn't be able to transmit over long distances, only to interface with the machines."

"Yes," Sheppard said. "According to law, it has to be a unit that exists separate from the user's body. There are exceptions. The law allows limited use of direct neural interface by the military."

"Like my ocular implants," Hal said. "The ones that connect my vision to the sights of my weapons."

"Yes," Sheppard said. "The other exception is bionic prosthetics, as I mentioned earlier. The mind has to have a way to connect with the bionic parts in the body."

"If everyone in society had synthetic reality transmitters already implanted in their heads," Pirate said, "it would be possible to create a whole world of zombies."

"Which is what Gogue is trying to do now," Jaina said, "what my parents are helping him to do."

"Yes," Sheppard said. "I've met several of those zombies back on *Vector*. Their bodies are intact, but Gogue had total control of them. Only the victims and God Himself know where Gogue has sent their minds. They might be relaxing on a quiet beach or burning in some computer-generated hell."

"And with the whole world wired into his network," Hal said, "he could send everybody to la-la land and take control of everything."

"Or keep them around to do his bidding," Sheppard said, "and reward them by letting them spend time in computer-generated paradises."

"Or punish them," Jared said, "by causing them to experience their most terrifying nightmares."

"And you could use anybody in the network as a spy or an assassin," Neema said. "A wife assassinates her husband. Children monitor parents. They would not even know when they were doing it."

"So those kids Astrolus sent after us really didn't know what they were doing?" Hal said.

"Their first experiments were on juvenile delinquents," Neema said. "Their parents were willing to do anything to change their behavior. When they saw the change, they were so impressed they didn't ask questions."

"How many bionic people do you think there are running around in the world now?" Zapper asked.

"A few hundred thousand," Sheppard said.

"I just had this horrible vision," Zapper said. "An army of bionic zombies."

"I'd prefer not to think about that right now," Sheppard said.

"So with that implant installed in Wendy's head," Pirate said, "Gogue could send or receive messages anytime he wished to?"

"Yes," Sheppard said.

"And when Wendy was experiencing those hallucinations," Pirate continued, "her mind was actually communicating with a synthetic reality body in an environment Gogue had created in cyberspace."

"Right," Sheppard said.

"And what was her body doing?" Pirate asked.

"Except for the time she broke the mirror," Sheppard said, "her body seems to have been inactive."

"But it didn't have to be," Hal said. "If I'm understanding you, he could have controlled her, made her do anything he wanted her to."

"Like kill us all in our sleep?" Tori said.

"Yes," Sheppard said.

"Then why didn't he?" Zapper asked.

"He didn't want you dead," Sheppard said. "If he had, he could have accomplished that by bombing you from space. He was mainly interested in capturing Neema. That's why he let you make it to *Vector* station before he captured you. He thought you were delivering her right into his hands."

"But I knew what he was doing," Neema said. "I knew, but he did not realize I knew. That allowed me to stay one jump ahead of him."

"And the drugs they're giving Sheppard and Wendy should neutralize the implants?" Hal asked.

"For the time being," Jaina said. "Those implants are organic in nature. It's possible that they might eventually build up an immunity to the serum we're using to neutralize them."

"Can't you just remove them?" Zapper asked.

"It will be tricky and dangerous," Jaina said. "The usual procedure would be to inject nanites into the brain to destroy them, but they might be designed to fight back. We have to make sure their defenses are neutralized before we remove them. It's a little like defusing a bomb."

"Great," Hal said.

"How soon before Wendy wakes up?" Pirate asked.

"About an hour," Jaina said. "Her condition was more advanced than Sheppard's. Her body had had more time to adapt to the implants."

"And we all have them?" Pirate said.

"Everyone who went inside that bunker when we fought Astrolus last Christmas," Jaina said. "Tori and I were still outside. The rest of you were captured and injected, but the police were able to pull you out before the implants had had time to incubate. Wendy and Jared were in the bunker longer."

"But Jared's body rejected the implants," Pirate said. "He had some kind of immunity."

"His mind shut itself down," Jaina said, "while his body fought off the implants."

"And it put him into a coma for three months," Zapper said.

"Exactly."

"So what's next?" Pirate asked.

"We're headed for Titan," Sheppard said. "Preston seemed to think we'd find answers there. The trip will take about two months at maximum speed."

"What if the Earth can't hold out that long?" Mike asked.

"Preston's lead is all we have to go on," Sheppard said, "Unless Neema has a better suggestion."

"No," Neema said. "I agree with you."

"All right," Sheppard said. "I'm going back to my cabin for a while. Between those treatments and the torture Gogue put me through, I'm still feeling pretty bad. Dismissed."

"Wait," Pirate said. "You never told us what happened to you back there."

"No," Sheppard said. "I didn't. I'll talk about it when I'm ready. Dismissed."

Most of the team stood up to return to quarters. Jared and Neema remained snuggled close together, content in each other's company.

"You two make me sick," Zapper said.

"Zapper says he's happy for us," Jared said.

"How sweet of him," Neema said. "He always was a faithful friend."

"Hah," Zapper said.

"Jaina," Pirate said. "Would it be okay if I stayed with Wendy until she wakes up?"

"She's in recovery," Jaina said. "It should be okay, if you don't think she would mind."

"Thanks," Pirate said.

"By the way," Jaina said. "I told you it wasn't Landers' Syndrome."

* * *

Wendy sighed, moaned softly, and turned her head.

"Wendy," Pirate said. "Wendy, are you awake?"

Wendy opened her eyes and closed them again. A smile touched the corners of her lips.

"Hi," she said, her voice weak.

"Hi," Pirate said. He sat down on her bed and brushed her hair out of her face. "How do you feel?"

"Tired," Wendy said, "but okay."

"Jaina said the treatment went perfectly," Pirate said. "This should be the worst one. The rest of them won't be that bad."

"Good," she said. "I'm glad you're here. I'm glad you didn't give up on me after the way I acted." She reached out for his hand. He took her right hand in both of his hands and held it.

"It's okay," Pirate said.

"I thought I was going crazy," Wendy said. "I was afraid to tell anyone. I was actually relieved to find out about the implants. I'm just glad I didn't hurt anybody." Tears came to her eyes. "I'm glad nobody died because of me. My fault we were captured on *Vector*."

"You didn't know," Pirate said. *Neema knew*, he thought, but he didn't say it out loud. Pirate liked Neema and was happy for Jared that he had finally met the woman who had haunted his dreams--how many people got to experience that?-- but he was not sure he approved of the way Neema had used the Intrepid Force as decoys. She had, he supposed, been hardened by the original Neema's memories of life as a freedom fighter in a police state. Even so, the thought of using his friends as decoys did not sit well with him. He would have to have a talk with Neema about that.

Pirate started to say something else to Wendy, but she had fallen back to sleep. He sat on her bed, held her hand, and treasured a perfect moment in an imperfect world. The problems back home on Earth seemed far away.

* * *

Sheppard crept into the *Intrepid*'s small auditorium and found it empty. He walked down the center aisle that ran between the rows of seats, seated himself on the front row, and lowered his head.

"Computer," he said softly. "Load prayer chapel."

"Specify religion."

"Christian," Sheppard said. "Protestant Revivalist."

Soft music began to play. A kaleidoscope of soft colors formed abstract patterns on the screen.

Sheppard sighed.

"Computer," he said. "Do you have the Smokey Mountain Retreat program?"

"That program is available," the computer said.

"Play it."

The image on the screen was replaced by an image of misty green mountains and water falling over rocks. An acoustic guitar began to play "Amazing Grace."

"Thank you," Sheppard said.

"You're welcome," the computer's voice answered.

Sheppard lowered his head, felt himself lifted up by the strumming of the guitar and the sound of flowing water. He pictured himself sitting by that quiet river in the mountains, tried to picture Christ sitting there beside him. He tried to form words but they didn't come.

The door opened and closed again. Sheppard heard footsteps in the aisle. Someone was coming.

Maybe, he thought, *if I pretend not to notice them they'll go away.*

"Say, Rev," Zapper Martin spoke up. "Are we about to start the prayer meetings again?"

Sheppard looked up. Zapper had seated himself across the aisle.

"I--uh," Sheppard began. "Well, I really hadn't planned on it. Why?"

"I don't know," Zapper said. "The team used to enjoy 'em. It was part of the routine, ya know. Ahadri really seemed to get a lot out of 'em."

Sheppard nodded.

"With things being like they are," Zapper said, "I think we could all use a little inspiration."

"A lot has happened to me since the last time I saw all of you," Sheppard said. "I don't think I'm qualified to be a minister anymore."

"Why?" Zapper asked. "You play too many strip poker simulations?"

"No," Sheppard said. He laughed. "No, I haven't been playing too many strip poker sims." A strange look crossed his face. He turned and looked at Zapper. "Why would you ask that? Why that particular sin?"

"What?" Zapper said. "No reason, Rev. Just a random sin."

"I see," Sheppard said.

"So what did you do?" Zapper asked.

"I denied Christ," Sheppard said, "denied my faith and told that monster he was my lord and master." He closed his eyes, shook his head.

"Why'd you do that?" Zapper asked.

"He threatened to kill someone if I didn't," Sheppard said.

"Seems to me," Zapper said, "you just did what you had to do."

"I denied Christ," Sheppard said.

"Sometimes there just ain't no good solution to things," Zapper said. "You do your best, but you just have to wing it."

"Still . . . ."

"Look," Zapper said. "If you put a gun to my head and made me get baptized, would I really be a Christian?"

"No," Sheppard said.

"All right then," Zapper said. "If those weirds put a gun to somebody else's head and made you say you worship Gogue, how come that counts? That don't seem right to me."

"Zapper," Sheppard said. "There might actually be a good point in there somewhere."

"Look," Zapper said. "I don't know a lot about religion, but we're trying to save humanity here and some of these people could use a preacher 'long about now."

"Feed my lambs," Sheppard said.

"What?" Zapper said.

"Feed my lambs," Sheppard said. "After Peter denied Christ, Jesus came to him and told him 'Feed my lambs.'"

"Well, there you go then," Zapper said. "I know you need a little time to recover, but we sure could use some of those prayer services." He stood. "I'll let you get back to your praying."

"Zapper," Sheppard said. "Thanks."

"Hey," Zapper said. "No problem."

"And Zapper."

"Yeah."

"No more strip poker sims."

· "I'll try to cut back. I keep losing anyway."

CHAPTER 33 : Planet of Ghosts

"How long have you been standing here?" Pirate asked.

"I can't stop looking at it," Wendy said. "It's one of the most awesome things I've ever seen."

Wendy had been standing on the shady observation deck for hours. It was one of the few zero gravity sections of the ship. When the blast doors were open, thick glass windows looked out upon the infinity beyond. Magnetic boots kept the deck's visitors from floating away.

Pirate stood beside Wendy and looked out. She slipped her arm around him, squeezed up to his side. They stood holding each other and looking out.

The wondrous sight of the planet Saturn had held most of the crew spellbound since the *Intrepid* had arrived there. Saturn was not the only ringed world in the solar system, but it was certainly the most spectacular. Almost every child searches for the end of a rainbow in the hope of seeing one up close. Saturn's colorful rings spun in an immense circular plane of kaleidoscope patterns. Glacier-sized chunks of ice, sparkling in the light of the distant sun, drifted in an eternal circle around a swirling sphere of gas that was big enough to swallow several hundred Earth-sized planets. Looking across the surface of Saturn's gleaming rings of ice was like staring across an infinity of glaciers in a dark, eternal, and stormy northern sea. Lightning flashed across the rings in beautiful and terrible arcs. It cast shivering patterns across the surface of those rings. Saturn's constellation of moons danced around the planet with delicate precision. The largest of these, Titan, was larger than the planet Mercury. It had an atmosphere of mostly nitrogen and methane.

"Captain Butler," Echo Yazzi said. "Nancy?"

"Yes?"

Butler pulled from her reverie. She pulled her eyes from the screen and looked around at the bridge crew.

"Yes, Echo. What is it?"

"We found the wreck," she said.

"Any signs of activity?" Butler asked.

"No," Fairbanks said. "The *Arthur Conan Doyle* reported some kind of signal. We're not getting anything."

"But you're sure it's the same wreck?" Butler asked.

"How many wrecks could there be down there?" Fairbanks asked.

"There may have been some recent additions," Butler said.

"This one's old," Fairbanks said. "It looks like it's been here for centuries. It's the same one."

"How could something like that stay hidden for so long?" Yazzi asked. "We've been sending probes here for years?"

"Cloudy atmosphere," Fairbanks said. "And the thing's half buried in mud."

"Tell Pirate and the others we've arrived," Butler said. "Assemble the Intrepid Force in the meeting room in an hour."

"Yes, ma'am."

* * *

"We've all been over the logs from the *Doyle*," Nancy Butler said, "so I don't have to warn you about the danger. None of us knows exactly what he or she is walking into."

Zapper stirred in his seat as the captain spoke.

"The prospect of landing on Titan is both thrilling and terrifying," Butler continued. "Few humans have ever made it this far out. Under ordinary circumstances, this would be the adventure of a lifetime. The possibility of finding evidence of alien life aboard this wrecked ship makes it doubly so.

"Unfortunately, these are not ordinary circumstances. Our planet is under siege, and we may be its last hope. We are hoping to gain knowledge that will help us in our fight to save Earth from whoever or whatever has it under siege."

"Because of his experience as a former member of Intrepid Force," Butler said, "I have agreed to allow Mr. Sheppard to lead this expedition. If this were a scientific expedition, I would insist on going down myself. Because of the nature of the threat we are facing, I am sending Mr. Sheppard down instead."

"I'm not a scientist," Sheppard said, "But I have nothing but respect for Dr. Butler, and the scientific method. I hope we make discoveries that will fill textbooks for years to come, but our first order of business is to save the people back home. We've been preparing for the past month, so there's not much more to say. Get your gear. Report to landing vehicle A-Four in five minutes. Dismissed."

* * *

Pirate Eisman was strapped into the *Victoria* soaring over the dark surface of an alien world. Narrow canyons twisted through gray rock like wrinkles on the surface of a brain. Ghostly clouds of methane brushed across the heavy glass ports on the side of the ship. Glistening droplets clung to the glass. They gathered into writhing streams that flowed back along the contours of the glass. Saturn's ringed glory hung eternally poised at the edge of the world. It filled nearly a quarter of the tangerine sky. The experience of visiting an alien world had always exhilarated Pirate. He remembered seeing Venus for the first time. Its mountains shimmered with glistening lead from molten metal rains. The sight of Saturn had been breathtaking. Now he was soaring over Titan.

"There it is," Echo Yazzi said through a helmet microphone. She was strapped into a heavy shoulder harness in the cockpit. Sheppard rode beside her.

Pirate peered down through the mist at a debris field that stretched for nearly a mile. The larger chunks were mostly cylindrical and hewn of gray metal. The smaller pieces looked like parts of machinery, twisted hunks of sheet metal, or the broken up parts of a fuel system. The ship's crash landing had cut deep gashes in the frozen ground. Methane rains had softened the edges, but they were still visible. The debris field looked flat from above, but it was really on a steep slope. Just over a narrow ridge of mountains was a flat plateau lying on the edge of a foggy pool of liquid methane.

"Take us down, Echo," Sheppard said. "Be careful."

"Yes, sir," Echo said. The panel sang as she punched in the command. Landing thrusters fired, and Echo monitored the lander's descent on brightly colored panels.

Sheppard was still haunted by Echo Yazzi's resemblance to her twin sister. He had watched Jasmine die in a recorded message Gaith Corbalew had sent to torment Lancing DeFalco. Jasmine Yazzi was not the only person to die at Corbalew's hands on the day of his escape, but her casual execution was certainly among the most callous murders Sheppard had ever seen Corbalew commit. He still cringed every time he thought about it.

The *Victoria*'s long, insect body touched down beside the steaming sea of methane. This was the same site the crew of the *Arthur Conan Doyle* had chosen.

Sheppard unstrapped himself and moved though a hatch in the rear of the cockpit. The men and women of the Intrepid Force were already squeezing into their space suits.

"Hey!" Zapper said. "Watch those hands!"

"Sorry," Jaina said. "There's not much room in here."

The spacesuits they were pulling on were hard suits that flexed only at the joints. They had liquid heating and cooling systems that could be adjusted for extremes of heat and cold. Each crewperson's helmet had its own light and camera. Sheppard pulled on his own hard suit. He twisted the helmet into place and switched on the electronics. He pressurized the helmet to test the seal. Readouts indicated no problems.

"Is everybody ready?" Pirate asked.

"Let's go," Sheppard said. He looked around at the others to see if his communications system was working. "Everybody be careful."

"Yes, sir."

Sheppard and the rest of the team exited, four at a time, through the ship's two airlocks. Hal emerged from a separate hatch. Instead of his usual exobot, he was driving a prototype surface exploration unit. It had tracks like a bulldozer and long robot arms.

Pirate stepped out beneath a dark sky. The frozen ground crunched beneath his boots. He felt a sense of exhilaration. He was really on Titan, really on that distant moon. The ground was dark gray, almost black. It was scattered with frozen chunks of rock.

"Who would have thought," Jared said, "with all the adventures that we used to have around Crane Island, that we'd ever end up here."

"It's beautiful," Neema said, "and, at the same time, very lonely."

The horizon burned with orange light, but the sky directly overhead was dark gray. The sun was an orange disk the size of a tennis ball. Saturn hung eternally above the weathered horizon. The big gas planet reflected in the dark surface of the methane cauldron beside the surface party. Pirate looked around. There were, he noticed, several faded sets of corrugated footprints leading away toward a winding pass that ran between mountains.

Tori released a fleet of fan-powered explorer probes into the cold fog. There were six of them. They were saucer-shaped and about a foot in diameter. The probes would serve as scouts and alert them to unseen dangers.

"Nancy," Sheppard said. "This is Sheppard. Our helmet cameras are on, and Tori has just released the probes. Are you getting everything?"

"You're all coming through fine," Butler said. She sat uneasily in the captain's chair staring into a bank of monitors that ran along one wall of the bridge. Fairbanks and the rest of the bridge crew were there with her.

"Can you hear me, Mom?" Zapper asked.

"I hear you just fine, darling," Butler said. "Audio's coming through fine."

"Darling," Hal mumbled, and then sniggered.

"I heard that," Zapper said.

"Let's make sure they're all working," Fairbanks said. "Everybody sound off when I call your name." Fairbanks went through a roll call of the team. Except for a few minor adjustments in volume and gain, communications worked flawlessly.

"It looks like the crew of the *Doyle* went through that mountain pass," Sheppard said. "Let's start there. Mike and Tori will stay with the ship as we discussed."

"It's about three hundred below zero down there," Dr. Sanchez said from the ship's bridge. "Is everybody warm enough?"

"Temperature readings are all around seventy degrees," Fairbanks said, studying the readouts.

"We feel fine, Doc," Hal said. "It's like a spring day."

Pirate and the others began to walk. The gravity was light-less than one-sixth that of Earth. It was closer to the microgravity Sheppard and some of the others had experienced on Earth's moon. They shuffled along the surface in slow motion leaps and hops. Step and glide, step and glide, step and glide. There was a certain rhythm one had to keep. Stopping in mid-glide could cause a stumble.

"Mr. Sheppard," Fairbanks said suddenly through the helmet transmitters. "One of Tori's probes just picked something up at the edge of that mountain pass. We're moving in closer."

"What does it look like?" Sheppard asked.

"It's a body," Fairbanks said. "Jaina is approaching it."

"Over here," Jaina said. Since the message came through Sheppard's helmet radio, it was difficult to determine direction. Sheppard looked up and saw a spacesuit-shrouded figure waving from the narrow path that ran between the mountains.

Sheppard stepped and glided. Finally he stopped, dug in, and ran into Zapper. Both of them tumbled to the frozen ground in a clattering tangle of spacesuits. Sheppard felt a moment's irritation.

"Sorry," Zapper said. "Still getting used to this gravity."

"It's all right," Sheppard said as he rolled to his feet. He grabbed Zapper's upper arm and hauled him to his feet.

Then he saw what Jaina had found. Lying against the wall of the pass, frozen to the surface of Titan, was a dried mummy in a ruptured space suit. It looked completely human. The mouth was splayed open in an eternal and exaggerated scream. Its gloved fingers clawed at the frozen rock beneath it.

"It's one of the *Doyle*'s crew," Fairbanks said from orbit. "That's their insignia on the shoulder patch."

"Looks like he was backing away from something," Jared observed. "He was shot through the chest. The entry wound is in the front."

"We're analyzing Jaina's scans," Dr. Sanchez said from orbit. "We'll compare his dental records to what we have on the *Doyle*'s crew and see if we can identify him."

"I want to know what killed him," Captain Butler said.

"Other than a gaping hole through his chest," Zapper said.

"I meant I want to know what he was shot with," Butler said. "That remark put you on my bad list, young man."

"Ah, come on," Zapper said.

"I've got it," Sanchez said. "His name was Benchley."

"Do you know what kind of weapon killed him?" Sheppard asked.

"It was a beam weapon," Sanchez told him.

"No surprise there," Zapper said.

"Zapper!" Sheppard snapped.

"Sorry."

"The blast took out nearly every organ in his chest cavity," Sanchez continued. "His heart's completely gone. It looks like it was blown completely away."

"The edges of the wound are cauterized," Jaina added. "Some of the bone mass was completely vaporized. We're looking at a concentrated beam of intense heat. Several thousand degrees."

"At least he went quickly," Wendy commented.

"How resistant are our suits to beam weapons?" Sheppard asked. "Jared? Hal?"

"In short bursts," Jared said, "the carbon nanotubes in these suits would be enough to dissipate the heat of most hand-held beam weapons. Based on the size of the wound, I'd say that's what this man was hit with."

"What about a sustained burst?" Sheppard asked.

"To vaporize bone, the center of the beam would have to be pretty hot," Jared said. "Like Jaina said, it would be several thousand degrees. These suits would probably protect us for about five seconds. The glass in our face masks in the exception. The blast shield would have to be down to protect your head."

"Fairbanks," Sheppard said, "Is there any sign of movement from any of the probes?"

"None, sir," Charles Fairbanks said.

"Let's not take any chances," Sheppard said. "Lower blast shields. Switch to digital imaging."

Pirate rolled his helmet's blast shield down and locked it firmly into place. A full color image of the landscape came up on an internal viewscreen. The image was practically indistinguishable from the reality of peering through the helmet's face plate. It was a little clearer though. The contours of the rocks were more distinct. Pirate would have preferred to see a new world through the glass with his own human eyes, but this place clearly had its dangers.

Following faded footprints left by the *Doyle*'s crew, Sheppard's party edged carefully through the winding path that led between the mountains. The *Intrepid*'s bridge crew and the men and women still aboard the landers kept a constant watch over the readouts from the probes. They would alert the surface party if they saw any sign of movement. The dark, dreary path was bordered on both sides by steep walls of eroded rock.

"This place makes me edgy," Hal said. "It seems dangerous somehow."

"Finding that body back there didn't help things either," Pirate said. He brightened the computer-generated image inside of his helmet and found himself in a world of murky gray surrounded by fog.

"*The valley of the shadow of death,*" Sheppard said. "I've preached on the twenty-third Psalm hundreds of times, but I never really understood that verse until now."

"Fairbanks," Jared said suddenly. "Any signs of movement?"

"None," Fairbanks said. "We'd have alerted you immediately."

"I know," Jared said. "Sorry."

"What's wrong, Jared?" Butler asked.

"I feel like we're being watched," Jared said.

"We're not detecting anything," Fairbanks said. "Not from the probes or our long range scans either."

"Whoooooooooo," Zapper started making ghost noises.

"Who wants to kill him first?" Hal asked.

"You're almost out of the pass, Jared," Butler said.

"That's a relief," Pirate said when the party stepped out of the narrow pass and into the light. Spread out below them was a steep and heavily eroded plain littered with gray metallic debris. Pirate counted six large cylinders scattered around the plane. One ended in what looked like a nose cone. Twisted shards of metal scattered the ground. A ruptured tank lay half buried in Titan's cold hydrocarbon mud.

"I'm guessing this thing started out as a long, cylindrical tube," Zapper said, "It looks like it broke apart when it hit the planet."

"That's reasonable," Jared said. "It may have been assembled in space from separate, prefabricated cylinders. When they hit the ground, they split apart at the joints."

"I guess we'll start with the closest one," Sheppard said.

They moved carefully down the slope. Wendy bent over and picked something up.

"Pirate," she said. "Look at this!"

"What did you find?" Sheppard asked.

"A self-heating meal," Wendy said. "Beef tips, gravy, and assorted vegetables."

"The package is in English?" Pirate asked.

"Wendy," Captain Butler said. "Hold that closer to your helmet's camera."

"Yes, ma'am," Wendy said. "According to this, the dinner was manufactured by Swift and Cooley Food Services of Atlanta, Georgia."

"It must be from the *Doyle*," Hal said.

"Here's another one," Pirate said. "Beef stroganoff. It's still sealed. Best flavor when eaten before January 12, 2110."

"A thirty-six year shelf life," Zapper said. "Not bad. Might not taste very good by then, but not bad."

"Do they have any Japanese food?" Mike's voice chimed in. He had been monitoring them from the lander.

"There's a six pack of beer over here," Hal said. "Kyoto Genuine Draft."

"Are you serious?" Jaina asked.

"Yeah," Hal said. "Want some?"

"Grow up."

"She ain't old enough to drink," Zapper said.

"That looks like part of a cargo container over there," Sheppard said. "It must have burst apart when it hit."

They found more artifacts scattered along the hillside. Among them were a green coffee mug, a pair of coveralls, and a striped throw pillow.

"None of this is looking very alien so far," Hal said.

"It's got to be from the *Doyle*," Jaina said. "Right?"

They reached the first of the battered cylinders that had made up the ship's crew quarters. It was not until they were standing at its base that they realized how big it truly was. The cylinder was roughly eighty feet in diameter. The sides were pitted and burned. There was a dark trace of something that looked like writing, but it was mostly covered by a layer of carbon and dust. At the end, they could see that the interior was broken into floors and walls. There were six decks, like six floors of a building. The cylinder had landed at an angle. Someone walking around inside would find themselves standing on tilted floors. The hallways on each deck were sealed. Six pressure doors--one for each floor--ran down the middle at about a fifteen-degree angle from the ground. There was a single large, rectangular door in the side.

"Hey," Zapper said as his spacesuit shrouded form approached. "There's writing here."

"Can you read it?" Sheppard asked.

He brushed away a layer of carbon and with his hand.

"Yeah," Zapper said. "It says *Airlock*."

"More English," Pirate said.

"How is that possible?" Captain Butler asked. "I thought this wreck was supposed to be hundreds of years old."

"Good question," Zapper said.

"Who did the dating analysis of the wreck?" Pirate asked.

"A whole team of our finest people," Captain Butler said. "We may need to get another sample though. There could be something in the atmosphere that corrupted the scans."

"No," Neema said. "I don't think so."

"Let's get that airlock open," Sheppard said. "Hal."

"I'm on it," Hal said. The robot hands of his exploration rover had laser torches, screwdrivers, and other assorted weapons attached to the fingers. Hal went to work on the door. "I think I've got it," he said. "Now."

The door blew open.

Zapper cursed involuntarily. Jaina gasped. Sheppard crossed himself. Inside the airlock were three bodies. They were ancient, mummified. Their skin had turned to black leather, but their heads were still covered with hair. Their uniforms were faded and rapidly falling apart with age.

"I've seen this," Wendy said suddenly. "I've been here before."

"When?" Pirate asked.

"In a nightmare," she said. "I told you about it."

"I remember," Pirate said.

"Jaina," Sheppard said. "Run some scans. Are they or aren't they human?"

"Hold on," Jaina said. "Sanchez, are you running this through?"

"Yeah," he said. "We're getting it. Here. We're sending the results now."

"They're human," Jaina said. "The one on the right has twenty-eight teeth. Female. Cranial scans fall within established norms for homo sapiens sapiens. Caucasoid features."

"What's this sapiens sapiens business?" Zapper asked.

"They're completely modern humans," Jaina said. "Not cro magnon or some other humanoid variant."

"Why would you have cro magnon astronauts?" Zapper asked. "Cave men didn't build starships."

Jaina ignored him and scanned a second figure. "This one is male," she reported. "Evidence of mixed African and European ancestry. Cranial bone structure also well within homo sapiens sapiens norms. These people were human."

"Are they from the *Arthur Conan Doyle?*" Sheppard asked, "or are they part of the crew of this ship?"

"These bodies are centuries old," Jaina said. "Advanced mummification. The estimated age of those bodies fits with our earlier estimates of the age of the ship. That wreck is over a thousand years old."

"That's impossible," Sheppard said. "Isn't it?"

"Twelfth century people didn't have this technology," Pirate said. "And I doubt they had the English word 'airlock' either. There's only one other explanation I can think of."

"It's from the future," Neema said.

"The faulty scans theory is easier to swallow," Captain Butler said. "Time travel is theoretically impossible."

"Then your theories are wrong," Neema said. "This ship is from the future. Surely you must see that."

"Let's not debate this anymore," Sheppard said. "We need a look inside."

"You know, Gene," Captain Butler said, "I can't help thinking about those old Egyptian tombs; how a curse was supposed to fall on anyone who violated one of them."

"What killed these people?" Wendy asked.

"Scans indicate asphyxiation," Sanchez answered from orbit. "They ran out of breathable air."

"Are we ready to go in?" Pirate asked.

"Hal," Sheppard said. "Is the airlock still working?"

"We've still got power," Hal said.

"Let's try to preserve the original atmosphere," Sheppard said. "I'll take Jared, Neema, and Jaina with this first group."

"I want to go," Wendy said.

"So do I," Pirate said.

"The airlock only holds four or five people," Sheppard said. "We'll all go, but we'll have to go in groups."

Jared, Neema, and Jaina squeezed into the cab with Sheppard. He pressed a button on a murkily glowing control panel and the outer door slammed shut.

"Nancy," Sheppard said. "I hope you're wrong about that curse."

"Me too," Captain Butler said.

The airlock pressurized. The inner doors opened on a dark corridor. A few dim rays fell onto the floor's metal grating, but they couldn't see anything else.

"Adjust the light levels on your masks," Jared said. The lights came up on a spartan corridor. Debris was scattered along the floor. The false color viewers in their helmets showed a long hallway lined with doors. Because of the way the cylinder had landed, the floors were sloped at a fifteen-degree angle. They were covered with black metal grating. There was a body in a pressure suit about twenty feet down the hall.

"What's the atmosphere like in here?" Sheppard asked.

"I wouldn't recommend taking off your helmet if that's what you're suggesting," Sanchez answered from the ship.

"There's still some oxygen in the atmosphere, but it's pretty cold in there."

"He's wearing a spacesuit," Jared said. "They must have lost pressure before the crash."

"Jaina," Sheppard said. "Why don't you examine this body while we wait for the others."

Sheppard, Jared, Neema, and Jaina walked down the dark corridor to the still figure in the pressure suit. A hole had been bored through the chest and out the back. Jaina scanned the body.

"Let me guess," Sheppard said. "Beam weapon. Intense heat."

"If you'd bet money on your guess, you'd have won," Jaina said. "Same kind of injury as Benchley, the man from the *Doyle*."

"Is this one of the *Doyle*'s crew?" Sheppard asked.

"No," Jaina said. "He's one of the original occupants too."

"What about that hole through his suit?" Sheppard said. "Is it the same weapon that was used on the man from the *Doyle*?"

"The damage is identical," Sanchez said from orbit. "I don't know if it was fired from the same exact weapon, but the technology is the same."

"So something murdered this person a thousand years ago," Captain Butler said. "And the same weapon was used on that man from the *Doyle*?"

"That's what it looks like."

"Did the rest of you get that?" Sheppard asked.

"Yes, sir," Hal said, placing emphasis on the *sir*.

"Do you think it came from this?" Neema asked. She had found a pistol lying in the hall. The main body was cylinder-shaped.

"Hold it up to your helmet camera," Sheppard said. "Fairbanks, see what you make of it."

"Be careful," Jared said. "There might be fingerprints."

"Got it," Fairbanks said from the *Intrepid*. He fed the scan into the ship's computer.

"Why was this man wearing a space suit?" Captain Butler asked.

"Someone may have turned off life support," Jared said. "Or he might have come in from outside."

"It's a beam weapon," Fairbanks said, reading out the results of the scan.

"No kidding, Sherlock," Zapper muttered from outside where he was waiting. It came through the speakers.

"Shut up, man," Mike said from the lander.

"Polymer shell," Fairbanks continued. "Iridium. I'm not familiar with the power source.

WHIIIISHHHH!

The airlock doors opened a second time. Pirate, Wendy, and Zapper stepped into the corridor. Hal, in his bulky suit, would have to wait for the next cycle.

Pirate scanned the dark hallway. Sheppard, Jared, and the others were about twenty feet ahead of them gathered around the body in the pressure suit.

"I know this place," Wendy said. "I've been here before."

"In a nightmare," Zapper said. His helmet's blank face mask hid the rolling of his eyes. "You're starting to sound like Jared."

"Gogue was inside my mind," Wendy said. "He showed me things, terrible things. In one of the visions, I was in this corridor. I think I was part of the crew of this ship."

"Are you sure this is the same hallway?" Jaina asked.

"I was here," Wendy said.

"Why would Gogue send you pictures of this ship?" Pirate asked.

"To torment her," Neema said. "To parade clues before her face without explaining him. I think you call it a game of cat and mouse. It's something he likes to do."

"Yes," Sheppard said. Memories of his time aboard *Vector* rose up like bile. "I can testify to that. What else did you see, Wendy?"

"These doors," she said. She took a few steps and stopped, pointed at the door. "I think this was Darnell's room."

"Let's start opening doors," Sheppard said. "We may not like what we'll find, but we've got to know what's in there. Be on guard for any sign of trouble."

They had expected the door to be locked, but as soon as Wendy touched the latching button, the door rumbled and slipped aside. Wendy's breath caught in her throat.

The room looked like a mummy's tomb. The walls were covered with posters of Egyptian symbols. A statue of Anubis stood on a box in one corner. A still figure lay on the bunk. His hands were arranged on his chest and a golden mask had been placed over his face.

"Darnell," Wendy said. Tears rose up in her eyes, and she wasn't sure why.

Jaina scanned the body.

"Caucasian male," she said. "Late teens."

"What killed him?" Sheppard asked.

"Poison," Jaina said. "Probably an overdose of something from medical."

"Suicide?" Jared asked.

"Possibly," Jaina said, "but not necessarily. I'm seeing evidence of bruises and a concussion. It looks like he fought someone and lost."

"You say you saw this boy in a vision?" Sheppard said. "What do you remember about him?"

"His name was Darnell," Wendy said. "He made everybody call him Dokanuchu. He was young, but I got the impression he was very smart--a genius. I think he was some kind of computer engineer. He loved simulation games. Especially military strategy games."

"That would fit," Pirate said.

Jared snapped open a plastic case he found on the floor. Inside was a flat, rectangular object with a row of buttons along the bottom.

"This looks like a *padd*," Wendy said, referring to the hand held, touch sensitive reading and writing devices they downloaded books into. "I wonder if it still. . ."

The face of the object crackled. A picture of a library shelf appeared on the screen. The names of books were clearly visible on the spines.

"Books," Pirate said. "This was a collection of books. This was his book shelf."

Jared touched the spine of one of the books. It flew off the shelf and opened to the first page with a sound like pages turning.

"*The Art of War* by General Sun Tzu," Sheppard said. "Interesting."

Jared touched a button. The face of an Asian man in ancient armor appeared beside the text and began to speak as though he were addressing a young pupil.

Jared thumbed through other books in the young man's collection. Some of them were technical manuals about computer programming, synthetic reality, and artificial intelligence. There were fantasy and science fiction novels. Tolkein's *Lord of the Rings* series was there as were Asimov's *Foundation* novels. Jared pulled up another volume.

How to Conquer the World.

"Now this is interesting," he said.

"What is it?" Tori asked from she ship. "Hold it where I can read it."

"It's a guide to a simulation game called *Rubicon*," Jared said.

"What's the object of this game?" Sheppard asked.

"You travel through time," Jared said, "and set up empires. The one who conquers the planet wins. It's kind of like the old game of *Risk* only there's a time travel element."

"No way," Zapper said. "That's got to mean something."

"What's the copyright date on it?" Pirate asked.

Jared paged back.

"2105," he said.

"That fits with Neema's theory," Sheppard said. "If this ship really is from the future, how did it get here?"

"You may want to read this," Jaina said. She held up a faded magazine. It was printed on some type of recyclable plastic and brittle with age.

Solar System Today, the banner on the cover read. The cover graphic showed a massive ship blasting off through space. "Main Story: Launch '09."

"Let me see that," Zapper said. He reached for the magazine.

"DON'T TOUCH IT!" Jaina yelled.

Zapper pulled his hand away.

"Were you going to pull it out of my hand?" Jaina asked. "This magazine is fragile, Zapper. It's about to fall apart."

"Sorry," Zapper said.

"According to the date on the cover, it's from June 12, 2109," Neema said.

"Over thirty years in the future," Pirate said.

"This article's about a space mission," Jaina said. "The first manned interstellar flight."

"Interstellar?" Sheppard asked. "To another solar system?"

"Exactly," Jaina said. "It also says DeFalco scientists discovered life on a planet about a hundred light-years from here."

"DeFalco?" Sheppard said.

"Yeah," Jaina said. "Apparently they're still a major player in space exploration."

"Remind me to buy more stock," Zapper said. "Does that count as insider trading?"

"They sent probes all over the solar system using something called a Scanlon-Marston Drive," Jaina continued.

"Some kind of faster-than-light travel?" Pirate asked.

"In a way," Jaina said. "It generates a field that opens tunnels through space/time."

"Wormholes?" Neema said. "Hyperspace travel?"

"Apparently," Jaina shrugged. "A ship called the *Lightbringer* was supposed to be the first manned vehicle capable of faster-than-light travel. After several successful test flights, scientists planned a shakedown cruise to a solar system a hundred light years away. The *Lightbringer* was scheduled to depart, with much fanfare, from high Earth orbit."

"*Lightbringer*," Sheppard said. "That's ominous."

"Why ominous?" Pirate asked.

"The name *Lucifer*," Sheppard said, "if you translate it into English, means lightbringer or lightbearer."

"What's it doing here?" Pirate asked. "Does the article say anything about time travel?"

"No," Tori said. "There is a sidebar here about the Marston-Scanlon drive, though. Some scientists theorized that it might be used for time travel--or maybe even to visit alternate universes if they exist."

"This ship's not supposed to be here," Jared said. "It was an accident."

"Here's a picture of the crew," Jaina said.

"Let me see," Wendy said. Jaina gently passed the old magazine to Wendy. Wendy pulled the open page into the light of her helmet lamp.

Twenty men and women in sleek black uniforms stood lined up along a metal catwalk.

"There," Wendy said. She pointed to a young woman who stood leaning against the rail. "That's the girl I saw."

"Are you sure?" Zapper asked. "That's a pretty small picture."

"I'm not sure of anything right now," Wendy said.

"Is there a list of names?" Pirate asked.

"No," Wendy said.

"We need to cover more ground," Sheppard said. "Let's split into groups, but stay together. I don't think there's anybody else around, but something about this planet feels unsafe. I don't want any of you wandering around alone."

"I know what you mean," Pirate said. "It's like walking through a haunted house."

"Or a graveyard," Wendy said.

WHHIIIIIISSSSH!

The airlock in the hall opened. Nearly everyone jumped.

"Hal," Zapper said. "That better be you out there."

"It's me," Hal's voice said.

"We're gonna have to hang a bell on you," Zapper said.

"Wendy," Pirate said. "You thought you'd seen this ship in a dream, some kind of vision. Were there any other places you remembered?"

"Yes," Wendy said. "The girl in the picture. I think her name was Arwen."

"Like the character in *Lord of the Rings*?" Pirate said.

"Her quarters are near here," Wendy said. "Just a few doors down."

"Why don't you and Pirate start there," Sheppard said. "We'll try opening a few of the other doors and move on to the deck above us."

"I'm staying here," Neema said.

"Fine," Sheppard said. "Jared can stay with you."

"I wouldn't trust those two alone," Zapper said.

"They're in spacesuits, you fool," Jaina said.

"Wendy and Pirate are going to one room," Zapper said. "Jared and Neema are staying here. This is turning into a couples thing."

"Don't even suggest it," Jaina told him.

"Tori," Sheppard said. "Hey, Tori."

"Right here," Tori replied, transmitting from the lander.

"Is everything all right outside?" Sheppard asked.

"Fine," Tori said.

"If there's any sign of trouble," Sheppard said, "I want to know immediately."

"That's my job," Tori said.

"I've already said that, haven't I?" Sheppard said, abashed.

"At least five times," Tori said. "Not that I'm counting."

Pirate followed Wendy down the hall to the quarters she had seen in her vision. Wendy touched a lighted button on a keypad beside the door. The door rattled open. Wendy stepped inside, Pirate at her elbow, and gasped. Lying on the bed, arranged much the same way Darnell had been, was the still body of a young woman. Her gray, withered hands were folded on her bosom. A burial mask covered her face. Lying on the pillow beside her head was a hand-held recording device with a screen. Wendy picked it up. Her hands, she realized, were trembling. She touched a button. A hissing storm of pixelated noise filled the screen. Suddenly it congealed into a crystal clear image of a young woman's face.

"Wendy?" Pirate gasped. "It's you."

"It's her," Wendy said. "Arwen. That's the girl I saw in the mirror."

"He's taken over the ship," the girl in the video said.

A burst of static.

". . . restored life support for the moment," she continued. "I think I'm the last one left alive."

She looked like Wendy, but her eyes were pale blue and her voice was softer, more hesitant.

The image froze, pixelated, then reformed.

". . . overridden self-destruct. I'm going to try to send a power surge into the Scanlon-Marston field generators and collapse the wormhole."

The message froze, pixelated, and fell apart again. This time it didn't return.

Pirate looked down at the floor. Just beneath the edge of the bed he saw a small, rectangular piece of metal with the DeFalco logo--some future version of it--emblazoned across one edge. Straining against the bulk of his spacesuit, he knelt down and picked it up. It was a name plate. *Arwen Eisman.*

* * *

Pirate and Wendy called the others together and played back the recorded message.

"'He's taken over the ship,' she said," Jaina repeated Arwen's words. "Who did she mean? Who had taken over the ship?"

"Gogue," Neema said. "I found more recordings in Darnell's quarters. I know what he is."

"Sheppard!" Tori's voice came through Sheppard's helmet speakers. "SHEPPARD!" She sounded panicked.

"Yes, Tori," Cockrum said. "What is it?"

"It's the *Intrepid*," she said. "We've lost contact with them."

"*Intrepid*, this is Gene Sheppard. Come in, please. Somebody answer!"

There was no response.

"When did you lose them?" Sheppard asked Tori.

"They were circling Titan," she said. "They'd passed over the horizon out of sight when we lost them."

"Something may have gone wrong with communications," Sheppard said.

"We dropped a ring of satellite probes around the planet so we wouldn't lose touch when the ship passed over the terminator," Echo Yazzi told him. "They're still up there and, from what I can read here, they're still transmitting."

"It's Gogue," Neema said. "He's found us."

CHAPTER 34: Marooned

"*Intrepid*, this is Dr. Jaina Benedict. Come in, please. Come in!"

They had been crowded into the lander for six hours. Jaina had been glued to the communications console the whole time.

"Give it up, Doc," Zapper said.

"It could be some kind of technical glitch," Tori said. "A problem with communications."

"It's possible," Sheppard said, "but it's looking less and less likely as time passes."

"Something has happened to them," Neema said. "They were either captured or destroyed."

"You've dealt with this Gogue longer than we have," Sheppard said. "Which do you think it is?"

"He's not wasteful," Neema said. "He would not destroy a ship if he could avoid it. He would rather add it to his armada."

"Unless capturing the additional ship cost him ships," Hal said.

"What about Captain Butler and the crew?" Mike asked.

"You've seen what he does to people," Sheppard said. "He'd probably add them to his army of zombies."

"Unless killing them had greater dramatic effect," Pirate said. "He seems to have a flair for drama, for extravagant cruelty."

"Yes," Sheppard said. "He definitely has that."

"So," Pirate said. "What are we going to do if the *Intrepid* doesn't come back?"

"The lander can get us into space," Hal said, "but it's not built for interplanetary travel. There's no way it could get us home."

"Could we hitch a ride on an ore freighter?" Zapper asked.

"An asteroid smasher?" Hal said. "Gogue seems to have captured every one in the sector."

"One of two things is going to happen," Pirate said. "Either Gogue is going to leave us here to die or he's going to send someone after us. If he leaves us stranded here, how long could we hold out?"

"There's enough air in this shuttle to keep us alive for about a week," Echo Yazzi said.

"Does that include the oxygen used in the spacesuits?" Pirate asked.

"No," Echo said. "That would keep one person alive for another week. We've got twelve people."

"We've got to find a better alternative," Sheppard said. "Can this shuttle recycle air?"

"No," Echo said. "We do that on the *Intrepid*."

"There's some air on the *Lightbringer*," Pirate said. "It's a thousand years old and probably pretty stale."

"We can filter it," Hal said. "They've probably got some bottles stored somewhere too."

"Provided they weren't all destroyed in the crash," Pirate said.

"We'll have to go back over there and do a search," Sheppard said.

"Should we leave somebody here to protect the lander?" Pirate asked.

"This lander's got deflection systems and particle cannons," Echo said. "And it's not stuck in one place. Don't worry about us. It's you guys who will be sitting ducks."

"Ducks with teeth," Zapper said.

"What about food and water?" Pirate asked. "How well stocked are we?"

"It won't go far with twelve people," Echo said. "The nutrition bars will last for a while, but it's the water that concerns me."

"We can recycle our urine," Zapper said.

"You would be the one to think of that, Zapper," Mike said. "What is it about you and bodily fluids?"

"There should be water somewhere on the *Lightbringer* too," Sheppard said. "It may be frozen or contaminated, but it's a start. Everybody suit up. Let's get started."

"Wait a minute," Hal said. "Isn't there water ice on Titan?"

"Yes!" Sheppard said. "You're right."

"And you can distill oxygen from water," Jared said. "It may be slow with our equipment, but it might just work."

"Then let's collect some ice," Zapper said.

Sheppard and the Intrepid Force climbed back into their exploration gear. They tested the seals, watched the gauges.

"That's it," Pirate said. "Let's go."

"Watch our backsides, Pocahontas," Zapper told Echo.

"I'll whip yours," she said, "if you call me Pocahontas again."

"Typhoon," Mike said.

"Volcano," Zapper replied.

Five minutes later Sheppard was leading Neema and the Intrepid Force through the dark maze of canyons that led to the wreck site. Pirate kept looking up between high canyon walls at the tiny, snaking wedge of smoky orange sky overhead. *We're like ants down here,* he thought.

A light flashed on the viewscreen inside Pirate's helmet. Echo Yazzi's face appeared, postage stamp size, on a tiny inset window at the edge of Pirate's viewscreen. The others, he realized, were receiving the same message.

"Look sharp!" she said. "I'm reading multiple objects coming around Titan. They're headed this way. They should be visible on the horizon in about twenty seconds."

"Do we have time to get back to the lander?" Sheppard asked.

"No," Echo said. "They're coming too fast. You have to try to make it to the *Lightbringer.* We'll give you cover. Firing up engines. Powering deflection systems. Cannons armed. We'll come get you, Intrepid Force."

"Be careful, Echo," Sheppard said.

"I'm always careful," she said with a quick smile. "Hang on. We'll be right there."

Echo's face vanished.

"Come on," Sheppard said. "Power up weapons and deflector systems and run for the ship."

They charged through the canyon's dark passageways for just over a minute. Their suits were bulky, but the gravity was light. They stepped out into the open. The wreck of the *Lightbringer* lay spread before them, a vast debris field. The lander hovered against the orange sky. Its thrusters hissed and blew off steaming clouds. Bright flood lamps lit the frozen ground beneath it. A line of bright objects glistened over the mountains. They were coming closer.

The flash of fire spattered against the lander's deflection field, sent it spinning off its axis. Thrusters howling, the ship banked, righted itself, and returned fire. The sky overhead filled with soaring mechanical drones. Laser beams flashed through Titan's cold atmosphere.

"Echo!" Sheppard yelled. "Get out of here. You can't fight them all."

Hal's exobot unleashed its mechanical wrath.

"Get inside," Echo yelled. "I'll cover you."

"Go," Sheppard said. "Everybody into the wreckage."

The drones descended on the wrecked ship. Pulsed tracer beams ripped through the foggy atmosphere as they swarmed the *Lightbringer* like angry bees. They targeted the hatches, the airlocks, the places where the hull was weakest. They rained the debris field around the wrecked ship with blistering pulses of fire.

"Belay that!" Sheppard cried. "Back into the canyons! Back into the canyons!"

A troop carrier fell from the flashing heavens. It opened its hatches, deployed human troops. They jetted through the atmosphere in black hard suits with jet packs.

The Intrepid Force fell back into the canyon's dark maze. Energy bursts blasted away at the rock formations overhead. For the next twenty minutes they scampered through the dark labyrinth seeking caves to hide in, rocky overhangs for protection. They returned fire--fought back as well as they could--but they were outnumbered and outgunned.

After twenty minutes of leaping, shooting, dodging, hiding, and shooting again--twenty minutes of breathless, uncoordinated action--the canyons fell silent.

"Are they gone?" Zapper asked. He climbed out from behind a large rock.

"Looks like it," Hal said. His cannons were aimed at the narrow crack of sky overhead.

"Everybody sound off," Sheppard said. "Pirate."

"I'm here."

"I heard Hal and Zapper. What about Wendy?"

"I'm here," Wendy said. "Pirate and Jaina are with me."

"Mike? Jared?"

"I'm here."

"I'm here."

"Reverend Sheppard," Mike said. "Is that you?"

"It's me," Sheppard said. Mike's spacesuited form was standing at a point where the canyon curved sharply to the right.

"I just saw something crash around the corner," Mike said. "It looked like a ship."

Sheppard followed him with weapons raised. The canyon split into a Y. Ready for anything, Sheppard and Mike peered guardedly around the corner to see what had crashed there. They came around the corner into a wide clearning. Just ahead of them was a battered metal shell. It was the lander, their own lander.

"Echo!" Sheppard cried. "ECHO! STEPHENS!" The wrecked craft lay against a large rock. Scorch marks covered the sides in black, spray paint patterns. They ran to it.

"What is it?" Pirate asked from somewhere else. "Are they all right?"

"We're okay," Echo's voice said, "but we've been hit bad. We're taking on methane."

"The hull's breached," Hal said grimly as he came around the corner behind them.

Steam filled the cabin as Titan's chilling soup of nitrogen and methane spewed through into craft's warm, internal atmosphere.

Hal concentrated a laser burst onto the lander's cracked hull. He fed a shard of metal into the beam, welded the crack through a cloud of steam.

"Atmospheric pressure has stabilized," Echo said. "That's the good news. Now we've got to filter out the methane. It really stinks in here."

"Hey, folks," Zapper said. "I'm back at the crash site. We've got a problem."

"What is it, Zapper?" Sheppard asked.

"It's the *Lightbringer*," Pirate said. "The sealed compartments we found." Pirate and Wendy were standing beside Zapper looking out at the cluttered debris field. Steam rose from the starship's wreckage.

"Yes, Pirate," Sheppard said. "What about them?"

"They shot them full of holes," Pirate said. "Blew out the airlocks."

"You can forget about getting any air out of that sucker," Zapper said.

"So we're stuck with whatever is left in the lander," Sheppard said. "And in our suits."

"That's not going to last very long," Echo said. "If the *Intrepid* doesn't come back for us, we're dead."

"Maybe we can make it into orbit," Wendy said. "Maybe there's an asteroid smasher they missed. We could send out a signal and hitch a ride."

"The propulsion system is wrecked," Hal said. "This lander's not going anywhere."

"They could have finished us," Zapper said. "Why did they leave? Why are we still alive?"

Jared emerged from the canyon behind Pirate, Wendy, and Zapper.

"Neema's gone," he said. "They took her."

CHAPTER 35: Final Thoughts

Jaina Benedict crept stealthily among the sleepers. Locked snugly away in pressure suits and bubble helmets, they lay in silent rows on the lander's tilted-back seats. In drug-induced comas, they needed less oxygen. The scarce air supply would last longer that way. Jaina turned them to prevent pressure sores and found herself hoping someone would wake up. She knew better.

"Recorder on," Jaina said.

"Recording," a filtered male voice answered. Jaina was glad to hear a voice, any voice, in those circumstances.

"Personal Log," she began. "Dr. Jaina Benedict recording. It has been over a week since the *Intrepid* vanished from orbit, since attacking robot drones destroyed most of the exploration team's oxygen supply. We had reserves, but not enough to last for long. We're trying to distill enough oxygen from melted water ice to replace what we're using, but it's taking too long. For the eighth consecutive day, I am awake and alone. I envy the others. They're all sleeping peacefully. No fear. No loneliness."

She looked down at the instrument panel in front of her.

"The first night, I dreamed the drones had returned. They captured us, placed us in synthetic reality chambers. I woke up gasping, afraid of every sound."

She stopped, hesitated.

"I'm--I'm fairly sure it was a dream. The airlocks were sealed and the cameras didn't record a break-in. Everyone was lying exactly the way I left them. It had to have been a dream."

She wrung her hands nervously.

"I've also had dreams of rescuers in spacesuits. They come in smiling, glad to have found someone still alive here. Then I wake up to the sobering realization that they're not here, that they probably never will be."

She looked around.

"I don't know why I'm doing this," she said. "There doesn't seem to be any reason for it. Why extend all of our lives until the last possible moment when there's no chance of a rescue? Who are we kidding? We're over 800 million miles from home."

She looked down at her own readouts.

"I don't have much air left," she said. "Only enough for a few hours. Only a few hours. The rest of my life."

Jaina sat down in a reclining chair. She leaned back and put her feet up. The screen in front of her looked like a picture window. Titan's barren landscape stretched out before her.

"I could inject myself with the same drug I used on the others," she said. "I might be able to stretch out my life for another day or two, but why? Why extend my own life when there's no hope of rescue? Recorder off."

Jaina sighed. She got up, went around to her sleeping patients. She turned them and checked their vital signs one last time.

"Recorder on," she said.

"Recording."

"The patients all seem to be doing well. They should outlive me by two or three days. Maybe more. Who knows?" She sat back in the padded reclining seat, put up her feet, and lay back. As though looking out a window, she gazed at the screen at the lonely moonscape, the close, jagged horizon, the sky of orange smog, and the glorious ringed planet. "It's so beautiful here," she said. "My parents never believed in a God. I never really did either, but sitting here I can't help but wonder and hope. If there is a God, how could He leave our world in the hands of something like Gogue? On the other hand, Sheppard used to say God's face was written across the universe. Lying here, I can almost believe it. If there is a God, I hope it's the one Sheppard used to talk about. I always liked Him."

She lay talking into the recorder as the hours slowly ticked past. It was good to have something to talk to. She hoped someone might find the recorder one day and share her last thoughts, her last moments of life.

"My eyelids are getting heavy now," Jaina said. "If I fall asleep now, I'll never wake up. Somehow that doesn't bother me. Goodbye, everyone. Goodbye, Pirate, Wendy, and Jared. Good night, Zapper, Hal, and Mike. Goodbye, Tori. I wish I could say I'll miss you. Goodbye, Jonas. I hope you're alive somewhere. Goodbye, everyone else."

Jaina yawned. Her eyelids closed. Moments later she drifted soundly off to sleep. A light began to flash on the monitor board in front of her. Jaina didn't react. Klaxons engaged, their howling voices warning of the approach of intruders. Jaina didn't awaken. The airlock engaged as someone breached it from the other side. Moments later it popped open.

* * *

Jaina Benedict felt someone holding her hand. She moaned softly. Gentle fingers stroked her forehead, smoothed back her hair. She forced her eyes to open. Bright rays of light burned them. She shut them tightly and tried, more slowly this time, to open them again.

"She's coming around," a man's voice said.

"Jaina," another man said. "Jaina, can you hear me?"

"Jonas?" she said. Her mouth was so dry she could hardly speak. Her tongue felt like sandpaper. "Jonas?" she squeaked.

"Yes, Jaina," the voice said. "It's me."

"Thirsty," she said.

"You're thirsty?"

She nodded.

"Wait." She heard the figure raise up. He squeezed her hand and placed it gently on her chest. She was in bed--no longer wearing a pressure suit. Someone had bathed her, dressed her in clean, dry clothes, and tucked her into bed.

"I'm going to raise you so you can drink," Jonas Cockrum's voice explained. Jaina opened her eyes. The light didn't hurt as much. Cockrum was leaning over her. He held down a switch as whining servos tilted the upper half of her bed. Then he placed a cup into her hands and raised the straw to her parched lips. She sipped water, felt it on the dry leather of her tongue.

"Is she all right?" Jaina heard someone ask. She squinted into the light and saw Pirate, Wendy, and Zapper standing at the end of the bed watching her. Jared was pacing an aisle at the far end of the room. Jaina was in a hospital, a spaceship's medical bay. The equipment looked old and bulky. It was functional but not state-of-the-art. The ship, she could tell, was an older ship, but it looked well-maintained. The medical bay was about twenty feet long and broken into semi-private cubicles by half-walls.

"She's fine," Cockrum said. "Everyone seems to be doing fine."

"Except for the diaper rash," Zapper said. "Eight days in a space suit. Sheesh!"

"Where are we?" Jaina asked.

"Aboard Corbalew's ship," Zapper said.

"Corbalew!" Jaina gasped. She started to get up.

"Easy," Cockrum said. He placed his hands on her shoulders.

"The ship he used to attack Venus," Pirate explained. "Cockrum's engineers have managed to repair some of the technology Gogue's people installed."

"So Corbalew's not here?" Jaina asked.

"Naw," Zapper said. "Of course not."

Cockrum smiled enigmatically.

"But where in space are we?" Jaina asked.

"Still in orbit around Saturn," Cockrum said. "We've been tailing the *Intrepid.*"

"What are you doing out here?" Jaina asked. "How could you possibly be here?"

"It's a long story," Cockrum said. "We left Venus a few days after the attack on Earth. Preston told us he thought we'd find answers on Titan. Obviously he was right."

"They barely found us in time," Pirate said.

"Did you find Neema?" Jaina asked.

"No," Pirate said. "She's still missing."

"They've had her for eight days," Jared said. "Eight days! Can you imagine what they've put her through?"

"That poor girl," Zapper said.

"I hope we're not too late," Wendy said.

Jared's face fell when she said it.

"Don't worry, man," Zapper said. "That girl's a fighter. If anybody can make it, she can."

A hatch opened. A boy in his teens stepped in. He had long, light brown hair and high cheekbones. Pirate knew, the instant that the saw him, that he had seen the boy's face before, but he could not remember where.

"Lex," Cockrum said. "Come in. Intrepid Force, I want you to meet Lex Marston."

"Lex Marston?" Jared gasped.

"From the pictures in Uncle Enoch's museum?" Pirate said. He remembered the pictures: black and white photographs from a hundred years in the past.

Lex looked from one stunned face to the other.

"This is Jared," Cockrum said. "And this is Pirate Eisman. He's the great-grandson of Ian and Joanie."

"Joanie?" Lex said, his voice shaky. "My sister?"

Cockrum nodded. The life seemed to leave Lex's body. His knees buckled. He stumbled backwards onto the bed across from Jaina's.

"It's really true then," he said. "I'm in the future, and everyone I knew is dead."

"Not everyone," Cockrum said.

"I'm glad to know you, Pirate," Lex said earnestly as he fought to control his emotions. "Glad to know all of you."

"Jared and I grew up in Crane Island," Pirate said. "We'll be happy to take you back there if you want to go."

"Yes," Lex said. "I'd love to go."

"I think my Uncle Enoch will want to see you too," Pirate said.

"Enoch?" Lex said. "Enoch Henry? He's still alive?"

"Yes," Pirate told him. "He is still alive."

"I think we'd better get everybody together," Jared said. "Neema and I learned some things on board the *Lightbringer*, things you all need to know."

"I'll tell Sheppard," Cockrum said.

* * *

Twenty minutes later, Cockrum and Sheppard assembled the Intrepid Force in the *Vanguard*'s multipurpose recreation lounge. Most asteroid mining ships had spartan living areas, but Corbalew had outfitted the room with couches, cushions, and draperies. It looked like something from a sultan's palace. Sheppard and the members of Intrepid Force all wore light blue crew uniforms Cockrum had pulled from ship's storage. Tori wore the smallest uniform they could find for her, but still had to roll up the sleeves and pants legs. Lex Marston and Jolie Harrison, his attorney, joined the meeting.

"You're sure about this?" Cockrum asked. He took a sip of coffee from a ceramic mug.

"Yes," Jared said. "I'm certain."

"Gogue is a machine?" Jolie Harrison asked.

"No," Jared said. "He's a computer program. He resides in a machine."

"A computer program," Lex said. "Like a character in a synthetic reality program?"

"Yes," Jared said. "One of the programmers on board the *Lightbringer* was a master of artificial intelligence programming. The Gogue personality is, as you say, a character."

"So this man was a saboteur?" Cockrum said.

"No," Wendy said. "He was a boy who loved to play military strategy games."

"One of his favorites was a variation of an old game called *Risk*," Jared said. "It's called *Rubicon*."

"Like the river Caesar crossed," Cockrum said.

"In this game," Jared said, "the Rubicon is the river of time."

"What's the object of this game?" Cockrum asked.

"Players try to capture the world," Jared said. "They can travel through time and build their power across the centuries."

"So Darnell created an opponent for himself," Wendy said. "The ultimate general, the worst tyrant he could imagine."

"What do you get," Zapper asked, "when you cross Genghis Khan, Hitler, Napoleon, and Maltuvius with the Antichrist?"

"Back in my time," Lex said, "people used to write computer programs that could play chess. You're saying that's what Gogue was?"

"Yes," Wendy said. "Darnell, the boy who created Gogue, couldn't see how dangerous he was."

"Like keeping a crocodile as a pet," Zapper said.

"Exactly," Wendy said. "He kept making him smarter, more cunning, and more ruthless. Arwen tried to warn him, but it was too late. By the time she knew what was happening, Gogue had already taken over the ship's computer systems. He had overwritten them with his personality."

"And that gave him total control," Sheppard said. "He could imprison the crew in their own quarters, cut off communications, shut down life support . . ."

"Or direct the robot drones the ship used for repairs and exploration," Jared said. "Turn them into killers."

"And now he's taken over every computer on Earth," Pirate said. "Our encryptions were no match for his technology."

"And he can copy himself into every computer in the world," Hal said. "There's no way to stop him."

"That's not entirely true," Jared said. "Gogue was designed to run on a twenty-second century computer with more memory and faster processors than any computer late twenty-first century scientists have ever built. He has created aliases--simplified versions of himself--to run on the older, slower computers of the twentieth and twenty-first centuries, but they're only shadows of the original Gogue. They don't have his abilities, not even close."

"So he has to have computers from the future to run his software?" Tori asked. "Is that what you're saying?"

"Exactly," Jared said. "Imagine trying to run today's software on a thirty-year-old system. Gogue uses a twenty-second century artificial intelligence matrix."

"How many of those are there?" Zapper asked.

"According to the *Lightbringer*'s schematics," Jared said, "there were three of them aboard the ship. We found one of them. It was badly damaged."

"So there are only two computers in this time that can contain Gogue's consciousness," Cockrum said, "his soul, if you will?"

"That thing doesn't have a soul," Sheppard said.

"No," Jared agreed. "Not a soul as you and I understand it. He has no consciousness, no feelings, but he has been programmed to react as though he does. He deliberately torments and provokes his enemies."

"Yes," Sheppard said. "Yes, he does. It's funny. I can make theological arguments against Gogue having a soul, but I could almost swear he's demon-possessed. That kind of evil doesn't come from the cool calculations of a machine."

"You underestimate machines," Jared said.

"Okay," Sheppard said. "So what can we do to stop him?"

"The answer seems obvious," Pirate said. "Destroy the computers that contain his software. The trick is finding them and getting to them."

"We have another problem," Jared said. "The drive system from the *Lightbringer* is missing. I think Gogue may be constructing his own time machine."

"For what?" Zapper asked. "Earth is beaten. It's on the ropes. What does he need a time machine for?"

"*Rubicon*," Jared said. "He can play the game as many times as he needs to to conquer the world. "

"There's only one problem," Sheppard said. "He doesn't know how to travel through time."

"But he did," Cockrum said. "Obviously his ship did have the capability."

"He has the capability, but not the knowledge," Jared said. "His trip through time was an accident. The ship's drive system had the ability to open wormholes, tunnels through other dimensions. That was the only way they could ever reach another star system in a human lifetime. Gogue was opening one of those wormholes when Arwen sabotaged the ship's computers. The wormhole destabilized, and the ship was thrown out of control and back through time."

"In the simulation I was trapped in," Lex Marston said, "the Corbalew character kept asking me if I knew the secret of time travel. He was almost frantic about it."

"Do you think there's any chance he'll figure out how to recreate the accident on his own?" Cockrum asked.

"He doesn't have to," Jared said. "He already has it."

"What?"

"He's got Neema," Sheppard said.

"She'll die before she gives away that secret," Jared said. "That's why we've got to hurry."

"He won't let her kill herself," Sheppard said. "He'll put her into some kind of synthetic reality nightmare and trick and torture her until she breaks."

"And he's had her for nine days," Pirate said. "God help her."

"Jared," Wendy said. "What about your link to Neema's mind? Have you sensed anything?"

"No," Jared said. "Nothing. But there's something else you should know."

"More bad news," Zapper said.

"The time travel formula is hidden on board the *Intrepid*," Jared said.

"What?" Tori said. "Where?"

"I'd rather not say just yet," Jared said.

"You don't trust us?" Zapper asked.

"After some of the things we've been through," Sheppard said. "I don't blame him."

"You're saying Neema hid it somewhere on the ship?" Pirate said.

"Yes," Jared said.

"Do you think Gogue knows it's there?" Hal asked. "He may not know what he has."

"That's why I have to get on board that ship and steal or destroy it before he gets the chance," Jared said.

"That technology could put us years ahead in space exploration," Jaina said. "Think of what we could learn."

"It was technology this generation was never meant to have," Sheppard said. "We can't let ourselves be tempted by it."

"The Tree of Knowledge," Zapper said. "It's the Garden of Eden all over again."

"That was the knowledge of good and evil," Sheppard said.

"How many people has Gogue killed?" Wendy asked. "Millions? Hundreds of millions?"

"A lot," Zapper said.

"What if we could stop it from happening?" Wendy asked. "Go back into the past and keep it from happening?"

"Or send a message back," Pirate said. "Maybe we could warn Neema."

"Okay," Sheppard said. "So we've got three mission objectives here. First we have to find the artificial intelligence modules--the artificial brains--that contain Gogue's consciousness and destroy them, second, we have to keep Gogue from developing time travel capability and escaping into the past . . ."

"That's two objectives," Zapper said.

"No, it's not," Tori said.

"Keep him from getting the capabilities," Zapper said. "Keep him from escaping into the past. To keep him from getting the capabilities, we've got to get to the *Intrepid* and find out where Neema hid the secret. To keep him from escaping, we've got to find his time ship."

"He's right," Sheppard said. "Different tactics are required to accomplish them. Those are the second and third objectives then. Thank you, Zapper."

"No problem," Zapper said.

"And the fourth objective is to rescue Neema," Jared said.

"And Captain Butler and the rest of the *Intrepid*'s crew," Sheppard said. "I won't argue over how many objectives that is."

"Our problem," Pirate said, "is what to do first. We don't know whether he's found the data Neema hid on board the *Intrepid*."

"Or made Neema talk," Zapper said.

"Or if he's finished building the time ship," Pirate said.

"Right," Sheppard said. "If he already has the time travel formula, breaking into the *Intrepid* wouldn't stop him. If the time ship isn't finished anyway, we don't have to worry about disabling it."

"So basically," Zapper said, "we've got to find Gogue's base, break in, and make things up as we go along."

"Essentially," Sheppard said. "We'll send Jared onto the *Intrepid*. He'll be responsible for retrieving whatever Neema has hidden there."

"And hijacking the ship," Jared said. "At the very least, it will serve as a diversion."

Cockrum and Sheppard looked at each other.

"What do you think, Jonas?" Sheppard asked.

"It's risky," Cockrum said. "The *Intrepid* can't stand up long against their weapons, but I don't think Gogue will destroy it if he can capture it."

"All right," Sheppard said. "Jared will board the *Intrepid*. I'll send two other people with him. Tori will assist with the technical details. Mike will watch both of their backs."

"Our ninja protector," Tori said.

"At your service," Mike said. He bowed gravely.

"The rest of us," Sheppard continued, "will have the dual responsibility of finding Gogue and freeing the hostages."

"What about the time ship?" Hal asked.

"That will be my job," Cockrum said. "The *Vanguard* will be responsible for disabling or destroying the time ship."

"Will we have time to get our strength back before we find the base?" Pirate asked. "We're not exactly at our fighting best."

"I don't know when we'll find them," Cockrum said. "Maybe in the next few minutes, maybe a few days from now. I know you're not at your best, but the people on board this ship are the only hope humanity has right now."

"Not that we're under any pressure here," Zapper said.

"There may be a medical solution," Jaina said. "I've got stimulants that can give us almost superhuman strength and endurance."

"What's the downside?" Pirate asked.

"They keep you going for a few hours," Mike said, "After that they leave you wasted. Repeat injections can be fatal. That's why they're banned from martial arts tournaments."

"That's the trade-off," Jaina said. "If the battle lasts more than a few hours, none of us will be in any condition to fight."

"I'm not worried about a few hours," Zapper said. "If we live through the first five minutes, we'll be lucky."

"Maybe we're using the wrong approach to finding Corbalew," Sheppard said.

"How do you mean?" Cockrum asked.

"We're hunting," Sheppard said. "Maybe we should try fishing instead."

"Bait him," Hal said. "Lure him out."

"Yes," Sheppard said. "Exactly."

"I think I know how," Lex said. "It will take a couple of hours to set up. And I'll need Preston's help."

* * *

Dressed in identical black life support suits--suits designed to be worn underneath spacesuits--Sheppard and the Intrepid Force packed into the tight EVA (extravehicular activity) ready room and watched the monitor screens. Gray hard suits hung, suspended from metal frames, against one wall. With their large heads and hunched backs, they looked like aliens hanging on hooks in some horror movie meat locker. Flat monitor screens and shelves of silver gray tubing took up the remaining space.

The adjoining room was lined with metal lab tables. The members of the team took turns sitting and lying on them during the tense hours of waiting. The room was dull gray and sparsely furnished. The pallid lighting gave the room a cold, sterile look. The floor was covered with a black rubber mat that was worn through to the metal in spots.

As the rest of the team stood around the EVA room's monitor screens, Pirate looked over his shoulder and saw Wendy sitting by herself on one of the lab tables. She was holding a portable video unit and staring into the screen. Pale light played across her intense features.

Pirate left the others staring at Saturn's bright rings and craggy satellites, crept around the table behind Wendy, and peered over her shoulder at the weathered video unit and at the tiny ghost who moved on the screen. Her urgent voice, tinny and distorted, floated across time.

"He's taken over the ship. SKKKKTTT--restored life support for the moment. I think I'm the last one left alive. SKKKTTTT . . . overridden self-destruct. I'm going to try to send a power surge into the Scanlon-Marston field generators and collapse the wormhole."

Pirate put his arms around Wendy's waist and his chin on her shoulder.

"Who was she, Pirate?"

"A girl from the future who looks like you," Pirate said, "and has my last name."

"And your eyes," Wendy said. "The same frosty shade of blue. Is this our daughter?"

"It may be a coincidence," Pirate said. "We never found any records that told who her parents were."

"Jaina could analyze her DNA," Wendy said. "Then we would know."

"Maybe," Pirate said. "Would you want to know?"

"I don't know," Wendy said. "Yes, I think I would."

"Even if the test results turned out to be positive," Pirate said, "she might not be our daughter. Not the 'us' we know anyway."

"What do you mean?" Wendy asked.

"Scientists at least admit the possibility of alternate futures," Pirate said. "Neema claims she used to be able to detect them. Arwen Eisman may be from another time line, a world of what might have been."

"I like her," Wendy said.

"I do too," Pirate said. "She was smart and pretty. I'd like to think my daughter would be like that. I keep feeling sad for her, like I've lost someone close to me."

"I know," Wendy said. "I wish we'd at least had some kind of funeral for her."

"Me too," Pirate said.

"Is that what's destined for us, Pirate?" Wendy asked. "We get married, have a daughter, and then lose her sometime in her twenties?" Her dark eyes looked hopelessly, profoundly sad.

"No," Pirate said. He moved over onto the table beside her, put his arm around her. "I can't believe there's no way we could warn her, no way we could stop it from happening. That's why I keep hoping she's from an alternate future. I mean, she almost has to be, doesn't she? We would never have let her go on that mission knowing what we know."

"Maybe we died before we could warn her," Wendy said. "Or maybe we tried to warn her, but she wouldn't listen."

"There's so much we don't know," Pirate said.

"If we lose the battle with Gogue," Wendy said, "none of this will matter. We'll both be dead."

"You keep hoping for an early death," Pirate said, "and you keep surviving."

"Just unlucky, I guess."

Pirate looked around at the dingy room with its pale lighting and metal walls. He looked at their friends, friends they had faced death with, in the adjoining room. He pulled Wendy closer, and they sat in silence for a while.

* * *

Dr. Chambers found Jaina Benedict in an alcove in the ship's medical lab. Her hand-held medical scanner was plugged into a dock on one of the ship's medical computer ports. A three dimensional schematic of a human brain and spinal column rotated slowly on a flat viewscreen.

"Can I help you?" Chambers asked.

"No," she said. "I was just finishing something up."

"It's a courtesy," Chambers explained, "to ask for permission to use the ship's medical equipment."

"I'm not going to break your equipment by playing with it, doctor," Jaina said.

"I never said that you would," Chambers said.

"If I were twenty years older," Jaina said, "would I still have to ask permission?"

"Is everything all right?" Sheppard asked. "I noticed you were missing and went to look for you. We may have to launch at a moment's notice."

"Dr. Benedict is not a member of our medical staff," Chambers said.

"What staff?" Jaina said. "There's just you and Dr. Rampillai?"

"I don't mind her using our equipment," Chambers continued, "but I'd appreciate it if she would notify someone first. That is proper protocol."

"He's right, Jaina," Sheppard said. "It's professional courtesy."

"All right," Jaina said. "I'm sorry. I just needed the equipment for something."

"Is there anything wrong?" Sheppard asked. "Anything I should know about."

"I don't think so," Jaina said. "I just--"

"What is it, Jaina?"

"It's probably paranoia," she said. "but I did some neural scans of the group. The first night we were stranded on Titan, I had a dream that Gogue's forces had come back. After what happened to Wendy, I wanted to make sure we weren't all carrying live neural implants in our heads. The last thing we need is Gogue controlling our minds."

"Did you find anything?" Sheppard asked.

"No," she said. "The scans were negative. I guess I was just being paranoid."

"Dealing with Gogue will make you that way," Sheppard said. "You did the right thing, Jaina."

Klaxons sounded in the hallway. Sheppard spun around and tapped the communications panel beside the door. Cockrum's face appeared on the screen.

"What is it?" Sheppard asked. "What's wrong?"

"Gogue just responded to our hails," Cockrum said. "I thought you were in the EVA ready room."

"On my way," Sheppard said.

CHAPTER 36: Meeting the Enemy

"As you can see," Corbalew said, "the reports of my death were quite exaggerated. My captors did not want my allies finding out I was still alive."

"I see you've managed to retake the ship," Gogue said.

"Yes," Corbalew said. "With the help of my faithful army. I'm afraid the ship is not in perfect working order, and we're a bit low on supplies. Do we have your permission to return to base?"

"Yes," Gogue said. "I'll transmit the coordinates."

"I have the boy, Lex Marston," Corbalew said. "Stefan, as we know him. His secrets are safe, and I have more to share with you. I'm afraid, however, that the science of time travel was not one of his specialties."

"A pity," Gogue said.

"So you still have not been able to discover the secret on your own?" Corbalew asked.

"The simulations we have run have not been able to develop a stable wormhole into the past," Gogue said.

"What about the girl?" Corbalew asked. "Were you able to capture her?"

"Yes," Gogue said. "She has been most difficult . . . most uncooperative."

"Unfortunate," Corbalew said. "I may be able to assist you in persuading her."

"Not likely," Gogue said. He seemed angered by the suggestion that anyone else might succeed where he had failed.

"Oh, my," Corbalew said. "Don't tell me you've killed her."

"No," Gogue said. "She lives. For the moment."

Sheppard and the Intrepid Force watched the exchange from the flat screen of the EVA ready room.

"He's good," Zapper said. "Do you think we fooled him?"

"Preston got the face and voice prints from the simulation Gogue used to persuade Lex Marston," Sheppard said.

"But what about access codes and passwords?" Hal asked.

"They managed to get those from the real Corbalew," Sheppard said. "Cockrum's got him in the cargo hold."

"What?" Wendy said. "He's alive?"

"He's in a REGEN tank in one of the cargo bays," Sheppard said.

"A REGEN tank?" Zapper said. "They're treating him? Healing him?"

"They have their reasons," Sheppard said.

"You can't trust anything he says," Wendy said. "Any access codes you get from him will only lead us to our deaths."

"I feel the same way," Sheppard said. "I just hope we're both wrong."

"Or that Gogue plays along long enough for us to get within striking distance," Pirate said.

"So what do you think, preacher?" Zapper asked. "Do you think God's on our side?"

"I believe in a God who loves us," Sheppard said, "but whether we're destined to win this battle isn't for me to say."

"But what kind of God would leave our planet in the hands of that thing?" Jaina asked.

"God's ways don't always make sense to us," Sheppard said.

"What's the use of a God like that?" Jaina asked. "What good is He?"

A look of horror crossed Sheppard's face.

"What's wrong?" Mike asked.

"Gogue asked me the same kinds of questions," Sheppard said. "Over and over and over. Just for a moment I wondered if my escape from him was just another one of his illusions. I wondered if I was still in that room on *Vector*."

* * *

Two tense, breathless hours crept by. Cockrum sat, bolt upright, in his seat on the bridge. Saturn's glistening rings, once so beautiful, looked cold and menacing now. The blackness beyond them concealed an ancient horror--not a dark angel cast down from heaven's glorious realm but a deadly bit of computer code cast down a wormhole from an unrealized future.

"How close to the coordinates Corbalew gave us are we now?" Cockrum asked. He had asked the same question five minutes before.

"Practically right on top of them," Halloran, one of the bridge officers, said.

"I'm getting something," Tyler, another of the bridge officers said. "Actually I'm getting nothing. There's a dead area ahead of us."

"The blind," Cockrum said. "Red alert. That's got to be it. Red alert. Ready all weapons."

Red warning lights came on in corridors throughout the ship.

"Intrepid Force to EVA pods," Sheppard said to the young men and women in the ready room around him. "We may not get but one shot at this."

"I wonder how close Gogue will let us get before he discovers Corbalew's not really in command," Tyler said.

A tremor shook the ship.

"This close," Cockrum said. "Battlestations!"

"Drones," Tyler said. "We've got drones."

Metallic reflections filled the dark void around the ship.

"Come now, Mr. Cockrum," Gogue's voice said, suddenly coming through the ship's communication grid. "You didn't really believe it would be that easy, did you?"

"No," Cockrum said. "But I hoped."

The ship's deflection field activated. The ship bucked as bursts went off all around it. The lights went out for a moment, then came back.

"That's their power dampening field," Lex Marston said "It looks like our modifications are working."

"You've saved our lives," Cockrum said.

"Pull up!" Tyler cried.

Halloran, the helmsman, turned to look at Cockrum. Cockrum nodded. He keyed in the command. Thrusters fired. The nose of the ship swung sharply upward. G-Forces ground down on the bridge officers, pulled them against their shoulder and lap restraints. The ship shot out over the top of a large dish-shaped object. They had not been able to see it from the front, the side that was pointed toward Earth. Once they had flown past it, they could see a space station and a fleet of ships tucked safely away in its shadow. The front surface was, among other things, a giant screen that projected what was behind it-- everything in the visible light spectrum, at least. This was the blind that Cockrum had spoken of.

"That's *Astor* Station," Halloran said. "It was placed in Saturn's orbit so explorer ships could refuel and repair damage to their ships."

"It went missing six months ago," Cockrum said. "Three expeditions failed to find it."

"Now we know where the refits have been taking place," Pirate said. He and the rest of the team were wearing spacesuits and climbing into EVA pods. The small one-person vehicles seemed more like clothing than ships. Pirate seated himself, snapped the restraints into place, and touched a button on the control panel to power up the instruments.

"Intrepid Force to EVA pods," Cockrum repeated.

"Cockrum," Sheppard said. "We're all suited up and ready when you are."

"I've got to go to the bathroom," Zapper said.

"Hold it," Tori told him.

"We've taken out most of the drones," Cockrum said from the bridge. "They're launching ships."

"This is it," Sheppard said. "Launch EVA pods."

The metal hook on Pirate's EVA suit hauled him through a long, dark tunnel. Pirate felt a rush of acceleration and found himself in space. Robot probes were exploding around him. Without an atmosphere to contain them, the explosions were quick, bright, and silent. Pirate felt the thrill of fear, and realized he was helpless. He was hanging in space with only the thin walls of a tiny pod to protect him.

Help me, God, he thought. That was all he had time for.

Pirate felt his pod buck and he found himself spinning out of control. He had only an instant to study his situation. The others were around and beside him. Wendy was only a few meters away. His pod narrowly missed hers as it rolled past. He was falling toward *Astor* Station. The computer-controlled thrusters on his ship were fighting to compensate, spitting bursts of gas through side-mounted jets. Pirate saw his world with slow motion clarity. He could see the *Intrepid* docked silently at one of the station's ports. There were other vehicles docked there as well. Most of them were Interplanetary Guard ships and asteroid smashers. Pirate thought he recognized the

355 / INTREPID FORCE

Arthur Conan Doyle there too. Saturn hung, breathtaking and glorious, overhead. Glistening in the distant sunlight, its rings looked fragile and ethereal. Bottomless black void lay beneath them. Pirate's pod righted itself, stopped spinning. Suddenly a spherical probe fell directly into Pirate's path. The lasers on his pod engaged automatically. Shards of debris peppered his suit's hull like burning hail.

"Pirate!" Zapper yelled. "Hey, Pirate."

"I'm all right," Pirate said.

"We're almost there," Hal said. "Everybody stay sharp."

Pirate felt braking thrusters engage. Crushing, nauseating force ground down upon him. Black spots appeared before his eyes.

WHA-CHUNK! Pirate's pod struck the station's hull, engaged magnetic feet. Pirate breathed a sigh of relief. He was relieved to have made it this far and hoped everyone else had.

Pirate saw a flash and thought he felt the station move beneath him. Chunks of twisted metal spiraled away from a gash in the station's side. Cylindrical cargo containers spun out into space. According to plan, Hal had blown the lock on one of the station's cargo bays. The cargo bays had large doors that opened into space and airlocks that separated them from the station's internal hallways.

"Everybody inside," Hal cried. "I'll cover you."

Pirate engaged thrusters, pushed away from the station, and coaxed his pod laterally along the hull until he reached the cargo bay. He could see the pods of his teammates skirting across the hull and dropping through the hatch.

"Hurry!" Sheppard yelled. "We've got company."

Pirate could see Hal's pod hanging in space behind him. His weapons ports flashed. A shadow fell across them. Pirate turned his head sideways. He could not get a clear view of what was behind him, but thought he could make out the edge of a spaceship's hull. *There was a ship back there. It was targeting them.*

"Intrepid Force," Cockrum's voice said through their helmet radios. "Stand by. We've got your back."

A bright flash lit up the ship's hull. The shadow of the approaching ship dropped away.

"Cockrum's got their attention," Sheppard said. "Everybody inside."

Pirate dropped through the open cargo bay. Plastic cargo cylinders floated past him. Others were tethered to the wall by netting. Pirate could see four other EVA modules already inside. Sheppard, Wendy, Zapper, and Jaina had made it. Hal was still outside.

"Hal," Sheppard said.

"That's it," Hal said. "I'm coming in behind Pirate."

"Everybody prepare to ditch EVA pods," Sheppard said. "Head for the airlocks. We can expect to meet some opposition on the other side."

Pirate maneuvered his pod toward a section of wall. The magnetic feet engaged. With his tether firmly attached, Pirate ejected his pod's canopy. He disengaged his restraints, twisted free, and swung out onto the cargo bay's wall. Magnetic grips on the soles of his boots seized the wall. Pirate reached back into the pod and pulled what his friends called "the magnetic ski pole" from its socket beside the hatch. The pole had a hand grip on one end and a magnetic gripping foot on the other. The device had been developed by astronauts to help them maneuver quickly in zero gravity. By attaching the magnetic foot and swinging on the pole, they could "pole vault" through a ship faster than they could run through it with magnetic boots and with greater control than swimming through the air allowed.

As Pirate swung away from his EVA pod, he saw scorch marks running along the rear of the pod. There was a jagged gash in the heat-resistant ceramic tiling. His throat tightened. One side had been blown out of the main thruster assembly. His pod had taken a hit by fire from one of the robot probes that were floating around outside of the station. He had been inches away from death, and he had never realized it.

Pirate joined Sheppard, Wendy, Zapper, and Jaina at the airlock. Zapper had already torn the cover off the control panel and was inserting devices into the machinery inside. Hal soared up beside them, his long legs looking spindly as he kicked through vacuum in zero gravity. The airlock sprang open, and they all climbed in. Hal slammed the door behind them.

"Power up weapons," Sheppard said. "Everybody back away from the door." He pulled out a concussion grenade and twisted it. Lights came on as the device armed itself.

A green light came on over the airlock's inner doors. Pirate, Wendy, and the others backed against the wall as the metal doors opened. A barrage of laser blasts burned through the opening. They struck the airlock's rear hatch. Hal tossed the concussion grenade. A shock wave tore through the station. The laser barrage ceased.

Pirate started to peer around the corner.

"Wait," Hal said. "Let me have a look first."

He stuck his pistol around the corner. The site was tied to the implant in his optic nerve. He could see what the gun "saw."

"Oh, man," Hal said.

"What is it?" Tori asked.

"We've got drones," Hal said. "A lot of drones. I'm tossing another grenade, and we're going in."

I wonder how the other group is doing, Pirate thought.

* * *

Jared, Mike, and Tori stepped out of the *Intrepid*'s airlock and into the dark ship. Tori jerked the cover off an access panel and jammed a plug into the connection port she found there. Her fingers flew across the control pad she had pulled from her tool box. Colored icons flashed across the pad's flat screen.

"I've got the cameras locked into a loop," she said. "If anybody looks at the monitors, they'll see an empty ship. I've also locked down the airlocks."

"Life support's still operating," Jared said. "That's good." He twisted off his helmet.

"It's sad seeing the *Intrepid* like this," Mike said. "It's like another ship."

"I know," Jared said. "Everything's familiar, but it all seems wrong."

"Let's get to the armory," Tori said. Duplicates of all Intrepid Force uniforms and equipment were locked away in the *Intrepid*'s armory.

"I'm heading straight for the bridge," Jared said. "We may not have much time."

* * *

There were explosions going off all around the ship. Thrusters spun the battered asteroid smasher out of harm's way. The *Vanguard* returned fire. The heads of the ship's laser turrets spun like deadly lighthouses spitting hot rays of death across the dark ocean.

"Minimal damage," Halloran said, "but they're backing off."

"How are those refits working?" Cockrum yelled.

"We've neutralized the dampening field," Tyler said. "We've confused their targeting sensors. They're firing at ghosts images."

"He's sending out more ships," Halloran said. "Asteroid smashers. The *Carnegie* and the *Bessemer* just pulled away from the station."

"Keep circling the station," Cockrum said. "He won't hit us with anything big if there's a chance of wrecking the station."

"Mr. Cockrum," Halloran said. "I've got a call coming in from Dr. Chambers in medical. He says it's urgent."

The ship darted wildly to the side as an explosion grazed its hull.

"Does he know what we're facing up here?" Cockrum replied.

"He says it's about the Intrepid Force."

"Tyler," Cockrum said. "Launch the decoys!"

"Yes, sir."

"Put Chambers on," Cockrum said.

Another explosion shook the ship.

"Cockrum," Chambers said.

"Yes," Cockrum said. "What is it?"

"A little while ago I caught Dr. Benedict analyzing neural scans of the team," Chambers said. "She told me she was afraid they'd been infected with some kind of mind-controlling implants. She said the scans were negative."

The ship bucked again.

"We're being shot at up here," Cockrum said. "What's the problem?"

"I just analyzed the scans she took myself," Chambers said. "They're positive."

"Positive?" Cockrum said.

"They're infected by mind-controlling implants," Chambers said.

"The whole team?" Cockrum gasped.

"Everybody but Jared."

"You're saying she misdiagnosed the scans?" Cockrum said, not believing it.

"I'm saying she never ran them," Chambers said. "It was a false memory."

No.

"Halloran," Cockrum said. "Contact the Intrepid Force. Emergency!"

* * *

The interior of *Astor* station was a dark maze of gray metal lattices, support beams, metal staircases, catwalks, and elevator tubes. The labyrinth seemed to go on forever and to lead nowhere. The Intrepid Force had been running, dodging beam weapons, and returning fire on shadowy attackers for what seemed like hours.

"Where are we?" Zapper asked. He scanned the walkway above them for signs of movement.

"I don't know," Pirate said. "This doesn't match any of the schematics I downloaded."

"What?" Jaina said. "Are you saying we're lost in here? That you downloaded the wrong schematics?"

"No," Pirate said. "There were pictures of the outside as well as the inside. Those were a perfect match. Once we stepped through the airlock, everything turned strange."

A concussion beam struck Pirate's deflection field. Hal's exobot sidestepped a beam that was aimed at him. He returned fire with both hands, his blazing tracer flares lighting the way as his projectiles blasted apart one of the overhead balconies. There was no one on them.

"What are we fighting here?" Zapper said. "No people. No bodies."

"Jaina," Wendy said. "Did you analyze those neural scans you took of us?"

"When she scanned us for implants?" Zapper said.

"Of course I analyzed them," Jaina said. "The scans were negative. We were clean. All of us."

"There was a sound I used to hear just before I had one of those illusions," Wendy said. "A sound like a ringing handset from my communications center. I heard that sound when we were coming through the airlock."

"So what are you saying?" Zapper said. "That all of this is a simulation? That none of it's real?"

"Have you ever seen a space station with this much wasted space?" Wendy said. "The schematics don't match."

"Jaina," Zapper said. "Who analyzed the scans you ran on us?"

"I did," Jaina said.

"Who else did you show them to?" Zapper asked.

"I . . . ," Jaina paused. "Look. I thought I was just being paranoid." She looked down.

"Who else did you show them to?" Hal asked.

"No one," she said. "I didn't show them to anyone."

"Did you ever notice," Zapper said, "how real smart people never have any common sense?"

* * *

"I've found something," Tyler said as the *Vanguard* arched around the station. "It's a second blind."

"No wonder they stopped firing at us," Halloran said. "They didn't want to hit it. We're coming around it now."

Behind the blind was a single ship. It was partly enclosed in a construction dock and surrounded by construction drones.

Tyler scanned the ship. The *Vanguard*'s computers assembled a three dimensional model from the data. The ship's model sat--slowly rotating to display every angle--on one of the side screens. Data from the scan poured into the margins on either side of the image. The ship was long and ugly with huge engines, an instrument package where the computer core and scanning equipment would be, and storage bays for drones and other equipment. Two enormous cannons were mounted on the front.

"Where are the crew quarters?" Tyler asked.

"He doesn't need a crew," Cockrum said. "He can run the whole ship himself."

The vessel was held together by I-beams of space-forged steel. There was a name plate welded to the side:

Rubicon

"That's it," Cockrum said. "The time ship. How close is it to being able to launch?"

"It's hard to tell without schematics of the finished ship," Lex said, "but it looks like everything is there."

An energy burst struck the ship, sent it spinning away from the blind.

* * *

"Mike has your invisibility armor," Tori said. "And I've got my nanoprobes back."

"Good," Jared said. He didn't look up. He was sitting at a computer station on the second level of the *Intrepid's* dark bridge. Mike and Tori were standing on the deck beneath him beside the captain's chair. The room was three stories tall. The front wall was dominated by a huge curved viewscreen. Individual workstations--consoles filled with screens, buttons, knobs, and levers--were stacked into railed catwalks along the walls. The floors of those upper level catwalks were made of black metal grillwork.

"How's it going?" Mike asked. "Where are you?"

"I've broken into the *Intrepid's* computer core," Jared said. "I'm going through files."

"Can we hijack the ship?" Tori asked. "Run it on automation?"

"Yes," Jared said. "It shouldn't be a problem."

"What about Neema's time travel secrets?" Mike asked. "Weren't you going to look for those first?"

"Yes," Jared said. "They're here."

"Here?" Mike said. "Where?"

"In the *Intrepid's* computer core," Jared said. "Neema's ship uploaded them before it was destroyed. They were scattered throughout the system, hidden in other files."

"So what do we do with them?" Tori asked.

"If we can beat Gogue and keep him from downloading them into his ship," Jared said, "we may be able to use the time ship he's building to send a message into the past. We might be able save all of the people Gogue killed."

"But if we can't beat Gogue," Mike said, "we've got to make sure he doesn't get this data."

"Right," Jared said, "That's why I need you to help me rig a switch that will fry the *Intrepid*'s computer core."

"That shouldn't be too hard," Tori said. "We'll have to uncover the main memory core, run a few cables from one of the power couplings."

"Let's get to it," Jared said. "We may only have a few minutes."

* * *

After wandering through the *Astor*'s dark maze for what seemed like days, Pirate, Wendy, and the others found the entrance to what looked like a temple--or maybe a gaudy Las Vegas casino. Flaming torches burned from braziers on either side. Tall columns of machined metal stood tall on either side of a rectangular passage. Overhead was an arch with burning letters flashing across it:

LOOK UPON MY WORKS, YE MIGHTY,
AND DESPAIR.

CHAPTER 37: Showdown of Shadows

Sheppard, Pirate, Hal, and the rest of the team stood at the temple's entrance for a moment and wondered what secrets they would find within. Had their enemy finally decided to reveal himself?

"Look upon my works, ye mighty, and despair," Hal said as he read the flashing letters above them. "Pretty dramatic."

"It's a quote from a poem," Sheppard said.

Between the columns was a staircase of white marble leading upwards. They could make out a human figure standing at the top. A row of fluted marble columns stood in a line behind him. Between them was a dark sky streaked with meteors.

"Come on up," the figure said. The voice was male. His back was to them, but he did not seem surprised by their approach. Warily they climbed the stairs and found themselves standing in what looked like a Greek temple or an image from mythology. Beyond the pillars was a dark sea. Blazing clods of pitted stone plummeted down from the sky, struck the sea, and sent up sizzling geysers of steam. The sky, they saw, was full of spaceships.

"Mag, huh?" the man said. "Magnum opus ad infinitum." He turned around. He was young--eighteen or nineteen years old. There was a wreath of leaves encircling his head.

"Darnell?" Wendy gasped. "Is that you?"

"What?" the young man said. "You don't recognize me?" The face was not an exact copy of the young man from Wendy's vision. The chin was squarer, the skin was darker, and the muscles were enlarged, but the resemblance was unmistakable. His eyes flashed red.

"Gogue," Sheppard said. "The yin to the yang. The dark mirror."

"Very good, Reverend Sheppard," Gogue said. "Very good."

"Darnell used himself as the model," Wendy said. "The personality matrix."

"Only without a conscience," Sheppard said. "Without a soul."

"A soul?" Gogue said. "Hah!"

"What is this place?" Pirate asked.

"It's an image, stupid," Gogue said. "Haven't you grasped that by now?"

"No," Pirate said. "I meant, what does it represent?"

"It's my temple," Gogue said. "My holy of holies. You've been good enemies. I wanted you to see it before I killed you."

"Why kill us?" Wendy asked.

"Because it's who I am," Gogue said. "It's who I was programmed to be. I might be willing to spare you, Wendy. I could always use a queen to rule at my side."

He gestured. Wendy's outfit morphed into the garb of a Martian princess from one of Edgar Rice Burroughs' *John Carter* novels. A jeweled tiara decorated her brow. Bits of metal and flowing cloth were held to her body's flowing contours by chains. They left plenty of bare skin showing between them. Ornate bands encircled her wrists and ankles. A long, jeweled sword hung from her hip.

"A teenage boy's fantasy," Jaina said. "It's a wonder he left her any clothes at all."

"Don't tempt me," Gogue said.

"Darnell must have liked Arwen," Wendy said. "That's why Gogue tormented her."

"And you too, *Mom*," Gogue said. "You're so much like her. More fun in some ways. She was such a little mousy-mousy sometimes."

Mom? Wendy thought. *So Arwen was my daughter?*

"Listen," Pirate said. "Since you can kill us anytime you want to, why not have some fun. Let us take you in a game. If we lose, you can do whatever you want to with us."

"I can already do whatever I want with you," Gogue said.

"Right," Pirate said. "But if we win, you have to release us from this simulation."

"Who says I have to?" Gogue said.

"Don't you like to gamble?" Pirate said. "It's not a challenge if there's no way to lose, and it's not a game if you don't have any stakes."

"It does sound interesting," Gogue said. "What do I get if I win?"

"Whatever you want," Pirate said. "We can't stop you."

"Yes," Gogue said. "But why should I play you for something I already have?"

"Because it's your nature," Sheppard said. "It's what you were created to do."

"How true," Gogue said. "How true. All right then. I accept your challenge. A battle to the death. You against my champions. Let's make this interesting." He gestured. Their clothing changed. "Costumes and powers based on your old uniforms. And new names.

"The Intrepid Force versus the Soldiers of Purgatory. Starring Pirate Eisman as the Centurion."

Pirate wore a uniform of black leather and golden metal.

"You have a strength rating of 3, an invulnerability rating of 7, a tactical rating of 10, plasma bursts with an attack rating of 10, and limited flight capability."

"Reverend Sheppard stars as Elisha Thunder, an angelic warrior from the heavenly realms."

Sheppard was dressed in a white tunic with baggy pants, a golden belt, and boots that looked like liquid gold. His hair was white. He had a golden helmet and a sword in his hand.

"Strength rating 9, invulnerability rating 9, tactical rating 10, sword has an attack rating of 8, and limited flight capability."

Gogue went through the same ritual with the rest of the team. Zapper became Johnny Lightning whose bolts had an attack rating of 10.

Wendy became Cyberia, a deadly machine woman with the ability to transform her cybernetic body into any number of shapes. She was horrified by the grotesque appearance Gogue had given her. She was bald and gaunt with long, metal claws.

Jaina became Nightingale, a dark-hooded presence with the ability to heal wounds or start deadly epidemics. Hal became the Warwolf, a thirty-foot-tall mechanical beast. The resemblance to the armor he had used in the old stunt show was obvious but exaggerated.

"This is so much fun," Gogue laughed to himself. "Now your enemies, the Soldiers of Purgatory.

"Chamelious, a reptilian assassin with the ability to blend in with his surroundings." A rotating hologram of a dark, slinking shape appeared in midair as Gogue described him.

"Aurelia, with her aura of death."

Aurelia had blue skin and armor and a glistening blue aura that extended from her body to ensnare foes.

"Xenius, with her deadly speed and accuracy."

Xenius was an elfin woman with pointed ears, lightweight body armor, and an arsenal of hand weapons.

One by one Gogue described each of the foes. He went into painstaking detail about strength ratings, invulnerability ratings, special abilities, and so on.

"He sounds like a guy who's played too many simulation games," Zapper said. "Mama always told me they would warp my brain."

"Now, my intrepid warriors," Gogue said. "Descend the stairs into the shadowy realms of purgatory. Your foes await you."

* * *

The *Vanguard* had stopped spinning. Emergency bulkheads had fallen into place and latched. Emergency hatches had sealed. The wrecked ship was no longer spewing atmosphere into the void, no longer vomiting people and equipment though its gaping wounds. Emergency lights flashed, blood red, through coils of smoke. The acrid tang of burned plastic filled the ship. Founts of flame-suppressing foam spat floating white snakes. They wriggled through the darkness and broke apart into white globules. Artificial gravity was out.

Cockrum looked around the ruined bridge. Tyler and Halloran floated out of their alcoves. They looked, Cockrum thought, like disembodied spirits. He halfway expected to look behind them see their riddled bodies lying splayed against their flashing consoles. Lex Marston clung to the arms of his chair and stayed at his post. His eyes were haunted. How many friends, how many worlds, would he have to lose before this nightmare within a nightmare finally ended?

Echo Yazzi, the young Navajo woman from the *Intrepid*, popped through one of the hatches in the back of the bridge. She looked like she was swimming through smoke. She had a pistol in one hand.

"They're boarding us, sir," she said. "What do we do now?"

"May I have your attention," Cockrum said, holding up one hand as he spoke into a goose-necked microphone. His voice echoed through the ship's dark hallways. "The *Vanguard* has been disabled, and is now being boarded. The ship is coming apart. Under other circumstances, I would order the crew to abandon ship. Out here, there is no one to rescue us, no safe haven to escape to. Defend yourselves by any means at your disposal. Nothing will be said against anyone who chooses to surrender. May God watch over us and over our planet. Cockrum out."

"So that's it?" Echo said, not believing what she had just heard. "We just sit here and wait for them to take us?"

"Not necessarily," Cockrum said, "but going head to head with them is no longer an option. Now we have to resort to guerilla tactics. Hit and run."

"That's more like it," Echo said.

"Tyler," Cockrum said. "Can we still track the boarding parties?"

"Yes, sir."

"Good," he said. "There are two people on board this ship that Gogue's men will be looking for. One of them is Lex Marston."

Lex turned at the mention of his name.

"The other is Gaith Corbalew."

"Corbalew?" Echo gasped. "He's here? Alive?"

"He's in a REGEN tank in Cargo Bay 13," Cockrum said.

"You're keeping him alive?" Echo said. "After all the people he killed? My sister was a hostage. He shot her through the head and hung her on the wall of an escape pod with a data slide in her mouth."

"Echo," Cockrum said. "I know . . ." He put his hand on her shoulder.

"No!" she said, slapping his hand away. "You don't know anything, man."

She sprang toward the hatch, grabbed the rails on either side of it.

"Where are you going?" Cockrum asked.

"What do you care?" she snapped. She touched a button, and the hatch rumbled open. Echo dove off into the smoke and vanished.

"Echo!" Cockrum yelled. He leaped into the air, drifted to the door, and caught the rail beside it. Squinting, he strained to see through the tendrils of smoke and fire suppressant that filled the corridor beyond. Echo was gone.

* * *

The first battle had been fierce. Aurelia's energy field had destroyed Wendy's right arm. Chamelious had pummeled Pirate relentlessly before Zapper's silvery bursts of lightning had forced his retreat. His black, reptilian shape had vanished into the dark maze, melding with the shadowy catacombs of Gogue's computer-generated purgatory.

Xenius, the female warrior elf, had battered Jaina with her quarterstaff. Hal's energy bolts had sent her cartwheeling away. An armored warrior on horseback had sliced into Hal's armored shin with an energy-charged axe. Pirate had blown him out of the saddle, and Hal had stomped him.

A red demon with a censer full of exploding fire gems had burned his was through Sheppard's protective aura before a strategically-placed jab from Sheppard's sword had caught him by surprise. Shrieking and writhing, he had melted into a cloud of red smoke and vanished.

"That was nasty," Sheppard said.

"First blood to the Intrepid Force," Gogue said, suddenly appearing in a doorway behind the team. As soon as he had delivered his proclamation, his body wavered and vanished.

"How long is this going to go on?" Jaina asked, her voice strange and inhuman like the shrouded form in which Gogue had cast her.

"As long as he wants it to," Zapper said, his voice deep and heroic.

"Why did he have to make me look like this?" Wendy said. She looked down at the stump of her bionic right arm. A tangle of scorched cable and wiring hung just above where her elbow joint had been. Wendy's voice, unlike Jaina's, was the same. Coming from the pale lips of the bald Cyberia, it seemed strangely out of place.

"Don't think about it," Sheppard said. "Just keep going."

"I know it sounds crazy," Hal said, "but try to enjoy it."

"Enjoy *this*?" Jaina cried.

"It's a game," Hal said. "In order to win it, you have to get into it, to fight with heart and spirit. Be competitive."

"He's right," Pirate said. "It's the only way we'll ever make it out of here."

"All right," Sheppard said. "Let's go. Next round."

* * *

Magnetic boots sucked against the deck with every step, then released, as a faceless parade of death-dealing soldiers stamped their way through the *Vanguard*'s dark halls. Their insect voices chirped discordantly, muffled by the black fishbowls on their heads. Fiery bursts from their rifles burned through anyone who dared oppose them.

"Where's Corbalew?" they demanded of anyone they captured. "Which deck is Corbalew on?"

Finally they got their answer. When they emerged from the elevator tube outside of Cargo Bay 13, Echo Yazzi was waiting for them. Wailing like an avenging spirit, she launched herself through the air. Concussion beams leaped wildly from the weapons in her hands. They tore into the patrol, slammed them to the deck.

Red flashes from beam weapons danced through the foggy air. They tore into Echo's floating body. She stopped moving. She hung in midair like a broken doll or a helium balloon until one of the raiders shoved her aside. She flew into a bulkhead, bounced off, and hung, weightless and wilted, in the wake of her attackers. Their bright beams burned through the cargo bay hatch. They opened the door and stepped into darkness.

* * *

Tori and Mike stepped through the hatch into the *Intrepid*'s bridge.

"The kill switch is ready," Tori said. "I've got it wired into the bridge controls. I'm pulling up the menu now."

"Great," Jared said without looking up from the console in front of him..

"How's the hijacking coming along?" Mike asked.

"I can't get the engines to initialize," Jared said. "I think he's overriding us."

"Is there any way to launch the ship manually?" Mike asked.

"Yeah," Tori said. "You have to do it from engineering."

"Do you know how to do it?" Jared asked.

"I think so," Tori said.

"You think so?"

"Yeah," Tori said. "Yeah, no problem. I can do it."

"Mike," Jared said. "Go down there with her. I'll hold the bridge."

An alarm sounded from Jared's workstation.

"What was that?" Tori asked.

"Trouble," Jared said. "We've got a boarding party. They're breaking through the main airlock. Get down to engineering. Hurry!"

"Are we staying with the plan?" Mike asked.

"Yes," Jared said, "but we have to hurry."

* * *

The hatch opened. Dark shadows fell across the corrugated deck plating of Cargo Bay 13. Gogue's forces scuttled through the open hatch like black ants. They pointed their beam rifles left and right, scanned for intruders.

Corbalew's REGEN tank stood on a raised platform in the corner. The greenish fluid within glowed beneath the lamps that encircled it. Corbalew's shrouded body was almost completely healed now. His long hair floated wildly in the green liquid around him. He saw his armored rescuers. A ghastly smile crossed his pale features.

"Well, gentlemen," his voice said from the box beside him. "I see my liberation is at hand."

"Guess again," a young woman's voice said.

Corbalew peered through the fluid, through the glass walls of his chamber, into the dark cargo hold beyond. In the red light that flowed through the outer hatch, he could see a figure standing by the cargo bay's controls. It was a young woman in a blood-soaked uniform. She had black hair and Native American features. Blood was pouring down the side of her face from a wound on her temple. Their eyes met. A look of horror crossed Corbalew's face, horror and recognition.

Dear God. It's the girl I killed.

"Echo!" Richard Preston cried as he pushed through from the hall outside. "NO!"

The men in the boarding party started to turn. Echo Yazzi grabbed the hatch release lever with both hands, threw her feet against the wall, and pulled for all she was worth. The roof of the chamber split asunder. Saturn's ringed majesty floated against the backdrop of cold eternity.

Corbalew's tank lifted from the floor, held in place by tubes. Gogue's armored soldiers leaped for the tank. One of them struck it and ripped the tubes from their moorings. A flying cargo container struck them, sent them plummeting out into space. Soldiers, guns, and cargo fell out into the void.

Richard Preston clung to Echo Yazzi's small body with all the strength he had. Tumbling through space, he had managed to snag one of the webs of cargo netting that kept crates within from floating out of the hatch every time the ship took on new cargo. Preston felt the skin on his face growing tight. Capillaries in his face were starting to burst. Numbing cold engulfed him.

I'm going to die now, he thought. *This is it. It's over.* The thought did not bother him as much as he felt it should.

The plastic hooks that held the netting in place were starting to pull free. Preston looked out into space at the ringed planet before him. He wondered if his body would be pulled down into Saturn's atmosphere or if it might become part of those bright and beautiful rings. Preston smiled. His eyes burned. His vision blurred. Saturn vanished, the wind subsided, and darkness swallowed the cargo hold. Echo Yazzi was still in Preston's grasp. He tried to breathe but could not fill his lungs.

* * *

"Nasty suckers," Zapper said. He looked both ways down the narrow corridor.

Pirate's charred body lay bleeding on the deck. He shook his head and rose to his feet. The wounds closed, but his ornate Centurion uniform was still battle scarred and blackened with soot.

"This is my last resurrection," Pirate said. "Next time they kill me, I'm out of the game for good."

"I can heal you," Jaina said, "as long as the wounds aren't mortal. I can't bring you back from the dead."

"Can you help me?" Wendy asked. Her bionic legs had been sliced out from under her. Her clawed left arm was the only extremity she had left.

Jaina sat down beside Wendy. She slid the bionic legs into place and waved her hands over Wendy's body as she had done with others earlier, but the mechanical legs refused to re-attach themselves.

"It doesn't seem to work on machines," Jaina said. "Just flesh and blood. I'm sorry."

"Chamelious," Zapper said. "That stinking lizard. If I see him again, I'll fry his tail."

A column of smoke and flame spun up from the floor in front of them. Pirate trained his hands on it, prepared to launch plasma bolts.

"This is the last round," Gogue said, appearing in the flame. "Make it a good one."

He vanished in a flash of fire and smoke.

"Leave me here," Wendy said.

"No," Pirate said. "You couldn't defend yourself."

"I'll carry her," Sheppard said.

"Better let me do that," Hal said.

"What difference does it make?" Zapper asked. "None of this is real anyway."

"Wendy's only got one life left," Pirate said. "We don't know what Gogue will do with our real bodies if we get killed in here."

"All right," Zapper said. "Good point."

Aurelia and Xenius attacked. Aurelia's cloudy aura engulfed Jaina. Xenius, the elf-woman, threw out a handful of explosive pods. Pirate and Zapper dodged around them. Hurling plasma bolts and lightning blasts, they returned fire.

* * *

Jared heard explosions in the hall and knew Tori and Mike were out there fighting for their lives.

I've got to try to help them, he thought. Then he looked down at the glowing button on the console before him. The kill switch. Frying the ship's computer core was the only way to keep the formula for time travel from falling into Gogue's hands. Jared saw green lettering form on the screen of the workstation beside him:

DOWNLOADING. 10%

DOWNLOADING? No! Gogue was downloading the files Neema had hidden in the computer.

Jared sprang for the kill switch and stabbed it with his finger.

DOWNLOADING. 12%

The switch had not worked. Gogue was still downloading the data, the precious secret.

"No!" Jared cried. He pounded the console with his fist. The door imploded.

Jared switched on his invisibility shield and powered up the concussion nodes that were mounted on the backs of his wrists. A body shot through the air, struck a bank of machinery, and lay still on the deck plating beneath him. It was Tori. Her helmet had been ripped away and his face was horribly blistered on one side. Her eyes were open but glazed. Her body shivered. She looked to be in shock.

A gigantic metal shape leaped through the hatch and into the room. It unfolded to its full mechanical height.

* * *

"This is it," Zapper said. "The throne room."

Hal was already inside, his massive shape filling the dark chamber. Pirate, Jaina, and Zapper bounded in after him, their weapons ready. Sheppard, the heavenly warrior, still carried Wendy's wounded cybernetic body over his shoulder. He raised his sword but hung back. Jaina filled the air with toxic smoke. Pirate and Zapper aimed their curled fingers into the dark spaces around them. They searched for signs of movement.

Chamelious dropped from the ceiling, his fluid reptilian body melting suddenly out of the darkness. He dropped onto Hal's back and sank his claws into the hump behind the craggy robot head.

"Get him off me!" Hal cried. "He's taking me apart!"

"STOP!" Pirate and Zapper both yelled at the same instance.

"What is it?" Sheppard asked. "What's wrong?"

"That's Jared," Pirate said.

"Yeah," Hal said. "It's the same trick he used on me at the stunt show."

"YOU LOSE!" Gogue roared, his voice shaking the very walls of the chamber.

Pirate, Zapper, Hal, Jaina, Sheppard, and Wendy all found themselves standing frozen on the marble steps of Gogue's temple. Blazing rocks were still falling from the spaceship-filled sky. The sea was still erupting with steaming geysers. Gogue paced back and forth, wagging his head, shaking his finger.

"You almost got us," Sheppard said. "Almost tricked us into killing our friends."

"I don't have to have your cooperation to kill them," Gogue said, "but it would have been more fun that way. It doesn't matter. You still lose. All of you still lose."

* * *

Hal's giant exobot stood frozen in the center of the room as Jared sat on its shoulder ripping out control chips. The boarding party poured into the room behind him. They wore the same black armor and helmets that the rest of Gogue's forces wore, the same armor and helmets Corbalew's troops had worn during the battle on Venus. The glass in the helmets was black, opaque, but there was still something familiar about those figures.

NO.

Jared had assumed, at first, that Gogue's forces had somehow captured Hal and taken his armor. Now he knew the truth. It really was Hal inside the armor, and the figures beneath him. . .

"Get him off me!" Hal cried out from inside the armor. "He's taking me apart!"

"STOP!" two of the figures beneath him both yelled at once.

"What is it?" the figure in the door asked. "What's wrong?"

"That's Jared," one of the figures beneath him said. The voice belonged to his close friend Pirate Eisman. He would recognize it anywhere.

"Yeah," Hal said. "It's the same trick he used on me at the stunt show."

Jared felt relief begin to wash over him. Then the figures froze and stopped talking and a concussion burst struck him between the shoulder blades. Jared tried to grab one of the catwalks as his armored body plummeted to the deck plating beneath him. He caught onto a rail with his left hand and held on for about two seconds before his fingers slipped free. He fell the remaining ten feet to the floor and felt the breath explode from his body as he landed hard on his armored back.

Jared raised up. He was only inches away from Tori's still form.

Pirate, Wendy, Zapper, Jaina, and Sheppard lifted away their helmets and stood facing him. Hal flipped a switch, lifted away the headpiece of his exobot, and smiled. All of them were smiling, but the smiles were cold and inhuman. These were not the smiles of his friends. Gogue was smiling through them. Their personalities still existed, but their bodies were no longer their own. They were puppets now, sleepwalkers. Their souls were, for all practical purposes, trapped in some synthetic reality prison.

Jared's hand went to the control panel beside him. A flash of pain engulfed him. He fell, senseless, to the deck plating and lay still.

CHAPTER 38: Silence

"What's going on here?" Pirate asked. He was dressed in black body armor and standing on the *Intrepid*'s bridge. Jared lay sprawled on the control panel in front of him. Hal's exobot towered over him and Zapper was beside him.

"Jared!" Wendy cried from behind him. "Tori!"

"We did this to them," Zapper said. "Gogue made us do this to them."

Pirate ran to Jared's still form. He twisted away the invisibility suit's gray mask. Jared's eyes were closed, and he was still breathing.

He's still alive," Pirate said.

"So's Tori," Sheppard said. "Thank God."

Pirate's eyes wandered to the workstation behind Jared, to the letters on the screen:

DOWNLOAD COMPLETE.

"Download complete," Pirate said. "What were they downloading?"

"I don't know," Zapper said. "But it can't be good."

The *Intrepid* was silent around them, silent as a tomb. A dark shape, lit by the pale light of the corridor behind it, stumbled through a hatch.

"Mike," Zapper said. "Is that you, man?"

"Yeah," Mike said. His voice was a ragged whisper. "It's me."

"Mike!" Wendy said. "Are you all right?"

"Sure," Mike said. "Everything's great." He stumbled to a chair and collapsed into it.

"We're sorry, man," Zapper said. "We didn't know it was you."

"I know," Mike said. "I figured that out."

"This is weird," Zapper said. "Everything's too quiet."

"Why did Gogue let us go?" Sheppard said. "We were beaten. He had us on the ropes?"

"Time travel," Jared groaned.

"What?" Jaina said. "What is it, Jared?"

"Time travel," Jared said. "Got--got the secret of time travel. Downloaded it."

"Who downloaded it?" Zapper asked.

"Gogue!" Jared said. He tried to stand. Pirate and Zapper helped him to his feet.

"Neema had hidden the secret to time travel in the *Intrepid*'s computer core," Mike explained. "We were trying to keep Gogue from downloading it."

"What's going on outside?" Zapper asked.

"I wish I knew," Pirate said.

Sheppard sat down at Captain Butler's workstation and began to flip switches.

The giant screen in the front of the room came suddenly to crystalline life. It looked, for an instant, like the front wall of the room had vanished and left the *Intrepid*'s bridge open to space.

Saturn, resplendent as ever, hung glowing in space. Probes, ships, and bits of debris drifted lazily past.

"*Vanguard*," Sheppard said. "Come in, *Vanguard*."

There was no response.

"*Vanguard*," Sheppard said again. "Are you there?"

"*Vanguard*," a familiar voice finally answered. "This is Cockrum. Is that you, Gene?"

"Yes," Sheppard said. "It's me. What's going on out there?"

"I wish I knew," Cockrum said. "The ship's been wrecked and boarded, but our boarding parties seem to have lost interest."

"Lost interest?" Sheppard said. "What do you mean by that?"

"I mean they're all wandering around like they're in some kind of a daze," Cockrum said. "They don't seem to know where they are or how they got here. What's going on over there?"

"I don't know," Sheppard said. "We're all on the *Intrepid*'s bridge."

"Is everyone all right?" Cockrum asked.

"We've had some injuries," Sheppard said. "But everyone's alive."

"Did you find Neema or Captain Butler?" Cockrum asked.

"Not yet," Sheppard said. "I'll keep you posted."

"Try to find out what's going on over there," Cockrum said. "Keep us posted."

"Sure," Sheppard said. "Sheppard out."

"Tori's awake," Jaina said, "but she's got a pretty serious concussion. I'm taking her to the sick bay."

"I'm goin' with her," Zapper said. There was a sick expression on his face. "I'm the one who took Aurelia down."

"You didn't know it was her, man," Mike said. "Tori would understand."

"Was it them we were fighting the whole time?" Wendy asked.

"You came through the airlock and hit us," Mike said.

"The airlock," Zapper said. "The cargo elevator. I thought something about it seemed familiar."

"We'd better get going," Pirate said. "Do you need help with Tori?"

"I've got her, man," Zapper said. He lifted Tori to his shoulder. "She don't weigh that much."

"Be careful," Sheppard said. "We don't know what's going on here. We've got to get back into the station and see what's happening there."

Pirate looked around at Wendy. With her brown hair and young skin, she was a beautiful young woman again and no longer a cybernetic zombie.

"Wendy," he said. "You look great."

"Thanks," she said. "I feel pretty good too." She held up her hands.

WHHHHSSSSHHHHH!

The airlock opened. Servos pulled the doors aside. With weapons raised, Sheppard and the Intrepid Force stepped into *Astor* station. The lights were on, but the hallway before them was deserted. Hal's exobot lumbered out of the airlock behind them. He could not raise up to his full twelve-foot height.

"This is what the schematics showed," Pirate said, indicating the corridor in front of them. "Eight foot ceilings. Narrow hallways."

"An ordinary space station," Sheppard said. "Be careful."

"Why don't we start opening doors?" Pirate said.

"Sounds like a good place to begin," Sheppard said. "Just be careful."

The rooms along the hallway were all empty and completely unfurnished.

"There's nothing in any of these," Pirate said. "It's like they never finished moving in."

"Let's go on to the next hallway," Wendy said. "There have to be some answers here somewhere."

The electric doors at the end of the hall hissed and snapped open. Captain Nancy Butler and Charles Fairbanks stepped through. There were about twenty other people with them. Sheppard spun around and aimed his beam weapon at them.

"Gene!" Captain Butler yelled. "It's us."

Sheppard lowered his pistol and breathed a sigh of relief.

"What's going on here?" Fairbanks asked.

"That's what we're trying to find out," Sheppard said.

"We have to find Neema," Jared said.

A communications panel lit up.

"You will find her in the station's medical lab," a disembodied voice said.

"Who's there?" Sheppard demanded.

"My name is Balthazar," the voice answered. "I am an interactive computer program from the twenty-fourth century."

"It's the computer from Neema's ship," Pirate said. "I thought she said it had been destroyed."

"Can you show us the way to the station's medical lab?" Jared asked.

"I can," Balthazar's voice replied.

* * *

"Neema!" Jared cried. "Neema! What's wrong with her?" They had found Neema unconscious and strapped to an examining table. She lay beneath a bright light in the center of a dark room. The lighting assembly was mounted on a swiveling metal arm. It looked like the head of a dragon that was holding Neema in the grip of its paralyzing death stare. The expression on her face was serene, angelic. Her eyes were open but sightless.

Jared ripped away the restraints that were binding Neema, pulled her into his arms, and raised her into a sitting position. Her eyes were blank. She was breathing but completely unaware of her surroundings. Her lips were dry and cracked.

"What did that monster do to her?" Sheppard asked. He thought of his own captivity, of the torture he had endured at Gogue's hand.

"She's catatonic," Sanchez, the *Intrepid*'s medical officer said.

"That's how you were after Astrolus captured you," Pirate said. "Your brain had shut itself down."

"It was Neema's way of protecting him," Wendy said. "What if this is the same thing?"

"Balthazar," Pirate said. "Are you there?"

"I am here," the voice said from the comm panel.

"Neema seems to be catatonic," Pirate said. "We think she's shut down her mind to keep Gogue from controlling her. Can she do that?"

"Yes," Balthazar said. "She does have that ability."

"Do you know how to wake her up?" Jared asked.

"Are you prepared to tend to her needs?" the computer's voice asked.

"Yes," Jared said. "I'll care for her."

"Then I will awaken her now."

Neema blinked, gasped, and began to look around.

"Are you all right?" Sheppard asked her.

"Where are we?" she asked.

"*Astor* station," Jared said. "Around Saturn."

"What happened to Gogue?" she demanded.

"We haven't heard from him in the past hour or so," Pirate said. "We were hoping you knew."

"Did he download the files from the *Intrepid*'s computer core?"

"I'm afraid so," Pirate said. "Jared tried to stop him, but he tricked us into helping him."

"It's okay," Neema said. "I meant for him to download the files. I had hidden Balthazar there."

"He's overwritten Gogue's personality," Pirate said as the truth came to him, "like a computer virus."

"I prefer to think of myself as an upgrade," Balthazar said.

"So everything Gogue controlled," Sheppard said, "Balthazar now controls?"

"Exactly," Balthazar said.

"What about the fleet in orbit around Earth?" Hal asked.

"It has been disarmed," Balthazar said.

"So all that about the time travel formula was just a ruse?" Pirate said. "Bait?"

"A Trojan Horse," Hal said. "We thought we were here to keep Gogue from downloading what was on that drive. Instead of that, we tricked him into drinking poison."

"And all of us were decoys again?" Pirate said.

"Yes," Neema said. "You were so good at it before."

"How do you like that?" Hal said.

"So it's over?" Wendy said. "Gogue is finished?"

"I know," Neema said. "It doesn't seem possible. I've lived in his shadow my entire life. Can I really be free?"

CHAPTER 39: Loose Ends

Sheppard stood at the window of *Astor* station's spaceport and watched as shuttles from the *Vanguard* and the ships that had fought her drifted across the void to the station's docking port.

"Two of the enemy ships got away," Sheppard heard Jonas Cockrum explaining to Pirate and Wendy.

"What about Corbalew?" Wendy asked.

"We found his REGEN tank floating in space," Cockrum said. "It was empty."

"Do you think he's dead?" Pirate said.

"With Corbalew," Cockrum said, "you can't afford to make that assumption."

Sheppard heard the sounds of shuffling feet as another shuttle's load of passengers came through the last security gate. Some of these were hospital patients. They were lying on robot-guided floating medical beds. Sheppard recognized one of the patients and made his way through the crowded room to the aisle in front of the gate.

"Preston," he said as he approached the gaunt figure on one of the beds. "I never got the chance to talk with you earlier."

"Sheppard," Preston said. "I can barely see you." The whites of Preston's eyes were bloody red. His skin was covered with bruises and purple blotches.

"I'm not surprised," Sheppard said. "Next time you decide to take a space walk, wear a suit."

Preston laughed.

"Everybody keeps telling me that," he said. Preston stretched out a hand. His fingers were slender and birdlike, almost feminine. Sheppard took them in his own thick fingers.

"I hear you saved somebody's life," Sheppard said, "that you're something of a hero."

"I was at the right place at the wrong time," Preston said.

"Don't believe a word he says," the young woman walking beside him said. She had strawberry blonde hair and a heavy southern accent. A teenage boy with long, light brown hair stood beside her.

"This is Jolie Harrison," Preston said. "She's my attorney-- and my friend. And I think you already know Lex Marston."

"It's good to see you both," Sheppard said.

"Can you believe it's over?" Jolie Harrison said. "I'd about given up hope."

"Even when we're faithless," Sheppard said, "God is faithful."

"If you had told me that when we were back on Venus," Preston said, "I wouldn't have believed it. Now it almost seems possible."

"You were sure you would be killed," Sheppard said, "but you made it through after all."

"Which one is your daughter?" Lex Marston asked.

Preston squinted, scanned the room with his red eyes.

"There," he said. "Beside Cockrum."

"Wendy," Sheppard said. "You never told her."

"After everything I put her mother through," Preston said, "everything I put her through . . . ."

"There's plenty of guilt to go around," Sheppard said, "and plenty of grace to cover it all." He turned around. "Wendy."

"No," Preston whispered.

"Wendy," Sheppard said. "Come over here. There's somebody I want you to meet."

"Excuse me," Wendy told Cockrum and Pirate. She walked across to the hovering bed where Preston lay.

"Wendy," Sheppard said. "This is Richard Preston."

"Preston," Wendy said. "We met back on Venus."

"The traitor who turned himself in," Preston said.

"And saved all of us by sabotaging Corbalew's ship," Wendy said. "I remember you."

"Tell her, Richard," Jolie Harrison said. "She needs to know."

"Tell me what?" Wendy asked.

Preston waited for a moment, took a deep breath.

"Your mother and I were married once," Preston said. "It didn't last long."

Wendy waited a moment before replying.

"She never told me," Wendy said. "It--it must have been before I was born."

"Yes," Preston said. "About nine months before." Tears filled his red eyes. He began to weep in shuddering gasps.

Wendy stood, eyes wide, staring at the gaunt figure in the bed. Sheppard placed a fatherly arm around her.

"Are you all right?" he asked.

Wendy nodded, but tears were already starting to form in her own eyes. She had known her father was an actor, that he had been wealthy once but had lost everything to drugs. That was all. Richard Preston had struck her as odd, pitiable, and tragic. The thought of him as her parent would take a long time to get used to.

"Thank you for telling me," Wendy said. She clasped Preston's hand briefly. Harrison, sensing that the conversation had ended, led Preston's floating bed away to sick bay.

"Are you all right?" Sheppard asked again.

"I don't know," Wendy said. "This is so strange."

"I wish you were my daughter," Sheppard said. He kissed the top of Wendy's head.

"I do too," Wendy said. "It would be easier to accept. He's so . . . so strange."

"Give him a chance," Sheppard said. "He's been through a lot."

Lex Marston excused himself and walked over to join Cockrum and Pirate. He had questions for Pirate, questions about Joanie, Enoch, and Crane Island. He was walking toward them when he saw a face in the crowd, a face he had thought never to see again. She was tall and blonde with a Nordic kind of beauty. Jared Thomas was walking beside her.

"Lex Marston!" Neema said, excited. "You're here. So this is how it happens."

"Nina?" he said. "Is that you?"

"Neema," she said, smiling. "Nina was another name I used once. It is good to see you, Lex."

"You--you haven't changed," Lex said. "Not at all."

"Neither have you," Neema said. "Here we stand, two immortals."

"I've lost just about everyone," Lex said. "Are you going to stay here or are you going to leave again?"

"I'm staying," Neema said, "but I have to say goodbye to a friend."

* * *

"Good luck, Balthazar," Neema said. Sheppard and almost the entire Intrepid Force stood with her in *Astor* station's observatory and communications center. The room was round with lighted instrument consoles encircling the lower level and a holo-dioramic dome filling the space above them with stars, floating ships, and Saturn's ringed majesty.

"Goodbye, Neema," the voice from space said. "I'll miss you."

"And I'll have your twin to keep me company here," Neema said. "It hardly seems fair."

"I have your personality matrix and genetic code stored in my databanks," Balthazar said. "You may not be the last of your kind, Neemanissa Arita. You may yet have sisters."

"Take care of yourself," Neema said.

"Goodbye, Neema."

About a hundred kilometers from *Astor* station, a dark and stormy hole opened in the empty fabric of space. A silver needle, an obelisk of I-beams, metal grids, and oversized cylindrical engines, dropped through that hole and vanished. The *Rubicon*, Gogue's time ship, was gone.

"So what will happen now?" Pirate asked. "Do you think he'll be able to stop Gogue from killing all those people?"

"Yes," Neema said, "but it will not be in our world."

"An alternate universe?" Jared said, "another timestream with alternate versions of each of us?"

"Yes," Neema said. "And that makes me both happy and sad."

"I understand sad," Wendy asked, "because it won't help the people in our universe. But why happy?"

"Because she's from a future that won't exist," Pirate said. "We stopped Gogue, prevented his rise to power. There won't be a Neema in our twenty-fourth century because her world won't exist."

"So, Reverend," Zapper said. "What does that do to your theology?"

"Creation just keeps getting bigger and more mysterious," Sheppard said, "and every time we think we're close to understanding God, we realize just how far we've got to go."

"So alternate universes don't shoot holes in your faith?" Zapper asked.

"No," he said, "but they do open the door to some pretty interesting possibilities."

"Like what?" Zapper asked.

"Like what if everybody could have the total freedom to accept or reject God," Sheppard said, "but out of all those universes, all those realities, at least one version of each of us could still choose to love Him. At least one version of each of us would make it to heaven. It's probably not watertight theology, but it does sound good."

"Can we call home from here?" Pirate asked. "I've worried about my family since this whole thing started."

"I think that can be arranged," Cockrum said.

* * *

They stood in spacesuits beneath a foggy, orange sky. Saturn watched silently from its ringed realm above the jagged hills that lined the horizon.

"For nearly ten centuries this ship has served as a kind of burial chamber," Sheppard said, "a resting place for the bodies of the men and women who served on board the *Lightbringer*. Until now this has not been a peaceful resting place. Even in death, these men and women have been overshadowed by the malevolent spirit responsible for their deaths. Though their souls have long since departed, their bodies have remained in the shadow of Gogue's dominion and their names have been lost to all who might have known and loved them."

The others stood at attention as Sheppard scanned the words he had written from the screen inside of his helmet.

"We don't have any way of returning these people to their loved ones," Sheppard said. "We have no way of knowing if they are our own unborn children or the children of our twin brothers and sisters in some mirror universe. Whoever they were, we have gathered here today to honor their memory, to call out their names before God, and to commit their bodies to this now-liberated world as their final place of rest."

Sheppard nodded.

"Positions," Hal said.

Pirate and Wendy, Echo Yazzi, Captain Butler, and an assortment of others from the Intrepid Force and the crews of the *Intrepid* and the *Vanguard* raised their rifles to the cold sky.

"Captain Jerome Lem."

The weapons fired. A bright flash lit up riddled remains of the Lightbringer and the surrounding debris field.

"Arwen Eisman."

The weapons fired. Pirate and Wendy looked at each other through the face plates of their helmets. Both had tears in their eyes.

"Darnell Dark."

The weapons fired.

"Terrence Davidson."

The weapons fired.

An hour later an armored lander blasted off into Titan's murky sky.

"Goodbye, Arwen," Pirate said softly as he stared out through the thick and frosted glass. "I hope I get to see you again." Thrust pulled him back into his seat.

* * *

"We've been through some hard times," Sheppard said. "Shadows of a tribulation yet to come. A dress rehearsal for an apocalypse."

Sheppard arranged his notes on the lectern in front of him and looked out onto the *Intrepid*'s bridge, at the faces of Cockrum, Preston, Captain Butler, Lex Marston, and of his well-loved students. The dark face of space, the gleaming sun, and the distant planets filled the giant screen behind them.

"The death toll on Earth," Sheppard said, "has turned out to be surprisingly light. We believed it to be in the millions. In reality, we only lost a few thousand. Much of the carnage we saw played out on television was simulation only, computer generated smoke and mirrors. Some of it wasn't. Our prayers go out to the people who lost loved ones in the attacks on Los Angeles, Washington D.C., Berlin, and Moscow."

Sheppard paused, shuffled through the papers in front of him.

"Keep on," Zapper said. "You're doing fine."

"Thank you," Sheppard said. "This dark challenge has served to show many of us what we are truly made of. Some of us thought we were weak and found out we were strong. Some of us thought we would never deny our faith, but lost our strength in the face of fear. And some of us learned from that experience that our strength comes not from ourselves, but from God."

Sheppard sighed, cleared his throat.

"And some of us have realized that life is too sweet to waste and that love is too sweet to be denied. That brings us to the purpose of our gathering here today. I tried to talk them into waiting until we got back to Earth, but they wouldn't have it. Who could blame them? And so, dearly beloved, we are gathered here today, in the light of Saturn's rings, farther from home than most human beings have ever journeyed, to join Jared Lawrence Thomas and Neemanisa Arita in the holy and sacred union of marriage. Will the groom please rise and join me here."

Jared stood and joined Sheppard at the lectern.

"I haven't performed a wedding in a while," Sheppard said. "This one is special. We thought humanity was at the end of it's road. It turns out we may still have some road ahead of us after all. All rise in honor of the bride."

"All this pageantry," Neema whispered to Pirate. "It seems so immodest."

"It will be over before you know it," Pirate said. The doors at the rear of the bridge opened. Pirate and Neema hooked arms and started down the aisle as the wedding march chimed, with full orchestration, through the speakers.

* * *

The *Intrepid*'s dining hall had been decorated with colored paper and artificial flowers. A bowl of fruit punch and a tiered cake had been arranged on a table at the front of the room. The receiving line had been short. Jared and Neema were sitting together at the head table.

"Look at them," Mike said. "They don't know there's anybody else in the world."

"That lucky snake," Zapper said.

"Yeah," Mike said. "Couldn't have happened to a better guy though."

"Don't be too jealous," Hal said. "Those two have a long road ahead of them. Marriage isn't as easy as single people think."

"Look at Neema and tell me that," Zapper said.

"My wife was good-looking too," Hal said.

"Did you ever talk to her?" Mike said. "Is your little boy okay?"

"I finally got through to 'em," Hal said. "They're fine."

"Then why do you look so sad?" Mike asked.

"'Where were you, Daddy?'" Hal said. "That's what he kept asking me."

"Did you tell him what you were doing?" Mike asked.

"I tried to explain it to him," Hal said. "He didn't understand. He just kept asking me why I wasn't there."

"Ah, kids," Zapper said. "They don't appreciate anything you do for them."

Sheppard and Cockrum stood in a corner of the room watching the others.

"It was a beautiful ceremony," Cockrum said. "You delivered a good message."

"Thanks," Sheppard said. "It's been a while since I conducted a wedding."

"I just spoke with Security Chief Rotwang back on *Vector* station," Cockrum said.

"How is everything there?" Sheppard asked.

"They're recovering," Cockrum said. "Not everybody who served Gogue was controlled by those implants. They're still rooting out collaborators. I don't know if we'll ever find them all."

"So we've still got a lot of work ahead of us," Sheppard said. "Why am I not surprised?"

"There's something else Rotwang told me," Cockrum said. "Something I wanted to ask you about."

"What is it?" Sheppard asked.

"Rotwang wanted me to ask you how you managed to escape from those bonds in the interrogation room," Cockrum said.

"I was pretty delirious at the time," Sheppard said. "I guess I just kept pulling against them until they broke."

"Those bonds were designed to hold Lars Brunkert," Cockrum said. "They should have been unbreakable, even to a cyborg."

"Sometimes the people who design the bonds don't take willpower into account," Sheppard said.

"Maybe not," Cockrum said. "So that's all that happened? You just kept pulling until they broke? Was there anything else?"

"My memories are pretty hazy," Sheppard said. "I was delirious, delusional."

"I just wondered," Cockrum said.

"Why?" Sheppard said. "What's going on?"

"Well," Cockrum said. "Rotwang asked if someone else had helped you escape. He said those bonds had been twisted apart from the outside."

Sheppard thought of Ahadri's face, of his deep and comforting voice. He swallowed hard and fought back tears.

"Listen," he said. "I'll see you later, Jonas."

"Where are you going?" Cockrum asked.

Sheppard didn't answer. He didn't trust himself to speak as he left the dining hall and made his way across to the ship's observation lounge to gaze out at the face of God.

Sheppard gazed back at the planet Saturn. Titan had shrunk to the size of a star. Sheppard remembered his last moments on the cold moon. Most of the others had returned to the *Intrepid*, but Sheppard had remained behind. Firing up a laser torch, he had carefully stenciled a blazing red inscription into a piece of the *Lightbringer*'s battered hull plating. The metal had cooled to a dull gray but the inscription remained:

> I met a traveller from an antique land
> Who said: Two vast and trunkless legs of stone
> Stand in the desert . . . Near them, on the sand,
> Half sunk, a shattered visage lies, whose frown,
> And wrinkled lip, and sneer of cold command,
> Tell that its sculptor well those passions read
> Which yet survive, stamped on these lifeless things,
> The hand that mocked them, and the heart that fed:
> And on the pedestal these words appear:
> "My name is Ozymandias, king of kings:
> Look upon my works, ye Mighty, and despair!"
> Nothing beside remains. Round the decay
> Of that colossal wreck, boundless and bare
> The lone and level sands stretch far away.
> ~Percy Bysshe Shelley

Then, in flowing freehand script he had added one last thought:

> *. . . And, lo, I am with you always, even unto the end of the world.*
> ~Jesus of Nazareth, Matthew 28:20

Coming Soon:
Intrepid Force:
Heritage

ABOUT THE AUTHOR

Timothy D. Wise is a professor of management and marketing at Southern Arkansas University in Magnolia, Arkansas. He was born in Panama City, Florida, but has lived in North Louisiana and Southern Arkansas most of his life. He has written and illustrated stories since childhood. *Intrepid Force* was the first to be published. Wise received four degrees from Louisiana Tech University in Ruston, Louisiana. During his time there, he was active in the Baptist Student Union, and did summer ministry work in Washington D.C. and on the big island of Hawaii. He earned his doctorate in business adminstration in 1995. Founding his own studio and publishing company, *Professor Theophilus' Emporium of Imagination, Inc.*, began the realization of a long-time dream. Wise is already at work on a third *Intrepid Force* novel and a graphic novel adaptation of the first novel. He also has plans to publish *Season Out of Time*, a young adult novella.